CAPITOL MURDER

A NOVEL

WILLIAM
BERNHARDT

BALLANTINE BOOKS • NEW YORK

Copyright © 2006 by William Bernhardt

All rights reserved.

Published in the United States by Ballantine Books, an imprint of The Random House Publishing Group, a division of Random House, Inc., New York.

BALLANTINE and colophon are registered trademarks of Random House, Inc.

Library of Congress Cataloging-in-Publication Data

Bernhardt, William.
  Capitol murder : a novel / William Bernhardt.
    p. cm.
  ISBN 0-345-45149-X
  1. Kincaid, Ben (Fictitious character)—Fiction.   2. Attorney and client—Fiction.   3. Trials (Murder)—Fiction.   4. Chicago (Ill.)—Fiction.   5. Tulsa (Okla.)—Fiction.   I. Title.

PS3552.E73147C37   2006
813'.54—dc22   2005053173

Printed in the United States of America on acid-free paper

www.ballantinebooks.com

First Edition

2   4   6   8   9   7   5   3   1

Text design by Meryl Sussman Levavi

To Joss Whedon

It's not the genre that matters;

it's what you do with it.

Much madness is divinest sense
to a discerning eye—
Much sense the starkest madness.

—EMILY DICKINSON

Love makes you do the wacky.

—TY KING

Prologue

In my dream, I'm alone in my bedroom. The window is open and there's a breeze, gentle, but ominous; cool, but foreboding. I'm dressed in nothing but a sheer full-length nightgown, white—always white—with a dangerously provocative décolletage, my neck entirely exposed. I feel shivers coursing down my spine and gooseflesh on my arms. At first I think it must be the wind, but then I realize there's something more, something lurking just outside my window. All I can see is a billowing fog, insubstantial, shapeless shadows that cross my windowsill and enter of their own accord. I am terrified, but at the same time exhilarated by my intense desire to know what will happen next.

When he materializes, he is barely two feet away. He stares down at me with eyes that are piercing, relentless, but also calming and nurturing. They invade me, deep down into my soul and I feel violated, swept away, breathless. I already love this man, this creature, his jet-black hair, his tall gaunt frame, his pale translucent skin, even his thin lips, slightly distended on either side. I give myself to him willingly, heedlessly, aching for his touch. He takes a step toward me, then another, never once moving his eyes from mine. After what seems an eternity of wanting, he lays his hands upon my shoulders. I want to scream, not from terror but from pleasure, from the sheer overpowering rapture of the moment. My knees weaken but he holds me firm, one strong arm around my waist, as his mouth draws close to me, nearer and nearer still, and his mouth descends with an excruciatingly sweet slowness toward my neck . . .

When it finally happened, it was nothing like that, yet everything like that, everything in every way that mattered. I was not in my bedroom, but somehow our clandestine location, in these ornate surroundings he so appropriately calls a church, lent a sense of danger that magnified my yearning to crazed, almost unbearable proportions. I was dressed in a dark ceremonial robe, not a nightgown, but my seducer made short work of that, releasing each clasp with his pale, gelid fingertips, while never once releasing me from the hypnotic gaze of those unrelenting ebony eyes.

"I'm yours," I whispered, more to myself than aloud.

"And I will have you," my companion replied.

"I want you to know," I said, my voice choking, my tongue thick with desire, "that this is my first time."

A barely perceptible rise to the corner of my companion's lips exposed a flicker of incandescent white teeth. "And your friends?"

"They're different," I answered. "I don't know if they're ready. But this is what I've always wanted, what I've dreamed about." My hunger was so powerful I could barely think, barely breathe. "Please take me. Take me now."

I watched as the object of my longing drew near to me. When I first felt teeth electrify my flesh, I could not help but let out a cry.

"You are not ready," my companion said.

"I am," I insisted, desperate to propitiate my master. "Please don't go. Please. I just—it caught me by surprise, that's all. I've never felt anything like that before. Never felt anything so . . . overwhelming." I was gasping, begging, a cat in heat, consumed by this internal inferno that I could not quench. "Please give me another chance."

"As you wish, my child." This time, when he made contact, I

winced, but did not flinch, did not gasp, did not pull away. As my companion slipped inside me, I felt so many sensations and emotions at once I could not identify them all: fear, pain, violation—but also an ecstasy, a mind-chilling bliss. The penetration went deeper, then deeper still, turning me inside out, bringing to life parts of me that had never been touched before. I was overcome by a rush of unbridled passion, and a sweetness I had never imagined possible. I had slipped the bonds of this mortal plane and found another place, a higher dimension of unspeakable pleasure.

I don't know how long the sensation lasted: an hour, a minute, a moment. I had lost the ability to stand, to speak; I was in a place that transcended time. I was aware of some commotion, some attempt to interfere, but it was all so distant, so remote, and my master's minions were strong enough to prevent any interruption. I was so far gone the spell could not be broken—not until I felt my own hot blood trickling down my breast.

"Was it all you dreamed it would be?" I heard him ask.

"Oh yes. Oh yes yes yes."

"I'm glad. Farewell, sweet Colleen."

"What?" I said, trying unsuccessfully to raise my head. "What's happening?" I was slurring, listless; a numbing torpor enveloped my entire body. "I feel . . . weak."

"Of course you do." My companion swooped me up and laid me gently on the altar, cushioning my head. "You're dying."

"But—why?" I managed to murmur.

"So that you will live again," was the reply. "So that we will become one."

My consciousness faded. I heard footsteps, near and far, but the bleeding did not stop. I realized that I was covered with blood. How could anyone bleed so much and still live? This was not the way it was supposed to happen. This was not the way my dreams ended. But that is the problem with dreams, isn't it? Somewhere between the conception and the execution is a vast abyss. And the name of that abyss is Death.

Part One

Too Much Information

1

TULSA, OKLAHOMA

As Ben Kincaid peered at his client through the acrylic screen, he was startled by how appealing, how downright cute she still looked. Usually, the first few weeks behind bars took a terrible toll on first-time inmates. The lack of sunlight, the coarseness of the company, the absence of hair care and beauty products, the low-watt institutional lighting, the inevitable depression—all conspired to make the newly incarcerated appear as if they had emerged from the ninth circle of hell.

But not Candy Warren. Somehow Candy had managed to retain her fresh-faced charm. When her father first introduced her to Ben, he had compared his daughter to Lizzie McGuire—perky, effervescent, goofy but lovable. Two weeks in the slammer and a switch from Gap jeans to TCPD orange coveralls hadn't changed any of that. She was still adorable. She even had her hair up in pigtails.

"So you've talked to my daddy?" she asked, speaking into the telephone receiver that allowed them to communicate.

"Yes," Ben answered. "He's worried about you, of course. But I assured him we would do everything we could. And I got him the present you wanted to send. The Hilary Duff poster."

"Oh, that's wonderful." Ben loved the way her nose crinkled when she laughed. "Can you believe it? The man is in his sixties, and he's crazy about this girl who's barely a teenager. Isn't that wild?"

Ben could think of a different word for it, but never mind that. Always refreshing to have a client who still cared about her parents. "I have some good news for you. To my utter surprise, DA Canelli has made an offer."

"An offer?" She lifted her chin, giving those pigtails an endearing bounce. "What kind of offer?"

"A plea bargain. A chance to avoid trial."

"Assuming I plead guilty."

"To a lesser charge. Yes."

Candy kneaded her hands. Ben noticed that her fingernails were painted electric pink. "But what will my daddy say?"

"What will he say if this goes to trial?"

"Aren't I entitled to my day in court?"

"Yes. But that day is fraught with risk. Canelli is offering you a sure thing."

She sat up straight, throwing her shoulders back. "I can't do it. I can't take the easy way out. I owe that much to my daddy. And while we're talking about this, Ben, I want you to do something about those newspapers."

Ben didn't follow. "Which newspapers?"

"All of them. Have you read the articles they've been printing?" Creases flanked the bridge of her nose. "File some kind of lawsuit against them."

"On what grounds?"

"What grounds?" she said with great indignity. "They've been saying horrible things about me. They're libeling my reputation! Destroying my good name!"

Ben shook his head. "Candy . . . you're—"

"Ben, don't. You know I have labeling issues."

"Nonetheless—"

"Ben, I don't want to hear—"

"Candy . . ." Ben cleared his throat. "You're a hit man."

She gave him a stern look. "Excuse me?"

"Sorry. Hit *person*."

"Better." Her face hardened; the adorable factor vanished. In the space of a second, she went from Lizzie McGuire to Lizzie Borden. "Now, what are you going to do about those goddamn newspapers?"

Ben drew in his breath. "Nothing. A libel suit would be frivolous, given the circumstances, detrimental to your criminal case, and so utterly stupid that if you really want to do it, you're going to have to find yourself another lawyer."

She glared back at him with eyes like Uzis. "Then what do you suggest?"

"I suggest you take the DA's deal." He hung the phone receiver back in its cradle. "Be seeing you, Candy."

Christina McCall sailed through the front doors of her law office with an air of insouciance, bouncing with each step, whistling as she walked. Jones, the office manager and part-time oracle, did his best to interpret the signs. He could tell she was in a merry mood, not only from the whistling, but also because she was dressed less like an attorney and more like, well, Christina. She was wearing a short, pleated skirt, knee-high boots, and a clinging sweater ornamented with irregular patches of fake fur.

"I'm guessing you didn't get that outfit at Saks," Jones commented.

"Dear Jones," she said smiling, "Don't you know? This is all the rage amongst the *jeunesse dorée*."

Jones didn't know what that meant and wasn't interested enough to ask. "Is there a reason why we're whistling this morning?"

Christina beamed. "Because it gives me a happy."

"Uh-huh. May I assume from this unsuppressed display of jocularity that you must've beaten Ben at Scrabble last night?"

She stopped at his desk in the lobby and snatched the pink message slips from her spindle. "Jones, Jones—you're so passé. We're long past the Scrabble stage."

"'Zat a fact," he said dubiously. "Might I have the temerity to suggest the possibility that he actually . . . kissed you good night?"

"Jones, Jones, Jones!" She leaned across his desk, still grinning. "You are such a busybody."

"I'm just trying to stay up-to-date on this putative romance."

"And I'd love to continue this delightful raillery, but—"

"Look, I'm trying to run an office," Jones said, raising his chin. "It's my job to know if anything potentially damaging to the firm is developing. So I'm naturally concerned when the firm's two attorneys make the incredibly boneheaded decision to start dating each other. But if you don't want to tell me anything, fine. I don't care."

A few seconds of silence passed. Christina stared at him. Jones drummed his fingers.

"All right, so I do care. Don't make me grovel. Tell me already."

Christina fluttered her eyelashes. "Dear sweet Jones. Don't work yourself into a swivet. I'll tell all. Ben and I are so past the good night kiss stage." She gave him a pronounced wink. "Way way past. What a libido that man has."

"Really. I thought Ben was more glibido."

"Huh?"

"All talk and no action."

"Well, you are . . . totally wrong."

"Glad to hear it. I guess." As Christina bounced toward her office, he added, "But I notice there's no ring on your finger."

Her neck stiffened first; the rest of her body soon followed. She slowly pivoted on one heel. "That . . . doesn't mean . . . anything. We haven't been dating all that long."

"Oh? Seems to me it's been . . ."

"Just a little over a year." She paused. "With, like, ten years of foreplay. Look, he's a typical nineties male. Afraid of commitment."

"Wake up and smell the calendar, Chris. The nineties were over a long time ago. Your boy is stalling."

"He isn't stalling. He's just . . . Ben." Her fingers fluttered through the air. "You know how hard he was hit by that Ellen mess, how she betrayed him. That's how he sees it, anyway. And that business with Belinda Hamilton didn't help any."

"And Keri Kilcannon."

"Ugh." Christina's face twisted into a grimace. "Did you have to bring her up?" She sighed. "I keep telling myself this romance isn't hopeless, that eventually we'll take the next step. But how long can I wait for this man to come to his senses?"

"Hearing that old biological clock ticking?"

"Yeah. The one that tells me I probably won't live past one hundred and ten. And that may not be long enough."

"I feel for you. Truly."

"What would you know about it? You and Paula fell in love right off the bat."

"We didn't get married right off the bat." Jones's eyes twinkled. "But I knew it was going to happen. Knew the first moment I laid eyes on her."

"And you've been happily married ever since. How did you know? How could you be sure? Give me a test."

"That's easy enough. Has he ever told you he loves you?"

She frowned, then stomped across the lobby to her office.

Jones leaned back in his chair and closed his eyes. "That's what I thought."

Ben crept into the lobby, carefully opening and releasing the door so the automatic chime would not sound. When was he going to have that private-access elevator to his office installed? Answer: probably sometime after he actually made some money, a goal that perpetually eluded him. And it wasn't because of his profligate ways, either. In all his years as a lawyer, he'd tried dozens of cases, mostly with some degree of success, settled a multimillion-dollar tort case, written two books, inherited a boardinghouse, and rarely spent a dime on himself. But he still only barely managed to keep the firm afloat. And for the most part, it was his own fault. And he knew it.

Which was why he was tiptoeing past his office manager's desk, hoping Jones kept his attention fixed on his computer screen. He felt certain that Candy Warren would take the DA's offer. He also felt certain that as soon as her father found out about it, he would refuse to pay Ben a dime, which would make her the third no-pay in a month. The only check he remembered seeing recently had come from the government for a court-appointed representation, and that hadn't amounted to enough to take his staff to the Golden Arches for a burger and fries. No, he definitely didn't need to have a confrontation with Jones this early in the morning.

As he turned stealthily down the corridor to the private offices, he saw that Christina was already in. His spirits got an instantaneous lift, as they always did when he saw her. He almost said hello—then thought better of it and returned to stealth mode. They'd had a wonderful time together the night before, absolutely blissful: takeout from Right Wing, a new episode of *Says You!* on the radio, and some extremely gratifying snuggling. But when the evening came to an end; and they stood at the door together, and he'd given her one last goodbye kiss about as many times as was possible without it becoming ridiculous, she paused, held him at arm's length, and waited.

He knew what she was waiting for. And the pathetic thing was, he wanted to comply. But he couldn't make himself do it. No matter how hard he tried. So he bumbled something inane about what a "swell girl" she was, and she left.

Yes, he was definitely tiptoeing past her door, too.

He slid into his desk chair and thumbed through the mail Jones had left. Bills, bills, and more bills. A possible case in Creek County against a crop-dusting school. A small-time Internet florist that wanted to sue its fulfillment service. Nothing remotely interesting. Nothing likely to make him rich overnight. And nothing that was ever going to help him work up the nerve to do right by—

"Christina!" He sat upright, startled by her sudden appearance. "What—"

She marched past his desk, grabbed him by the shoulders, raised him to his feet, and planted a big wet one right on his lips.

"Ub—dub—what—"

"Yes, yes, I know your rules. No smoochies in the workplace. But today I think you've earned an exception. I just got word from the courthouse. Father Beale is going to be released!"

"You're kidding!"

"You know I wouldn't joke about something like that. He's been wrongfully incarcerated for far too long. It's an embarrassment to the entire state."

"So our appeal finally worked."

"Appeal, schmiel. It was your book that did it." Not long after he had tried Father Beale's case—and lost—Ben began writing his second nonfiction book. It had finally been published about a month before, and the sales had been considerably better than those for his first book—which meant they were at least in two-digit numbers. *Bad Faith* had also generated a fair amount of media attention, especially in legal circles.

"The governor, archconservative that he is, couldn't help but get involved after you turned up the heat, Ben. People were calling for Father Beale's release all over the state—heck, all over the nation. Greta van Susteren devoted an entire hour to the case, for Pete's sake. Make no mistake, Ben—this had nothing to do with any judge, jury, or legal argument. You made this happen."

"Well . . . I'm glad he's getting out, anyway." Which was putting it mildly. Father Beale had been Ben's childhood priest, a man he loved dearly for all his faults. Losing his case had been a devastating blow. "I want to be there when he's released."

"I knew you would. I've made all the arrangements."

"Great. That's just . . . great." Ben had been trying to avoid her eyes, but something about Christina made that impossible. Whether he wanted to or not, his gaze returned to her long strawberry-blond hair, her freckled nose. She was half a foot shorter than he was, and yet everything she did, everything she said exuded confidence and fortitude. "Look . . ." He hesitated. "About last night . . ."

Her eyes turned up. "Yes?"

"I just—I just wanted you to know that—that—"

"Yes?"

Ben felt beads of sweat trickling down the sides of his face. "That you were totally robbed by that *Says You!* fake definition round. I mean, who on earth would know that *babbing* was some kind of eel fishing? Arnie has a way of bluffing that takes everyone in. And—and you shouldn't feel bad about missing that one."

Her head moved slowly up and down. "Thanks, Ben. Appreciate that."

A large crew-cut head bobbed into the office. "Hey, you guys got the TV on?"

It was Loving, their investigator. A huge man, built like a storage freezer, but at heart as soft as a new pair of Hush Puppies.

"No," Ben answered. "Why? Oprah going to help you find fulfillment by buying some book?"

"Nah. Somethin' really excitin'. On C-SPAN."

Something exciting on C-SPAN? Ben thought. That'll be the day. "What about?"

"Come see for yourself. It's that Senator Glancy guy."

"Glancy?" Christina turned her head. "Don't you know him, Ben?"

He nodded. "Went to law school with him."

"Friends?"

He shrugged. "His family knew my family. Titans of Nichols Hills, that sort of thing. But no, he and I were never particularly close. My mother is constantly comparing us, throwing his success in my face."

"Why? Because he was a successful and fabulously wealthy oil magnate and then got elected to the Senate, and you're a—a—"

Ben waited. "Ye-es?"

"—a . . . increasingly prominent attorney. Let's go see what Loving is talking about." She did a quick about-face and headed out of the office.

Ben almost smiled. Smoothly done, Christina. Very smooth indeed.

Ben and Christina stared at the small television set in the office lobby, their lips parted. Even in black and white, it was difficult to believe. Or stomach.

"And you say they've been running this all morning?"

"Oh yeah," Loving replied. "You know how these news guys are. They get their hands on somethin' this good, they're gonna find some reason to play it over and over again. Before, the talkin' heads were usin' it for a discussion of character issues. Now it's some kinda chitchat about employer ethics. It's all just a big dog-and-pony show so they can run the tape."

Loving may have a homespun way of expressing himself, but Ben knew he wasn't wrong. In a previous age, the press, of their own volition, declined to ever print a photo of FDR in a wheelchair or using leg braces. Today they would show . . . this. Repeatedly.

"How did they get it?" Ben wondered aloud.

"No one seems to be sure. They said the tape showed up on a C-SPAN reporter's desk."

"I am so totally disgusted," Christina said. "I mean, an *affaire de coeur* is one thing, but this—"

"Jiminy Christmas," Ben groaned. "They're starting it again."

Christina's lips pursed. "Let's just hope they resist the temptation to use slow motion."

The video was black and white and grainy, but it was still clearly Senator Todd K. Glancy, D-OK, in the foreground, wearing a blue business suit. Kneeling before him on a sofa was a brunette woman who couldn't possibly be older than her early twenties. She was wearing nothing but lacy undergarments, a black push-up brassiere, and panties connected by a garter strap to fishnet hose, like something you might see in a Victoria's Secret store window. No, Ben thought, it was too tacky for Victoria's Secret. Maybe Frederick's of Hollywood. No, still too tacky. Maybe Ashlyn's Adult Toy and Costume Shop.

The lead anchor appeared on the screen, a somber expression on his face, continuing his prosaic commentary. "Again, we want to caution our viewers—what you are about to see will shock you. We are airing this only because it is clearly newsworthy, and because it could have profound ramifications for the future of this country. Nonetheless, if there are any impressionable minors in the viewing area, or for that matter anyone who might be offended by graphic sexual content, we strongly urge you to remove them, or to turn off your television immediately."

Brilliant lead-in, Ben thought. Guaranteed no one on earth would be changing the channel. Especially impressionable minors.

As the tape began, the audio was staticky, but captioning at the bottom of the screen helped fill in the gaps. The young woman on her knees bore a lascivious grin. "I've been watching you all day," she said, breathily. "Trying to contain myself. But it's been hard. You are so hot."

"Am I?" Glancy replied.

"Oh yes. God, yes. You're a firecracker. Every woman in the office dreams about getting a piece of you."

Glancy's voice softened. "Tell me more."

"I've heard them talking about it, the secretaries, the other interns. How incredibly sexy you are. The fantasies they have about you. How they cream every time they get a whiff of you. How they'd give anything—anything—just to get you inside them."

"Does that include you?" he asked, a sickening, raffish expression on his face.

As if to answer, with both hands, she pushed in on her bosom, which was already all but spilling out of the brassiere. "What do you think?" she asked, in a coy, singsong voice. "Brand new."

"Which," Glancy replied. "The bra or the boobs?"

"The bra, silly." She put her finger in her mouth, sucked on it, then pulled it out, slowly, biting down on her nail just before she finished. "The whole outfit. I've been wearing it under my suit all day. Just waiting for you. Waiting till we had a chance to be alone together. You like?"

"Yeah," Glancy replied. Because the camera was focused on the woman and the sofa, his head was now off the top border of the screen. "I like."

The woman lay back against a sofa cushion with her legs slightly spread. "You want to show me how much you like it?"

"I think I can do that." His hands moved below the screen, but it was obvious he was pulling down his pants and advancing toward her.

The woman's eyes ballooned. "Oh God. I didn't mean—I—You're—"

"Waiting for you, baby." She leaned back as if to lie down, but he held her by the shoulders and pulled her closer to him. Pixilated masking obscured his groin area. "Show me how bad you want me, baby."

"Oh, honey, I—I—can't—" She was staring at him—staring at his pelvis—with unmasked horror. "I can't—put—that—"

"Sure you can, baby." He pulled her closer to him, even though she was visibly resisting. "I'm your Sugar Daddy, right? Your all-day sucker. You said you wanted me inside you. Here's your chance. Get to work."

"Oh God, Todd, I—" As he pushed her face nearer to him, the pixilated masking spread from his groin to cover most of her head, but the audio continued uninterrupted. "Please, I—I—mmph—"

Her voice was obscured by a series of gagging noises. The captioning couldn't possibly transcribe this dialogue, but it didn't matter. No matter what language viewers spoke or wrote, they would have no trouble interpreting this scene.

The man's head was still off screen, but his torso stiffened. "Oh yeah. Oh yeah, baby. That's it. That's exactly it."

"Mmmph—mmm—" She was struggling, but with his arms locked around her, there was nowhere to go. Her eyes, the only part of her face that wasn't obscured, were wide and panicky.

"Just a little more, baby. We're almost there." His hips started rocking. "Oh my God. Oh yes. Oh yes." He began to shout, twisting back and forth. "Oh yes! Oh yes yes yes yes *yeeeeeessssss!*"

When he was finished, he leaned back, releasing her, and pulled his pants up. He smacked her once on the side of her left buttock. "Thanks, sweetheart."

As soon as she was free, the woman rolled over. Her head was out of the camera frame, but the audio made it clear she was retching, then gasping for air, then retching again, her body convulsing with each new upheaval.

And then, abruptly, the tape ended, replaced by the image of the commentator who had introduced the piece. "And there you have it. Cynthia, what do you think?"

She didn't need to speak. The expression on Cynthia's face effectively conveyed what she thought. "Well . . . ," she began slowly, "of course, dressing up or playacting during sex is not that uncommon. The domination–subjugation model is a common facet of many people's sex lives, and some forms of . . . punishment, such as spanking, while arguably aberrant, are not that unusual. But what we just witnessed on that videotape, particularly given the persons involved and the apparent absence of consent, went far beyond the bounds of . . . of . . . I mean, did you hear the girl vomiting? He obviously—"

Ben switched the television off. "Ugh. Too much information."

Loving's lower lip protruded. "I was kinda interested . . ."

"I think we've seen enough. I don't need the color commentary."

Christina had a hand pressed against her mouth. Her face had turned a greenish tint that, Ben noted, did not go particularly well with the red hair. "Are you okay? That was rather gross."

"Übergross," Christina corrected him. "What do you think will happen to Glancy?"

Ben puffed out his cheeks. "Well, for starters, I think he's probably going to be dropped from my mother's Christmas card list."

The phone rang. A moment later, Jones held his hand over the receiver and whispered across the lobby. "Ben? It's for you."

At the moment, Ben had an overwhelming desire to brush his teeth. "Is it something that can wait?"

Jones shook his head fiercely no.

Something about the expression on his face made Ben's Spidey-senses start tingling. "Who's calling?"

"It's from Washington. As in DC."

All heads slowly turned toward Jones. Ben made his way to the phone. "Where in Washington?"

Jones pointed toward the caller ID screen on his phone console. "The U.S. Senate, that's where." He pushed the receiver firmly into Ben's hand. "I think you'd better take the call."

2

Washington DC, the Next Day

Ben was crushed with disappointment as they exited the overpass for I-395. Even though he knew they were nearing Capitol Hill, the neighborhood was, to put it politely, a dump. They were surrounded by all the hallmarks of abject poverty: low-income housing, trash in the streets, rampant graffiti, broken chain-link fences, homeless people holed up in cardboard boxes. He spotted two teenage boys in stocking caps huddled between homes, doing what looked very much like a penny-ante drug deal. Ben had read that DC had an astronomical crime rate, and gazing at this neighborhood, he didn't doubt it.

Jones turned onto C Street, and the view gradually improved. Shantytown gave way to tall narrow brick townhouses, one squeezed closely up against the next. He could believe that congressional staffers could conceivably live here, although he was beginning to understand why most members of Congress had places in the suburbs.

"We've arrived," Jones said at last. "And we're early. Let's take a spin around and see the sights."

Ben gazed at the shimmering image of the Lincoln Memorial in the famed Reflecting Pool. Magnificent. The cherry trees were in bloom, and the Main Mall was dotted with picnickers, families tossing Frisbees, and aging hippies handing out flyers. They whizzed by the Holocaust Museum, then the Vietnam War Memorial—the first one. Ben marveled at its sheer stark blackness. A perfect commemorative of a stark black war, he thought. And all those names.

"There it is," Jones said, pointing ahead of them. He was driving the rental car down New Jersey Avenue, and doing an admirable job of it, maneuvering through the frenzied DC traffic. They raced past the corner of Independence and South Capitol.

Ben didn't need Jones's help to spot it—Capitol Hill, the white sculpted dome glistening in the bright sunlight. A magnificent work of architecture. Again Ben felt his heart swelling. Gazing at this fabulous construction, it would be easy to become a superpatriot. Especially since, from this distance, you couldn't make out any of the people who inhabited it.

"This is the House side," Ben said. "We need to get around to the north—that's where the Senate is."

Jones complied. "Which building?"

"The Senate has three office buildings—the Russell, the Dirksen, and the Hart. Senator Glancy's office is in the Russell." He leaned forward and pointed. "That one." Jones turned toward First and Constitution Avenue.

"That's the side entrance where he told us to come in," Ben continued. "I've got our passes." Jones pulled up behind a cab stand. Ben, Christina, and Loving popped open their doors.

"Shouldn't there be some sort of formal greeting party?" Christina asked. "Team Kincaid has arrived."

"Guess all the heralds and buglers are momentarily occupied."

A sign by the curb informed them in no uncertain terms that although this was a valid drop-off point, anyone trying to park here would be immediately apprehended by surveillance guards. "Wait a minute," Jones said. "What am I going to do?"

"Guess you'll have to stay with the car," Ben replied, gathering his briefcase.

"What am I, the chauffeur? I'm a college graduate, Ben. A skilled professional."

"Sorry. I don't see any alternative. We'll call you when we're done."

Jones watched, teeth clenched, and the three of them clambered out of the car, leaving him behind. "Swell," he muttered under his breath. "We come all the way to Washington, DC, and once again I'm stuck at the children's table."

"Can you believe the security?" Ben whispered to Christina. They were standing in line, waiting for their turn to be scanned and searched by the officers posted at the X-ray and metal detectors.

"After 9/11? Yes, I can." She stepped forward, laying her briefcase flat on the conveyor belt, then waiting while the female Capitol police officer waved a metal detection wand from her head to her toe. "Would you think it funny if I told you I'm getting a real charge out of this?" The guard laughed, but not much.

Loving was next through the portal. He had to take off his shoes, then his belt, but he got through in a minute or two.

And then it was Ben's turn.

"Sorry for the inconvenience," the officer said, "but this is the seat of the American government. We can't be too careful."

"Right, right," Ben said, as he removed his college ring, then his belt, then the brand-new Harold's shoes he'd bought just for the occasion. His mother told him that important people judge you by your shoes.

"Thank you, sir. Appreciate your cooperation." The officer waved the wand over him again—and it beeped just as it reached his waist.

"Sir," the officer said, "do you have any, er . . . any studs?"

"Studs?" Ben tried not to raise his voice. He knew the man was only doing his job, an important job, but this was a little exasperating. "Of course not."

"He is a stud," Christina said quietly, from her vantage point, "but he doesn't have any."

Loving gave her a look but made no comment.

"What about any, um, any . . ." He cleared his throat. "Any implants?"

"What, like have I had my breasts augmented?"

"No, sir. I was talking about, um, you know, your . . . penile implants."

Christina covered her face with her hand.

"They have been known to set off the detectors on occasion," the officer continued. "Some are made of nitinol reinforced with a copper alloy, so when the machines are on their most sensitive settings, as they are today—"

"No," Ben said, with a sort of low growl, "I do not have—nor do I need—any . . . what you said."

The Capitol police officer nodded, his face a phlegmatic mask. He could've been a Vulcan, except that Ben couldn't shake the paranoid feeling that the man was laughing at him behind his eyes. "Then, sir, I'm afraid I'm going to have to ask you to remove your trousers."

"Remove my—are you kidding me?"

"No, sir. Regrettably, it is a necessary security precaution. We have a side room here you can use. We'll have to call for witnesses and a video crew."

"What!"

"Just to document that the proper procedures were followed. Can't be too careful, you know. Frivolous lawsuits costs the taxpayers billions of dollars each year."

"And how long will this take?"

"Oh . . . probably no more than half an hour. An hour at most."

"I have an appointment with Senator Glancy. I'm expected."

"Can't be helped. Security first, that's our motto. Now if you'll just step inside this room, there are some forms—"

"Jesus, Mary, and Joseph." With one angry flick of his wrist, Ben unfastened the button on his pleated slacks and released the zipper. The slacks fell in a bunch to the floor. Revealing the tail of his pressed white shirt. And a darling pair of boxer shorts, baby blue, with little red hearts all over them.

The officer's stony façade began to crack.

Christina grinned from ear to ear. "Now that's adorable. Did your mommy buy those for you, too, Ben?"

"Be. Quiet," he replied, through clenched teeth.

"I don't know why he's being defensive. Do you, Loving?"

The investigator managed to keep a straight face. "No idea."

"You work with someone for years, you think you know them, and then one day you realize they're wearing cutie-pie boxers with little red hearts all over them. Isn't that remarkable?"

"What I think is remarkable," Loving said, "is that this is the first time you've seen his cutie-pie boxers with little red hearts all over them."

Christina's smile diminished considerably.

"Here's the problem, sir," the officer explained. "Got a button stapled to the inside of the tail of your shirt. Metal button. Probably came from the store that way, and you never took it off."

"Does-that-mean-I-can-put-my-pants-back-on-now?" Ben answered without moving his lips.

"Of course, sir. Appreciate your cooperation." He laid down the wand and folded his arms. "And if I may say so, sir, I think those boxers really work for you. Bring out the blue in your eyes."

"Thanks so much," Ben said icily. He pulled up his trousers and grabbed his briefcase, then rejoined his companions. "Don't say it," he warned them. "Don't say a word."

"Of course not," Christina agreed. "Wouldn't dream of it." Pause. "But man—what a pair of thighs." She whistled.

"Christina—!"

"You're a regular Casanova, what with the sexy hearts and all. Wouldn't you say he was a regular Casanova, Loving?"

Loving nodded curtly. "Chick magnet. Big-time."

"I hope you're enjoying yourselves," Ben said, as they reached the central lobby. "Because when we get back to the office—you're both fired."

The generally jocund mood continued, much to Ben's chagrin, until they were greeted by an attractive blond teenager wearing a blue suit with a name tag.

"Mr. Kincaid? I'm Tiffany Dell. I'm a Senate page."

Ben shook her hand. "Nice to meet you."

"Senator Glancy asked me to show you to his office when you arrived."

"Oh, I'm sure we can find it. You—"

"Don't count on it, sir." She laughed, almost a giggle. "This place is a maze to the uninitiated. Took me a week to get the lay of the land."

"Still, you must have more important things—"

"Sir, running errands for senators is what pages do. It's, like, our job description."

"Very well," Christina said. "Lead on. By the way, love that suit."

"Thanks, but I didn't pick it out. It's the standard page uniform. You can't change it. We're not even allowed to wear jewelry. I try to do the best I can with it."

"You succeed. Helps that you're in great shape."

"I should be. On average, pages walk seven miles a day."

"Wow. You must be all muscle tone. Ben, I'm dumping you to become a Senate page."

Tiffany laughed. "I think you're over the age limit, nothing personal. And even though it's good exercise—it's exhausting. Back and forth between the houses, all day long. The underground tram barely helps. Though I'd rather be out and about than stuck in that tiny former cloakroom we call our headquarters." She led them around a corner and down a long marble hallway. "Do you have time for a quick tour? We don't have to stay in this building. Wanna see the Senate chamber? The antique desks? The photo op platform where Vice President Cheney gave Patrick Leahy the f-word? Or the West Front—that's where presidents are sworn into office. Statuary Hall? The Rotunda? Or the catafalque beneath—that's where they originally planned to bury George Washington, and where Lincoln and Kennedy and Reagan lay in state before burial. Did you know that the first Supreme Court chamber was in this building, before they got their own place across the street?"

"I did," Ben said, "and I'd love to see all that, but I think your boss is anxious to talk to us."

"All right. If your schedule lightens up, just ask someone to call for Tiffany." She turned toward a long narrow stairway and led the way.

Senator Glancy's office on the second floor of the Russell Building, Room S-212-D, was a study in chaos theory. Ben stood at the threshold and watched as more than a dozen staffers scurried back and forth, ants in an anthill, each with their appointed tasks, each on a path that intersected those of numerous others without quite colliding. Perhaps this was not the chaos that it appeared after all, Ben mused. Perhaps, as Mrs. Austin, his fourth-grade social studies teacher taught, this was Our Government in Action.

The office consisted of a large lobby with many chairs and a sofa, but only one desk. There were four doors to smaller inner offices, all of them open. Three were occupied; one, the largest, was empty. Ben assumed that was Senator Glancy's office and wondered where he was. Despite the embarrassing security kerfuffle, they had arrived almost exactly at the appointed time.

The fiftyish woman behind the desk was juggling two phones at once while simultaneously writing something on a yellow legal pad. Almost everyone in the room had a cell phone pressed to their ear or, worse, one of those near-invisible headsets that allowed them to walk and talk on the phone, but made it look as if they were muttering to themselves. Like the receptionist, they were all multitasking. Apparently their jobs required them to do three things at once, perhaps more. Ben wondered if the place was always like this, or only the day after a graphic, grotesque sex video featuring the boss hit the airwaves.

Not everyone currently in the office worked there. Ben spotted what appeared to be at least two civilians, one of them a father with three children clustered around his feet. "When am I going to get those tickets to the White House?" he kept saying, to anyone who passed near him. No one answered. Ben sympathized with the man, but he expected that visitor tours were not high on anyone's agenda today. Another woman was short, obese, and with such an evident mad-on that Ben was surprised the security guards let her through the door. She stood in the middle of the lobby and shouted, "When is my boy going to get his furlough? His dad's sick. I need him!"

The ants scurried past her. If they noticed, they gave no sign. A young woman with platinum-blond hair crossed right past Ben and stopped at the receptionist's desk. Despite her worried expression, she had an attractive face, with a slight overbite that made her appearance all the more endearing. She couldn't have been more than twenty. "I'm sorry to keep pestering you, Hazel. But I'm still having trouble with the Blue Beetle. I don't know if it's broken or if I just don't know how to work it."

"Probably a combination of both," the woman replied, holding her hand over the voice end of one of the phones. "I'll check it out as soon as I can."

"The senator said he wanted these memos out immediately."

The receptionist gave her a long look. "I'll check it out as soon as I can."

While the young woman was momentarily still, Ben seized the opportunity. "Excuse me, can you help me?"

"No," the woman said, frowning. "I can't help anyone. This is my first day here and I'm proving myself totally useless."

"Your first day? Good grief, what a time to start work."

"Yeah. I'm filling in for you-know-who, since she didn't turn up for work today. Not that anyone was surprised."

Ben was able to put the pieces together. By yesterday afternoon, the press had revealed that the young woman in the video with Senator Glancy was none other than one of his office interns, a relatively new hire named Veronica Cooper. She was probably deep in hiding, dodging reporters. This young lady was taking her place.

"Tough situation to be plunged into," Ben said, hoping that if she warmed up to him a bit he might actually persuade her to take him to the senator. "You have my sympathies."

"Hey, I'm not complaining. I wanted this job. I wanted it three months ago when it first became available, but Veronica beat me out. Career-wise, this is a great opportunity. Sanity-wise, it's a disaster. The phones have been ringing nonstop. Just getting past the press corps stalking the office was a challenge."

"We had to meet that challenge ourselves," Ben explained. "By the way, I'm Ben Kincaid. I'm an attorney."

"Shandy Craig," she replied, shaking his hand. "I'm a baby intern."

"Shandy," Christina repeated. "I like that. Is it Scottish?"

"Oh, it isn't my real name. But that's what everyone calls me. Since I was a kid."

"I'm supposed to have a meeting now with the senator," Ben explained.

"Good luck. Everyone from the minority leader on down has been trying to talk to him today, and no one has managed to do it. I think he's lying low until he figures out how best to deal with this mess."

"Yes, that's what he told me he planned. In part, that's why I'm here."

"You'll need to talk to Amanda Burton. She's the senator's PR director. She keeps his calendar. Makes sure he's where he's supposed to be. She'll be able to tell you where he is. If you can get her attention."

Christina stepped forward. "Mind if I ask a question?"

Shandy held up her hands. "All I was supposed to do was run the automatic-pen signing machine. I don't know anything more about that video than you do."

"No, not about that. I was just wondering—what's the Blue Beetle?"

"I believe he was a comic book hero in the forties . . . ," Ben said quietly.

They both stared at him for a moment, then Shandy laughed. "Is that where it comes from? I didn't know. The Blue Beetle is what they call the senator's obsolete copying machine. He insists on having all his memos printed in blue ink—and this is a senator who still hasn't figured out how to use e-mail, so we're talking about a lot of blue ink."

"Why blue?"

"He says it's a friendly color. A larger percentage of the American population says blue is their favorite color than any other. Personally, I don't care what color ink he uses. I just want to make copies. I've got a prepared statement I'm supposed to distribute to about a billion news agencies, and I can't get it photocopied."

"Loving?"

The burly man stepped forward.

"Would you mind helping this first-day intern see if she can get her copier working?"

"'Course not. Let's go, Shandy."

The young woman hesitated. "Is he some sort of . . . repairman?"

"Well," Christina answered, "actually, he's a private investigator. But he's been fixing Ben's copier for years. Yours should be a piece of cake."

"I don't know. This machine is pretty old. The senator is renowned for his thriftiness."

"I bet it isn't as old as Ben's," Christina replied. "Ben is renowned for his impoverishedness."

Loving strolled off with the attractive young intern—not appearing at all displeased with the goodwill assignment, Ben noted. He and Christina crossed the anthill toward the office with the nameplate reading AMANDA BURTON. Unfortunately, just as Ben was about to step in, she came charging out, almost toppling him in the process.

"Hazel? Where the hell is that speech?"

The receptionist immediately put both lines on hold. "I'm doing the best I can. The phones have been ringing constantly and—"

Burton placed her hands akimbo. She was thin—too thin, as far as Ben was concerned—and her obviously tailored suit accented her nearly nonexistent waist. She wore fashionable thin black rectangular glasses and kept her raven-black hair pinned to the back of her head. Not exactly Ben's type, but she was undeniably eye-catching. "Eighty-six the phone calls. Didn't I tell you to make this your number one priority?"

"Yes, but when I'm getting calls from the top brass—"

"I can solve that problem." Burton reached down and yanked the cord out the back of Hazel's phone console. "In this office, Hazel, I'm the top brass. You will not replace that cord without my permission. You will not get my permission until you have finished that speech."

"But—we're expecting a call from the president."

"I don't care if we're expecting a call from God." She leaned in close. "Like it or not, Senator Glancy is going to have to make a public address today. And I think he just might like to read what he's going to say before he says it. So get to work. *Capice?*"

Hazel lowered her chin. "Yes, ma'am."

Ben and Christina observed the entire scene. "So," Christina said, "you want to approach her, or shall I?"

Ben hesitated. "You know . . . she does seem to be more your type . . ."

"Somehow I had a hunch you'd say that." Christina marched up to the woman, and Burton did a sidestep to maneuver around her. Christina grabbed her arm tightly and held her in place.

"Excuse me? Your hand is on my arm."

"Yes. Lovely jacket, by the way." She tilted her head backward. "This is Ben Kincaid, and I'm his partner, Christina McCall. We have an appointment with the senator."

"No, you don't."

"I can assure you that—"

"I can assure *you*," Amanda said, glowering, "Ms. Whoever the Hell You Are, that if the senator had an appointment with you, I'd know about it." She shrugged off Christina's hand. "I keep the man's calendar. He doesn't go anywhere unless I tell him to."

Ah, Ben thought, the power behind the throne. Or at the very least, the ego behind the throne.

Christina was trying to be patient, but Ben could tell it was a strain for her. "We set up this appointment with the senator himself just—"

"Doesn't matter," Burton said, holding the flat of her hand between them. "Today all our appointments have been canceled. As you've no doubt heard, we have important issues to deal with."

"But that's why we're here. We—"

Burton's cell phone chirped. She flipped it open and checked the caller ID.

"It's very important that we—"

"Talk to the hand, lady." She turned her attention to the phone. "I know you have, Maury. I know I owe you one. But this isn't the one. I can't say anything until . . ." She closed her office door behind her.

Christina stared at the closed door, fuming. "If I killed her," she said, "do you think you could get me off on justifiable homicide?"

"Probably," Ben said. "But let's not go there."

"Are you Kincaid?"

They both turned and saw a small wizened man in a wheelchair. His hair was gray and not ample. Even through his trousers, his legs appeared atrophied, and he wore extremely thick glasses. Ben guessed he was around sixty, but given the obviously poor state of his health, it was difficult to know for certain.

"I'm Ben Kincaid, and this is my partner, Christina McCall. You are . . ."

"Marshall Bressler, at your service. I'm Todd's AA." He noted their blank faces. "That's short for administrative assistant. It's like being chief of staff. I'm the top dog. After the senator himself, of course."

Ben frowned. "I was under the impression that Ms. Burton—"

"No, she just thinks she's the top dog." He grinned a little, and Ben couldn't help grinning back. "Amanda came on during the senator's last reelection campaign. The idea was that we needed to reach out to a younger, female constituency, so I hired her to show this old geezer how to do it. After the campaign, we kept her on staff. Mostly she's in charge of media relations."

"She's a spin doctor," Christina said.

"Yup. Which explains why she's so frazzled. If ever Todd needed a good spin, this is the day. But she still reports to me, and the only person I report to is Todd."

"He must have a lot of faith in you."

Bressler shrugged in a self-effacing way. "I've been with him since the get-go. Managed his first campaign for Oklahoma County DA, and every campaign since. Even after a traffic accident seven years ago did this to me." He gestured toward his useless legs.

"I'm sorry," Ben said quietly.

"Don't be, son. Hasn't slowed me down a bit. I still work as hard for Todd as I ever did—maybe more. I think it would be fair to say he has a lot of faith in me. And I have a lot of faith in him." He pursed his thin lips. "Which makes these recent developments all the more distressing."

"Senator Glancy called me yesterday," Ben said. "He's concerned about a possible legal action. Maybe a sexual harassment suit, since Ms. Cooper did work under him."

"There's also a possibility of censure from the floor of the Senate. Even possible expulsion. He's going to need some astute legal advice." Bressler rolled in even closer. "Can I be honest with you?"

"Of course."

"I didn't want him to call you in. You or your partner."

"Oh."

"Nothing personal, son. But this is serious business. He needs the best there is, not some chum from law school. But then I started doing a little research on you. Even read one of your books last night. You've done pretty well for yourself."

Ben felt his face burning. He was never good at accepting compliments and always changed the subject as quickly as possible. "Well, thanks, but if you want to hire other counsel—"

"Let me finish, son. What Todd told me was that he thought it was important that we hire an Oklahoman—not some fancy-pants DC or New York City lawyer—and that he thought you had one of the best, if not *the* best, reputations of any lawyer in the state."

Christina's eyes brightened.

"And I'm not just talking about your win–loss record, although that's pretty damn impressive. I'm talking about your personal reputation. I talked to folks, and what I got over and over was that Ben Kincaid was a man with integrity. A man who wouldn't lie to or mislead the court, not even to defend a client. The world's most square-shooting geek. A veritable saint."

Ben shuffled his feet. "I'm sure that's an exaggeration."

"I hope not, son. Because a saint is exactly what we need right now. The news media is going to forget all the good Todd has done for the poor, the homeless, battered women, since he came to Washington. They're going to try to make him out like he's a devil. And who better to convince them that he's not—than a saint?"

Ben tugged at his collar. All this beatific talk was making him uncomfortable. He just tried to do his job as well as he could. He was no saint. Heck, once, when he was ten, he stole a comic book from Crest Groceries.

"So," Christina interjected, "can we see the senator?"

"Of course. You folk need to have a good chin-wag about how he can best defend himself. He's waiting for you now in one of the Senate cafeterias."

"Really?" Ben arched an eyebrow. "That must be . . ."

"Awkward? Not for Todd. Ballsiest man who ever lived. I think he wanted to do it as a test. See who would sit with him, talk to him. And see who was distancing themselves, shunning him, acting as if he's already been expunged. A senator needs to know who his friends are. Especially in times of crisis." He pivoted his chair toward the door. "Come on. I'll show you the way."

"Oh—let me." Ben raced around behind the wheelchair to help—but found there were no handles. "Aren't there usually . . ."

"Not on my chair, son."

"I'm surprised they make them—"

"They don't. This one was custom-built for me. The senator's wife, Marie, had it designed and paid for it herself. Birthday present, not six months after my accident. Special executive edition. See? A sliding tray I can fold across to use as a desk. A compartment under the armrest for holding documents and files."

Ben pointed to a recess at the end of the right arm. "Even a cup holder."

Bressler shook his head. "Cell phone charger."

"Okay, now I'm impressed. But still—no handles?"

"I don't need anyone to push me. I push myself."

"I didn't mean any offense. Usually—"

"I know, son. But I've taken care of myself all my life. Not going to stop now just because of this little accident. Now let's get to that cafeteria. I think I can smell the bean soup from here."

3

He wasn't hiding, not at all. Ben had to give him credit for
that. To the contrary, Senator Glancy was sitting alone at a
table square in the center of the main Senate Dining Room, a linen
napkin in his lap, slowly sipping a drink. It would be virtually impossible for anyone to pass through the room without seeing him,
and, as Ben watched, several men he recognized as fellow senators
did come by and pause briefly to smile, say a few words of encour-
agement, slap Glancy on the back. But none of the women, Ben noticed. None of the women in the room came within three tables of
him.

"Let me introduce you," Bressler said, as he wheeled his way
through the maze of tables to the senator. "Todd," he announced,
"your legal eagles have arrived."

Glancy immediately sprang to his feet, his hand outstretched.
"Ben! Great to see you again. How long has it been?"

"Well . . . a long time."

"Too damn long. Particularly given all the good work you've been doing." He shifted his gaze. "You must be Christina McCall."

She nodded and took his hand, wincing slightly at the grip. "Good to meet you."

"The pleasure is all mine. Ben told me he was bringing his partner. He didn't tell me she was a beauty."

Christina's lips parted, but she remained silent, nonplussed.

"I hope you don't mind me being blunt. I know we're supposed to keep our mouths shut about such things these days. Don't want to be accused of being sexist. Or worse, get slapped with a sexual harassment lawsuit. Which is why I've asked you to come here." He glanced down at his administrative assistant. "Marsh, will you join us for lunch?"

"Are you kidding? With all the pandemonium upstairs? I'll grab a Snickers bar on my way back to the office." He swiveled his wheelchair around and headed out.

"Great guy," Glancy said, as soon as Bressler was out of earshot.

"Certainly seems like an asset," Ben commented.

"You don't know the half of it. I wouldn't be here today if it weren't for him. Brilliant strategist. Like one of those chess players who can anticipate what's going to happen six moves ahead. And so loyal. He's always stuck by me—even after his accident. His legs are paralyzed."

"Permanently?"

"I'm afraid so. He tried physical therapy—I went to the sessions with him myself. Didn't take. He'll never walk again. And yet, he's never let it get to him. Never complained, never indulged in self-pity. He works out regularly—he's very fit from the waist up. You might wonder why he bothers. Well, I'll tell you why—because this is a man determined to take care of himself. The epitome of self-reliance. Never married, never even dated, as far as I know. And given his current physical condition, probably never will. But he's still the most productive person I've ever met."

"What a profile in courage," Christina said. "No wonder you've kept him all these years."

"I'd do anything for the man. Anything at all. But enough about Marsh. How the hell are you, Ben?"

"Can't complain."

"Your mom still in that huge mansion in Nichols Hills?"

"Oh yeah. She'll never move."

"My folks are the same way. Jesus—how long has it been—ten, twelve years?"

"Something like that. Since law school."

"Right. How come we didn't hang out together more?"

Ben shrugged uncomfortably. "Oh . . . I suppose we just traveled in different circles."

"Yeah, like you were in the 'make-good-grades' circle and I was in the 'party-down-pretty-mama' circle."

"Well, I don't know . . ."

"You were on law review, weren't you? And you won the big Moot Court competition?"

"That was a long time ago."

"You did all that while I was schmoozing profs and local politicians. My dad wanted me to take over his oil empire, of course, and I did for a while. But I always had my sights on the political arena." He snapped his fingers. "Didn't we intern at the DA's office at the same time? You worked with Jack Bullock."

"Yes. But I . . . left early."

"Right, I remember. Your father passed on. That must've been tough."

Glancy obviously didn't know or didn't remember the half of what had really happened, and that was fine with Ben. "It was. But I moved on. And you launched that crusade to stiffen the sentences for domestic abuse. Launched your political career while you were still an intern. Not even out of law school."

"I was very fortunate. Everything just fell into place. I've been lucky—I know that. Until now, anyway."

The assistant restaurant manager appeared with a pen and order pad. "Three for lunch, Senator?"

"Exactly, Jonathan. What delectable viands have you got for us?"

"It's Hawaii Day, sir."

Glancy turned to Ben and explained. "Here in the Senate Dining Room, the menu is based on the food of a chosen state. Different state each day. They rotate through all fifty of them, then start over again. Equal time for every senator." He turned back toward the manager. "Good God, I hope this doesn't mean we have to eat poi."

The manager smiled slightly. "No, sir. I would recommend the grilled mahimahi, mango and coconut on the side."

"Sounds good. Ben?"

"I'm . . . not much of a fish eater. And coconut makes me break out in hives."

"Sounds like you should have the bean soup."

"I've heard the Senate is famous for it. Must be quite good."

Glancy and the manager exchanged a look. "Not really. And there are potentially embarrassing aftereffects, if you plan to be around people later in the day. But it's like jumping out of an airplane. Once you've done it, you can spend the rest of your life telling people you've done it. Christina?"

"I'm not afraid of fish. Mahimahi for me."

"Done," the manager said, making sparse notes on his pad. "I'll have that out right away."

"Thank you, Jonathan." Glancy smiled as he departed. "Wonderful man. Keenly mediocre dining room, but great service. Did you see what a straight face he kept? As if he hadn't seen the video. But we know better, don't we? And that's what we need to talk about. Ben—"

Glancy was interrupted by another man whom Ben recognized. A congressman from Arkansas, he thought.

"Hanging in there, buddy?"

Glancy turned, beamed, and put out his hand. He had the gift, Ben thought. When he was talking to you, his attention was entirely focused on you, as if nothing else in the world existed. "Best I can. What are you doing on this side of the dome, Shawn?" That was the name, Ben recalled. Shawn MacReady, R-AR.

"Just schmoozing. Given any more thought to what we talked about day before yesterday?"

"Believe it or not, Shawn, I've had a few other things on my mind."

"I can imagine. Anything I can do for you?"

Glancy chuckled. "Yeah. Vote no."

"I hope it doesn't come to that. Remember the wisdom of the ancients: *Illegitimis non carborundum.*"

"Sorry, Shawn. My Latin is a little rusty. Any chance of a translation?"

MacReady smiled. "Don't let the bastards get you down."

"That must be gratifying," Ben remarked, after MacReady departed. "When people stand by you. Even after . . . something like this."

"That perfidious cockalorum?" Glancy snorted. "Don't be fooled. Politicians can be civil without actually being friendly. He's just consolidating support for his latest Arkansas boondoggle. He's got no business being here in the first place—he's a congressman, not a senator. But he thinks because he heads the Appropriations Committee, that puts him on par with us." He smiled at Christina. "Don't mean to sound snobby. But it's kind of like a legal assistant who acts like a lawyer."

"Heaven forbid," Christina deadpanned.

"Why is leading the Appropriations Committee such a big deal?" Ben asked.

"Because they decide what gets paid for and what doesn't. We can pass a bill and the president can sign it, but unless the appropriators earmark money for it, it isn't going to happen. So MacReady gets to play Big Man on Campus, for a little while, anyway, and we're all forced to engage in a gigantic horse trading session, endless pieces of pork in exchange for the munificent gift of funding our own legislation."

"It's a miracle you can pass anything."

"Truth is, most of our legislation passes by huge majorities. Small wonder, given how long and hard the process is just to get a bill on the floor."

"Mind if I ask a question? Why isn't *he* sitting with you?" Ben tilted his head toward a tall young man, early thirties, with close-cropped brown hair and a blue suit, sitting alone in the corner. "I would think the junior senator from Oklahoma would've been the first to offer a few consoling words."

"Brad Tidwell?" Glancy shrugged. "He's a Republican. He's

waiting for instructions from his masters. He won't speak to me until he has permission. He won't do anything inimical to his own career agenda."

"Must make it hard to work together."

"We don't. Never have. He's arrogant, contumacious, and jingoistic—exactly what we don't need in these troubled times. And a major-league whiner. Says he can't get any good assignments because I'm in the way. Wants to be the senior senator so bad he can taste it. The man is worthless, and I don't say that just because he's in the opposing party. He's set some kind of Senate record for fatuous remarks designed to please special interests. I don't think he can remember what his personal beliefs were, if he ever had any."

After the food was served, the three of them finally got down to business. "My chief concern," Glancy explained, "is that the Republicans will use this as a tool to engineer a putsch."

"Excuse me?"

"A coup d'état. To put me out of office, maybe even influence the upcoming presidential election."

"You're not planning to run, are you?"

"My prospects don't look quite as good as they once did, huh? But that won't stop them from slinging charges of 'typical Democratic immorality' at whoever does run, and using me as Exhibit A." He inhaled deeply. "So, can I assume you've both seen the video?"

Ben nodded. "Any idea where it came from? Or who leaked it to the press?"

"None. Looks like a setup to me. Someone wants to bring me down. Like Watergate, or Monica Lewinsky. Start with a molehill, then try to make a mountain out of it. Send in your lackeys to bloviate."

Ben's face reddened. "To . . . um . . . um . . ."

"Relax, Ben, it's nothing dirty. It's a word President Harding used. Means 'to speak verbosely or windily.'"

"Oh . . . right. Why didn't I know that?"

"Because you've spent the last decade in the courtroom, not the Senate."

Christina cut in. "Sir," she said slowly, carefully measuring her tone. "I . . . don't think what I saw in that video can be characterized as a molehill."

Glancy shrugged. "It was sex between two consenting adults."

"Was it? What happened . . . toward the end. Didn't look to me as if she wanted that at all."

"Did you see what she was wearing? How she looked at me? Did you hear what she said? She was hot and heavy and raring to go."

"But—"

"She wanted sex," Glancy continued. "She consented to sex. And the fact that it may not have been the precise sex act she anticipated does not turn it into a rape case. Consent is consent."

Christina fell silent.

"Marshall has already spoken to the DA. They have no intention of pressing any criminal charges."

Ben jumped in. "So you're only worried about civil actions."

"And the political ramifications, yes."

"Do you think it's likely that this . . . Ms. Cooper would bring a charge of sexual harassment against you?"

"She disappeared from the office as soon as the story broke and didn't show up for work today. We haven't been able to contact her. Who knows what anyone will do if you wave enough money in their face? Remember Paula Jones? She waited years before she brought her case against Clinton. Why sue all of a sudden? Because a Clinton-hating right-wing organization adventitiously provided funds to cover her legal expenses, that's why. And the Republicans then used that little indiscretion to try to bring down the president. They appointed an obviously biased 'independent prosecutor' who blew over fifty million in taxpayer dollars prying into Clinton's sex life, and Clinton ended up getting impeached over it. They'll try the same thing with me—try to turn me into the scandal du jour. Some of the more vulpine members of the current administration are already calling for me to resign, but that isn't going to happen. I worked too damn hard to get where I am. I'm not going to give it up over this pip-squeak."

"There's nothing I can do to prevent someone from filing a suit," Ben said.

"Yes, but if she does, you can crush it dead before it gets out of hand. I've followed your career, Ben. You're smart, you're hardworking, and you've got credibility. People believe you. That work you did up in Chicago on the Tony Barovick case—absolutely brilliant. And very well covered by the media. You came out smelling like a rose, even though you had a supremely unsympathetic client. How many defense attorneys could've pulled that off? I think that case made you the best-known attorney from the state of Oklahoma."

"And, ironically," Christina interjected, "the poorest."

"Anyway, that's why I want you working for me. If you can defend a violent gay-basher and come out looking good, my case should be a cinch."

"You can't be sure of that, Todd. I'm new to this town. I'm not even licensed to practice here."

"Big deal. We'll line up some token local counsel and get you admitted *pro hac vice*. The bottom line is this: if you tell the judges this case is frivolous, they'll listen, and we can get rid of it before the right-wing nudniks turn it into a political football."

"The plaintiffs will try to make you out as some sort of sexual predator. The Senate lothario. Anything to back that up?"

"Like what?"

"Prior incidents. In the office or elsewhere."

"Absolutely not."

"Todd," Ben said slowly, "you're a lawyer. You know how important it is to tell your counselor everything. The good and the bad."

"Ben, there's nothing. So what do you think? Will you go to bat for me?"

"I can't guarantee anything."

"Sure you can. You can guarantee you'll do your damnedest. That's all I can ask of anyone." His eyes shifted slightly. "And I want you working right beside him, Ms. McCall."

Christina shifted awkwardly in her seat. "Senator . . . I'm not sure I should be working on this case. I—"

He held up his hands. "I know. You think I'm a scum bucket. You think I forced that intern to perform a vile sex act against her will. Veronica wasn't like that. I'd been with her before—she was a poster girl for saying 'no' when she meant 'please God yes.' But you don't have to believe me. In fact, I don't want you to believe me. I think it'll be good to have a skeptic working with Ben, someone to play devil's advocate. That could be very valuable when we're planning our strategy."

Christina's head tilted slowly to one side. "If you say so."

"I know so. I also know that—"

He was interrupted by a burly man, sandy-haired, with a bright tie and a pin-striped suit that was way too flashy for Ben's taste. He seated himself in the fourth chair at their table without asking. "How's it hanging, Todd?"

Glancy did not appear particularly pleased or amused to see his visitor. "Oh, fine. Just a day like any other," he replied, rolling his eyes.

"Todd, we've got to talk about the Alaska bill."

Glancy brought Ben and Christina into the picture. "This is Steve Melanfield of Kodiak Oil. He's a lobbyist." He frowned at his new guest. "I didn't think they allowed lobbyists in here."

Melanfield grinned. "Just a matter of greasing the right palms."

Glancy turned back to Ben. "You have to understand that in DC, there's a certain hierarchy. The president is at the top, of course. Then the Senate majority leader, the Speaker of the House, et cetera, et cetera. And lobbyists fit in . . . well, somewhere beneath the carnival geeks. You know, the guys who bite the heads off live chickens. There's no one lower. Except the NRA lobbyists."

Melanfield was unfazed. "Come on, Todd, let's be friends. I'd think you could use a pal right now. Especially one who could put a lot of loot into your campaign coffers." He paused. "Or your defense fund."

"And you're willing to give that to me?"

"Damn straight."

"And all you ask in return?"

"Is that you reconsider your position on the Alaska wilderness bill. It's your opposition that's keeping the bill from getting out of committee."

"You know what that bill would do."

"Yeah, I do. It would allow us to stop being dependent on foreign oil. Which would allow the U.S. to stop meddling in the Middle East in a never-ending series of conflicts that only increase anti-American sentiment and kill thousands of U.S. troops."

"By turning what is quite literally the last untouched wilderness preserve in the fifty states into a noisome oil refinery."

"We've spent billions in the Middle East—"

"Inveighing against foreign policy I don't support won't persuade me to change my vote, Steve. I won't do it. Not for your money or anyone else's."

"You know it's going to happen, Todd. Eventually. Just a matter of time. When the people want oil bad enough, they'll demand that their politicians find it, quick. And that'll mean bye-bye, Alaskan preserve."

Glancy sighed. "The sad thing is, you're probably right. But it's not going to happen on my watch. Now push off, will you?"

Melanfield rose to his feet, no longer smiling. "You're making a big mistake, Todd. Mark my words—you'll regret this." He left the room.

"I think you just made an enemy," Ben said.

"You can't be a senator without making enemies. But a man has to draw the line somewhere, even in this day and age, when politics are dominated by big money. Can you imagine—letting the last untouched American wilderness be destroyed by oil companies? This is the country that invented conservation, the whole idea of preserving land from development. We had the first national park system in the world. And slowly but surely we've let that American ideal be eroded. Logging in the national forests. Commercial sponsors in the national parks. And now this. Well, I'm drawing a line in the sand. Whatever it costs me."

"At least he's a lobbyist, not a senator."

"Right. Which means he has a lot more clout."

"What?"

"Sorry to disillusion you, Ben, but lobbyists run this town. There are more than fifteen thousand of them running around any given time of the year. And they have enormous influence."

"Because of their campaign contributions?"

"Money is good, no doubt about it. But what these guys really have that makes them indispensable is information. They can determine whether a senator comes off as an out-of-touch dodo or a sapient policy analyst."

"But your staff—"

"Is overworked and underpaid. You have any idea how many thousand of bills we have to consider every year? No one could possibly be knowledgeable about all of them. But if the media catch you with your pants down, even once, they'll crucify you. So we call on lobbyists to give us the quick and accurate info we need to seem informed. That's the true source of their power. Pissing one off, any of them, can have serious repercussions."

"Nonetheless," Ben noted, "you just did it."

He looked out the corner of his eye and smiled. "Like the distinguished representative from Arkansas said. Don't let the bastards get you down."

4

Shandy hadn't intended to invade anyone's privacy. She just needed a few moments to herself. Sure, she wanted this job—had fought for it, in fact. Had done everything imaginable to get it. But what a day to start work! There had been almost no orientation, not even instructions on how to work the coffee machine. The moment she returned from the senator's committee meeting and the keenly disturbing aftermath, that rhymes-with-witch Amanda (Shandy didn't like to use sexist terms, even to herself) had shoved a pile of phone messages into her hand and told her to return the calls—without telling anyone anything. Good luck with that.

"But what position is the senator going to take?" "Will he consider resignation?" "What's the reaction from his wife?" All Shandy could do was repeat over and over again, "I'm sorry, but we have no comment on that at this time." A machine could have performed the job. And a machine wouldn't have minded the hostility she met in almost every instance.

After that, Amanda had her reviewing and revising the press releases she'd drafted, a pointless exercise since Amanda was obviously the type of person who couldn't take criticism from anyone. Then she had to make copies on that pathetic copying machine. Then she had to conference with a delegation from each party. Ironically, Senator Glancy's party turned out to be far more hostile. She could tell the Republicans were enjoying this, savoring the opportunity to bring down someone who had been mentioned as a possible national ticket player. The Democrats, on the other hand, felt disgusted and betrayed. Why would Amanda send her on these no-win missions? Two explanations leapt to mind. First: she figured Shandy couldn't tell them anything because she didn't know anything, and second: Amanda didn't want to face them herself. If Amanda had any hint of what Shandy had seen after the committee meeting, she'd have kept her under lock and key, but Shandy didn't know what to think about all that yet, so she kept her mouth shut.

Shandy knew that as soon as Amanda spotted her again she would give her another unpleasant assignment—something as bad as or worse than what she'd been doing all morning—so she told Hazel she was stepping out to get some fresh air, just so she could have a minute or two to collect her thoughts and slow the onset of insanity. She didn't think anyone (other than Amanda, if she found out) would mind. After all, they had told her where the senator's hideaway was during the interview, and she had been there before. She knew it was quite nice—it had a sofa with a foldout bed, a television, a fridge stocked with soft drinks, even a faux fireplace. So she quietly wound her way down the stairs and into the basement, through the circuitous maze of passageways that led to the private hideaway.

Unlike the wide-open passages aboveground, down below the corridors were narrow and claustrophobic, made all the worse by the discarded furniture and equipment that lined the way, some of it junk so old she didn't even know what it was originally designed to do. Stacks of yellowed paper, dented file cabinets, exposed wiring and rusted pipes: this was The Land That Time Forgot. She winced at the incessant clatter made by the electrical units, plumbing, and bizarre ancient subterranean air-conditioning tunnels. Finally she arrived at the hideaway, desperate to rest her feet, close her eyes, and just relax for one precious moment. She opened the door and stepped inside.

Her scream was so loud it could be heard all the way down the winding corridors and even upstairs, despite the rattling of the pipes, the humming of the exposed electrical wiring, and the sucking of the ancient air-conditioning tunnels. She screamed and screamed and when she finally stopped, it was not because she was no longer terrified, but because she was unconscious.

5

The first time Ben and Christina visited Senator Glancy's office, the scene had been chaotic. When they returned after lunch, it was empty. They were baffled—until the police officer posted inside escorted them downstairs.

"Where is this they're taking us?" Ben asked.

"My hideaway," Glancy explained, his lips pursed. "In the basement. The best of all possible Senate perks—and one of our most closely guarded secrets. A private haven far from the madding crowd, but close enough to the action that you can still make it upstairs in time for a roll call vote. Just a little place you can use to avoid lobbyists or tourists or anyone else. No one is supposed to know about them—they don't show up on the maps. Not even the Senate floor plan. But all the top senators have one. Dianne Feinstein used hers as a temporary office during the anthrax scare of '01 and the ricin scare of '04. Hell, in his prime, Tom Daschle had six of them."

When they finally arrived, the narrow hallway was congested by so many people it was difficult to pass through. The door to the hideaway had already been restricted with yellow crime scene tape. Hazel was there but not much help; her hands covered her face, which was streaked with tears. Most of the other staffers were equally distraught. Only Amanda appeared to have kept her head. She was facing down a mildly overweight man in a tan suit and white shirt, arguing with him about some topic they couldn't discern.

"What the hell happened?" Glancy muttered, soaking it all in. "Did the White House send cops out to look for a semen-stained dress?"

"There must be more to it than that," Ben said quietly. "A lot more."

"Why?"

"That man Amanda is talking to? He's a police detective."

"How can you tell?"

"Because I've spent a lot of time around detectives—and they didn't put this crime scene tape up for decoration. Something happened, and judging by the flurry of coveralled crime tech personnel in there, it happened in your hideaway."

"How could anything happen here? I've been in the cafeteria for hours."

"I don't know. Let's see if we can find out. Christina, try to get to one of the uniforms. I'll work on the detective."

They split up. Ben moved beside Amanda and the detective and waited for a pause in the conversation, which given the speed at which Amanda bellowed, was a fairly long wait.

"Who else had access to this location?" the detective asked.

"Only members of the staff. No one else would even know it existed."

"And I've met all the staffers here. Is there another office?"

"We have a secondary office a few blocks from here. At the Democratic headquarters."

"Why so far away?"

"They're full-time fund-raisers. They make cold calls, stay in touch with major donors, that sort of thing."

"You keep a separate office just for that?"

"No choice. Federal law prohibits fund-raising calls from a government office or on a government phone. Just ask Al Gore."

"Excuse me," Ben said, cutting in. "May I ask what happened here?"

The man looked at Amanda, not at Ben. "Who the hell is he? Is he on my list?"

"He's . . ." She waved her hand in the air. "Actually, I don't remember his name. He's the senator's lawyer."

"My name is Ben Kincaid. Why are the police here? What's happened?"

The detective scowled. "Like Glancy doesn't already know?"

"No, he doesn't."

"Then what a coincidence that he just happens to show up with a lawyer in tow." He snorted.

Ben did his best to control his temper. "Would someone please tell me what happened?"

The man reached past his bulging belly into his jacket and removed a black wallet, then flashed his badge. "I'm Lieutenant Albertson, DCPD. Homicide."

Ben felt his pulse quicken.

"We found the senator's missing girlfriend doing a headstand in the senator's hideaway. On the sofa, with her face wedged between the cushions. And her legs sprawled backward over the edge. And a nine-inch gash in her neck. Huge blood loss. Does that answer your question?"

"Is she dead?"

"You betcha. That's why we call it a homicide."

"May I see the crime scene?"

"No."

"May I speak to whoever found the body?"

"No."

"I'd like to receive copies of all your preliminary reports."

"Hell, no."

"Why not?"

"Why should I?"

Ben knew he was staring at a brick wall, and nothing less than a cannonball was going to get him through it. He realized how spoiled he had been, working in Tulsa, where his best friend and former brother-in-law was a homicide detective. Mike usually kept him involved and shared pertinent information, even when it infuriated the prosecutors. Obviously he was not going to get the same courtesy from this detective.

He retreated to the doorway, where he found Glancy with Christina. "They found a corpse."

"We know," Christina said. No surprise there. Christina was infinitely better at working people than he was. "I got the skivvy from the hunk posted outside the door. It's Veronica Cooper. The young woman in the video." Both Ben and Christina slowly turned toward Glancy.

"What are you looking at me for? I didn't have anything to do with it! I've been in the cafeteria with you, remember?"

"And before that?"

"I've been in and out of my office. At a committee meeting. In case you didn't notice, we've had a fairly busy morning. I haven't had time to come down here. But anyone could've gotten in."

"Anyone could have, maybe, but why would they?" Ben surveyed the scene. The videographers were making their visual records, the hair and fiber teams were crawling on their hands and knees searching for trace evidence, and a chemical ID team was coating the floor with luminol. "I don't know how to tell you this, Todd, but that serious problem you had? It just got a hell of a lot worse."

The police officers wouldn't cooperate with Ben at all, but they couldn't evict him, at least not beyond the perimeter of the crime scene tape. Ben suspected they really didn't want to; they knew that if he left, Glancy would go with him, and they wanted the senator on tap. So far there had been no questioning. Albertson was probably waiting until he knew as much as possible before he started interrogating their most likely suspect.

Christina continued to schmooze the officer at the gate and anyone else whose ear she could bend. She was amazing. Never once did she do anything that could be called flirting, but at the same time she had an instinctive knack for making people like her, for figuring out the best way to loosen someone's tongue. At the end of the day, she would have more insight on the situation than Ben could get in a week.

Ben was still standing outside the door when the coroner's team took the body out of the office. They seemed nervous, and Ben could understand why; it was a fair bet they'd never been asked to haul a corpse out of the U.S. Senate before. At one point an assistant stumbled and the top sheet slipped. Glancy averted his eyes. Ben didn't.

Her face was ashen and gray, but there was no doubt that it was the woman in the video. She was wearing more clothing now, but not that much more. Her white blouse was open three buttons down, exposing her neck and a significant amount of cleavage. She was wearing a short but professional-looking skirt, red and blue plaid, and red pumps.

Once the sheet was replaced and the corpse removed, Glancy turned back around. "My God," he whispered. "Who would've done this to her?"

Ben had no answer for him. But he suspected that every law enforcement officer in the room did, and that it was an answer Glancy was not going to like.

Christina pulled a chair beside Hazel, the receptionist, and tried to comfort her. She was still sobbing, blowing her nose, wailing about "that sweet girl who never wanted to hurt anyone," a dolorous expression engraved on her face.

It was really no business of hers, but Christina noticed that no one else in the office was paying Hazel any attention. Certainly not Amanda, who still bore a stony expression and periodically thrust herself into the police officers' paths for no apparent purpose other than being an irritant. She overheard a conversation between Lieutenant Albertson and his sergeant in the corridor. They didn't know she was with Ben; neither even looked her way as they talked.

"What do you make of it?" the sergeant asked in hushed tones.

"Got no idea," Albertson answered. "It's too crazy. But the evidence all points in one direction."

"Think he did her in there?"

"The CSIs haven't found blood anywhere else."

"I guess you noticed she wasn't wearing panties."

"Be hard to miss."

"Think Glancy decided to go back for seconds? Maybe she didn't like it, and—pow."

Albertson grunted. "Hard to know. A man who would do what he did in that video is capable of anything, far as I'm concerned. Think we've got enough?"

"Hell, yes."

"Me, too. Let's do it."

Christina raised her arms, not dramatically, just enough to get Ben's attention. While he was watching, she locked her fingers around each wrist, pantomiming handcuffs. Which probably wouldn't mean anything to anyone else. But they'd been working together for a long time. He'd get the message.

"Senator Glancy," Lieutenant Albertson said, as he strolled casually toward the senator and Ben, a friendly expression on his face. "I think I'm ready to ask you those questions now. Shouldn't take too long."

"Of course," Glancy said. "Anything I can do to help." He glanced at the still-blood-soaked sofa, his eyes filled with regret. "I tried to warn that girl."

Ben's eyes widened.

"Warn her?" Albertson asked. "About what?"

"Don't answer," Ben interjected.

The lieutenant and Glancy both stared at him. "Beg your pardon?"

"You heard me. Don't answer."

"Well, then let me ask this," the lieutenant said. "How long have you been in this building today?"

"Don't answer," Ben insisted. "I'm cutting this off now. No more questions."

Glancy protested. "But, Ben—"

"You heard me. Don't say a word."

Albertson frowned. "May I ask on what authority you're impeding this investigation?"

"I'm Senator Glancy's attorney. And he has the right to remain silent, as you very well know, even though you seem to have forgotten to read him his Miranda rights."

"It was my understanding you were representing the senator with regard to a civil matter, not a criminal one. As for the Miranda rights, this is not a custodial interrogation. We just want to ask the senator a few questions."

"What do you take me for?" Ben shot back. "I'm his attorney in all regards until you hear otherwise. He's not talking and that's—"

"Excuse me, may I be of service?" It was Marshall Bressler, suddenly wheeling up beside them.

"Where did you come from?" Ben asked.

Bressler smiled. "The entire building is wheelchair-accessible, Ben. Including the basement. Federal law." He looked up at the police lieutenant. "I'm the senator's top aide. His administrative assistant."

"All we want is to ask the senator a few questions."

Ben jumped in. "And I absolutely forbid it."

Bressler gave Ben a stern look. "Failure to cooperate with a criminal investigation is a serious matter. We could get all kinds of bad press."

"I agree," Glancy said. "I don't see any reason not to assist the police, Ben. If I can help them find the man that did this—"

"Don't kid yourself, Todd. They think they already have."

"What? Are you suggesting—"

"No, but they will."

Lieutenant Albertson tried again. "It would be very helpful if we could just get clarification on a few points about the senator's whereabouts and—"

"He's not talking."

"Is that right?" Albertson said, exasperated, addressing the senator.

"You heard what I said," Ben said forcefully.

"You're just a counselor, Mr. Kincaid. An adviser. He can take your advice—or not. It's his call." He paused. "You know, my uniforms tell me there are about, oh, two billion reporters outside waiting to see what happens next."

"What is that supposed to be?" Ben bellowed. "A threat? Blackmail? Any attempt to deny my client his Fifth Amendment rights is impermissible under *Miranda v. Arizona* and sanctionable by—"

"Yadda, yadda, yadda." The lieutenant ignored him. "So what's it going to be, Senator? Do you come clean, or do we go outside and inform the world that you're not talking?"

Glancy paused, pursed his lips, exhaled heavily. It was obviously a difficult decision for him. "It goes against my every instinct not to cooperate with a legal inquiry." He sighed. "But I suppose I have to respect my attorney's experience in these matters and do as he says."

"Have it your way." He waved to his sergeant. "Senator Glancy, you are now under arrest on a charge of murder in the first degree. Sergeant Reasor, handcuff the man."

"That won't be necessary," Glancy said.

"I'm afraid I insist."

"Why?" Ben said. "Just to humiliate him on the six o'clock news?"

"Standard operating procedure." He leaned into Ben's face. "I gave you a chance to save face, wiseass. Now your man pays the price."

"You'd already decided to arrest him. You were just trying to get a few pre-Miranda freebies and we both know it."

The sergeant handcuffed Glancy, then pushed him toward the door and down the corridor.

"I can run interference for you," Ben said, as they approached the swarm of reporters waiting at the top of the stairs. "Hold up a newspaper. Keep them from getting TV footage."

"Please don't," Glancy said, and a moment later he had his television face on while a hundred bright lights shone down on him and a thousand questions were shouted at once. "This is all a terrible mistake," Glancy said. "I intend to cooperate with the investigation fully, so we can find out who really committed this atrocity. And then I'll be back to work, serving the best interests of my constituents, in no time at all."

But even as he watched the man perform like the pro he was, Ben knew he was wrong. This wasn't going away anytime soon. If it went away at all.

Part Two

The Judicial Evidence Is All-Embracing

6

WASHINGTON DC, FIVE MONTHS LATER

Ben thought he was beyond the point where anything that took place in, at, or near a courtroom could surprise him. After the trial in Chicago—an emotionally and politically charged hate crime, covered blow-by-blow by the media nationwide—what could possibly be more difficult? He thought he'd seen it all.

He was wrong.

The federal courthouse was swarming with reporters. That was hardly startling. The so-called Glancy's Glen had established itself in the courthouse parking lot almost immediately after the senator was arrested. Scores of reporters representing all the media were there, making daily, sometimes hourly updates with the majestic stone pillars of the courthouse as a backdrop. According to the experts, the media stronghold outsized the famed O. J. outpost. Every pretrial proceeding, no matter how minor, had been covered in detail: every docket hearing, every pretrial motion, every judicial conference, no matter how trivial. The reporters would deliver their reports in somber tones, usually concluding with a small pivot toward the courthouse and a reference to how "no one would know for sure" what happened to Veronica Cooper until the parties gathered in this building "for a final reckoning."

What did surprise Ben as he and Christina stepped out of their taxicab was how expertly the area surrounding the courthouse appeared to be organized this morning. Ropes cordoned off the central flight of steps leading to the front doors. There were protesters present, firebrands from the left and the right as there had always been, but somehow they had been pushed far to the rear, far enough that not even the loudest of them would be heard once the minicams started rolling. Ben recognized many of the people standing closest to the ropes—including several of the senator's staff members and friends, such as Amanda Burton and Shandy Craig. A podium had been placed at the top of the stairs with several microphones already in place.

As Ben gazed at the assembly, Marshall Bressler rolled up beside him.

"Got to hand it to the DC authorities," Ben said with genuine admiration. "They've got things much more under control than their counterparts in Chicago did."

"Forget the authorities," Bressler replied. "Congratulate Senator Glancy's advance team."

Christina raised an eyebrow. "What's an advance team?"

"I can tell you haven't had much experience with politics. These days, advance men—many of whom are women, by the way—are the lifeline of any politician. At least any politician who wants to be one for very long. Ever since Kennedy/Nixon in 1960, the need for specialists to orchestrate and control how candidates are presented by the media has been readily apparent."

"I haven't seen any advance men in the office."

"We're not talking about paper pushers. We're talking about highly skilled media consultants who command top dollar—because they're worth it. They pander to the press, marshal the allies, outwit the enemies, cozy up to the Secret Service, prepare itineraries, arrange photo ops, plan motorcades, hang bunting and banners and, most important, anticipate every contingency. Politics is not immune to

Murphy's Law—anything that can go wrong, will. The advance men deal with all unforeseen developments and overcome them."

"And they did—" Ben waved his hand toward the general assemblage. "—all this?"

"Of course. Believe me, they've been working on it for days—obtaining permits, snuggling up to the courthouse officials, confabbing with Amanda and the rest of the staff on how we wanted our man presented. Remember, most people will be seeing Todd today for the first time in five months, ever since he was incarcerated in the district jail."

"Your people put up these ropes?"

"Who else? They wanted to make sure the senator could make a dignified ascent, without interference. Why do you think all the protesters and right-wing tub-thumpers—some of whom were bused in from Maryland by the Senate majority leader's staff, by the way—have been shunted off so far from the action? All the cameras will get are Todd's supporters."

"Is this really necessary? The potential jurors are already sequestered."

"They're not concerned about the jury, Ben. That's *your* job. They're concerned about the voters, and not just the ones back in Oklahoma, either."

"Surely Todd doesn't still think he can run for national office."

"Our polls indicate that the video hurt us with female voters, but much less so with males, especially those under the age of forty-five. If you can make it look as if Todd has been the victim of political calumny, an unscrupulous plot to entrap him with another woman then frame him for murder, you might well win us back those female votes. Women sympathize with underdogs and martyrs—people they believe have been treated unfairly."

"Speaking as a woman," Christina said, "and for that matter one who doesn't believe Senator Glancy killed Veronica Cooper, I still wouldn't give the man my vote if he personally kissed my—"

Ben clamped his hand over her mouth. "Minicams, Christina. Big powerful microphones. Talking out loud bad."

Christina clenched her teeth and remained silent.

A few minutes later, a black van from DC's Central Detention

Center rolled up to the curb and Senator Glancy stepped out of the back. He raised one arm into the air, and all at once the crowd went wild, cheering, calling out his name, whistling and thumping their feet. Ben felt more like he was at a rock concert than a murder trial. At any moment he expected someone to hold up a lighter.

"What did I tell you?" Bressler said, winking. "Advance men."

Glancy's intern, Shandy Craig, stepped out of the crowd and tugged at his sleeve. "Hair check."

She scrutinized him carefully, then minutely adjusted the lie of his salt-and-pepper bangs.

"Teeth."

Glancy flashed them for her.

"You're clean. Go get 'em, tiger."

Glancy jabbed his thumb back toward Shandy. "Is she the best, or what? Love that girl. Are we ready?"

"We are," Ben answered. "But I'm afraid this isn't going to be a very pleasant day for you."

"We'll make the most of it. Anything's better than that hellhole where they've been keeping me. I don't know where people get these ideas about politicians going to country club prisons. The DC jail is the pits."

Having visited him on several occasions, Ben knew this was true. It was a no-perks enterprise operating on a constrained budget. The visitors' room didn't even have separated chambers; every time Ben talked to Glancy he had to shout to be heard over the clatter of all the other attorneys and relatives.

Glancy turned toward the crowd and flashed them a grateful smile—the kind of million-watt grin that gets men elected to public office and keeps them there—then moved with calm and grace toward the front steps. As negotiated with the incarceration officials and the prosecution in the spirit of fair play, Glancy had been provided with a freshly pressed suit and grooming equipment, and his keepers remained several paces behind him out of camera range, so he could enter the courtroom looking like a senator—not a murderer. As he passed by, dozens of people thrust out their hands, and he shook a few, though never slowing his advance up the stairs. Ben couldn't help but admire the style, the savoir faire that allowed a

man in such dire circumstances to emerge looking more like a re-
turning astronaut than an accused murderer.

Once he reached the top of the stairs, Glancy started toward the
podium.

With a subtle sidestep, Ben blocked his progress. "Wait a minute.
We need to move on to the courtroom."

"I'm giving a press conference," Glancy said, smiling. "I'm a
politician, Ben. It's what we do."

"No way," Ben replied, standing firm. "I told you. You say
nothing unless and until we put you on the witness stand."

"This is a critical moment, politically speaking," Glancy explained. "The press has been building toward this for months. They
expect me to say something. I can't let them down."

"Listen to me," Ben said, keeping his voice down so the mikes
surrounding him wouldn't pick it up. "This is not a campaign.
You're on trial for murder. Under the new federal execution act, the
jury has the option to give you the death penalty."

"But the potential jurors have already been sequestered, right?
They won't be able to hear what I say."

"True, but—"

"Please excuse me." His face remained calm. To anyone who
couldn't hear what was being said, it would look as if two close
friends were having an amiable chat. He started again toward the
podium.

"Todd." Ben held his arm. "When I agreed to take on this murder case, you agreed that you would follow my instructions. To the
letter."

"As regards the case, yes. As regards my career—well, I think
my political advisers are more qualified to make those decisions,
don't you?"

"Todd, if you endanger—"

"I'm not going to say anything that will help the prosecution, or
that will even directly relate to the case." He gently removed Ben's
hand from his arm. "You know how to play your game, Ben, and I
respect that. Now let me play mine."

Glancy squared himself behind the podium. He started to speak,
but another round of cheers and applause erupted, drowning him

out. Ben wondered what his advance men had done to trigger that. Paid off a wino? Goosed a maiden aunt?

"My friends," Glancy began. Even in these circumstances, something about the way he said it, his crisp mellifluous voice, the way he looked squarely into the camera as he spoke, made you want to believe it. "I thank you for your support during these troubled times. I particularly thank those of you who have been so kind to my wife, Marie. My lawyer won't let me talk about the case—and you know how those lawyers act when they don't get their way."

The crowd laughed heartily. What was all this "those lawyers" jazz? Ben wondered. Hadn't Glancy picked up a JD way back when, too?

"Nonetheless, I can assure you that when this is over—and it will be over soon—I will be back to work, doing what I've always done: defending and protecting the best interests of my constituents." The resultant swell of cheers and enthusiasm almost drowned out his closing. "Thank you again for your support. See you on the other side."

Loving drummed his fingers on the desktop. He circled Jones's workstation, pacing trails into the burgundy carpet. He checked his watch. He gazed at the view of the Main Mall out the north window of their borrowed office space. He shuffled through his papers and daily reports. And then he sat back down and drummed his fingers some more.

"Would you cut that out!" Jones said, finally.

"Huh? What?"

"Everything! All of it. The pacing, the fiddling, the drumming. You're driving me insane!"

"Short drive," Loving muttered. "Why are you so touchy?"

"Because I'm swamped! As you may recall, the trial we've been prepping for the past five months began today. I have a mound of motions and other paperwork to deal with."

"Didn't Glancy hire a team of big-firm lawyers to do that kinda stuff?"

"Yes, a magnificent beau geste designed to show his gratitude to Ben—that hasn't helped in the least. A bunch of twenty-eight-year-olds in starched shirts billing three hundred dollars an hour. Give me a break. I'd rather do it myself."

Loving frowned. "Least you can make yourself useful."

"You're the resident hawkshaw. Don't you have some investigating to do?"

"I've been investigatin' for five months. And I haven't come up with squat."

"No theories?"

"Oh, I got lots of theories. The Trilateral Commission runs this town—they're behind all the big power plays. There's basically thirteen old men who run the world."

Jones resisted the urge to roll his eyes. He'd long since become accustomed to Loving's endless supply of conspiracy theories. "Got anything Ben could conceivably use in court?"

"Nah. I've interviewed all the witnesses. Everyone who might know somethin' about the case. Looked under every rock. And struck out each time." He was interrupted by a computer chip rendition of the William Tell Overture. "'Scuse. That's my cell."

Jones turned back to his screen. "Probably Ben wanting me to run him over some pencils or something. As if I had nothing better to do."

"Yeah?" Loving said, as he snapped open the phone.

The voice on the other end was low and whispery. "You the one looking for intel on the Cooper killing?"

Loving's eyes widened. "Yeah, I am. Who's this?"

"That's not important."

"I gotta call you somethin'."

"Fine." There was a short, bitter laugh. "Call me Deep Throat."

Loving felt his heart race. "Like—in that movie they showed at my brother-in-law's bachelor party?"

"The—what? No, like in—never mind. You don't need to call me anything. But I can help you."

"How?"

"You want Glancy to get off, don't you?"

"That's our goal, yeah," Loving said, not quite answering the question. Having seen that video several times too often, he personally had a hard time getting worked up about whether Glancy was convicted. This was a job he was working for Ben, period. "How can you help?"

"The secret to saving the accused," the voice continued, "is finding out more about the victim."

"I've investigated the victim. For months. I know where she grew up and what her favorite colors were and what grades she made in junior high science. I've talked with her mom. I know everything about the woman."

The softness of his voice gave his chuckle an eerie hollowness. "No, you don't. Not by a long shot."

"Okay, hotshot, tell me what I don't know."

"Not over the phone."

"Oh, puh-lese."

"Will you meet me? Someplace safe?"

"What is it with you Washington clowns?" Loving said. "Can't you ever just talk to someone like a normal human being?"

"No, I can't. If he found out—"

"If *who* found out?"

"I can't tell you that. But if you'll agree to meet me . . ."

"Fine." Loving acted exasperated, but in reality he was elated. It was a lead—or at least the promise of a lead. Even if the guy was a kook, which was the most likely case, it would give him something to do. "Where you wanna meet?"

"How about the Reflecting Pool. You're already near, right?"

"Where exactly? It's a big pool."

"I can't specify a location. I have to remain fluid. To keep watch for people who might recognize me."

Loving felt his patience draining. "Then how am I gonna find you?"

"You won't have to. Just leave your office, right now, walk across to the Pool, find an empty bench, and make yourself comfortable." He paused. "When it's safe, I'll find you."

The courtroom was as silent as a vacuum while all assembled waited for the judge to arrive. It was almost like a wedding: the supporters of the defendant were seated on the right side of the courtroom behind the defense table, next to the jury box. The prosecution, the deceased's family, and most of the press sat on the left. No cameras were allowed in the courtroom, but there were record numbers of notepads, sketch artists, and laptops with padded keyboard silencers and Wi-Fi transmitters that beamed each word back to a receiving station in Glancy's Glen.

Ben also spotted a number of Glancy's fellow senators in the gallery. Presumably they got first dibs on the limited seats, if they wanted them. The Republicans had excoriated Glancy from the moment the body was found. The Democratic support was lukewarm at best: "I'm optimistic that when the truth is uncovered, we will find that Todd did not commit these horrific acts, despite appearances. But let me make it clear that I do not condone sexual harassment in the workplace . . ." That sort of thing. Although a motion to censure had been brought, it was tabled for the time being. Independent counsel had been appointed to investigate whether any violation of federal law "or Senate protocol" had occurred—but as yet, nothing had been done. They were all waiting to see what happened in the courtroom. Glancy had resisted calls for his resignation; if for no other reason, his replacement would be chosen by Oklahoma's current governor, a staunch Republican. Given how close the balance between the two parties was in the Senate at the moment, the outcome of this trial could affect far more than the future of Tom Glancy; it could quite literally affect the future of the nation itself.

No pressure there, Ben thought, muttering under his breath. None at all.

"Judge Herndon should be here soon." Ben said. "Know him?"

"Ben, I know everyone in this town," Glancy replied calmly. In dramatic contrast to the nervousness Ben was experiencing, the defendant was maintaining his usual implacable sangfroid. "Herndon is a Republican, alas. Been around a long while. Used to be in private practice, then he helped George Bush the First raise a lot of campaign dough and got himself appointed to a federal judgeship. He's still active in the Republican machine. I'm surprised he hasn't moved higher than the district court by now. It suggests several relevant possibilities."

"Such as?"

"Either he likes it where he is, or there's a reason he can't get anything better."

"Heads up, Ben," Christina whispered. "Enemy at five o'clock."

Ben's esteemed opponent, federal prosecutor Paul Padolino, headed his way. Padolino was a calm man, eminently reasonable, quiet and laconic, unlike most prosecutors. To Ben's knowledge, he had not indulged in excessive gamesmanship and had not held repeated press conferences despite the fact that he reportedly had political ambitions. Nonetheless Ben knew that as soon as the judge's gavel sounded, they would both relinquish all pretense of civility and begin a titanic struggle, each desperate to come out the victor.

Padolino paused at the defendant's table, nodded politely to Christina, then looked Ben square in the eye. "Life, incarceration at the upscale prison in Arlington, possibility of parole in eight years."

"You call that an offer?" Ben said. It was his standard reply to all plea bargains; the only thing it meant was that he needed more time to think.

"I call that the best you're going to get. The prison I'm offering has tennis courts, for God's sake. A nine-hole golf course."

"Sorry, but—"

"Ben, once the trial starts, there's no stopping it. All offers are off the table."

Ben turned toward his client.

"No conversation required," Glancy said, holding up a hand. "I did not commit this atrocity. I will not plead guilty to it, not if your offer was one day of community service at a candy factory."

"And there you have it," Ben said.

"I'm not kidding, Ben. This is our final offer."

"And we're declining."

Padolino's cool melted a bit. "You're both being irrational. I'm trying to do you a favor!" He stomped back to his table.

Despite Padolino's protest, Ben suspected he wasn't all that surprised by their decline of his offer, or disappointed. No trial lawyer who'd come this far wanted to pack it in before it started.

Barely a minute later, Judge Herndon emerged from his chambers, preceded by his bailiff.

"Oyez, oyez, oyez," the bailiff chanted. The judge took his seat. The trial had begun.

Leave immediately, the man had said. When it's safe, I'll find you, he'd promised. So where the heck was he?

Loving sat on a bench on the south side of the Reflecting Pool, crossing his legs from one side to the other, staring at the passing joggers, watching the squirrels in the trees, bored to tears. He'd never been good at sitting still. The view was lovely, not only the

Pool but of the Lincoln Memorial at the opposite end and all the cherry trees lining the perimeter. But he hated waiting, and he hated all the oh-so-mysterious cloak-and-dagger baloney. That wasn't how they operated back in Tulsa.

He checked his watch. He'd been sitting for more than an hour. Even if he didn't have any other decent leads—or, for that matter, any indecent leads—this was more than he could bear. The guy obviously wasn't coming. Maybe he'd give up on the chump and pay a visit to Honest Abe. There was a man you could count on.

He started to push himself to his feet, and just as he did, he felt a pair of hands slap down on his shoulders and shove him back down onto the bench.

"Don't turn around!" the voice commanded, stifling Loving's natural instinct.

"Why not?"

"I swear, if you turn around, I won't tell you a thing."

"Fine. I won't look at your pretty face." At least, not yet. "So whaddya got for me?"

"A name." He was breathless, making an effort to stay low-key and quiet. But it was definitely a man. "Colleen Tomei."

Colleen Tomei. Loving ran the name through his cranial database a few times. He'd heard it before, but where? Oh—right. "She was a friend of Veronica Cooper's. I tried to track her down. Never found her."

"And there's a reason for that." Loving could feel his informant twisting from side to side, as if checking to make sure he hadn't been spotted. "She's been eliminated."

"Eliminated? Whaddya mean?"

There was a long pause. Loving could feel the hands on his shoulders lightening. Was this guy planning to bolt? Because if he did—

"Look, I can only stay another minute. I've taken too many risks as it is. If he found out—"

"There you go again. Who?"

The voice behind him barreled onward, ignoring the question. "There were four of them: Veronica, Colleen, Amber, and Beatrice. Four DC girls who liked to party. But they got into some weird stuff. Seriously weird stuff."

"Like drugs? Bad boys?"

"That's not the half of it. Just listen, okay? They got in over their heads, seriously kinked, and that's why you're never, ever gonna find Colleen. But there's still a chance for the other two. If you move quickly."

"And why do I hafta move quickly?" Other than the fact that Ben's trial had already started.

"Because you're not the only one looking, idiot. Do you think he doesn't know? Do you think he can risk them talking? After what happened to Colleen?"

"I'm sorry, man, but you're not makin' any sense."

"I don't have time to make sense!" Loving felt the hands on his shoulders trembling. "Look, I've got to get out of here."

Loving almost turned. "And suppose I don't let you leave?"

"Then you don't get the only lead you're ever going to get!" he said, raising his voice. "I don't know where Amber is, but I know how you can find her. And I'll tell you. If you promise you won't turn around. Won't move a muscle, and will give me a full minute to get away."

"And what makes you think I'd keep that promise?"

"Because I checked you out before I called. You're a man of your word, that's what I hear. Is that right?"

Loving didn't answer.

"Will you keep the bargain?"

Loving sighed heavily. "I'll keep the bargain. But why are you helpin' me?"

"Because this has got to stop, man. I mean, it was fun at first. I really went for it. It appealed to my dark side, you know? Made me feel like I belonged. But this—what's happened now—God. It's just got to stop."

"Can't you stop it?"

The man laughed. "Me? Against him? Jesus!" Loving felt the hands lifting from his shoulders. "Look, I'm making tracks."

"The lead!" Loving shouted. "You never gave me the lead!"

There was a moment of hesitation. "Martin's Tavern, after dark. Through the back door, down the alley. Look for an escort service."

"An escort service!"

"When you get there, ask for Lucille." His hands rose off Loving's shoulders. "I'm outta here."

"Wait!"

"Remember your bargain!" the man hissed, and Loving could tell from the sound of his voice that he was already moving away.

Blast! He should look, he knew he should, any other investigator would. But the man had played him perfectly. He'd given his word. He wasn't going to break it.

As soon as his watch told him the minute was up, Loving jumped to his feet and looked all around. No trace of the informant. Or, to be more accurate, no one he could positively identify as the informant, given the large number of people surrounding the Pool.

What had the man been babbling about? Who was this person he was so scared of? And what could those four party girls have been involved with that could lead to Veronica Cooper's murder in the U.S. Senate?

He didn't know. Didn't have any idea. But at long last, he had a clue. Or a chance of one. If the man wasn't totally whacked, or playing him. Or covering up something by leading Loving in the wrong direction. It was impossible to know.

Only one thing was certain. Tonight Ben was going to have to schlep his own gear back from the courtroom. Loving was going tavern-hopping.

7

Even though the federal courts gave attorneys far less leeway during jury selection than the typical state court, and even though the questions were screened in advance and were asked by the judge himself, not the lawyers, jury selection was still an unbearably time-consuming process. This was a murder case, after all—potentially a capital murder case, and one involving a very well-known public figure. It was nearly impossible to find a juror who did not know the defendant or who was not familiar with the case. The best Ben and Christina could hope for was twelve people who claimed that they had not yet made up their minds as to his innocence or guilt and who would not do so until all the evidence was presented. Which was how it should be in every case, of course, but Ben wasn't kidding himself that this was anything like every case.

The stickiest point of discussion, of course, was the video. Everyone had already seen it, but just in case they hadn't, Prosecutor

Padolino was desperate to show it to them during voir dire. Not for evidentiary purposes, of course—that would be wrong. He just wanted to be sure the jury wouldn't be so shocked by the graphic content—especially when the network pixilated masking was removed—that they would be unable to adjudicate the case without bias. Yeah, right.

Ben did rather like the way the judge conducted the jury questioning. Judge Herndon was a tall man, lean, with a slow, studied expression reminiscent of Gary Cooper in *High Noon*. He knew Glancy was concerned that the judge would show partisan bias, but as he conducted his measured, careful jury questioning, Ben saw few indications of favoritism. Maybe it was because he knew the press was watching, but he appeared determined to observe each and every punctilio of federal criminal procedure.

Lawyers were forever shading and slanting their jury questions, attempting to preview their case during voir dire. None of that from the judge. He toed the line, never once giving any indication how he felt about any of the parties, the matters at issue, or even the damnable video. He asked his questions simply and for one purpose—to determine if anything in the venireperson's background, beliefs, or personality would make him or her an unsuitable juror. Did they know any of the parties, object to the senator's political positions, or have a past experience with romance in the workplace? He let the jurors talk back, even ask questions of their own—something an experienced trial attorney would never risk. Christina took down some of the jurors' most noteworthy remarks:

"Any woman who wears underwear like that is asking for it. End of story."

"Will the senator be questioned about his surgeries? Because I think he's had some kind of surgery. And I'm not talking about circumcision."

"I'd like to know what time of day it was. If it was during work hours, that means the taxpayer was paying for it. Maybe he was, too, I don't know. But if it was the taxpayer, I'm angry."

"Did the senator vote to send our boys to the Middle East? 'Cause if he voted for that one, you better get me off this jury right here and now."

"Only thing I want to know is where the girl got that outfit. I mean, not that I would ever wear anything like that. I was just, you know. Curious."

"Way I see it, them boys up in Washington been screwin' us for years. What's so special 'bout this one?"

In a few instances, the judge removed prospective jurors *sui sponte*. The woman who was way too interested in the deceased's undergarments, for instance. But for the most part, he left it to the lawyers. After each round of questioning, Ben and Padolino approached the bench and quietly informed the judge who they wanted replaced. Ben took most of his cues from Christina—although he was able to deduce that the "angry taxpayer" needed to go on his own. Time and experience had proven to him that Christina had a preternatural gift for understanding people—far greater than his own. By the time he had a juror's name down, Christina had figured out her age, socioeconomic background, political persuasion, sexual preference, and whether she was a cat person or a dog person. Christina wanted a jury composed principally of ailurophiles—cat people. He had no idea why. But he didn't argue.

Eventually both sides used up their peremptories. After that, they had to come up with a good reason to remove a juror, persuasive arguments why an answer indicated bias. And they found that Judge Herndon was not easily persuaded. Maybe it was his usual resistance to prolonged jury selection; maybe it was because he knew the eyes of the world were on him and he was determined not to come off as a Judge Ito who let the lawyers push him around. Either way, eventually the questions and the challenges bottomed out and they had twelve jurors and four alternates.

"Opening statements at nine A.M. sharp," the judge informed them. Then he thanked the jurors for their cooperation and gave them detailed preliminary instructions. They would be sequestered for the length of the trial.

"What do you think?" Ben asked as he returned to the defendant's table. "Did we get a good jury?"

"I think you did the best you could with what we drew," Christina said.

"What does that mean?" Glancy asked. "Do they like me or are they going to hang me out to dry?"

"My name's Christina, not Sibyl," she replied. "The outcome will depend on what happens when the witnesses take the stand."

"I still don't understand why we couldn't ask if the jurors were Republicans or Democrats," Glancy groused. "That's the most important question—certainly the most relevant. And the judge never asked it."

"Because it is totally impermissible, even in this case," Ben answered. "There are about a hundred cases on point. Courts have to follow precedent—previous rulings on the same issue. Even the Supreme Court."

"So you're telling me the Supreme Court followed precedent when they butted into the 2000 election and made Dubya the leader of the free world?"

Ben turned his eyes toward his legal pad. "Let's stay focused on the case at hand, shall we?"

Of all the two-bit gin joints in the world, Loving mused to himself, this was about the only one Ben hadn't already sent him to—always in the hope of rooting out the truth by exploiting Loving's knack for worming information out of the bottom-feeders of society. Ben didn't like bars, had a coughing fit whenever someone lit up, and couldn't lie to save his soul, so he needed someone else to handle these assignments. Loving got that. But someday he was going to draw the line. That day would not be today, however. He wasn't going to pass this one up just because of the décor.

Which was actually quite nice, as it turned out, a step up from the usual haunts he ventured into in search of unfound knowledge. Martin's Tavern, in Georgetown on Wisconsin Avenue, was a national landmark dating back to 1933. The look of the place appealed to Loving—lots of dark stained wood, very colonial, from the booths to the long oak bar that flanked the north wall. And the waiters wore distinguished green jackets—pretty swank for a tavern.

Loving scanned the clientele as he passed through the building. Looked like a sports bar, except he saw a lot of people who might actually be capable of playing a sport rather than simply watching one on the tube from behind a mountain of six-packs. He wouldn't mind stepping up to the bar for a quick quaff himself, but not while he was on duty. He had to keep his wits about him. As he'd learned long ago—when you're working one of Ben's cases, you should prepare for the unexpected. Which was of course, by definition, impossible.

He found the rear door and the alleyway his mysterious informant had mentioned without any trouble. It was dark and squalid and had a penetrating stench. Loving didn't know how often the garbage was collected back here, but it wasn't often enough. He kept tripping over trash can lids or stepping into squishy lumps he couldn't identify, which was probably just as well. The alley seemed to cut through the better part of a city block, but most of the back doors weren't labeled, so he had no way of knowing which one might lead to the purported escort service, much less to the mysterious Lucille. He might still be walking back and forth in that alley if he hadn't spotted a man exiting quickly from one of the doors, hitching and adjusting his pants as he walked, a euphoric smile on his face.

Ah, Loving thought. One of *those* kinds of escort services.

He knocked on the door, wondering if he needed a secret knock or handshake. Fortunately, that didn't prove necessary. The door opened a crack. A pair of dark female eyes became just barely visible. "Yeah?"

"I'm here to see Lucille," Loving replied.

"Does she know you're coming?"

"Darn! I forgot to call ahead. But—"

"She isn't seeing any more clients tonight."

"Are you sure? Maybe if you asked, she—"

"I'm sure. She . . . had a bad experience. Asked for the rest of the night off. But we have other escorts on duty tonight. What are your requirements?"

"My . . . uh, requirements?"

"What exactly were you looking for? We have other redheads. Other large-breasted women. Much larger, in fact."

Loving squirmed. "No, it, uh, has to be Lucille."

The crack in the door began to narrow. "Try again another night, cowboy. If you want to avoid disappointment, make an appointment."

Loving thrust his toe forward, stopping the door.

The woman's face turned cold. "Look, buddy, I'm not alone here. You may think you're hot stuff, but I've got three guys inside just as big as you who'll rip your—"

"I don't want any trouble," Loving assured her. "I just gotta talk to Lucille."

"Then come back another night. There's no way—"

"Tell her it's about Amber." It was a shot in the dark, but he had to try something. "Tell her I'm looking for Amber."

The two coal-black eyes in the narrow slit stared at him for a long moment. A good thirty seconds passed before Loving heard the sound of the door chain being released.

"You can come inside. But stay in the lobby. I'll ask Lucille if she's up to it." She held up a finger. "You better not be screwing with us."

"Gosh, no," Loving said. "I wouldn't dream of . . . trying to screw with someone here. At the escort service."

She gave him another long look. "Back in sixty seconds. Don't go anywhere."

Senator Glancy had recommended the Four Georges at the Georgetown Inn for dinner; he'd even made the reservation himself on Ben's cell phone and told the maître d' to put it on his tab. He wasn't attending himself, since the federal marshals collected him as soon as the jury was dismissed, but Ben and Christina opted to take his recommendation—and his free meal. They were seated in the elegant and somewhat exclusive George II room—apparently senators had pull in this town, even when they were currently residing in a holding cell. The room was decorated in a desert motif: palm trees, or something that looked like them, brick-laid walls painted a sandy hue and ornamented with several variegated mosaics. They didn't have to sit on the carpet or wear turbans, but the low tables and the belly-dancing music still conveyed the desired ambience.

"Heard anything from Loving?" Christina asked. She had changed into a turquoise dress with a hip-hugging waist that was positively lovely. Even some nice bling—a faux pearl necklace and earrings.

"Barely." Ben was wearing the same suit he'd had on all day. Of course, he had only three, and the dry cleaning at the Watergate wasn't that speedy, so he couldn't afford to be extravagant. "He did leave me a message. Thinks he's got some kind of lead on Veronica Cooper's friends."

"'Bout damn time, as my father used to say." She flagged the waiter and asked him to refill her club soda. "You know how little we've got, and the prosecution has a mound of evidence. Not to mention public opinion—a general populace predisposed to convict. Everyone commentator and quidnunc in the city is talking about this case."

"Because of the video?"

"Because this is a nation where news has been supplanted by gossip. Because most people would rather think the worst of their elected officials than the best."

"There is that . . ."

"And I don't care what the judge says in court. As soon as the jurors see that video, in its full and unexpurgated form, the burden of proof will be on us."

"We don't have to prove he's a hero. Or even a nice guy. We just have to prove he's not a murderer. I think we should all but ignore the video, admit the affair. Focus on the murder, the forensic evidence, the bizarre appearance of the corpse in the hideaway. Glancy's alibi."

"Padolino will do his darnedest to bust that alibi."

"Just the same, that's where we should concentrate our energy. That's where Padolino has some holes in his case. We should make the most of it." He fidgeted with his fork. "Did I mention . . . that's a very attractive dress you're wearing tonight. Have I seen it before?"

She flashed her usual fulgent smile. "This is what I always wear when we go someplace nice."

"So that would mean . . ."

"You've seen it twice."

"Well . . . it looks . . . particularly nice tonight." He wanted to slap himself. Ben, you smooth talker. More talk like that and she'll be putty in your hands.

"You're sweet. But I've had it for years. It's getting worn. I should go shopping."

"Well, we are in DC. After the case is over . . ."

"Maybe if we win. And you actually collect a fee this time."

"Christina . . ."

"Just joshing, partner." She reached across the table and squeezed his hand. "You know I care nothing about monetary gain. Why else would I work with you?"

"I think our only danger is that Glancy will spend too much on associated counselors. How many people are technically a part of this defense team now?"

"I think we're up to ten, counting the local counsel that have been assisting on the paperwork and document review, the DNA expert, and the appeals expert."

"Both of whom are totally unnecessary at this time."

She nodded her agreement. "My theory is that Glancy wants to have more lawyers than O. J. and Jacko combined. It's an ego thing. And if he can afford it . . ."

"Whatever. Just so they're invisible in the courtroom. I don't want the jury to get the idea Glancy is trying to buy his way out of trouble." He glanced at the list in the center of the table. "Did you want some wine?"

She arched an eyebrow. "Does this mean the Four Georges doesn't stock chocolate milk?"

"*Très* amusing. I just thought you might like a little stress-reducer." And as a matter of fact, yes, the waiter had whispered to him earlier that there was no chocolate milk, but she didn't need to hear that. What she needed to hear . . . well, he knew perfectly well what she needed to hear. So why wasn't he able to say it? "You know, Christina, I really . . . really appreciate your help on this case. You were invaluable in the courtroom today."

"That's what partners do."

"Read jurors' minds?"

"They complete each other. Make a whole greater than the sum of the parts. That's true for . . . all kinds of partners."

Well that was unsubtle, even for Christina, the Queen of Blunt. Ben cleared his throat and fiddled nervously with the menu until the waiter blessedly reappeared.

The menu selections were extremely rarefied for Ben's taste, but he managed to order something he was pretty sure involved beef; Christina had the grilled salmon. After they'd given their order and the waiter poured the Beaujolais, Ben pitched various approaches to his opening statement to Christina. She didn't like any of them. Too defensive, too exculpatory. The trick was to remind the jurors that this was about murder, not sex; to direct them to disregard the video without appearing to make excuses for it. "If I were you," she advised, "I'd just come straight out the first time I addressed them and say—"

"Excuse me."

Ben looked up and saw a middle-aged man with a salt-and-pepper goatee standing next to the table beneath one of the pseudo-palm trees. He was staring at Ben with a crazed, walleyed expression. Ben didn't know who the man was, but he was certain he'd seen him in the courtroom earlier. "Yes?"

"Are you two the lawyers defending Thomas Glancy?"

"We're the lead trial counsel, yes." Ben pondered. Reporter? Police officer? Autograph hound? "We're working in affiliation with a number of—"

"Do you know who I am?"

"Uh, I'm . . . sorry, no."

"Maybe this will refresh your memory?" Before Ben had a chance to react, the man had grabbed Ben's wineglass and flung the drink into his face.

Ben reared backward, blinking, wiping the stinging liquid from his eyes. Great, he thought, now I'm down to two suits. Christina started to rise, probably planning to slug him, but Ben waved her back into her seat. The last thing they needed was salacious publicity on the eve of trial.

"So," Ben said, looking up at him, "you're . . . my dry cleaner?"

"I'm Darrin Cooper—Veronica Cooper's father, you son of a bitch." He spoke with such venom that spittle flew from his teeth. "Isn't it interesting that you didn't know? You've spent months looking for anything that might get that goddamn rapist off the hook, but you never bothered to talk to the victim's family."

"Actually," Christina interjected, "I did contact Ms. Cooper's family almost immediately after we took the case. I spoke to her mother; her sister declined to be interviewed." She paused. "I was told that Veronica was raised in DC by her mother—that her parents were divorced and her father lived on the other coast and hadn't seen her for years."

"What the hell difference does that make?" He glared at Christina, bitter and angry. Ben not-so-subtly moved her wineglass to the opposite side of the table. "She was still my little girl."

Ben tried to sound comforting. "Sir, I've never had children myself, but I can only imagine how devastating it must be to lose one."

"Don't give me that fake sympathetic bullshit. I won't take it from the man who's defending my little Ronnie's killer."

"Sir, you don't know that."

"The hell I don't. Everyone in the country knows it."

"If I've learned anything in my years of practice, it's that appearances can be deceiving."

"Don't try to bullshit me. Don't you dare try to bullshit me. You think I don't know why that monster hired you, Mr. Fancy High-Dollar Lawyer?"

Christina stifled a guffaw.

"You think I don't know what goes on in courtrooms? Listen to me, buddy. I know the way the world works. I've watched Court TV."

"I can understand your anger, sir. But I have to think that, deep down in your heart, you don't want revenge. You want to know the truth."

"I know the truth!" he bellowed, more than loud enough to attract the attention of the guests at the three other tables in the room, not to mention their waiter and the maître d'. Both were hovering on the fringe of the George II room, unsure how to handle the disturbance. "I know that goddamn rapist killed my little girl!"

"Look," Ben said. He was starting to lose some patience himself. He'd come here to plot strategy, not to deal with importunate relatives of the deceased. "I'm sure you didn't like what you saw in the video, but there is no evidence that their relationship was not consensual. To the contrary, it was obvious from her attire and manner and language that she was welcoming sex. She just didn't—"

"You filthy pervert!" He lunged. Ben dove out of his chair. Cooper narrowly missed him, smashing the wicker chair, then crashing to the floor.

That was more than enough opening for the maître d' to intervene, assisted by two large men who were either bouncers or the burliest guys this classy joint could find on the premises. They laid their hands firmly on Cooper's shoulders, raised him to his feet, and dragged him away. He was dazed, but not so much that he couldn't speak. "My little girl would never do that for anyone. He must've forced her to dress like that. Must've had some kind of hold on her. She would never act that way. Never!"

He continued ranting, all the way through the George III and the George Washington rooms, until happily Ben could hear him no more.

"Think he represents the viewpoint of the general populace," Ben asked, "or just those immediately related to the victim?"

"Let's hope the latter," Christina said. "Are you okay?"

"I'm fine. Just glad he didn't meet us in a dark alley somewhere. Which would've been the logical thing to do," he added, pausing thoughtfully, "if his goal really had been to hurt me."

The inside of the escort service was disappointingly bland—sparse and functional. Where was the red wallpaper, the overstuffed sofa, the piano player with a garter around his upper arm? Bordellos just weren't what they used to be. Or weren't what they used to be in John Wayne movies, at any rate. Lucille's room was equally inadequate—no lace, no vibrating or rotating bed, no mirrors on the ceiling. Resembled nothing on earth so much as a thirty-dollar room at a Ramada Inn. All very disappointing . . .

Except for Lucille herself. Lucille did not disappoint.

She was, as advertised, a large-bosomed woman, but then she was large all around. Not fat, but no petite supermodel, which was okay by Loving. He preferred women who still remembered how to use a knife and fork. She had huge curly red hair, like Christina's times three, done up in a sort of B-52 style all on the top of her head. She had wrapped a bathrobe around herself before he came in. Judging from the lines under the terry-cloth robe—or relative lack thereof—he adjudged that there was not much in the way of clothing on her. She was young, maybe thirty, but there was a profound weariness about her eyes. Loving guessed that she'd been plying this trade for half her short life.

For someone who'd "had a bad experience that night," she was uncommonly friendly. But then, Loving had noticed, girls with freckles were always friendly.

As soon as the dragon lady closed the door behind them, he opened his mouth to frame a question—but Lucille stopped him flat.

"Money up front. Two hundred big ones."

Loving blinked. "Did she explain that I just wanted to talk?"

"So what else is new? Lot of guys just want to talk. Some of them even come in here and sleep. Doesn't matter. I get paid by the hour, not the act."

"And you get two hundred bucks an hour?"

"Is that so much? The lawyers in this town charge more. And don't provide nearly so much service."

Well, he couldn't argue with that one. With some regret, he pulled out his wallet and laid the money on the table. He couldn't wait till he had to explain this expense to Jones.

"Good," Lucille said, tucking the money into her robe pocket. "Now where's my girl Amber?"

"That's what I'd like to know. I'm tryin' to find her."

"You a cop?"

"Absolutely not."

"Then what?"

"Do I hafta say?"

"No. And I don't have to talk, either."

Loving frowned. "You heard about the Veronica Cooper murder?" He saw a light in her eyes that told him the answer was in the affirmative. "I'm workin' for an attorney investigatin' the case." He opted not to identify which one.

"So what do you want from me?"

"I . . . I think Amber and Veronica were friends, right?"

Lucille didn't answer.

"I was hopin' Amber might be able to tell me somethin' about Veronica, somethin' we don't already know, maybe even about who did it or why she was killed."

"Why she was killed? Isn't it obvious?" Lucille looked at him strangely. "You must be working for Glancy."

"My boss is, yeah. And he doesn't believe Glancy did the deed."

"I'm sure he's being paid good money to believe that."

Loving shook his head firmly. "If my boss says he thinks some-one is innocent, then he thinks someone is innocent. And he's usu-ally right."

"So that's it? You're just looking to get your guy off?"

Loving hesitated. Obviously, something more was needed to loosen her tongue. "Well, I'm a little concerned. More than a little."

"About what?"

"About Amber." He took a shot. "Are you worried, too?"

Lucille slowly crossed the room, sat on the edge of her high-stacked bed, and crossed her legs, revealing a hint of hosiery. "Yeah. I'm real worried. I told the cops I was worried. But since no one's found a body, no one seems to care."

"I care," Loving said, seizing his opportunity. "And if you'll tell me what you know, I'll do my best to find Amber. That's a promise."

Lucille nodded. "Fair enough. Where do we start?"

"How do you know Amber?"

"Amber works here. Used to, anyway."

Loving felt his heart skip a beat. No wonder the dragon lady downstairs let him in. "Amber—worked for the escort service?"

"Is that so surprising?"

"Well—if she was runnin' with a congressional intern . . ."

"They were kids. Very nonjudgmental. Too stupid to be judg-mental, really. I don't know how they all hooked up, that whole gang, but they had fun together, and that was what mattered to them. They didn't care what anyone did to earn their bread. In fact, I suspect some of Amber's friends had the misguided notion that this was a glamorous and exotic line of work."

"And it ain't?" Loving said, unable to resist scrutinizing the line of her figure beneath the robe.

"No, it ain't. What, were you expecting to see Julia Roberts when you walked through the door? You can forget all that *Pretty Woman* BS. I'll grant you, this is not the worst way to make a living. We're in the service industry, that's how I see it. We provide a service that is apparently much needed. Facilitating a valuable social ex-change between two consenting adults." She paused. "But it isn't glamorous. And you're not going to end up with Richard Gere."

Loving drew her back to the main subject. "So you knew Amber well?"

"We had adjoining rooms. I was like her mother. I'm—a little older than she is."

"You don't look older."

"You flatterer." She slapped his knee with well-lacquered fingernails. "I knew we'd get along. I can make people, you know? And I liked you from the moment you walked into the room. Trusted you. I can't say I get that feeling very often. But in my line of work, you get to know what people are like. Develop an instinct for it. You have to, if you're going to survive long."

"I'll bet. So you knew Amber. And she knew Veronica?"

"They were friends. There were four of them, most nights— Veronica, Amber, Colleen, and . . . oh, what was her name? The mousy one."

"Beatrice?"

"Yeah, that was it. Anyway, they liked to do the nightlife thing. But toward the end . . . I don't know. I think maybe they were getting into something weird. Kinky, maybe."

And this coming from a woman who worked at an escort service. "Like what?"

"I don't know. And I asked, more than once. But Amber never gave me any details. Redecorated her room, though."

"Can I take a look?"

"Sorry. Boss lady had it all cleared out after Amber was AWOL for two weeks. But it was lots of candles and stars and weird symbols. Used a lot of red paint. Wasn't good for business—creeped the customers out, at least the ones who were sober."

"What kinda symbols?"

"Oh, I don't know. The main one was like this." Using her index finger, she drew a small loop in the air, then crossed the bottom of the loop with two short lines. "I don't know what that was supposed to mean. And she had this weird statue that she kept over her bed. Told me it was an incubus. You know what that is?"

"Can't say that I do."

"Neither did I, till she explained it. An incubus is a demon. Supposedly sneaks up on girls while they're sleeping and has sex with them."

"And she wanted this in her room?"

Lucille shrugged. "What can I tell you? Weird. I don't know

what it all meant. She started wearing lots of silver, jewelry and stuff. Dark lipstick. Big hoop earrings with an upside-down cross dangling in the center. And she started dressing in black—nothing but black."

"Why?"

"I don't know. Wish I did. The worst was when—when she told me she didn't want to be Amber anymore."

"She was gonna kill herself?"

"No. She was going to change her name. Said from now on I was supposed to call her Lilith. Lady Lilith, actually."

"Why?"

"She didn't say. I didn't ask. And I never followed her when she went out partying with those girls, though now I wish to God I had. I'd go get her myself if I knew where to look. Amber was such a good girl—so bubbly, happy, concerned about others. So full of life. But something happened to her. It's like someone—or something—sucked all the energy out of her. The light in her eyes faded. She became dull, listless. She didn't seem to care about anything any-more—including herself. She'd turned into a whole different kind of person." She brushed her hand across her eyes. "May sound stupid but—I loved that girl. She reminded me of myself when I was a little younger and—you know. A little smaller."

"Doesn't sound stupid to me at all." He reached forward and laid his hand gently on Lucille's shoulder. To his surprise, she pressed her hand down on his.

"You're good people." She looked up, and Loving saw tears in her eyes. "Do you really think you can find my Amber?"

"I can't promise nothin'. But I'll do my best. And I'm not too shabby at findin' things. Do you know the names of any of these clubs they frequented?" Lucille was still holding his hand.

"I know one. Found a matchbook in Amber's room when I helped clean it out. Place called Stigmata. I think I heard her party girls mention it once or twice. I don't know where it is."

"I'll find it."

"If there's anything I can do to help, you just let me know, un-derstand? And if you do find her—" Loving felt her hand press even tighter. "Would you bring her back here? Or have her call? Even if she's moved on to some other life, which I wouldn't blame her if she did. She had so much talent. Not like me. She could do better."

"I think you're sellin' yourself short."

"And I think you're way too sweet. So would you do that for me? Make sure I know she's okay?"

"It's a promise."

"Thank you."

She wasn't releasing his hand, and just standing there was getting somewhat awkward, so Loving sat beside her on the bed. "Mind if I ask you a question?"

"Depends on what the question is."

"What happened tonight? Why did you decide . . . not to work?"

"Oh. It's nothing that big. Par for the course, really. Tonight's a big Georgetown party night."

"Meaning . . . ?"

"You know. Frats. Alumni. Lots of politicos. Come down here for a big whoop-de-do."

"Sounds awful."

"Usually it's okay. And profitable. Lotta the time guys'll pay for the whole night then fall asleep. They'll be so drunk or drugged they won't be able to . . . you know. Get what they came for. Which is always a pleasant development."

"I see why you insist on being paid up front."

"Yeah. But tonight I got some jerk who'd been freebasing. Cocaine. Usually the boss lady spots the druggies and won't let them through the door. But in all the turmoil and excitement, this guy slipped through the cracks. Started running around the room, screaming that the devil was out to get him. He was gonna die and go to hell. Started breaking things. Hitting me. Nothing serious, but it shook me up pretty bad. Security boys got him out before he did any major damage, but still—"

"Musta scared the bejezus outta you."

"Well, enough to call it a night." She smiled. "How come I never get guys like you?"

Loving felt his face turning bright red. "I'm not really a party kinda guy."

"You've got a nice wife at home, don't you?"

"No. Not anymore."

"Someone let you go? Big mistake."

"That was how I saw it, but I guess she disagreed."

Lucille laughed. She brought a finger to the side of Loving's face, then slowly traced a line down his neck. "You know, if you really don't have a girl back home . . ."

"Yeah?"

She shrugged, creating a cascading ripple beneath her bathrobe that Loving had a hard time looking away from. "Well, I may not be as young as Amber." She leaned closer to him. "But I'm way more experienced. And you seem like the kind of man who appreciates . . . experience."

Loving stiffened. "Oh, well, I—couldn't—"

"You couldn't?"

"I mean—not that I couldn't. I could. You're darn right I could. If I wanted to."

She appeared crestfallen. "You don't want to?"

"I didn't mean that. I'm just sayin'—" He paused, his head turning to one side. "What am I sayin', anyway?"

"I'll make it worth your while," she said, slowly pulling Loving toward her.

"Of that I have no doubt. But my boss wouldn't approve."

"Is that your final answer?"

Loving tumbled onto the bed beside her. "Hell, no. Just makin' a statement for the record."

She smiled. "I'm glad. After all, you did pay for the whole hour." She loosened the terry-cloth tie and let her bathrobe fall. "And I would hate to see all that time go to waste."

The waiter brought Ben a replacement chair, and he had almost managed to sit in it when he heard a familiar voice. "My, but they'll let anyone in here, won't they?"

Ben sprang to his feet. It was Marie Glancy. The senator's wife.

"Are you referring to the guy they just hauled out of here, or me?"

She laughed, a little. Ben was glad to see it. He'd been talking and working with her on a regular basis these past five months, but this was the first time he recalled seeing her laugh, or even smile. "The former, I assure you."

"I didn't know you were here," Ben said. "Would you like to join us?"

"Thanks, but I know you two have work to do. And I'm here with friends. They're trying to be supportive. As if there was really anything they could do."

"I appreciate you being in the courtroom today. As I told you, it's very important that you be present, sitting in the gallery right behind your husband anytime the jury is around."

"On the theory that, if I've forgiven him, then they should, too?"

Ben craned his neck awkwardly. This was not an easy subject to discuss, especially with the betrayed wife. "More along the lines of, what he did was a private matter, to be dealt with by family. Not by the press. Not by the public."

"Ah. The Hillary defense."

"Well . . ."

"Don't worry, Ben. I understand. Totally. I won't do anything to jeopardize Todd's political ambitions."

Or yours? Ben had heard whispers at the Senate that Marie—a Georgetown political science grad, top of her class—had aspirations that went beyond being a senator's wife. Or even a first lady. She was not a naturally attractive woman, but she did the most she could with what she had, and Ben wondered if the ultimate result wasn't the best, politically speaking. She seemed sturdy and competent, not flighty or self-obsessed. She was from a good, well-to-do, old-money, blueblood East Coast family, the sort of whom Ben's mother would approve. Reportedly her family's fortune, combined with the considerable riches of Todd's own parents, gave Todd the stake he needed to build his career. Her reserved, cool demeanor was also a useful contrast to Todd's more earthy Oklahoma personality. What was it Christina had said? Partners complete each other.

"How do you think he's holding up?" Christina asked.

"I think he's doing admirably, all things considered," Marie replied. "I saw him before I came here, back in the slammer. I think he has been surprised by the harshness of the personal attacks on his character. He knows this is going to be a blow to his future plans. But he's dealing."

Ben nodded politely, but inside he was reeling. Since he'd come to DC, these people had never ceased to amaze him. The man was on trial for capital murder! But they rarely talked about the crime, much less the possible penalty. All they talked about were the political ramifications, as if this was just another scandal—the sort of thing every politician had to deal with at one time or another. Most of Ben's clients were terrified about the potential effect of the trial on their personal freedom. The Glancys seemed principally concerned with the effect of the trial on their approval ratings.

"And how about you?" Ben rejoined. "How are you doing?"

"I'm dealing, too. This isn't the first difficulty we've had. Probably won't be the last. You learn to roll with the punches. And come up slugging."

"I suppose you have to."

"That's exactly right. So why complain about it?"

"Still, I know these past few months have been . . . taxing. I've often thought criminal trials are harder on the accused's families than on the accused." Just as he had for the previous five months, Ben tried to warm up to the woman, but he found himself unequal to the task. Some things just couldn't be forced, he supposed. He should admire her resolve, her resilience, her legerity and wit. Many a time he had wished the spouses of his clients had more of those qualities. But he never sensed that Marie was masterfully containing the emotions seething inside her. More like she was . . . strategizing.

"You're doing a fine job taking care of Todd," she continued, gracefully filling the gap when no one else had spoken. "He really admires you, you know."

Ben did a double take. "Todd admires me?"

"Oh my, yes. Even before you came to represent him. He'd read about your cases or see you on television and he was so jealous. He's often said he'd be happier if he'd remained at the DA's office and stayed out of politics."

"I find that hard to believe."

"Well, frankly, so do I." She winked. "Todd's a political animal. Even if he doesn't want to admit it. But you're not, Ben. Anyone can see that at a glance. I think that's what he admires most about you. I think that's why he insisted that you be lead trial counsel. I'm sure you realize some of his advisers wanted him to go with high-dollar locals. 'Money talks,' that's the shibboleth this town lives by. Everyone wanted him to hire better-known DC big-firm big shots."

"I gathered as much."

"But he didn't. He has faith in you. As do I." The food arrived. She shook Ben's hand again, nodded at Christina, then left the room.

"Mind if I ask what you think of her?" Ben asked. Maybe Christina could assuage the uneasy feelings he had by offering a second opinion.

"I think she's biding her time," Christina said succinctly.

"Until this trial is over?"

"Until her husband's political career is over. So she can begin hers."

"So you believe the rumors."

"It's more than rumors, Ben. My sources tell me she's already bought her comfortable but affordable town house in New York. She's standing by her man now, because it's the savvy thing to do. But as soon as he's done playing politics, she'll start."

"Well, I suppose it's none of our business. I should focus on the task at hand."

"The opening statement dilemma?"

"Yes. I think I've figured out a solution to the problem."

"Which is?"

"You do it."

"Ben!"

"Don't fret, Chris. You'll be great."

"Ben, you can't just—"

"You'll be great. I know you will. And that will give me more time to review the witness outlines. Let's finish up here and get back to the hotel so you can start thinking it out. Though God knows, for what that hotel charges, they should write it for you."

"You know, Ben," Christina said, twirling a bite of salmon on her fork, "it is expensive, keeping two rooms at the Watergate. If you wanted, we could—"

"Move to that Motel 6 across the street? Maybe this weekend. We have too much to do tonight."

"Ri-i-ight."

Christina seemed faintly annoyed. Maybe he shouldn't have dropped the opening on her at the last minute? Well, he couldn't waste time worrying about it now. He'd been doing his best not to turn into a Valium case, but the immensity of this trial was overwhelming, and as always his insecurities were running high. Had he bitten off more than he could chew? He'd been flattered when Todd asked him to take the lead, but maybe it would've been better if he'd declined.

Ben had to put all that out of his mind. His client wasn't the U.S. government; it was Todd Glancy. And despite everything he had learned these past months, he did not believe Todd was guilty of the crime. He was convinced of that.

Now all he had to do was convince twelve other people.

Loving stepped into the alleyway, hitching and adjusting his pants, a euphoric expression on his face. Well now, he thought, that was a surprising turn of events. Might've been the most pleasant surprise in the history of his employment with Kincaid & McCall. Who said a private investigator didn't get any perks?

Should he go back through Martin's Tavern, or try to find a street outlet? He had a hunch this alley eventually emptied onto Wisconsin and might well put him closer to his rental car. From there, he could make a few phone calls, then start looking for this Stigmata joint.

He wasn't sure how much he'd accomplished, but at least he had some fresh information about Amber and one possible lead. He thought he was finally on the right track. And he'd made a new friend. It was always good to have friends.

Loving stopped. Had he heard something in the alley behind him? He turned and carefully scrutinized the darkness. It was hard to say with certainty, as pitch-black as it was here, but he didn't see anything. Probably his imagination. No one could possibly know where he was—no one but his mysterious informant, Deep Throat. Could they?

He resumed walking. The sounds of traffic whizzed by at lightning speed. Given what Lucille had told him, they were probably on their way to some party. Freebasing cocaine. Jeez, the stupid things people did to themselves. He would never understand that. Or, for that matter, why a sweet girl with a home and a mother and a perfectly good name—

He froze in place. Okay, that time he definitely heard something.

"Who's back there?" Loving barked. "You need somethin'?"

No answer.

Loving considered himself a solid sort, not easily given to flights of fancy. But this whole situation was starting to get under his skin.

He doubled his pace, just to be on the safe side. He could see the street now, and from there he'd find his car, then get his cell phone, and he'd check in with Jones and maybe even see if that club was open and—

The fist came out of nowhere, taking him by surprise. He had no time to duck, no chance to do anything to lessen the blow. Was it coming from ahead or behind? He wasn't sure, even as the fist drove into the left side of his skull.

Though groggy, he tried to focus. "What . . . is it? Wha—"

He couldn't be sure, but it looked like the lid of a garbage can rushing toward his face, battering him on the forehead. The back of his head slammed against the brick wall. He fell to his knees.

"What's—goin'—?" he mumbled, but it was no use. Consciousness was fading fast. He felt a hand grip the hair on the top of his head and knock him back against the wall one last time. After that, a deep black sleep shrouded his consciousness like fingers snuffing out the flame of a candle.

8

"Ladies and gentlemen of the jury: when all is said and done, this is a case about violation, in all its most repellent forms. Personal, sexual violations, yes. But even more so, violation of the employer–employee relationship, violation of women's rights. And perhaps most profoundly, violation of the public trust. Because as the evidence will show, the crime committed by the defendant, Todd K. Glancy, a United States senator, in the complex that is the seat, the very heart of our government, not only violated the poor young woman he abused and then murdered. Ultimately, Todd Glancy violated us all."

Ben was so close to being on his feet he could feel his toes twitch. This was supposed to be the opening statement in a murder trial, not a long-winded exegesis of women's rights in the work-place. Padolino was right on the line, almost but not quite verging from a permissible melodramatic summary of the crime to an imper-missible extrapolation of the crime to unrelated issues—a plea to find the defendant guilty not based upon the evidence but to "send a message." No doubt he had rewritten and rehearsed this opening endlessly, going just as far as he thought he could without being shut down.

"Let me apologize in advance for the unpleasant nature of some of the evidence I will be forced to present to you during the course of this trial. I don't want to, but I have no choice. Justice demands it. Much of what you see—some videotaped evidence in particular—will shock you, will tear at the very core of your soul. As well it should. But it is important that you fully understand the relationships of the parties, of the killer to his victim, and his proven attitude and behavior toward her, so that you can see as clearly as I do what led to this twenty-two-year-old woman's tragic death."

As Ben had anticipated, even though this was a capital murder case, Padolino was much more interested in talking about the alleged sex crime evidenced by the video. His lurid topic allowed him to avoid the usual bathetic cries for justice, and his considerable speaking skill prevented this lengthy talk from having the soporific effect openings often had on juries anxious to get on to the evidence. Padolino stuck to his strengths—the video could not be refuted, and it was guaranteed to repel anyone who watched it. Proving the senator guilty of murder was a trickier matter.

"Veronica Cooper graduated from the University of Virginia with high honors, receiving a BA in political science. It had been her dream to work in the national arena, so you can imagine her delight when she was hired by the distinguished senator from Oklahoma, a man considered one of the most promising, most up-and-coming members of his party. And then imagine her dismay when she found that her new job, her dream, required more than intelligence and hard work. Imagine her horror when she learned, as the evidence will show, that the senator extracted far more than legislative work from his interns."

Ben and Christina exchanged a glance. He was in effect arguing evidence of pattern or habit, that Glancy was an inveterate womanizer—evidence that could only be admissible given certain narrowly prescribed circumstances. But the irony was that he was arguing a pattern of sexual misconduct, which was not the crime for which Glancy was on trial. It was the crime for which Padolino intended to hang him, to make the jury despise him before the evidence relating to the murder was ever presented. Most of the opening proceeded in that manner. Ben was relieved when he detected the telltale signs— Padolino's approach to the jury rail, the lowering of his voice and the lengthening of his dramatic pauses—that indicated he was coming to his conclusion. He knew when it was time to stop—when the jury members understood what you were going to do but were still hungry for the details, before they reached the point of rhetorical satiety.

"As the evidence will show, Senator Todd Glancy met his intern in a secluded part of the Russell Senate Office Building and forced her to perform a repulsive sex act, documented by graphic videotape. The tape was leaked, the man was exposed, and suddenly his entire future, all his political ambitions, rested in the hands of that twenty-two-year-old intern whom he had treated so shabbily. The evidence will show that he met with her and attempted to buy her goodwill, or at least her silence, before the inevitable media deluge descended upon her. And when she refused to cooperate, he met her in his private hideaway and killed her, in a violent, bloody fashion. Once more showing his callousness, his utter lack of respect for her as a person, he tossed her body onto his sofa and left her." He paused. "And this from a man elected to the highest legislative body in this great land."

Padolino leaned across the rail, getting as close to the jurors as the judge would allow, looking each of them directly in their eyes. "Does this man deserve to be punished? I should say so. Does he deserve the greatest punishment it is in your power to decree? Again, I must answer yes. Because the magnitude of his crime was great. And the magnitude of his violation was even greater."

Loving awoke, head throbbing. Despite the darkness and the turbid haze swirling through his brain, he determined that he was affixed to a square-backed chair. He twisted a little each way, testing the degree to which he was bound. Damn tight, as it turned out. As his vision cleared, he was slowly able to make out the faint glint of silver emanating from his midsection.

Duct tape. Wouldn't you know it. Thanks to George W. Bush, every crackpot in America now had a roll of duct tape handy. Loving himself kept a backwoods survival cabin, a stockpile of fresh water and canned goods, and invested only in gold coins, but even he wasn't gullible enough to fall for the duct tape malarkey. Among other reasons, he knew that no matter how tightly you were taped, it was always possible to wiggle away—eventually. He could already feel some give around his right arm. There was a gap between the back of the chair and the back of his arm that was just loose enough to allow him to wriggle. Given enough time, he could get that arm free.

He continued twisting back and forth, but less than a minute later he heard the sound of a poorly oiled heavy metallic door opening and closing. The hollowness of the echo, combined with the visible concrete floor, suggested that he was in a large room—a warehouse, perhaps, or something like it.

He heard footsteps approaching. He reduced the wiggling, still doing his best to worm free, but careful not to let it become apparent.

A few moments later, a tall figure emerged from the darkness. He was about Loving's age, maybe a little younger. Thirtysomething. Black hair, with streaks of brown, tied into a ponytail in the back. Stubble. Wearing a navy-blue jacket over a light blue button-down shirt. Thin, wiry. Loving sensed a near-palpable tension bottled up, like a soda that had been shaken way too many times.

Loving decided to play it cool. "Thank goodness you're here. Someone tied me up and left me, I dunno how long ago. Have you got somethin' you could use to cut this tape?"

Loving was not surprised that the man didn't rush to help him. But he had hoped for at least a wry chortle. "Why are you looking for Amber Daily?"

"Who says I am?"

The man continued to stare at him. "Why are you looking for Amber Daily?"

Could this be the man Deep Throat had been talking about? The one he was so scared of? "I'm not lookin' for anyone. In case you haven't noticed, I'm duct-taped to a chair."

Loving could almost feel the man's rage. His nostrils flared; his chest rose. And yet his voice remained perfectly modulated. "Why are you looking for Amber Daily?"

"I'm a private investigator," Loving said, trying a different tack. "It's a job."

"What have you learned so far?"

"Not much. Why d'you care?"

"I need to know everything you've learned."

"And I need to take a leak, but at the moment neither one of us is gettin' what we want, huh?"

The man stepped forward with such suddenness that it took Loving by surprise. "Don't toy with me, asshole. I want to know what you've found out about Amber."

"Sorry. That information's strictly confidential. Rules of professional ethics."

Like a jaguar finally permitted to pounce, the man sprang forward, lowering himself on one knee. A flash of metal illuminated his hand.

As he inched closer, he pushed the switchblade against Loving's throat. "This is your last chance," he growled. "Why are you looking for Amber Daily?"

Christina had to give Padolino credit where due. He was a silver-tongued devil—heavy emphasis on the devil. He had written a magnificent opening, and delivered it to perfection, playing not only to the jury but also to the press corps he knew would carry his words to the millions of Americans following this high-profile case. Padolino was a gifted communicator.

Christina was not. Which was not to say she couldn't talk to people—she could. But she didn't have the fancy vocabulary, the silky tone, the square jaw, or even the earnest expression. Her strength was telling people what happened, straightforward and without embellishment. So that was what she did.

"Ladies and gentlemen of the jury, at this point you may well be wondering what this case is all about, so let me help you out. Is this case about a sex crime? No. Is this case about sexual harassment in the workplace? No. Is this a recall election for a U.S. senator? No. This is a murder trial. So everything that doesn't pertain to the murder—which would be about ninety-three percent of what the distinguished prosecutor just said—is not relevant. We all know about the videotape and we all know that there was an inappropriate"—she immediately wished she had said "illicit," a stronger word but one that would not stir memories of Clinton and Lewinsky—"relationship.

The defense will not even attempt to deny it. Not because we're proud of it. Far from it. It was disgraceful, as the senator himself would be the first to tell you. We will not discuss or deny that because it has nothing to do with the murder. It gives you no information, not even a clue, as to who killed Veronica Cooper. And that's what we're gathered here today to determine. That's the only thing that matters."

She paused and took a breath. It was hard to read people at the same time she was speaking to them. That was why she always preferred to let Ben do the big speeches—so she would be free to watch, to observe the expressions on their faces, the tiny twitches, the slight but ever-so-important rise of an eyebrow. She thought they understood what she was saying, that the courtroom should be focused on the crime at hand, the murder. But she wasn't at all sure they were receiving the subtext—that Padolino was manipulating them, using irrelevant matters to coerce a verdict based upon emotion rather than evidence.

"In his opening, the prosecutor made a great deal of the fact that the defendant is a U.S. senator, and I think perhaps that's appropriate, although for entirely different reasons. Although I'm sure he did not intend it, Mr. Padolino seemed to be implying that Todd Glancy should be held to a higher standard because he is an elected official. I will suggest to you, ladies and gentlemen, that the man has already been held to a vastly higher degree of scrutiny, and abuse, because he is a U.S. senator. This case is permeated with politics. If, as the prosecutor tells you, Todd Glancy wielded such great power, that is all the more reason why political opponents might want to bring him down, might orchestrate a scandal—or even a murder—to reap the political benefit. This is not mere idle speculation. As you hear the evidence presented by the prosecution, never forget to ask yourself the basic questions that have remained unanswered, that the prosecution still cannot answer. Who leaked that incriminating videotape to the press? Why does such a videotape even exist? The fact that it does, and that it was deliberately planted to incriminate Senator Glancy, tells you that even before the murder occurred someone—or some group—was working against him. And if we know that such a person or group might initiate a sex scandal for political purposes, is it so difficult to believe they might also arrange a murder? Again, ask yourself the fundamental questions. Why was she killed in the U.S. Senate complex—one of the most conspicuous locations for a murder imaginable. Why was the body left in the senator's own hideaway? Are we to believe the senator is so stupid he couldn't come up with a less incriminating place to commit a murder and leave the corpse? With all due respect, the theory of the case presented by the prosecutor in his opening statement simply makes no sense."

She took another deep breath. While not as smooth as the prosecutor, she spoke from the heart, and she hoped that it showed. Regardless of how bleak the case or how unsavory the client, she had never knowingly lied to a jury. She had to make them understand that. Not by what she said with her mouth. By what she said with her eyes.

"Ladies and gentlemen, I fear this is likely to be a long case, a complex one, tiring and confusing and, in the end, difficult to resolve. But I can tell you these two things for certain. First, the burden of proof is on the prosecution, to prove not that the senator was a bad person, but that he committed murder. And I can tell you one other thing. No matter what happens, no matter how bleak the outlook, no matter what evidence is revealed—I will not lie to you. We, the defense, will not lie to you. Not a fib, not a white lie, not an exaggeration, not the slightest little taradiddle. We don't have to. The prosecution cannot prove that Todd Glancy committed this murder." She paused. "Because he didn't."

"Whoa, whoa, pilgrim, let's calm down now," Loving said, staring at the switchblade pressed against his larynx. "No need to get excited. You didn't tell me this was urgent."

"Stop messing with me!" The man brought his free hand around and clubbed Loving on the side of his head. It stung—especially given that his head was already pounding—but it didn't hurt nearly as much as it might've. "Make no mistake, you pissant, I will cut your throat if you don't tell me what I want to know. Who hired you?"

Loving answered, but his response was so quiet the man couldn't make it out. Instinctively, he leaned in closer.

And that was when Loving whipped his free arm around and

clubbed the man on the side of the head. He tumbled backward. Loving grabbed his right hand, pressed his thumb down on the pressure point of the man's wrist. His fingers flew open and Loving grabbed the knife. Before the man had a chance to recover, Loving had cut himself free from the chair. The man tried to scramble back to his feet but Loving, hunched over him and empowered with the knife, held him down with one hand. "Not so fast, buckaroo," Loving said, shoving his face to the floor. "You know, I don't mind being questioned. Pretty much comes with the job. Sometimes I even answer. But I do mind having a knife pressed against my throat. Even if you didn't have the balls to cut me, you could've done serious damage just by accident."

The man squirmed under the weight of Loving's arm, but he couldn't get loose. Couldn't even come close.

"Might as well give it up," Loving said. "I don't need duct tape to keep you in line." He grabbed the man's collar and jerked him semi-upright. "Now, what's the big idea—clubbin' me over the head and tyin' me up?"

"I—I—I needed to know what you know. About Amber."

"And for that you were gonna slice me?"

"I needed to know why you were looking for her. I needed to know . . . anything about her. Everything about her."

"Why?"

"Why should I tell you?" the man said, finding a sudden reservoir of defiance.

"Because I'm the guy holdin' the knife now," Loving replied. "And I'm not afraid to use it. So here's your last chance, Buster Brown. Why were you pumpin' me for information about Amber?"

"Because—Because—" The man closed his eyes, swallowed. "Because I'm looking for her, too."

"And why are you looking for her?"

The man collapsed, his eyes watering up, his whole face transforming from anger to the darkest despair. "Because she's my daughter."

"I thought that went rather well," Marshall Bressler told Ben as he wheeled his chair toward a table in the rear of the courthouse cafeteria. Judge Herndon had called for a two-hour lunch break before the prosecution called its first witness. They had intentionally chosen a remote table at the far end of the room; they didn't want anyone, press or otherwise, eavesdropping. "I was surprised when you chose to let your partner deliver the opening, but she was a quite effective speaker."

"I thought Christina was awesome," Shandy said, her blond hair bobbing with youthful admiration. "Every time I stand up in front of a crowd of three people or more, I fall apart at the seams."

"Christina is full of surprises, that much is certain. It was a strategy call," Ben said. And the strategy was—don't give the opening if you can't think of one. "Christina has only been out of law school a few years, but she's light-years ahead of most, including some who've practiced longer than I've been alive."

"I don't doubt it. Pardon me." Marshall popped two blue pills in his mouth, then took a swig from a Styrofoam cup. "It's for the pain. Little reminder from my accident. Anyway, I thought the opening was a major success. Made a real impact on the jury."

"Unfortunately, I have to disagree." Amanda Burton swirled up to them, a whirlwind with a clipboard. "I just caught the latest poll reports on CNN. They replayed the openings word for word, using actors reading transcripts. Subsequent surveys indicated that while most Americans thought Senator Glancy had hired himself some good attorneys, nothing that was said changed their minds."

"That doesn't mean anything," Ben said. "No one wants to admit to a pollster that they were swayed by something a lawyer said. Our national cynicism toward the legal profession runs too deep. Nonetheless, in the courtroom, with a real live sequestered jury, it may be a different story."

Amanda shook her head, making an irritating, disdainful noise with her lips. "That's not what any of my research data indicate. We've seen no movement."

"Meaning—?"

"Meaning nothing you've done so far has changed the opinion of the general populace regarding the senator's guilt or innocence. And as you well know, every poll taken since the crime occurred has indicated that a plurality of Americans believe he is probably guilty."

"Again," Ben insisted, "being on a jury is entirely different from being quizzed by an anonymous pollster. 'Probably guilty' doesn't cut it in the courtroom, especially not when the attorneys are ramming 'guilty beyond a reasonable doubt' down your throat. Jurors don't have the luxury of indulging in cynicism or first impressions. They have to weigh the evidence."

"If jurors are human beings," Amanda insisted testily, "and although I did not attend law school, I believe that they are—then they are just as subject to bias and character assassination as anyone. Not to mention stupidity."

"I think juries get a bad rap," Ben shot back. "My experience is that whether they're manual laborers or rocket scientists, most jurors pay close attention and try to do the right thing."

"And my experience," Amanda said, now speaking in a tone that could be described as downright nasty, "is that most people are drones with no minds of their own who have to be told what the 'right thing to do' is. My sources indicate that we're not achieving that goal. Your entire approach to this case has been misguided. You've got a confused, incoherent farrago of highbrow theories that no one understands. You need to get down and dirty. You need to hit this upcoming cop witness and hit him hard."

"That would be a major tactical error."

She pounded her fists against her forehead. "God! I told Todd not to let you run this thing. Why is it he always listens to me—except when it really matters? You cannot go back into that courtroom with some mousy milquetoast cross-examination. You have to come on strong."

"That is, quite frankly, exactly wrong. The attack-dog approach will turn off the jurors, especially with a police witness."

"I'm not asking, Kincaid. I'm telling."

"Are you deliberately trying to sabotage your boss's defense?"

"All I'm trying to do is prevent this case from becoming a complete PR disaster."

"Tell you what," Ben said, doing his best to retain his cool, "I won't interfere in your PR work. And you stay the hell away from my trial."

"Excuse me. What are we talking about?" It was Christina, suddenly appearing at the end of their table.

There was a long pause.

Ben finally filled the gap. "We were talking about what a great job you did on the opening."

She beamed. "Really?"

Ben nodded. "You were magnificent."

Amanda buried her nose in her clipboard.

"You're Amber's old man?" Loving said, floored.

"Yes!" he gasped. "Robert Daily. I've been looking for her for months, ever since she disappeared. The police have been worthless—Veronica Cooper is the only one they care about. So I've been searching on my own, every night, going every place she once went, talking to people, asking questions."

Loving released the man's collar. "And you heard I was lookin' for her, too."

"I have a source inside the escort joint. He told me you were asking questions about Amber."

"So you bashed me over the head? Kidnapped me?"

"I just brought you here so we'd have a little privacy. It's a storage locker. I rent it year-round. I just—I just—" His eyes began to well up. "I just want to know what happened to my little girl."

Loving didn't have much doubt, but it was always wise to be cautious. "Have you got some ID?"

The man reached into his back pocket and produced a wallet. He showed Loving his driver's license, a host of credit cards. Sure enough—Robert Daily.

"Amber's my only daughter. And I've always loved her. Even after she ran away from home."

"When was that?"

"About a year ago. I eventually traced her to the escort service. Found out . . . how she'd been supporting herself."

Loving felt a gnawing at the pit of his stomach.

"Tried to get her to come home, but she refused. Claimed she loved her life, partying all night, turning tricks. Then she fell in with those other girls, Veronica and her friends. Then it became even worse."

"Worse than prostitution?"

"Much. That was when she started wearing all black—never

anything but black. Got her tongue studded. Got tattoos, even in places . . . girls shouldn't get tattoos. Had practically her whole back done—then started wearing backless dresses so everyone could see. And the tats were all weird stuff—symbols, signs, creepy occult crap. Last time I saw her, she wouldn't even let me call her Amber."

"Lilith," Loving said.

"Yeah, that was it. Lady Lilith. I couldn't get her to tell me much—she always ran away whenever I tried. Someone was messing with her head. And then one day, a little more than five months ago, she disappeared. Just like that. Not a trace of her. Not at the escort service, not anywhere else. Gone."

"And you've been lookin' for her ever since?"

Instead of rising, Daily tumbled back onto the concrete floor. His voice cracked as he spoke. "Her mother and I tried to be good parents. We did everything the books said. We didn't smother her. We tried to stay involved with her life, her friends, and activities. But somehow . . . it all went wrong. We screwed up."

"You shouldn't blame yourself," Loving said. He could see the man was on the edge. Some situations called for something other than his usual smashmouth approach. If Daily broke down, he'd be no use at all. "You can't explain the things kids do, huh? 'Specially teenage girls."

"I always told her I loved her. And now—now she's gone. I'm afraid—so afraid—that—"

"Come on," Loving said, lifting the man to his feet. "We're both lookin' for the same girl. Let's work together, whaddya say?"

Daily brushed the dampness from his eyes. "Then—you know where she is?"

"No. But I got a lead. I was on my way when you bashed me over the head." He smiled, then took the man squarely by the shoulders. "Now we can do it together."

9

Normally, in a case of this nature, for procedural reasons and to lay necessary evidentiary foundations, the first witness would be the person who discovered the body. Ben was not surprised, however, to find that Mr. Padolino deviated from standard procedure. The person who discovered the body, after all, was Shandy Craig, a member of the senator's staff. She would undoubtedly be called in time, and the prosecutor would do his best to use her as an example of how the senator favored putting young and pretty girls on his staff. For his opening witness, however, when he made his initial impressions on the jury, he wanted a witness who was squarely and unquestionably on his team—so he skipped Shandy and went straight to one of the police officers called to the scene, homicide detective Lieutenant Porter Albertson.

Padolino quickly established the man's credentials, his years of experience, and ran through the many commendations and promotions he had received for his work. The jury tolerated it, but it didn't really interest them, and Padolino clearly understood that. A cop was a cop—get on to the good stuff.

"When did you arrive at Senator Glancy's office?"

"About twelve thirty. Took us longer to get up there because of all the security precautions. We had to check our weapons, as well as anything else made of metal—down to the spare change in my pocket. They called back to the station to check us out. I kept telling the Capitol officers that a serious crime had been reported, but they didn't care. They weren't letting us in until they were certain we were who we said we were."

"When you arrived at the senator's office, what did you see?"

"Bedlam. It was a madhouse. People running like rabbits all over the place. The senator was gone and no one appeared to be in control. I'm accustomed to some disorientation after a major crime, but this was above and beyond the usual."

"Were all the members of the senator's staff present?"

"No. Some were at lunch. Some were down at the scene of the crime—the hideaway. And a couple were in their private offices, talking on the phone. Who they could be talking to at a time like that I have no idea."

Ben watched the witness carefully as he testified. He seemed friendly, open, and helpful, with none of the brusqueness or defensiveness that he had displayed at the crime scene. Was Albertson putting on a show then, or now? He also seemed uncommonly garrulous for a police witness. Ben knew they were trained to answer questions directly and succinctly—without giving the defense any help by adding unnecessary information.

"Did you find the deceased?"

"After a few minutes, yes. I located Shandy Craig, the young blond intern who discovered the body." Ben wondered if the descriptive term *young blond* was necessary, or even helpful. No, Albertson had been coached by the prosecutor to insert it, to remind the jurors that the senator was a cradle-robbing pervert. "She was really messed up, barely able to speak. Took forever, but I eventually got her to take us down to the basement hideaway."

"The door was closed?"

"Ms. Craig had apparently taken one look, screamed, and then—"

"Objection," Christina said, rising. "Lack of personal knowledge."

"Sustained," Judge Herndon said, in a tone that informed the jury that the objection was technically correct but of no importance whatsoever.

"But the door was closed, correct?" the prosecutor rejoined.

Christina didn't bother sitting. "Objection. Leading."

The prosecutor sighed wearily. Damn these defense attorneys and their constant attempts to enforce the rules. "I'll rephrase. Please describe the state of the senator's hideaway when you entered."

"The door was closed," Albertson said bluntly, obviously relieved to finally have it out.

"What did you do next?"

"Well, I opened the door, naturally."

"And what did you find?"

"The dead, blood-soaked upended corpse of Veronica Cooper."

There was a susurrous stir in the gallery, quiet, but no less chilling for it. Funny how that always happened, Ben thought, even though everyone present knew there had been a murder and knew how the body was found. When the fact of violent death is announced, a collective tremor runs through the assemblage.

Padolino winced slightly, as if he had not heard all this a hundred times. "Please describe her . . . position."

"Her face was between the sofa cushions," Albertson said, grimacing. "Facing me. She had been positioned so that her body fell behind her, against the wall. Like she was doing a headstand, but not very well. Her skirt was down, obviously, and she wasn't wearing undergarments, so she was . . . exposed. Her blouse was torn, two buttons were missing, and it was pulled down below her shoulders. There was a huge bloody gash in her neck. Not that it was still bleeding—the blood was dried and coagulated by the time I saw her. There was a large puddle of blood on the floor beneath her."

"Did her position seem . . . natural?"

Albertson looked up at his questioner. "Like she might've committed suicide by flinging her head into the sofa? No, it did not look natural. It looked like something I'd be surprised a contortionist could do. Like whoever left her there didn't care about her in the least."

"Objection," Christina said. "The witness is making suppositions and characterizations, not testifying as to what he saw and heard."

The judge made a dithering motion with his hand. "I think that comes . . . close enough to describing to the jury what he saw. Overruled."

As she had been taught, Christina sat down without a frown or protest, as if it didn't matter, or as if she had actually won the argument. Jurors were so easily confused by legal jargon; if you looked like you won, half of them would think you did.

"Did you find blood anywhere else in the hideaway?"

"No. We did a complete luminol wipedown. But we found no other traces of blood."

"So it would be reasonable to conclude—"

"Objection," Christina said, undaunted by her previous loss.

The judge didn't need an explanation. "The witness will stick to his own personal knowledge. We don't need any conclusions."

"Of course, your honor." Padolino adjusted his tie, then plowed ahead. "Lieutenant, I forgot to ask you earlier." Sure you did, Columbo. "Was Senator Glancy present when you arrived at the hideaway?"

"No."

"Was he there when you discovered the body?"

"No. We didn't see him until perhaps twenty-five, thirty minutes later. Most of the forensics experts were on site by then, and we'd begun searching the place. He'd been paged, but apparently he wasn't carrying his pager."

"And how did he react?"

"He took it in stride."

"What does that mean?"

"He said he was surprised, said he didn't know anything about it. But he didn't jump up and down or weep and wail or anything. He was very calm, especially considering the circumstances." He paused. "Not how I'd react if I found a surprise corpse in my private room, I can tell you that."

"Objection!" Christina said, turning on just the right amount of outrage.

The judge nodded. "I won't warn you again, counselor. The witness's testimony will be restricted to what he has seen and heard."

"Of course," Albertson said. "I'm very sorry, your honor."

"I instruct the jury to disregard the witness's last statement." As if such thing were possible.

Padolino continued. "Did Senator Glancy say anything of interest?"

"I thought so. He said, 'I—'"

"Objection!" Christina said, cutting him off. "Hearsay."

"It's an admission against interest," Padolino replied. "Bigtime."

"Nonetheless, your honor, the circumstances surrounding the statement do not suggest trustworthiness. The senator had just suffered a great shock. He probably didn't even realize—"

"From what I've heard," Judge Herndon said, "the man still had his head together. And I wouldn't buy that objection even if he hadn't. Overruled."

Christina sat down, expertly masking her disappointment. She hadn't expected to win that objection, but on something this important it would be negligent not to make an effort.

"What he said was," Albertson continued, "'I tried to warn that girl.'"

This time, the reaction in the gallery was one of total silence. Ben preferred the murmurings. They were less ominous.

Padolino continued. "Did you find anything of interest during your search?"

"Yes. The forensics teams uncovered—"

Padolino was smart enough not to wait for the objection. "Excuse me, sir. I'm asking what you yourself may or may not have discovered."

"Oh, right. The hideaway was pretty clean. Astonishingly clean, actually. Couldn't even get fingerprints."

Christina rose, but Padolino jumped in. "But you—Lieutenant Albertson. What did you find?"

"The only item of note that I found was the Gutenberg."

Padolino wrinkled his forehead as if he didn't understand. "Could you please explain what that is?"

"Sure. That's what I soon learned the senator—and everyone on his staff—calls his appointment book. Big thick thing. Like a Filofax, only more so. It's bound in black leather, and he's apparently had it for many years, and it shows—it's very worn. That's why they call it the Gutenberg."

"I see. A little joke. Did you find anything of interest in the, uh, Gutenberg?"

"Yes. Naturally, I opened it to the present day. I found that his committee had a meeting starting at nine that morning. A line down the side indicated he expected it to go well into the afternoon. Nonetheless, there was another entry, just below that one. I found he'd had a ten A.M. appointment."

"With whom?"

"Well, as you'll see, the book just says: 10:00, V. C."

Another stir in the gallery, louder than before. This was a detail most of those present probably did not know; it hadn't been in the papers.

"V. C.? As in Veronica Cooper."

Albertson leaned back. "Well, I assume he wasn't visiting with the Vietcong. For that matter, when I thumbed through the past month, I found numerous other meetings with V. C. Sometimes more than one a day."

Padolino nodded. "Thank you for your cooperation, Lieutenant." He turned toward the defense table. "Your witness."

Stigmata was nothing like Loving expected, but of course he'd never been to a Goth club and, for that matter, hoped to God there weren't any back in Tulsatown. Practically everyone was done up in the manner that Lucille had described—silver jewelry, body piercings, dark hair, pale makeup, ruby-red or ebony-black lipstick. And in the apparel department—lots of black. Black tops, black bottoms. Black fishnet bodices. Black leather.

What bothered Loving most was that, save for the few skimpily dressed women, most of the crowd favored an androgynous style that made it uncomfortably difficult to tell if he was scrutinizing the curves of a male or female. Black was a concealing color, and the silver jewelry and body piercings seemed entirely unisex. Plus, everyone was wearing black mascara, way too much. Was that supposed to be sexy? Loving thought they looked like they'd escaped from *Pirates of the Caribbean*. Standing there in a white T-shirt and a Casaba baseball cap, he felt like a whitebread turkey in the middle of Harlem.

"So this is a party bar?" Loving asked.

"More like the Little Shop of Horrors," Daily replied soberly. "And to think my daughter came here for kicks." He was standing just beside Loving, but the music was so loud he had to shout.

The lighting was low—and most of it came from the blazing torches hanging on the sides of the faux-stone walls, giving the place the ambience of a medieval castle. Chains of human skulls were strung together like bunting across the walls. Loving assumed they were fakes, but still . . . creepy. Several bright white spotlights periodically shone back and forth across the dance floor, creating a strobe-like effect. It was disorienting, disturbing, and made Loving more than a little nauseated.

"We should talk to folks," Loving said. "Let's split up. Meet back here in an hour."

Daily nodded, then headed off to the right, toward the dance floor. Loving pointed himself in the direction of the bar. Well, that was his lot in life, right?

Loving took a seat on the nearest bar stool. Given his fish-out-of-water appearance, he knew he'd have to work hard to get anyone to talk to him. He ordered a beer—which arrived in a medieval goblet with a pewter base depicting writhing naked figures. Just two stools down, he noticed a shapely young woman wearing— surprise!—black, top to bottom. Or so he first thought. On closer inspection via the mirror opposite the bar, he realized that a vast amount of what he initially took to be a body stocking was in fact black body paint, and that in reality she was not wearing much at all. Just black leather boots, a black sports bra, and, around her pelvis, a black leather thong.

"Howdy," Loving said. The woman looked up at him, gave him a quick once-over, then returned her attention to her drink.

This could be challenging. He wasn't going to get her attention with stupid bar glass stunts or by talking about dogs. He rummaged through his overcoat pockets, searching for something that might work in a joint like this. Until he found just the right thing. He pulled the parts out of his pocket, put both ends into place, let a few more minutes pass innocently by, then turned toward the woman in black and smiled.

"Wanna see a trick?"

"What?" she said, in a voice almost as husky as his. "Like you're going to pull a quarter out of my ear or something?"

"No, no. Somethin' much more interestin'."

"Thanks. I'll pass."

"Suit yourself," Loving said, but he went right on with his routine, checking out the corner of his eye to make sure she was watching. She was.

He pulled the large nail out of his pocket and pointed it toward his wrist.

"Oh, you might wanna scoot down a few seats," Loving said pleasantly. "Sometimes the blood kind of splatters around."

"What in the—"

"Think I can drive this iron spike through my wrist with my fist?"

Loving wasn't sure how to read her expression, but she wasn't turning away. "God, no. And even if you could—why?"

"I told you, it's a trick."

"Not one I care to see."

"You never know. Can't be worse than some of the stuff goin' down on that dance floor. Here we go." He poised the nail against his wrist and then, in a split second, brought his other fist down on the top of the nail, hard. The tip of a sharp bloody spike emerged from the other end of his wrist, piercing his shirt sleeve. Blood spurted in every direction.

"Oh my God," the woman said, leaning away but not, Loving noticed, moving away. "Are you in pain? How can you do that?"

"Like I told you. It's a trick." With a swift gesture, he removed the collapsible nail from the top of his wrist and pulled the separate, spring-loaded fake spike tip—triggered by the impact of his blow to poke through the hole he'd already cut in his shirt and split open a bag of red Karo syrup. "Had you goin', though, didn't I?"

Despite herself, the woman smiled. "So . . . that isn't really blood on your wrist?"

"Nah. Why?"

"Just . . . wondered." She turned away. "You are one seriously twisted dude, mister."

"Why else would I be here?"

"So you thought you'd win me over with that sick circus trick?"

"I dunno. Did it work?" He extended his hand.

Her grip was cold and limp. Loving didn't get the impression she was trying to be rude. She just seemed to have a body temperature lower than most lizards. "I'm the Duchess."

"Are you?" he replied. "I'm the Loving. You come here often?"

"Every night. But I've never seen you here before."

"Yeah, it's my first time. I didn't know the dress code." He noticed she had very long nails—not real, he hoped—predictably painted dark black. The red lines and glassiness of her eyes, her mildly slurred speech, her breath, all suggested to Loving that she was operating under the influence. Excessive amounts of alcohol. Or something.

"Actually, I'm here lookin' for a friend," he added. "Her name's Amber. Amber Daily. Do you know her?"

"I'm afraid I've never heard that odd appellation."

This from a woman who called herself *the Duchess.* "What about a girl called Lilith? Lady Lilith?"

Even though she tried to suppress it, he saw the flicker of recognition in the woman's eyes.

"So you know her?"

"I've known a Lilith."

"She's twenty-two, sandy hair—or possibly black, when she comes here. Look, her dad gave me a picture." He passed it to the Duchess.

She glanced at it, frowned, then passed it back, facedown. "She's one of the Chosen."

"What does that mean?"

"It means she's permitted up there." She pointed a long dark nail upward and across the bar.

Just to the left of the central dance area, Loving spotted an interior staircase leading to a room on the second floor. There were wall-sized windows on either side of the door, but drapes pulled across them obscured the view. "And what goes on up there?"

"Don't know. I've never been invited."

"Is going upstairs a good thing?"

"It must be. Once a girl is chosen, you never see her down here again. You never see her at all."

Christina came to the podium with a pretty good understanding of what she could get out of Lieutenant Albertson on cross and what she couldn't. It wasn't as if he were lying, after all. Slanting things to serve his prosecutorial masters, maybe. But his testimony was essentially accurate. She had to make what few points she could and then sit down.

"Let's talk about the Gutenberg, Lieutenant. You said it memorialized many appointments scheduled with V. C. And you assumed that V. C. is Veronica Cooper."

"Well, it stands to reason—"

"Did you investigate the possibility that V. C. could be someone else?"

"Given that I had a corpse bearing those initials right there in the hideaway—"

"In other words, no. You didn't investigate the possibility that V. C. was anyone other than Veronica Cooper. You didn't investigate at all."

"That's not true."

"Then why didn't you consider other possibilities?"

"Ma'am, when you've got a dead body right—"

"Are you familiar with Senator Collins of Minnesota?"

"I . . . think I've heard the name."

"Are you aware that his first name is Vincent?"

Albertson pursed his lips. "No."

"What about Senator Conrad from Alaska?"

"I . . . haven't had the pleasure."

"His first name is Verne. And he's on the same Health Committee as Senator Glancy. I would imagine they talk quite often, wouldn't you?"

"I . . . suppose."

"Did you ever ask Senator Conrad if he'd had any of those meetings with Senator Glancy? Oh wait—since you didn't even know who he was, I guess the answer to that would be no. Am I right?"

"I didn't talk to Senator Conrad. I saw no reason to do so."

"Because you'd already made up your mind who the guilty party was, long before you even began your so-called investigation. Probably the instant you entered Senator Glancy's hideaway. He was the obvious suspect, and it's always easiest to go with the obvious suspect. Are you by any chance a Republican, sir?"

"Check your coat?"

Loving and Daily whirled around and saw a young twentysomething man in a dark tuxedo and tails standing behind a counter. In total contrast to the rest of the club, he had red hair. And a lighthearted manner that was more twee than Transylvania. He almost smiled.

"It's hot in there," the man added, pointing to Daily. "Thought you might want to lose the jacket."

"Right, right." He shrugged off his navy-blue jacket and handed it to the man behind the counter.

"Mmm. Yummy, yummy."

Daily did a double take. "Huh?"

The man pointed. "Blood."

Daily glanced down and saw a dark red splatter on the right arm of his shirt. "Blast," he muttered. "Scraped my arm in that alley, Loving. Wouldn't have happened if you'd gone down easier."

"My apologies."

"Maybe I better keep the jacket."

"Whatever you say," the man replied, handing it back. "But you may be passing up your chance to make yourself Mr. Popular in there with the Gothettes."

"I'll take the risk." Loving headed toward the dance floor, while Daily slipped back into his jacket. "Do I detect a certain wry tone in your voice?"

"Who, me?" the man said, pressing a hand against his chest. "Far be it. I just work here."

"What's your name? If you don't mind me asking."

"Well, in real life, it's Joe. But in here—I'm Baron Orzny."

"Pleased to meet you, Baron. So—you *just* work here. You're not—"

"A member of this Gloomfest? No. Find me an opening at the Hard Rock Café and I'm gone."

Daily grinned. "Not your kind of people?"

"Aw, they're not that bad. Ever been to a biker bar?"

"No."

"Well, this is better. Certainly more stylish. Just keep reminding yourself it's all make-believe. Even when some of them seem to have forgotten."

"How does a person turn into a . . . Goth?"

"It's easy, man. Just remember the number one rule."

"And that is?"

"Become clinically depressed. Or look like you are, anyway. No smiles permitted, except for the occasional throaty growl of sensual pleasure. After that, it's all easy. Change your vocabulary. Instead of talking about 'blow' or 'wingspan' or 'hotties,' you talk about the 'ethereal,' or 'ectoplasmic dimensions' or 'life force'—also known to the Goth elite as 'psi.' A name change is equally essential. 'Heather' is out. 'Lucretia' is fashionable. Long hair is good, especially if it impairs the vision or obscures the face. The dress code—well, that part is obvious enough. The popularity of tattoos and piercings is equally self-evident. The latest rage is to have some body part pierced no one else has yet thought to pierce—and my, hasn't that led to some delightful spectacles."

"But—why would anyone want to do this?"

"Evidently it's fun, dude. I mean, look at them out there, writhing and twisting and doing that stuff they euphemistically call dancing. Mostly they just sort of sway—not in rhythm, but then this minor-key dirge-like music has no rhythm. Of course, they look ridiculous, but most of them are so stoned they don't know the difference."

Daily stiffened. "Stoned?"

"Look at the expressions on their faces. Look at their eyes. Do they seem normal to you? Maybe it's just the booze, but . . ."

"I didn't see anyone pushing on the dance floor."

"You think they want to be arrested?"

"Tell me where it's coming from."

"I'm not so sure that would be smart."

"Tell me!" Daily bellowed. As an afterthought, he added, quietly, "Please."

Baron Orzny hesitated. "You're looking for your daughter, aren't you, man?"

Daily nodded slowly.

The Baron blew out his cheeks, checked to make sure no one was listening. "Thought so. That's why I started talking to you in the first place. Look, the kind of action you're talking about isn't on the dance floor."

"Then where is it?"

Baron Orzny pointed to the far end to the club, past the dance stage, to a staircase in the rear leading up to a room overlooking the club. "Owner has a private place up there. Very exclusive. Only a few are admitted—just his close buddies, the goon squad, and some very young, carefully chosen girls. Every night his people scour the floor looking for new meat. After a girl goes up there and disappears for a while—she's like a whole different person. Changed. Personality, attitude, everything. And then they disappear."

"Amber," Daily said, under his breath. "How do I get up there?"

The Baron gave him a once-over. "Well, nothing personal, dude, but—I don't think you do. You're not really the owner's type."

"He'll have to make an exception."

"Hey!" He grabbed Daily's arm. "Don't do anything stupid. He's got all kinds of security."

Daily's teeth were set firmly together. "I'll find a way."

10

Although the ropes lining the granite courthouse staircase were still in place, Ben was pleased to see that the podium had been removed. The federal marshals delivered his client at a discreet location out of camera sight, and together they walked up the long steps.

"What," Ben asked him, "no press conference today?"

Glancy smiled, adjusting the lie of his bright red necktie as he walked. "First rule of politics, Ben. Never repeat yourself. The first post-incarceration press conference is an event. After that, it's yesterday's news. Buzz Aldrin was the second man to walk on the face of the moon. You remember what he said?"

"No."

"Which is exactly my point." Glancy smiled, waved, even signed an autograph book, all without ever slowing or tempting the marshals to intervene. "I've been meaning to say something about your taste in attire, Ben. I gather you're not exactly . . . up with the latest fashion trends?"

Ben tugged at the lapels of his jacket. "You think my suit is dated?"

"I think it's carbon-dated. And isn't that the same suit you wore on Monday?"

"I only have three. And one of them was stained by an outraged parent."

Glancy made a tsking sound. "Don't you realize you've been appearing on television constantly?"

"Yup. But I still only have three suits. And one of them was stained—"

Glancy held up his hands. "Let me see what I can do. I'll talk to Shandy. She's a wonderful girl, very devoted to me. She's been organizing my wardrobe. And you and I are about the same size."

"Thanks, but I'm perfectly happy with the clothes I've got."

"I'm not."

They passed through the massive front doors and headed toward the staircase. Elevators were too slow, too crowded, and too difficult for the marshals stalking them to control.

"I thought yesterday went rather well," Glancy said. Once again, Ben was amazed by his serenity, his apparent absence of fear or concern. It was as if they were discussing the progress of the World Series, not his trial on capital murder charges. "Didn't you?"

"Yes. Christina was magnificent. But of course, the prosecution is just getting started. Once they finish with the technical and forensic witnesses, they'll bring on the fact witnesses. That's when we have to be wary of surprises."

"Well," Glancy said, smiling, "I have a few surprises of my own."

"Could you please describe the condition of the body when you first saw it?"

Dr. Emil Bukowsky was the senior coroner for the District of Columbia. Ben gathered that due to his senior status, it was usually one of his assistants, not he himself, who handled courtroom appearances. This time, however, the prosecutor was accepting no substitutes.

"I found the body just as Lieutenant Albertson described—her head between the sofa cushions and the rest of her body bent behind her. No one to my knowledge had touched her or in any way altered the crime scene. And I arrived barely an hour after the police did. I would've been there sooner, but I was carrying a kit filled with metallic instruments, many of them sharp, so I encountered the same problems with the Senate security officers that the detectives had."

Padolino nodded. "Could you tell how long she had been dead?"

"I never attempt to make any precise estimates until the corpse is back in my laboratory and we've run a full battery of tests. There were, however, indications that she had not been dead for more than a few hours."

"And what were these indications?"

Bukowsky turned slightly to face the jury. He was one of the better medical examiners Ben had encountered—in the courtroom, anyway. He could talk to the jury without making it obvious he was doing so, could explain his findings without reliance on jargon or sounding as if he was talking down to them. "The absence of a strong odor, for one thing. Lividity, for another. That's the purplish skin mottling that occurs after death, when the cessation of heart functioning and gravity cause the blood to settle to the lower parts of a body. Unfortunately, in this case, I found that to be somewhat deceptive, given the position of the body and the fact that so much of the blood, most in fact, had escaped from the body."

"Were you able to make any findings regarding lividity?"

"Yes. With the corpse in question, there was very little. It was only slightly present in her elbows, on the backs of her legs and around her shoulders—she was upside down, remember. So the time of death was no later than ten thirty that morning. Probably closer to ten."

"Were you able to make any preliminary observations regarding the cause of death?"

"The blood loss immediately suggested exsanguination. It was only after further examination that I was able to confirm that she had bled to death. We did find unusually constricted vasoconstrictors in the GI tract and the kidneys. Her surface vessels had shut down—that's caused by the absence of blood volume. She had a greatly heightened level of epinephrine and norepinephrine in the tissue samples we took, which also indicates a sharply reduced blood volume."

"Was there anything unusual about the blood loss that you observed?"

"Yes. I noticed that much of the blood appeared to have dried from evaporation, rather than clotting."

"And what did that tell you?"

"It told me that, despite the size of the gash in her neck, she bled slowly. Almost completely, but slowly."

Ben could see the pained winces in the jury box. He didn't blame them. Everyone wanted to believe that she had died quickly. It would suggest that she hadn't suffered much.

"Could you please describe this large neck wound to the jury?"

"It was about six inches long—virtually the length of her right shoulder. And very deep. I even found markings on her clavicle—her collarbone. Marrow had actually seeped from the bone. Granted, her medical records showed the woman had some degree of osteoporosis—rare in someone that young, but not unheard of. Even then—to leave marks on the bone indicates a deep and severe injury."

"Would you please tell the jury what you did next?"

"After the scene had been thoroughly photographed and searched, I instructed three of my assistants to place the corpse in a body bag for removal."

"Were there any difficulties?"

"A few. Some of the blood had pooled under her buttocks, causing the body to stick to the wall when we tried to remove her. We had to be careful not to create any new injuries. But we managed it. And once we did, moving her was easy. I doubt if she weighed one hundred and ten pounds when she was alive. After all that blood and other fluid loss, she weighed considerably less."

Again Ben saw the jury avert their eyes, as if somehow not looking at the coroner would alter what had happened.

"Once I had Ms. Cooper's remains in my laboratory, I began a full battery of tests. Under magnification, I carefully examined each fragment of tissue from the wound, as well as the wound itself."

"Could you determine what caused the injury?"

"Yes. I found that the edges of the neck wound were consistent with the use of a wide, sharp-edged instrument. A knife, most likely. Possibly a chopping knife."

A knife? Ben pondered, not for the first time. How could anyone get a knife into the U.S. Senate?

"Did you discover anything else of note during the course of your examination?"

"I found evidence of recent sexual activity. Unfortunately, we were not able to recover any sperm or other fluids to perform a DNA analysis."

"Anything else?"

"Yes. When I took blood samples, I discovered that the woman had been given a significant dose of warfarin."

"And what is that?"

"A chemical anticoagulant. It prevents blood clotting."

"Is this something found naturally in the human body?"

"No. Not even in hemophiliacs. It had to be administered, and it explains a great deal. It significantly increased the likelihood that, absent medical intervention, she would bleed to death—especially given the size of the wound."

"And—" Padolino actually stuttered as he asked the question. "—would Ms. Cooper have been conscious during this . . . slow death?"

He nodded sadly. "Almost to the end. Helpless, probably. But conscious."

"And would she have experienced . . . great pain during this time?"

"Objection," Ben said, grateful for a chance to interrupt the flow. "Lack of relevance."

Judge Herndon nodded. "Sustained." Whether she felt pain did not in any way relate to the question of who killed her or how or why, but Ben knew this was a Pyrrhic victory at best. Everyone already knew the answer to the question.

"We've been here for hours," Daily said. "Feel at home yet?"

"Feel like I've stumbled into Cloud-Cuckoo-Land," Loving grunted, recalling the book he'd been forced to read in his tenth and final year of schooling.

"Entrance is still guarded," Daily noted, as he stared up at the two human Dobermans posted at the top of the stairway. "Same as last night."

"Two on the outside of the door," Loving observed. "At least two others on the inside."

"How can you tell?"

"I can tell."

Daily's lips tightened. "Hell of a lot of protection just to keep the rabble out of your private suite."

"I figure there's somethin' goin' on up there other than dancin'."

"You think—you think they've got Amber up there? You think they've got my little girl mixed up in some—some goddamn orgy?"

Loving gripped him tightly by the shoulders. "We don't know. Let's not let our imaginations go nuts here."

"Can you get us in?"

"I can try."

Loving felt eyeballs bearing down on him as soon as he took his first step upward, Daily just a few steps behind him. As soon as he reached the top, the two bulked-up bodyguards converged, blocking his access to the closed door.

"We'd like to go inside," Loving announced. "Got a message for the boss."

The two neckless brutes before him shook their heads in unison, left-right, left-right, like choreographed backup singers. "Gotta have an invitation," the man on the left barked.

"I'll just be a minute." Loving started for the door.

They cut him off—forcibly. The sandy-haired hulk on the right put his hand on Loving's broad chest and pushed him back, none too gently. "Gotta have an invitation."

While they were talking, a young woman sashayed up the stairs and slid between them. She couldn't have been more than eighteen, if that. Dressed in the requisite black, her top was a sheer webbing, more transparent than panty hose, and her skirt was so short Loving could spot her thong without even trying.

"Do we know you?" the left guard asked her.

"He's expecting me."

They gave her a quick once-over and let her pass, then re-formed the blockade before Loving could take advantage of the opening.

"You got a party goin' down in there?" Loving asked. "That's cool. But I'm not plannin' to party. I just—" He considered a moment. "I'm here to see Lilith."

The flicker of recognition on both sets of eyes was unmistakable. They knew her.

"So she's here?"

The bodyguard didn't answer. "You still gotta have an invitation, pal."

"That chick you just let in didn't have an invitation."

"Man, she was wearing her invitation. She's one of the Chosen, or will be. You're not. So run along before we have to—"

"Amber!" Daily shot forward, doing an end run around the thug on the left, then lunging for the door. But the guard was too quick for him. He blocked the entrance, catching Daily's head like a softball and shoving it to the ground. Daily fell, hard.

"That wasn't necessary," Loving growled. "All he wants—"

He was cut off by a sudden cry from the guard. Daily had sunk his teeth into the man's ankle. As he bent to swat his attacker away, Daily grabbed the guard's leg and pushed him backward. The other guard turned toward him, fists clenched. This was foolish and futile and Loving knew it, but he couldn't just stand there and let them kill his companion. He intercepted a kick aimed toward Daily's head, then caught the guard's fist in midair, squeezing it tightly until the guard backed down. Unfortunately, there was still the other guy, who wrapped his excessively muscled arm around Loving's throat. Just as Loving was considering how to deal with that, the door opened, and two more bodyguards rushed out.

Just as he had predicted. They were so hosed.

"Whass goin' down?" one of the new men asked.

"Nothin' we can't handle," the guard with the lock around Loving said. As if to prove his point, he reared back one booted foot and rammed it into Daily's face. His head whipped around so fast Loving was afraid he'd hear Daily's neck crack. Blood spilled from his lips.

"Take them out the back way," one of the new men grunted. He was taller than the others, and Loving got the impression he was in charge. At least of the goon squad. "Hurt 'em a little."

"With pleasure," said the sandy-haired one. His arm still wrapped around Loving's throat, he pivoted Loving around and walked him to a ramp in the rear, forcing him down to the back of the dance floor. The other man grabbed Daily by the hair, lifted him to his feet, punched him again in the kidneys, then followed his cohort downstairs. They wormed their way behind the dance floor to an emergency exit that opened onto a back alleyway. Loving felt a stunning blow to his ribs, and then he was tumbling face-first into the slime and grime of the slick concrete pavement. Daily fell just behind him.

"And don't come back," one of them growled. The two guards wiped their hands, then began to laugh, loudly and heartily, as they let the door slam behind them.

"You okay?" Loving grunted, as soon as they were gone. He was checking his teeth. He thought they'd loosened a molar.

"I'll live," Daily answered, several beats later, wiping blood from his face.

"Why the hell did you do that? Do you like having your butt handed to you?"

"I need to see my daughter," Daily said, through clenched teeth.

Loving sighed. "Yeah, I know."

"We should call the police."

"No."

"Why not? The police could get past those jerkoffs."

"But we've got no proof that any crime has been committed—"

"The drugs!"

"—and let's face it, if the cops start roundin' up drug users on the premises, they're gonna get Amber, too. Dependin' on how deep she's into this, she might go away for a long time."

Daily fell silent.

"Even if I rounded up an army of my own, by the time we got in, Amber would be gone. We need to enter without endin' the party."

"But how?"

"I've got an idea." Loving pushed himself to his feet, his back complaining all the way. He pulled out his cell phone and punched in a local number he'd had the foresight to memorize. "We're not done here."

During the break, Shandy Craig pumped Ben for information. Amanda Burton was present also, but after their contretemps of the day before, she'd been keeping her distance, which was okay by Ben.

"Do you think the coroner's testimony hurt us?"

Ben shrugged. "He said nothing I didn't expect. And I found some of what he didn't say quite interesting."

Shandy knotted her fingers together. "I don't know how you can stand this. I'm so tense I can hardly bear it. I didn't sleep at all last night."

"You get used to it." Which was a total lie. He hadn't slept much the night before, either.

"I've been getting offers," Shandy confided. "Other senators. Don't stay on a sinking ship, they say. But—I don't know—it just doesn't feel right. Todd needs me."

Todd, Ben noticed. Not Senator Glancy. Todd.

"By the way," she added, "I brought you some suits."

"I told Todd—"

"Oh, it's no sweat. He has more suits than I have shoes. And some of the older ones he can't wear anymore, anyway." She lowered her voice a notch. "He's put on a few pounds lately, as you've probably noticed." Ben hadn't. "Jail food, you know. Anyway, I think these will fit you just fine."

"Listen, I neither need nor want—"

"He'll be delighted to borrow them," Christina said, appearing out of nowhere. "Such a generous offer. Ben has been needing some sartorial guidance."

"That's pretty rich, coming from you," Ben said.

"What's that supposed to mean?" Shandy asked. "I think Christina is a very stylish dresser."

Ben smiled. "You haven't known her as long as I have."

Ben rarely crossed hard on the medical witnesses. In his experience, they were usually careful in their testimony, not prone to exaggeration, and frankly too damn smart to mess around with. Dr. Bukowsky was no exception, but Ben had pored over the coroner's various reports and records and he thought there was just a chance he might be able to do some good for his client. At any rate, in a case this desperate, he had to take every chance he had. It would either be a stunning triumph—or an abject failure.

"If I understand correctly, Doctor, you've placed the time of death after the start of Senator Glancy's committee meeting that day."

"Objection," Padolino said. "This witness has no knowledge regarding any committee meetings." The objection was sustained, as Ben knew it would be. Didn't matter. He'd given the jury Senator Glancy's alibi. They would remember it.

Technically, having established the alibi, he could sit down— what did it matter how death occurred, so long as they proved Glancy couldn't have done it? But Ben knew better than to pass up an opportunity to poke holes in the prosecution's case.

"You mentioned the large wound on the victim's right shoulder, Doctor. Why didn't you tell the jury about the other injury?"

The coroner blinked, leaned forward, as did several of the jurors. Very good. Ben was happiest when he knew people were paying attention.

"The other injury? I don't recall . . ."

Ben raised a thick stapled document. "This is your final autopsy report, isn't it?"

Bukowsky frowned. "Appears to be."

Ben flipped through the pages. "Here it is. On page twenty-two. 'Evidence of a small puncture wound barely a millimeter in width on the right jugular vein.'" He looked up. "That is what you wrote, isn't it?"

"It was a tiny anomaly."

"Meaning it was something you couldn't explain."

"I assume the vein was nicked by the knife—"

"Whoa, now. Let's rein in the horses. Didn't you tell the jury the murderer used a great big knife?"

"Yes, but—"

"How on earth could someone make such a small puncture wound with a thick chopping knife?"

"The woman bled to death. I can't see that this could possibly have any importance—"

"You mean you don't want it to have any importance, right? Because you can't explain it."

"Objection!" Padolino shouted.

Judge Herndon looked down sternly from the bench. "Mr. Kincaid, you will govern your conduct in accordance with the rules of decorum promulgated by this court. That kind of behavior might be acceptable in—" It was impossible to miss the note of derision in his voice. "—Oooo-kla-homa, but I will not tolerate it in my court-room. Are we clear on that?"

"Yes, sir. My apologies." Jerk. He turned back to the witness. "The fact remains. You can't explain the puncture mark."

"As I said, the knife might've nicked the vein—"

"Come on, Doctor. Isn't it far more likely that the vein was pen-etrated by something smaller than a great big chopping knife?"

"There's no evidence that another weapon was used on the woman."

"Sure, not now. Not after she's been ripped to shreds. But isn't it possible that there was evidence of another weapon before? Evi-dence that was obliterated by the slashing of her neck?"

"Your honor," Padolino said, "I must protest. This is idle specu-lation."

"An expert witness is allowed to offer an opinion, based upon his expertise," Herndon answered. Ben was glad to see the judge wasn't the sort to hold a grudge. "I'll allow it."

"All you have," Bukowsky insisted, "is a tiny, easily dismissed puncture wound—"

"Is that all I have?" Ben flipped through a few more pages in the report. "I read on page twenty-six that there was a cut on her tra-chea."

"Now, that could easily have been made by the knife."

"Yes, it could have. But my medical experts tell me that if her trachea had been cut with a knife while she was still alive, she would've aspirated blood." Now it was Ben's turn to lean forward. "Isn't that correct, Doctor?"

The doctor fell silent.

"I didn't quite get your response, Dr. Bukowsky. If her trachea had been cut while she was still alive, wouldn't she have aspirated blood?"

"It's . . . possible."

"Possible? It's a medical certainty! But she didn't aspirate blood, did she? Were there any traces of blood in her lungs?"

"No," the doctor said succinctly.

"And that means—" Ben paused, making sure everyone was with him. "At the time this woman was slashed on the throat, she was already dead or dying."

Bukowsky clearly was not prepared for this line of reasoning. "But—why would anyone cut her if she was already dead or dying?"

"To disguise the real manner in which she was killed, of course. Whatever it was that caused that puncture. The murderer obliterated the killing wound."

"I can't agree with that conclusion."

"Can't or won't?"

"Your honor," Padolino began.

Ben continued unabated. "Whether you agree or not, Doctor—you can't rule the possibility out, can you? It is an explanation consistent with the medical evidence. Right?"

His lips pursed. His tongue slowed. "I suppose it is . . . possible. But—"

"That's all I wanted to hear. Thank you for your candor, Doctor. No more questions."

After several failed attempts, Loving finally managed to get her on the phone.

"Lucille?"

"Well, hello there, sugah. Didn't expect to hear from you again so soon. But I can't say that I mind. You wanna come—"

"It's about Amber."

Her voice took on an instantly sober tone. "Is she okay?"

"I don't know. I can't get to her."

Lucille didn't hesitate. "What do you need me to do?"

Loving gave her the address. "We'll meet you out front. And Lucille?"

"Yeah?"

"Don't dress like you normally would. You gotta wear black—like the stuff Amber liked the last few times you saw her. And it needs to be kinda . . . trashy."

"Trashy poor, or trashy I-want-you-inside-my-pants-right-now?"

"Uhh . . . the latter, I think."

"Can do, sugah. Be there in an hour." She rang off.

Loving tucked his cell phone into his jacket pocket.

"What was all that about?" Daily asked. "Who was that?"

Loving allowed himself a small smile. "Our ticket inside."

11

After the coroner finished testifying, Padolino filled the day with brief, legally important but essentially uninteresting testimony, and Ben knew why. He wanted the jury fresh when he delivered his big wham-bam slammer. He'd been building up to it since jury selection—before, actually.

The video. Ben unsuccessfully had tried every motion imaginable to get it suppressed. There was no way to convince the judge that it wasn't relevant—since it so clearly was. To be sure, all but two of the jurors admitted that they had already seen the video—at least the somewhat expurgated televised version—and Ben very much suspected the other two had as well but didn't want to admit it because they feared it would get them booted. Didn't matter. To see some lascivious video on television about famous people you don't know is an event perhaps worthy of comment, but hardly a life-changing event. To see that same video in a court of law, with one of the featured players sitting right before you and the other one dead, is an entirely different matter.

Doing his time-filling belt-and-suspenders routine, Padolino called a barrage of technical experts: two hair techs, a fiber fiend, and a fingerprint specialist. They had all analyzed trace evidence in the hideaway and told the jury the same thing—Veronica Cooper had been killed there, and Todd Glancy had been present, probably on several occasions. Christina handled the crosses and did a fine job; Ben knew from experience that there was nothing on earth harder than crossing an expert. Just when you had them trapped, they hauled out some scientific gobbledygook and slithered to safety. Better to leave the jury confused than admit defeat. Christina kept them all on a short leash, but the only thing she couldn't do was change the undisputed facts. A clear picture emerged: Glancy arranged a meeting with Cooper in his hideaway to talk about the newly erupted scandal, maybe to pay her off, maybe to buy her silence some other way. When it didn't work, he killed her. Then he washed up and went back to work. The whole thing could've been done in fifteen minutes.

Glancy's only hope was his alibi. He had been at that committee meeting at the time the coroner claimed the murder occurred. As long as the alibi held, as long as the prosecution couldn't establish Opportunity, they still got game. But if they lost that, no amount of defense fancy footwork could bail them out.

Padolino called Everett Scott to the witness stand. As the jury soon learned, he was an off-air reporter for C-SPAN and had been for almost eight years.

"Mr. Scott, how did the videotape that has been entered into evidence as Prosecution Exhibit Twenty-three come into your possession?"

"It arrived in the mail."

"Did you have to sign for it?"

"No. It just showed up in my box with the bills and the advertising flyers." Scott was a thin man with glasses, long gangly arms, and brownish hair that he combed straight back from his face. A bit of a nebbish, really, Ben thought. But he hadn't expected a C-SPAN reporter to come off like Tom Cruise.

"Did the envelope bear a return address?"

"It did not."

"Was there a postmark?"

He hesitated before answering. "It had a DC postmark."

"An informant, perhaps?"

Scott did not reply.

"Mr. Scott," Padolino continued, "do you know who sent you the videotape?"

Again the hesitation. "I . . . do not know for certain who sent me the tape, no."

"But you have some thoughts about who might have sent it?"

"Objection," Ben said. "Calls for speculation."

Judge Herndon batted his pencil on his desk. "Well, I suppose that depends on the amount of evidence the witness has in support of his theory." He swiveled around to face Scott. "How sure are you that you know who sent it?"

Scott swallowed. "Your honor, I must respectfully decline to answer that question, or any other questions of that nature."

"You're pleading the Fifth?"

"I'm pleading a journalist's First Amendment right to refuse to identify his sources."

"That right, as I'm sure you know, is not one always recognized by the courts."

"I do know that." Scott pressed his hands together, wringing them. "But I won't reveal my sources."

"But if you're not certain—"

"Guessing would be even worse. I would be reduced to identifying numerous potential sources and contacts at the U.S. Senate, which would make it impossible for me to continue to do my job."

Undoubtedly true, Ben thought, in this era in which journalists ran with stories obtained from unnamed sources or insiders who "did not wish to be identified." Scott would lose more than just his sources if he named one. He'd become a pariah in the journalistic community.

Herndon leaned back and stared at the witness. "You're not going to back off, are you?"

"No, sir. I am not."

"Very well." He turned back to Padolino. "Move on to something else, Mr. Prosecutor." He paused. "I'll decide later whether to impose sanctions for contempt."

Padolino nodded and shuffled on to his next index card. "Did you take any actions to verify the accuracy of the tape?"

"I certainly did," Scott replied. "I would never recommend airing something like that unless I knew it was genuine."

"Please tell the jury what you did."

"We have our own voice analyzer in the C-SPAN office building. So I drummed up some old footage of Senator Glancy giving a speech, then compared the voice print with that of the man speaking in the videotape."

"And the result?"

"They matched. Perfectly. There was no doubt that Senator Glancy was the man in the tape. And by slowing the tape down frame by frame, we were able to capture a full-face photo of the woman whom he was with. With that photo," Scott continued, "we were able to confirm that his, um, companion was Veronica Cooper, an intern working in Glancy's office. At that point, the newsworthiness of the video was unquestionable."

"And did it bother you that you didn't know who had sent you the tape?"

Scott shrugged his shoulders slightly. "I would've rather known my source, but I'd confirmed that it was accurate information. So regardless of who the whistle-blower was, I realized the American people had a right to know about this . . . questionable conduct by an elected official."

"Indeed they do." Padolino looked up toward the bench. "Your honor, with your permission, may we lower the lights? It's time to show the video."

It seemed to take forever. Loving sat at the bar, nursing a 7Up, waiting as patiently as possible. A woman much older than he was sat on a stool behind him in between two girlfriends, all of them decked out in black.

"I was okay when Mark got the tongue stud," the woman was saying. Loving tried to block her voice out, but she had become his personal mosquito who wouldn't be swatted. "And then he got the navel stud, the nipple ring. I put up with it. But when he had his thing pierced—I mean, that's just gross."

"Why are you so uppity?" one of her friends said. "You had your boobs done."

"I did not have my boobs done."

"Oh, you so did."

"If I had my boobs done, I would've had 'em done a hell of a lot better than this."

"I liked Mark," the other friend said. "He was cute. Kinda like John Cusack, except fatter."

"And with a stud in his thing. I'm pretty sure John Cusack doesn't have that."

"And how would you know?"

Dear God, Loving thought, his eyes toward the heavens, I know I've done some evil deeds in my time, but surely never anything bad enough to deserve this. Where *is* she?

A high-pitched voice sang into his ear, "Here I come to save the day-y-y-y-y-y!"

Loving whirled around. Lucille.

"Will this do?" she said, patting the back of her head and shaking her hips in her best Mae West imitation.

"I kinda think so," Loving answered. She was decked out in black—black fishnet, mostly, with a leather skirt and strapless top. As if her hair weren't red enough already, she'd put on a big Lillie Langtry–style wig. She was wearing makeup twice as heavy as before, dark black lipstick and eyeliner. Some kind of glitter was streaked through her hair, and the black hip boots were a nice touch. She was an ample girl, perhaps not a born beauty, but she knew how to work it. And that was what they needed at the moment. "Man would have to be made of stone to say no to that."

"Still the flatterer." She tweaked Loving's cheek. "Shall we go for it?"

Loving showed her the way to the stairway leading up to the private room. The two guards posted outside were new, not the two who had booted him and Daily out on their first attempt, which was good. It would make this a little easier.

Lucille began sashaying up the stairs, shaking her hips, allowing her already too-short skirt to creep up with every step. Loving and Daily stayed a few steps behind. As before, as soon as they neared the top, the two guards converged in front of the door.

"Gotta have an invitation," the guard on the right said.

"He's expecting me," she said, following Loving's coaching.

The guard gave her the once-over and shrugged. "I don't remember seeing you around before."

"Trust me, sugah. I don't get dolled up like this for my own amusement. I'm one of the Chosen."

Apparently she fit the mold. He tilted his head toward Loving and Daily. "What about those two?"

"They come with me."

"I don't think so. Not his type."

"He'll like what they brought him."

"And what would that be?"

She singsonged her reply. "A little pick-me-up. Might be enough for you, too. Par-tay time."

The guard's eyes narrowed slightly. He turned to his partner. "I don't know about this."

Lucille brushed her hand down his chest, stopping just below his belt. "Play your cards right, sweetcakes, and I might have a little something for you, too."

He frowned, shrugged, then stood to the side.

Lucille opened the door. Loving and Daily followed in behind her.

They were inside.

At least Ben managed to thwart Padolino's plan to haul in a big-screen TV. He was still certain the jurors had all seen the video before, but no one outside the legal system and the C-SPAN offices had seen it like this—with no deletions from the sound track, without the pixilated blurring of Veronica Cooper's bared breasts or Senator Glancy's insistent genitalia. It was almost like a scene out of *A Clockwork Orange*; the entire room was forced to watch a porn video that was not the least bit sexy, but thoroughly repulsive. When they reached the part where Veronica began making the hideous gagging noises, Ben thought several of the jurors were going to be sick.

The reaction from the gallery was worse. When it was over,

Marie Glancy rose to her feet and ran out of the courtroom, her hand covering her mouth. Ben couldn't fault her for being upset. But showing the jury that she was upset effectively undid what little may have been accomplished by positioning her behind her husband, creating a show of support that all sixteen jurors now knew was a huge lie. Her hasty exit from her husband's side could be more damaging to their case than the tape itself.

After the proceedings adjourned, Marshall Bressler led the defense team out of the courtroom, wheeling his chair with a fierce intensity. "You're not going to cross?"

Ben shook his head. "No point. The reporter knows nothing I want the jury to hear. Best to get the damn tape out of their minds as soon as possible and move on to something else."

"Probably a smart move," Bressler muttered. "That man has had it in for Todd for years."

"Who?" Ben asked. "Padolino?"

"No. The reporter. Scott." He shot a quick glance over his shoulder. "Goes back to when Scott was covering the committee Todd chaired when the Democrats were in power and they were considering that health insurance bill. About seven years ago. You remember the one. Would've guaranteed coverage nationwide for anyone in need, mandatory coverage of controversial therapies for terminally ill patients. Scott's a bleeding-heart liberal and he really wanted it passed. But Todd buried it in committee—it was an election year and he felt he had no choice. Scott's been biding his time ever since, waiting for a chance to get back at Todd. Hell, he probably made that tape himself."

Ben's brow furrowed. He knew that Bressler was inveterately loyal to his senator, but this was sounding a little paranoid—more like one of Loving's conspiracy theories than anything that could really happen. "Big risk to take just to smear a senator."

"Compared to what? The push-polls Lee Atwater orchestrated to plant the rumor that John McCain's adopted Bangladeshi daughter was actually a bastard he sired in Vietnam? The out-of-state thugs Tom DeLay imported into Florida to screw up the 2000 recount? The forged letter Nixon's people used to push Muskie out of the race? You're not in Oklahoma anymore, kiddo. This is the big time. People here play for keeps."

"Hey, Kincaid!"

Ben saw the fist hurtling toward his face and jumped back just in time. His assailant tumbled forward, knocking Ben backward. Ben tried to scramble to his feet, but the man came at him again, this time landing a punch square in his stomach. Pain radiated through Ben's body. He tried to defend himself, but he was already wobbling and the sudden movement made him lose his balance. He tumbled back onto the floor, landing hard on the seat of his borrowed trousers.

"Defend this, asshole." The attacker reared back to deliver a swift kick to Ben's ribs, but before he had a chance, he was knocked to the ground—by Marshall Bressler's wheelchair. The man flew forward and hit the hard marble floor face-first. He groaned, unsuccessfully trying to push himself to his knees. A few moments later, two security officers arrived at the scene and grabbed him, cuffing his hands behind his back.

Ben rose, clutching his aching stomach. "Nice work with the chair, Marshall. You really know how to make that thing move."

He smiled a little. "It's my legs that are shot, not my arms. Who is this creep, anyway?"

Ben took a long look. "Darrin Cooper. We met at a restaurant a few nights ago."

"Is he . . . ?"

"Yeah. Veronica Cooper's father."

"Oh." Much of the anger drained from Bressler's face. "Well, that's different."

"Yeah."

One of the security guards addressed Ben. "We'll take him to our holding cell, sir. But we'll need you to come in and sign a complaint."

Ben waved his hand in the air. "I don't want to press charges."

The guard stiffened. "Sir, this is a federal courthouse. We take any threat to security very seriously. We can't allow—"

"I'm not pressing charges," Ben said firmly. "Just don't let the man in again, okay?"

The guard frowned, obviously not happy. "As you wish, sir."

"Thank you."

"This isn't over, Kincaid," Cooper snarled, glaring with his weird walleyed expression. "You can't go on working for the devil forever. There will be a reckoning!"

"With all due respect," Ben replied, "I think you need some grief counseling. In the worst possible way. I hope you'll take this chance I've given you to get some."

"Don't pretend kindness to me. You're doing Satan's work. Helping the man who butchered my little girl!"

Eventually the guards hauled Cooper out of earshot.

"Is that smart?" Bressler asked. "Not preferring charges? He doesn't have to get into the courtroom to get to you. How long till he shows up again to deliver another fist-o-gram?"

"The man lost his daughter," Ben said simply.

"The man barely knew his daughter," Christina interjected.

Ben nodded. "And that probably makes it worse."

Although there were several people in the private apartment, none of them looked up when Lucille entered, Loving and Daily close behind. In fact, no one even seemed to notice. They were in worlds of their own.

Loving heard a stream of air escape from Daily's lips. "Amber," he whispered.

There was a long sofa in the center of the room, parallel to a glass-topped coffee table littered with spoons and bongs and all kinds of drug paraphernalia. Various overstuffed chairs seemed randomly scattered throughout the room, most of them bearing men or mostly naked women—correction: girls—sprawled across them, all of the girls bearing heavy-lidded expressions, focused intently on some far-off place. One of them was bent forward over the back of a chair; the man standing behind had her hair in his fist and was pounding her with a steady, nauseating rhythm.

On the sofa, a thin, ashen-complexioned man sat with his legs crossed, a relaxed smile on his face, staring at nothing. Lying beside him, with her head buried in his lap, was a young woman wearing a man's shirt, naked from the waist down. Loving recognized her from the pictures he'd seen. It was Amber.

"My God," Daily whispered. He seemed unable to move, barely able to speak.

"It's like goddamn *Reefer Madness*," Lucille said under her breath.

Loving peered across the room, sickened, stunned, wondering what to do first, or next, or at all. The guards posted on the inside of the room were ignoring them, just as they no doubt had been trained to ignore everything that went on in here. But he didn't kid himself that he could get Amber out. He'd never make it to the stairs.

And the other problem was that Amber so clearly did not want out.

"Goddammit!" shouted the man behind the chair. Apparently he'd finished. "God, Vicky, that's good. You want some of this, Randy?"

The man on the sofa did not alter his placid expression. "Been there, done that."

"How 'bout yours? She ready to go again?"

"What do you think, my darling?" He put his finger under Amber's chin and turned her head to face him. "Ready for some sloppy seconds?"

Loving held Daily back with the flat of his hand.

She squirmed and stretched like a kitten, her eyes barely open. "Don't . . . know . . ."

"Daddy'll give you a little something more. Just to help you along."

"Yeah?" She slid off the sofa, curled up at his feet, and began to lick his hand. "Love Daddy." Chest extended, she shoved her tongue into his mouth. The kiss, if you could call it that, lasted for an eternity. Loving restrained Daily for the duration.

With a twitchy abruptness that made Loving's heart jump, the man on the sofa adjusted his gaze, apparently noticing the newcomers for the first time. He scanned Lucille, top to bottom, then smiled. "Want some X?" he slurred.

Lucille got her game together quick. She moved forward with an unsubtle body language that made it clear she had come to join the party. "You talkin' Ecstasy?"

He shook his head. "That's for the losers out there. We got the real X. The good stuff. Oxy."

OxyContin, Loving thought silently. A prescription pain reliever, basically morphine. And creeps like this one often mixed it with Spanish fly or other date rape drugs to make sure their prey got high and happy and submissive.

The man on the sofa rolled his hazy eyes. "So you want some or what?"

"I guess I could take a hit," Lucille answered.

"Hey!" Amber said. She sat upright, exposing herself. "I thought it wasss for me!" Apparently she was so far gone she didn't even recognize Lucille.

"There's plenty for everyone," the man on the sofa assured her.

"Cool," Lucille said. "Hit me."

"All you got to do is join the party. Come sit in my lap, beautiful."

Lucille did as she was told. Loving cringed, but he tried to comfort himself with the thought that she was used to doing disgusting things she didn't much like. The man on the sofa poured a white powder out of a vial into a spoon, then held the flame of a lighter beneath the spoon. As he stared at the flame, his pupils dilated. "Doin' a little cookin', bitchcakes. Gonna let you lick the spoon."

"You sshould let me go firsst!" Amber said, sounding like a petulant drunk.

The man set down the spoon for a moment and brought the flame next to her face. She screamed.

"Don't tell me what to do," he said flatly. "Just keep your ass on the floor and lick my hand."

Again, Loving kept Daily in check. The man on the sofa returned to his chemistry.

"What's with your friends?" the man asked Lucille, glancing toward Loving and Daily.

She tried to smile. "They're just looking for a good time."

"Are they cops?" He turned slightly toward Loving. "Are you cops?"

Loving took the succinct route. "No."

"You have to tell me if you are. Otherwise I can get you for entrapment."

Loving remained stone-faced. Bless television for the stupid ideas it put into the heads of slugs like him.

The man turned his bleary gaze back to Lucille. "Little old for you, aren't they?"

"I . . . think they like younger action," she replied.

He grinned. "Then they've come to the right place." He looked up, his eyes barely focused. "I can give you some X, for yourself or whoever, but it'll cost you. I don't get this stuff for free, you know."

"How do you get it?" Lucille asked. "You got a doctor?"

"Sweetheart—I am a doctor. I can get all I want." He handed Lucille the spoon.

Amber was too stoned to be smart. "I sssaid, I want to go first!" She reached for the spoon, but the man grabbed her arm, then slapped her across the face, so hard she fell on top of the coffee table. The glass cracked.

Loving wasn't fast enough this time. Daily tore across the room. "You son of a bitch. I'm taking my daughter out of here, and if you try to stop me I'll tear you apart!"

The two bodyguards were on him in a heartbeat. Damn! Loving swore silently. This is wrong, all wrong. But he had no choice. He rushed forward just in time to trip one of the guards before he got to Daily. While he was down, Loving stomped on the nerve center of the back of his neck. One down. The other one, unfortunately landed a roundhouse punch to the back of Daily's head.

All hell broke loose. The orgy was over; everyone moved at once. Even though most of them were dulled by drugs, they could turn into feral beasts with astonishing rapidity. Daily moved toward Amber, but the remaining guard blocked his way. Lucille tried to help him, but one of the other men swatted her with the flat of his hand. She tumbled to the floor. Then the two bodyguards from outside the door came racing inside.

Loving knew he had to hurry. He jumped over the coffee table and, before the guard pummeling Daily could react, thrust a fist square onto his nose. Blood spurted everywhere. The guard dropped to the floor like an anvil.

The man on the sofa wrapped his arm around Amber's neck. Loving gave him a chop just below the ribs; as soon as he loosened his grip Loving grabbed Amber by the arm and pulled her up to her shaky feet.

"Run," he said. "Understand me? Get out of here. Fast!"

He wanted to say more, but was interrupted by a chair busted across his back. Loving fell across the table and onto the sofa, knocking drug paraphernalia everywhere.

His back ached as if it were broken. He could see that Daily had clocked the creep who was doing Vicky, but two of the bodyguards were converging on him, one on each side of the overstuffed chair. Loving forced himself up, his back screaming in pain. He stumbled across the room, grabbed one of the men by the arm, and gave him a quick jab to the solar plexus. While he was doubled over, Loving kneed him in the chin. He went tumbling backward and smashed into the wall.

One left. Loving was in such pain it hurt to move, but he knew Daily wouldn't be able to take the man out himself. While Daily kept him occupied, mostly by acting as a punching bag, Loving raced behind him. Not very sporting, hitting a man from behind, but at the moment Loving didn't care. There was no telling how long it would be before one of the goons on the floor got up or more arrived. Loving swiveled his foot around and knocked the man's knees out from under him. Another blow to the front of the knees and he was down, howling in agony.

Loving leaned against the big overstuffed chair, heaving, gasping for air. He hadn't fought like that in ages, and for a reason. He didn't like to fight, didn't like to put himself into situations where it was necessary. A smart man always has an alternative, that's what Ben said. But when you're traveling with an idiot who's worried about his daughter, all bets are off.

Amber cowered beside the sofa. "Get your daughter," Loving huffed. "Get her out of here before it's too late."

But Daily didn't move. What the hell—? Loving pushed himself up, his back complaining bitterly.

Daily was pointing behind him.

He'd forgotten about the stonehead jerkoff on the sofa, dammit. He seemed so drugged and weak—

But even drugged and weak can be dangerous when it's holding a gun.

"Put that away," Loving bellowed. "You'll miss, and after you do I'll rip your throat out."

The man's hyperdilated eyes didn't blink. "Die," he said simply.

"Randy, no!" Amber threw herself across the sofa and grabbed the gun. "No!"

When the gun fired, her scream was like an ice pick piercing Loving's brain.

12

With about half an hour to go before the trial resumed, Ben motioned Christina into an empty jury room. She wasn't surprised. Even though they had been over everything a thousand times, she knew his personal insecurity levels were riding so high that he had an intense need to run through it again—not so much for her benefit as for his own peace of mind. As if there were such a thing as peace of mind when a trial was in progress, much less one of this magnitude.

"We couldn't just whisper in the hallway?" Christina asked. She had gone the extra mile this morning, perfecting her makeup, her hair, selecting her clothes. The cerulean blue of her jacket matched her vivid eyes and contrasted perfectly with her radiant red hair. No doubt about it—thanks to time, observation, and the Yoda-like influence of Ben's mother, she had learned how to dress herself up. When she wanted to.

"Did you see how many reporters are in the corridor? Those

high-powered microphones can pick up anything. And Marshall told me that Amanda was on the warpath. Apparently she disagrees with our decision not to cross yesterday's witness."

"How can we conduct a defense when we have a spin doctor analyzing every decision based upon how it will play on the evening news?"

"By avoiding her as much as possible. I've asked the appeals expert Glancy hired to babysit her. It's not like he has anything else to do." Ben placed his hand firmly on her shoulder. "So, you understand what you need to do next?"

"Perfectly. Are you ready to cross the distinguished senator for the opposition?"

"Ready as I'll ever be. There's not that much I can accomplish."

"You can prevent it from becoming any more lurid than necessary. This case has already had enough luridage. The courtroom should be declared a lurid-free zone."

"We're down on lurid."

"Very." She paused. "I mean, in the courtroom. In real life, between consenting adults, that's a different matter."

She leaned a little closer. Just before her lips reached his, Ben raised his hand. "Christina, we have to stay focused."

"I am focused," she said, her lips still hovering a breath away from his. "Oh—you mean on the trial."

"Yes, I mean on the trial. We have to be at peak efficiency, free of distractions. A well-oiled litigating machine."

"Right." She sighed, then drew away. "That's always been my dream."

"You know the plan. Let's get out there and make it happen."

She nodded, gathering her briefcase and following him out of the jury room. It was just dandy, she thought, that he'd mapped out this wonderful master plan for the case. But what was his plan for her?

Marie Glancy sat in the backseat of the limousine, her hand covering her eyes. Christina climbed in beside her, although given the size of the car they could be two feet apart and still both be in the backseat. Fortunately, the windows were tinted black so none of the countless onlookers staked out in Glancy's Glen could see inside.

Only the chauffeur was in visual range, and Christina could see he had been trained to be discreet. More than discreet, in fact. Invisible.

"I just can't do it," Marie said, her voice quavering. "I thought I could. I got dressed and came out here, fully prepared to march into that courtroom and do what you want me to do. But when I arrived, when I saw all those people lined up on the steps, all those cameras circling like vultures, ready to pounce on the slightest sign of weakness—I lost it."

"Marie," Christina said, "this is really not a matter that's open to debate. You have to go back into the courtroom. It's important that the jury see that you still support your husband."

"The jury saw me running out of the room in tears."

"And they will understand that. Any one of them might have done the same. When you return, it will be a sign that you've forgiven your husband's indiscretion. That you've reconciled. That you're still behind him one hundred and ten percent."

"Which is hogwash. All of it." Christina noted that the woman was able to cry, even to dab her tears, without ever once smudging her makeup. "There's been no reconciliation. We haven't even talked about it."

"If I may be blunt, Marie, I don't care about the reality of the situation. All I care about is what those jurors see. And what I want them to see is you, back there, in that courtroom."

The woman's eyes were misting. "You don't understand. You just don't understand."

Christina reached out and touched her hand. "I want to."

Marie shook her head, brushing away the tears. "Did you listen to the news reports last night? Did you hear what they were saying about me? About Todd's political future?"

"Sorry, I had work to do. But if you don't come back into the courtroom, I can't imagine that he has any political future."

"Maybe that's for the best," she said quietly. "Maybe we'd all be happier."

"Marie, I'm sorry, but we just don't have time for this speculation and hand-wringing. Court will be back in session in less than ten minutes. And you have to be there."

"No. I'm sorry. I understand what you're saying and I'm sure you're right. But I just can't do it."

"Do you want your husband to be convicted?" Christina hadn't meant to shout, but her voice came out much louder than she had intended. The question hung in the cold air between them like a poisonous balloon.

"Of course I don't."

"Then get over it already and get in there. Because if you don't, you'll do him more damage than any witness the prosecution has put on the stand or ever will."

"You're exaggerating."

"I'm not. As strong as the prosecution's case may seem, they don't have an eyewitness. They have to rely on circumstantial evidence and character testimony. But they couldn't buy character testimony any more damning than what you'll deliver if you don't appear in court today. That's the bottom line, Marie." She leaned forward, eliminating the possibility of Marie averting her eyes. "If you don't want your husband to die, you'll march your fanny back into that courtroom. Pronto."

"Get an ambulance!" Loving screamed, but no one was moving fast enough for him. He rammed the cell phone into Daily's hand and punched 9-1-1 for him. After that, he grabbed the gun from where it had fallen, ran out to the top of the stairs, and fired three shots into the ceiling. The crowd panicked; everyone ran for the door. Good. Loving wanted the place clear when the ambulance made the scene. There was a small risk of someone being trampled in the rush to get out the doors, but at this point he couldn't get too worked up about a decrease in the global Goth population.

When he returned, he found Lucille sitting on a chair, rubbing her sore face, and Daily hunched over Amber, tears streaming from his eyes, blood gushing from her neck.

"My baby," Daily whispered, breathing in broken heaves. "Please don't die. Please don't die."

In the corner of his eye, Loving saw the creep—Randy, apparently—swivel around and make as if he thought he might split.

Loving raised the gun. "One more step and I'll kill you dead. And enjoy it."

Randy slunk back into his chair.

Loving got another towel and tried to stop the bleeding from

Amber's neck, but he couldn't tie a tourniquet without strangling her. He couldn't tell how serious it was. It looked horrible, but he knew neck, head, and shoulder wounds always bled profusely.

If Amber died, the only remaining hope . . .

Even as he was thinking it, he saw her eyelids flutter.

Loving bent down on one knee, nudging Daily to one side. "I don't know how well you can hear me, Amber. I don't know if you can talk. But if you can—if you can do anythin'—please help me. Where's Beatrice?"

It could've been his imagination, but he thought he saw a tiny rise of an eyebrow.

"Beatrice?" Randy, the drug addict in the chair, began to chortle. "You mean that mousy cow with the fat ass?"

Loving felt his trigger finger tightening. God give him strength. "Do you know where she is?"

"Hell, no." He fell back against the chair, still laughing. "She cut out days ago, after we'd all had a turn at her and she'd had so much she couldn't see straight. You think we're weird. Now, that slut was into some kinky shit."

It was an accident, officer, Loving mentally rehearsed. The gun just went off . . .

So tempting. But he was in enough trouble already.

"Bee . . . Bee . . ."

Loving's eyes went wide. Amber was trying to speak. Blood caked her teeth and dripped from the corner of her mouth, but she was trying to speak.

"Cir . . . cle . . ."

Loving leaned in closer. "Circle? Sir Cool? What do you mean?"

"Circle . . . Thirteen . . ."

Amber's eyes closed, and Loving knew they weren't going to get any more out of her tonight.

"Amber!" Daily shouted. "Amber!"

Downstairs, Loving heard medics rush into the club. He ran to the top of the stairs to show them the way. "Up here! *Hurry!*"

The prosecution's next witness was Shawn MacReady, the Republican representative from Arkansas whom Ben had met briefly in the Senate Dining Room. Padolino spent a fair amount of time discussing the congressman's long and distinguished career, his personal triumphs, bills he'd written or sponsored that had populist appeal and thus might endear him to the mostly lower-middle-class jury. Ben was disappointed, though not surprised, that Padolino was also smart enough to point out that MacReady was a political opponent of Glancy's, a member of the opposition party and an antagonist on many high-profile pieces of legislation. Better to bring it out himself than to allow Ben to do it on cross.

"Sir," Padolino asked, "are you familiar with the Committee on Health, Education, Labor and Pensions?"

"Yes, sir. In relation to my work on the Appropriations Committee, I've had numerous contacts with their work and attended many of their meetings."

"And who is the current vice chair?"

"That would be the defendant. Todd Glancy. The senator from Oklahoma. He used to be the chair, until his party lost control of the Senate."

"That would be when Senator Waddington of Arizona shifted his party affiliation from Democrat to Republican."

"Yes. After twenty years in politics, the man finally saw the light." There was a mild titter of laughter in the courtroom.

"On September 26, the day that Veronica Cooper was murdered, was this committee in session?"

"It was."

"For how long?"

"We started at nine and worked straight through to lunchtime. Congressmen get very grumpy if we cut into their lunchtime." Another round of laughter. MacReady was displaying the charisma that had undoubtedly gotten him reelected so many times. His slight Tex-Arky accent made his quips all the funnier.

"And did Senator Glancy attend the committee meeting?"

"He did. The committee record shows he was present."

"Was he there the whole time?"

Ben felt his body tense. This was of critical importance.

"As far as I know."

Ben blinked. The prosecution was helping Todd establish his alibi?

"Would you know if he left?"

"Not necessarily. We were in informal session. People were running all over the place. Aides moved in and out, shuttling drafts and revisions. We were working on some proposed legislation on the government pensions problem."

"And you never saw Senator Glancy leave?"

"No. I don't worry much about what the Democrats are doing. Long as there are more of us than there are of them."

Another burst of laughter, enough to inspire Judge Herndon to rap his gavel and give everyone a stern look. This is as good as it could possibly get from this witness, Ben thought. If only Padolino would leave it alone and move on to something else. And to his great surprise, Padolino did.

Padolino held up a photograph of an attractive middle-aged woman with short-cropped brown hair and a long, angular face. "Sir, do you now or have you ever known a woman named Delia Collins?"

Ben shot to his feet. "Objection!"

Padolino was ready. "Your honor, this testimony is for the purpose of establishing a pattern on the part of the defendant."

"A pattern of what?" Judge Herndon asked.

Padolino arched an eyebrow. "Three guesses."

"Your honor," Ben said, moving rapidly toward the bench, "we briefed this issue in our motion in limine. It's in your file. You haven't ruled on it." Marshall had tipped Ben off about this possible problem in advance.

Herndon shuffled the paper around on his desk. "Oh, yes. Now I recall. Delia Collins."

"Then you must also know why this testimony is not relevant to any issue at bar, but could be extremely prejudicial to my client. I strongly urge the court to suppress any testimony regarding—"

"Nah." Herndon waved a hand in the air. "Sounds to me like the prosecutor can get it in as legitimate evidence of a habit or pattern of behavior such as might have been displayed on the day of the murder. I'll allow it, subject to subsequent reconsideration."

"But, sir, if we hear it in open court, it will be too late—"

"And if I find ultimately that the evidence is not relevant to the case, I will instruct the jury to disregard it."

A fat lot of good that will do, Ben thought bitterly as he returned to his table. Once this cat was out of the bag, it wasn't ever going back.

"Let me repeat the question," Padolino said. "Do you know a woman named Delia Collins?"

"Yes," MacReady answered. "She was a witness who gave testimony before the committee something like seven years ago on the MacReady-Friedman bill. That was the one that, among other things, would have invalidated the 'unproven or experimental techniques' clause from American health insurance policies in certain cases regarding terminally ill patients. Would have required insurance companies to pay for medical treatments even if said treatments were not yet FDA- or AMA-approved."

"Did you favor this bill?"

"I wrote it and co-sponsored it. Most of the men in my party supported it. But oddly enough, even though it seemed like something the liberals would embrace with both arms, Senator Glancy did not. And he was the chair of the committee at the time. And his people toed his line. The bill died in committee."

"Why was Ms. Collins testifying?"

MacReady acquired a more serious expression. "Regretfully, Ms. Collins herself was suffering from a terminal illness. Ovarian cancer, if I recall correctly. She wanted a new treatment developed by a medical researcher in Mexico City, a new drug cocktail that had shown some promise in fighting the disease. But it was new and experimental and expensive, unapproved by the FDA, and her insurance company refused to pay for it. She was not a wealthy woman, so she had no other means of obtaining the treatment. Her very dramatic testimony illustrated how serious the need for the MacReady-Friedman bill was. As far as she was concerned, when her insurance company said no, they effectively signed her death certificate." He stopped, sighed. "But as I said, the bill didn't get out of committee. And I believe I heard the poor woman died a few months later."

Ben could see the jury was mystified. This was all very interesting—but what did it have to do with the murder case? Unfortunately, he knew they would find out all too soon.

"Was that the last time you saw Delia Collins? The day she testified before the committee?"

MacReady cleared his throat. "Uh, no."

"Really. When did you see her again?"

"A few days later. Before the final committee vote was taken."

"And where did you see her?"

"In Senator Glancy's private office."

"Please describe the circumstances of this encounter to the jury."

MacReady frowned, shifted his weight, began to look uncomfortable. Ben suspected he was probably actually looking forward to this, but he didn't want it to show. That would be crass.

"I'd gone into Senator Glancy's office late at night. It was well past usual working hours, but the congressional clerk told me he hadn't left the premises. I wanted to take one last stab at persuading him to support the bill. I was even prepared to offer a little pork, let him slip in some appropriations money for another Oklahoma lake or whatever. Hazel—that's his receptionist, has been for years—wasn't at her desk. I suppose she'd gone home for the evening. So I just walked into the man's office. Door was shut, but so what? I never expected—" He stopped, coughed into his hand. "Well, I never expected what I saw."

"And what did you see?" Padolino prodded.

"The two of them were behind his desk. She was just visible on the right side. He was lying down and she was straddling him. His pants were pulled down and she wasn't wearing much, just some lacy understuff kind of like—" He gestured toward the television set, still in the courtroom from the viewing of the video. "You know. Like the other girl."

Ben glanced at the jury. Expressions ranged from small frowns to utter disgust.

"And were these two people engaged in . . . sexual relations?"

"Well," he replied, "I suppose that depends on whether you subscribe to the Clintonian definition of sex or the one we use back home in Arkansas."

"Can you . . . be a little more specific?"

"In my book, when a woman goes down on a man, that's sex."

Several members of the jury gasped—literally gasped. Marie Glancy covered her face with her hands.

"I . . . see," Padolino said. He was also wearing his strained expression of disgust, as if he were fighting to mask his revulsion. "They were engaged in fellatio?"

"I think that's the word for it, yeah. Like in that video. 'Cept he didn't appear to have forced himself on her."

"Objection," Ben shouted. Beside him, Glancy was maintaining a cool, expressionless demeanor. In their pretrial discussions, he had denied the incident ever happened. Even so, Ben was pretty sure he wasn't enjoying listening to this.

"Sustained," Herndon said calmly. "The jury will disregard the witness's last statement."

"Did they see you?" Padolino asked.

"Oh yes. Or she did, anyway. She made a feeble attempt to cover herself with her hands. He didn't move, didn't even get up. I think he was pretty . . . you know. Wrapped up in what they were doing."

"Were you surprised by what you saw?"

"Well, yes and no."

"Can you explain?"

"I knew she'd been in to see Glancy several times, presumably to persuade him to change his vote. I assume she went in that night for the same reason I did—to give it one last shot. Only he demanded a special quid pro quo from her."

"*Objection,*" Ben said, even more forcefully than before. "Pure speculation. Slanderous and totally unjustified."

"The objection will be sustained and the jury will disregard." The judge turned and looked sternly into the witness box. "You know the rules, Congressman. As I recall, you were once a trial lawyer yourself. One more trick like that and I'll find you in contempt and have your entire testimony stricken."

"I'm sorry, your honor," MacReady said with apparent contrition. "I didn't mean to say anything improper."

"Don't insult my intelligence." Herndon motioned to Padolino. "If you have any more legitimate questions, ask them. Get this over with."

"Yes, sir. Just one last question. Did Senator Glancy change his position on the insurance bill?"

"Nope. Didn't budge an inch, and all his little toadies followed his lead. He single-handedly killed a piece of legislation that might've done a lot of people a world of good. But no one could make him change his mind. Not even Delia Collins."

Which was worse? Ben wondered. If Glancy had changed his vote in exchange for a blow job, or if he took the blow job but still refused to change his vote?

"No more questions," Padolino said quietly.

The judge turned toward Ben. "Anything from the defense?"

"Oh yeah," Ben said, rising to his feet. "We're gonna be here a while."

Loving stood beside Daily, his hand on the other man's shoulder, hoping some of his inner tranquility would travel by osmosis into his companion's consciousness. So far it wasn't working.

"Please!" Daily insisted. "You've got to let me see her!"

The doctor shook his head. "I'm afraid that isn't possible." Dr. Aljuwani had a soft, sympathetic voice, not the voice-of-God demeanor Loving normally associated with surgeons. He was carrying a chart and wearing a white coat, all the accoutrements of the typical medical man, but he had also shown an enormous amount of patience. "We have to think of what's best for Amber."

"I am thinking about Amber!" Daily cried. "I always have been. I've been searching for her for months!"

"And now she is in our care. You have done your job. Please allow us to do ours."

Loving could feel the tension oozing from every pore of Daily's body. "Please. You have no idea how important it is that I see her."

"No, I do not. But I do know that her health is extremely fragile and that it is best that she not be disturbed. She is not conscious, at any rate."

"I don't care about that! I just want to see her!"

"And you will, my friend. I promise you that. Her chances for a full recovery are excellent. But she is weak. She has lost much blood. In addition to the gunshot wound, her bloodstream has been infected with excess amounts of a chemical that is, for all practical purposes, the same as morphine. She will likely suffer withdrawal symptoms, as well as severe respiratory problems."

"You said she would recover."

"I said that her chances are excellent. But we must take things slowly. Allow her body to recover its strength. For now, for her own safety, she must remain in the ICU. But I promise I will call you as soon as the danger has passed and it is safe for her to receive visitors."

Loving tried to be comforting. "He's right, you know."

Daily's teeth were clenched. "You have my cell number?"

"Indeed I do," the doctor assured him. "And I will call it just as soon as the time is right."

"You won't wait till it's convenient?"

"Indeed I will not. As soon as her vital signs are stable, I will call you."

"And that will be when?"

Dr. Aljuwani hesitated. "Perhaps twenty-four hours, if all goes well. I can't be certain."

"All right." His head hung low. "Thank you, Doctor. I'm sorry if I seemed—"

"Not at all. She is your own flesh and blood. I would feel the same if it were my daughter, I am sure." Aljuwani excused himself, leaving Loving and Daily alone.

"Hell," Daily muttered. "What am I going to do with myself between now and then? I'll make myself crazy."

"You're gonna get some sleep," Loving said firmly. "Then we continue the investigation."

"What? I've already found Amber."

"But don't you wanna know what happened to her?"

"Surely that creep from the club—"

"Didn't you hear what the police officer said?" Loving wasn't really surprised. The police had grilled them and Lucille for almost three hours, but the entire time Loving sensed that Daily's head was somewhere else. In that tiny room in ICU. "That creep Randy has already called in his lawyer. To represent him and his boys and girls. None of them is talking. Nor is anyone ever likely to. If we want to know what happened to your girl, we're going to have to find out for ourselves."

"And how are we going to do that?"

Loving hesitated a moment, watching the sun set through the wide panoramic hospital lobby window. It was almost sunset, the golden hour, his favorite time of day. Pity it had to be wasted on these tragic circumstances. "By findin' Beatrice. That's what your daughter wanted us to do."

"She was out of her head."

"Maybe. But did you see the way her eyes lit when I asked her? She may've been crazy with drugs, but I still think she was tryin' to help us. She's worried about her friend." Besides, Loving thought, finding Beatrice will be critical to Ben's case—in the event Amber never recovers.

"But what she said—it was just gibberish."

Loving shook his head. "I don't think so."

"Then what did it mean?"

"Well . . . I dunno. But if every answer was easy, the world wouldn't need private investigators."

"You've got nothing to go on! Two words."

"I've had less. Come on. Let's go see a friend of mine. If anyone can tell us what your daughter meant, he's the one."

"Congressman, have you ever thought about running for president?"

MacReady's head rose. Finally Ben had managed to ask a question he hadn't anticipated. "I'm happy where I am. But thanks for the recommendation, son."

"Come now. I've heard your name floated as a possible presidential candidate, and I don't even read the morning papers. There aren't many Republican senators with more experience or qualifications than you."

MacReady chuckled. "If we picked our presidents based upon experience and qualifications, the world would be a very different place."

"I've also heard Senator Glancy mentioned as a possible presidential candidate. Or perhaps a vice presidential running mate. Have you?"

"Objection," Padolino said wearily. "What possible relevance can this have to the case?"

"Goes to bias," Ben said, explaining what both of them already knew.

The judge nodded. "The witness will answer the question."

"I believe I have heard my colleague Senator Glancy's name bandied about," MacReady replied. "At least before this unpleasantness occurred."

"And what do you think about the possibility of your colleague Senator Glancy on a presidential ticket?"

He tilted his head to one side. "Well, I prefer my presidents a little more to the right, if you know what I mean."

"So you wouldn't want to see the senator on a presidential ticket. And a pretty good way to prevent that would be to present false testimony that gets him convicted of murder, wouldn't it?"

MacReady's eyes narrowed. "Are you saying I'm a liar, son? 'Cause I don't take too kindly to that."

Ben ignored him. This was his time to ask the questions. "Tell me, sir—after you witnessed this alleged incident in Senator Glancy's office, did you tell anyone?"

"Tell anyone what?"

"What you had seen. Glancy and Delia Collins . . . together."

"No. Why would I?"

"Well, for starters, it might've helped eliminate Senator Glancy's opposition to your bill."

MacReady appeared indignant. "I don't do business that way."

"Did you file a complaint with the Senate Ethics Committee?"

"I saw no cause for that."

"No cause? You all but said that you thought Senator Glancy had extracted sex under the promise of changing his vote. If that's not an ethics violation, what is?"

MacReady shrugged uncomfortably. "I had no proof. I was just . . ."

"Talking through your hat?"

"Suspicious. That's all. Suspicious."

"So even though you *suspected* a clear-cut ethics violation, and even though it would've been to your political advantage to reveal your suspicions, you kept quiet about this incriminating incident for seven years. Let me tell you, Congressman—that's what *I* find suspicious."

"Objection!" Padolino bellowed.

"Sustained." Herndon gave Ben a harsh look. "Watch yourself, counsel."

Ben plowed ahead. "Sir, where was the desk in Senator Glancy's office?"

"Same place it is today. In the rear center of the room, opposite the door, maybe ten feet back."

"And did you stay in the doorway or did you step inside?"

"Well, I obviously didn't step inside. You know what they say. Three's a crowd."

"And the couple you observed were behind the desk."

"Yes. But I could see her clearly enough. Just off to the side and above the desk."

"I don't doubt it. But since you said the other person involved was lying down on the floor and she was facing him—his head would've been behind the desk. How on earth could you see him?"

For the first time, MacReady hesitated momentarily before answering, which Ben took as a personal triumph. "Well, his feet and hands were sticking out the side."

"Could you see his face?"

"There was no doubt about who—"

"Please answer my question. Could you see his face?"

He sighed. "No, not as such. But it stands to reason—"

"That there was another person there. But you can't say for sure who it was."

MacReady rolled his eyes. "You're right. I suppose it could've been anyone in Senator Glancy's office, behind Senator Glancy's desk, having sex with a woman who wanted Senator Glancy's vote."

"Move to strike," Ben said, lips pursed.

"That will be sustained," Judge Herndon said, giving MacReady the evil eye. "Are you done with this witness, Counsel?"

"Very done, your honor." Oh so done. If he could've pulled MacReady off the stage with a hook, he'd have done it.

"Do you have any idea how busy I am?" Jones said, waving his arms in the air. "Any idea at all?"

"What's his damage?" Daily whispered into Loving's ear.

"Shh," Loving muttered back. Loving and Daily had come to Ben's borrowed office space near the courthouse. "I can handle it." He laid his hand on Jones's shoulder. "Jones, buddy, I know you're buried in paperwork. I know you've been fieldin' three times the usual motion practice. Just yesterday I heard Ben sayin' how invaluable you were. How he'd be nothin' without you."

"He did?"

Loving smiled, hoping Ben hadn't mentioned that Loving hadn't been in the office for days. "He did. Problem is—I feel the same way. I could spend days stompin' around the streets trying to track down this lead. Or you could probably figure it out in an hour. So you see why I came to you. I mean, I'm beggin' you, Jonesey. I'm on bended knee here."

"Oh, all right already," Jones said, his face wrinkling. "What's the sitch?"

Loving told him.

"Circle Thirteen? What the heck does that mean?"

"That's what we were hopin' you could tell us."

"And that's all you've got? Two words? Two very common words?" Jones turned to face the computer. "Jeez—this could take forever."

"I know," Loving said. "But even if it takes days, I'd appreciate it if you could—"

"Got it," Jones announced.

"Huh? What?"

"I Googled it. Broadband is a wonderful thing. Amazing the stuff you can come up with . . ."

"Just like that?"

Jones smiled, obviously feeling very superior. "I have tried to show you how to use the computer."

"I don't like the computer."

"Which is why I solved the mystery, and you didn't." Jones quickly scrolled down a webpage, scanning the text as he went. "Seems to be some sort of private club."

"I checked the phone book. There was nothing."

"I guess it's a very private club. Besides—Circle Thirteen isn't the name of the place. It's the name of a group that meets there." He continued scrolling. "Spooky-looking place. Spooky-looking people. Lots of black."

"What a surprise," Loving said dryly.

"They're trying to keep strangers from getting past the home page. This site isn't intended to be public—just a way for members to post messages privately, without leaving traces on someone else's server. You need a password to gain entry."

"Can you guess it?"

"I'll do an end run."

"What does that mean?"

"Means I'm going to sneak past their firewall and bust inside. I've got a little algorithm that might do the trick."

Loving looked at Daily. "Do you understand what he's talkin' about? Because I don't."

Daily looked back at him sadly. "Amber is the computer whiz in the family. As far as I'm concerned, it's just a big paperweight."

"I'm in," Jones crowed.

"Already?" Loving marveled. Jones was fast. Maybe he should consider not making fun of him at every opportunity. On second thought, *naah*.

"Oh my God," Jones whispered, his jaw dropping. "Oh my God."

"What?" Loving said, hovering behind him. "What's Circle Thirteen?"

Jones took a deep breath. "Well, it isn't a sewing circle. It's more like . . . a coven."

"A coven!" Daily stared at him in disbelief. "What are you saying? That they're witches?"

"Of course not. That would be ridiculous." Jones swiveled around and offered Daily his seat in front of the monitor. "They're vampires."

13

At first, there were no inhabitants in the small dark ceremonial chamber. It seemed like a chapel, despite being entirely devoid of Christian iconography. There was a stained-glass window just above and beyond the altar, but no light came through it, and the images, to the extent they could be discerned, were dark and grisly: portraits of bloodletting, blood sharing, and unholy acts of violence to women and children. The only cross, just behind the altar, was turned upside down, so that it pointed toward the earth rather than the sky.

Slowly, thirteen figures entered the room, single file. They were each wearing black hooded robes that covered them almost completely. Only the slightest traces of facial features were visible. They arranged themselves in the center of the room, lining the perimeter of a circle with a five-pointed star in the center.

A few moments later, another figure entered the room. The contrast was dramatic. This figure was smaller than the previous four, female, and moved haltingly, as if unsure what to do or where to go. Her robe was white. Tendrils of blond hair slipped from the front of the hood.

"Take your place in the pentagram," one of the hooded men said. His voice was deep and commanding, and the female obeyed without hesitation. She moved to the center of the circle and was surrounded by the hooded figures.

"Are you ready for the ritual to begin?"

Her hood trembled up and down, nodding.

"Speak!"

"Yes," she whispered. "I'm ready."

The man who had spoken, the tallest of them, stepped forward. He stood before her, gazing downward. He placed his hand upon her cheek, then slowly pushed the hood away, releasing an ample bounty of long golden hair and a face so young she could barely have been out of her teens. She stared, wide-eyed, as if she were powerless to look away from his piercing eyes. His thin blood-red lips turned upward, revealing a brief flash of incandescent white teeth. The other men began to chant in a low monotone, incanting some strange, numinous ritual in a language other than English.

"Kneel before me, woman."

She obeyed, lowering herself to the floor.

"Do you worship me with all your heart and soul and mind?"

"I do, my master." She leaned forward, abasing herself before the man in the black robe.

"Are you prepared to take your place in our brotherhood? To become one with the Inner Circle?" His booming voice reverberated through the tiny chapel.

"I am."

"Is it your devout desire to become one with the Sire? To enter into Holy Communion with him?"

"Yes," she said breathlessly. "Oh, yes."

"Very well, Beatrice. You may now disrobe."

Without apparent thought or reservation, she shook the robe off her shoulders. She was wearing nothing beneath. The folds of the robe gathered around her knees, leaving her entirely naked and exposed.

With such speed that it took everyone in the room by surprise, the man raised his hand and struck her face with the back of his fist. She tumbled sideways, halting her fall with an outstretched arm. He grabbed her by the hair and pulled her upright, then hit her again, even harder than before. A trickle of blood spilled from her mouth. A blue-black bruise began to swell. And then he hit her again.

"You are not ready," the man intoned, still clutching her hair. He hit her again, and her eyes fluttered closed. He threw her backward and she fell in a heap on the tile floor, her legs askew, her bloody face turned to one side.

"Leave her," the man said bitterly. "When she wakes, I will talk with her further. She can still be of service to us."

He left the room, and a moment later the others followed, leaving behind the young woman, her beautiful blond hair now sullied by the caked and sticky blood streaming from her broken nose.

"Bit rough on her, weren't you?" He removed his robe and carefully placed it on a coat hanger.

"For a reason," the man with the piercing eyes replied.

"But we need her to talk."

"Yes. But we also need to know that what she tells us is true."

"Naturally. But—"

"Complete subjugation of the will requires time. We must strip away her attachments to her former existence. Her world must become me. Her purpose for living must be to serve me, and me alone."

"How can you know she'll—"

"I know." The man had exchanged his dark hooded robe for a jet-black cloak. In the low lighting, he was almost invisible.

"That sounds good, in theory. But this is getting out of control. If she got away and talked to—"

"She will not. Never fear, my friend. Everything is completely in control."

"You're sure about that."

"I am." He turned, easing out of his chair as if his body had no solidity at all, as if it were pure liquid. "The sanctity of the Inner Circle will be preserved."

"You can't know that. What if she refuses to talk?"

He stepped closer to his companion, near enough that the much shorter man imagined he could feel heat emanating from those relentless black eyes. "I am the Sire, my friend. No one refuses to talk to me. No one refuses me anything."

14

Ben ducked into a side room, hoping to escape the throng of reporters in the corridor begging for a quote, wanting to know if the testimony of the distinguished congressman from Arkansas was "the final nail in Glancy's coffin." Ben didn't like to talk to the press before or during a trial, and he knew he couldn't come up with any answer that could give the situation a positive "spin."

He closed the door behind him, dropped into the nearest chair, took a deep breath—and realized he was not alone.

"Like vultures, aren't they?"

Ben was startled to see his opponent, Paul Padolino, sitting on the other side of the conference table, leaning back in one chair, his feet propped up on another.

"They are when you're a defense attorney. What are you doing in here?"

"Same as you. Hiding."

"Don't you have an office in this building?"

"Yes. Alas, the minions of the Franken-fifth estate know where it is. And by the way, the press doesn't just hassle defense attorneys. We get our fair share of grief on the prosecution side, too."

"It isn't the same. Defense lawyers are treated like pariahs. People assume anyone accused of a crime is guilty—especially if they're prominent. Which makes us the slime trying to get the guilty people off."

"Defensive, much?" Padolino asked, smiling slightly.

"Yes. And if you knew how many times I've seen the district attorney get it wrong, or take the easy way out, you would be, too."

Padolino shrugged. "Perhaps. But of course, you come from Oklahoma, where district attorneys hold press conferences to brag about how many people they've put on death row and forensic scientists falsify evidence to help them do it."

Ben cringed and quickly changed the subject. "I've noticed that you aren't going for the press conference routine much. Even though God has given you an incredibly high-profile case and public sympathy—and my informants tell me you have political aspirations."

Padolino smiled. "Whether I do or I don't, I believe criminal cases should be tried in the courtroom, not on the evening news. Besides, I could never compete with your boy's PR machine. Best to just stay out of its way." He reached into his coat pocket and pulled out a pack of Camels. "Care for a smoke?"

Ben blinked. "I thought all federal courthouses prohibited—"

"I won't tell if you won't tell."

"No thanks. I don't smoke."

"A little snort, then?" From the other side of his coat, Padolino produced a silver flask.

"Uh, no. I don't really drink much, either. Certainly not when—"

Padolino tossed his head toward the kitchenette in the corner. "Cup of jamoke?"

"Ohhh . . ."

"You're telling me you don't even drink coffee?"

"Well, the rumor is, it isn't actually good for you."

"Hell, Bressler was right. You are a saint." His smile made it come off funny, not mean-spirited. "But I don't think you're nearly as naïve or as gormless as you seem sometimes."

"I don't know what you're talking about," Ben insisted, then added, "but just for the record, I don't think you're the politically ambitious anything-for-a-conviction prosecutor you sometimes seem, either."

"Hey, have I treated you badly?"

Ben shrugged. In truth, he had not. He'd produced everything as required, at least so far as Ben knew, and had done so in a timely fashion. He'd given Ben access to all his witnesses. He hadn't engaged in *ad hominem* character attacks—well, not on Ben's character, anyway. Despite being given a case with numerous exploitable possibilities and public opinion vastly in his favor, Padolino had played it pretty straight. "No. You've been a model prosecutor, far as I'm concerned."

"I've had no reason not to be. Don't misunderstand—I'm not saying I don't want to nail your client. But I haven't got any grudge against you, so there haven't been any sneaky courtroom tricks, leaks to the press, any of that rot. And I plan to keep it that way." He pointed a finger. "I do intend to win this case. But I'm going to do it the right way."

"Fair enough."

"We're opponents. We don't have to be enemies."

Could I possibly clone this guy, Ben wondered, or take him home with me?

"You're wrong about the reporters, though. They really don't have it in for defense attorneys. Despite all the babble about the 'liberal media,' I'm not even sure reporters have opinions of their own anymore. All today's journalists care about is ratings. Circulation numbers. Popularity quotients. Nielsens. It's ironic, really. They criticize politicians for making decisions based upon poll results. But they do exactly the same thing."

"That's a rather heterodox viewpoint. Especially coming from a Republican."

"Answer me this: who did the press come down harder on? Reagan, during the Iran-Contra scandal, or Clinton, during the Lewinsky affair?"

"Clinton. By a mile."

"Right. Now let's weigh their relative importance. The Clinton scandal was about a man cheating on his wife. The Reagan scandal was, well, treason. Conducting secret foreign policy in direct contra-vention of Congress. And remember, you're talking to a very right-wing guy here. But the fact remains—the press didn't batter Reagan one one-hundredth as much as they did Clinton. Why? Because Reagan's popularity ratings were huge. Everyone loved the man. He was sweet and slightly doddering, like everyone's favorite grandfather. And everyone was overwhelmed with intaxication."

"What?"

"The euphoria induced by a tax cut, which overcomes people's recollection that it was their money in the first place. Anyway, at-tacking that sweet, senile old man with the dyed pompadour would've turned people off big-time. So the media softballed him."

"To be fair," Ben said, "Clinton did lie about the affair."

"Yeah, and Reagan lied about Nicaragua. Dubya lied about having a drunk driving record and he's been obscenely evasive about his past drug use. Why wasn't the liberally biased press all over that? Because dumb as the man is, he comes off on television as very lik-able, a regular guy. Clinton was smart and capable but not necessar-ily someone you'd want over for dinner; they could beat up on him all night long." He grinned. "That's your main problem in this case, you know, Ben. Everyone knows Glancy is smart. Very, very smart. You'd be much better off if you were representing an amiable dunce."

Ben glanced at his watch. "Fascinating as this is, it looks like it's time for us to get back to the salt mines."

"Right." Padolino swiveled his feet around and stretched. "One more question, though. That partner of yours. Miss McCall."

"What about her?"

"Are all the lady lawyers in Oklahoma that hot? 'Cause that sure isn't how we grow them up here."

Ben couldn't think of an answer that wouldn't insult someone, so he kept his mouth closed.

"My assistants tell me you and she have a thing going. True?"

Ben licked his lips, stuttered. "A-a thing? I don't know what that means."

"The hell you don't. Tell me the truth. Some of my people think you're working your mojo on that saucy little intern of Glancy's—"

"Shandy?"

"—but my investigators, the ones I really trust, say you and Christina are the item. One step away from wedding bells."

"Well, I—I wouldn't go as far as—"

"So it wouldn't bother you if I asked her out? Because I really want to ask her out."

Ben coughed, grabbed his briefcase. "I—I can't tell you what to do. Your business, not mine." He hustled toward the door, suddenly feeling more stressed than he had when he came in. "Enjoyed the chat. See you in court."

Loving sat by himself on the side of the cavernous wood-paneled room, eyes wide. He'd seen some pretty weird stuff in his time, especially since he'd started working for Ben Kincaid. But this joint was setting a new personal best for weirdness. Compared to this, the Goth club was a set from *Leave It to Beaver*.

The most prominent features of the room, so far as Loving could tell, were inlaid wood, low lighting, cobwebs, and dust. He had the impression that it had once been used for something else, but the former owners had stripped it clean, which explained why there was nothing hanging on the walls—no books on the shelves, no furniture other than the most rudimentary tables and chairs. The dust and cobwebs also signaled a lack of care, or perhaps just a décor that appealed to the members of Circle Thirteen.

As the hour passed, the room slowly filled with people. They were quiet, somber folks; even the ones who entered with a group tended not to interact much. They were here for a reason, Loving surmised, but unlike the habitués of Stigmata, they weren't here to party. As with the Goths, the attire of the denizens of Circle Thirteen tended to be predominantly black, but Loving saw none of the tongue-in-cheek, campy, Haunted Mansion spirit that he'd spotted at Stigmata. Here it was monotone black suits, even tuxes, floor-length drab dresses, some of them with a long train. There was no music, no dancing. Whatever it was these guys were planning on doing, they took it very seriously.

Loving and Daily had had no trouble getting in. This time they'd had the sense to dress in solid black, head-to-toe—Loving even forked over some cash for a pair of black high-top sneakers. There were no bouncers or bodyguards here, thank God. But if they didn't worry about security, did that mean nothing of interest would happen? Loving saw no signs of drugs or booze—not even smoking. Not that he was looking for trouble, but if they didn't encounter any, it probably meant they weren't on the right track.

"You think they're okay?" Loving whispered to Daily.

"Sure. They're clean-cut, law-abiding vampires."

"They did have a website, even if it was supposed to be restricted. I don't think they'd have a website if somethin' criminal was goin' down."

Daily scoffed. "Where have you been, Loving? I read in the *Post* about drug dealers that have their own websites, making deals, transferring funds via PayPal. They use code words to describe the goods, but the transactions are still taking place on the Web. The pushers' once ubiquitous cell phones have been replaced by instant messaging." He paused. "You know what instant messaging is, right?"

"Wrong. And I don't want to, either. Look, let's split up. We stand out enough individually. Together, we look too much like cops for anyone to talk to us."

Daily nodded and headed for the opposite end of the room. Loving walked over to a round table large enough to accommodate eight people. If he sat, maybe someone would join him, drawn by his animal magnetism. Did vampires have animal magnetism? he wondered. Well, then they'd be drawn by their sonar. Whatever.

He hadn't been sitting long before he was joined by a woman who appeared to be in her midthirties. She was very tall, very thin, with a clinging chemise that draped around her feet. Long jet-black hair almost reached her waist. Dark eyes, dark mascara. Since she didn't introduce herself, Loving decided he would call her Morticia.

"You're new," she said. It was not a question.

"Yeah," Loving replied, trying to size her up as he spoke. What would a nice girl like her . . . never mind. "I'm lookin' for someone."

"Oh, no, no, no." She wagged a finger back and forth. "Don't say that. They'll ride you out on the rails. Tell them you're interested in joining the Circle."

Well, this was going to be easier than he'd imagined. He hadn't even had to perform any silly circus tricks. "That's what I meant to say. I'm interested in joinin' the Circle. Any particular reason you're helpin' me?"

"We're destined to be together."

Loving blinked. "We are?"

"Yes. I knew it the moment I saw you sitting there. Well, I didn't exactly know it. It was more something I sensed, a psychic vibration, if you will. But I've learned to trust those vibrations."

That was a line he hadn't heard back at the Tulsa honky-tonks.

"You seem . . . more mature than most of our new recruits." She leaned closer, revealing a voluptuous bosom thinly veiled by her chemise. "I've been waiting a long time for some fresh blood. And I mean that in every possible way."

Loving felt an anxious tingling at the base of his skull. "So, you're a . . . a . . . member of the Circle?"

"I am."

"And that means . . ."

"Right." Her eyes come-hithered him in a big way. "But I assume that's a turn-on for you. Otherwise, you wouldn't be here."

Loving cleared his throat. "Like I said, I'm lookin' for someone."

And she smiled again, even more broadly than before. "You found her."

The prosecution's next witness was Steve Melanfield, the Kodiak Oil lobbyist Ben had first met in the Senate Dining Room. Funny how many of the people who were so friendly to Glancy five months ago ended up on the prosecution's witness list. Nature of the town, Ben supposed. Friends and enemies changed sides in a heartbeat. It was all a matter of who wanted what at any given moment.

Padolino established that Melanfield was a professional lobbyist, that he had been working for Kodiak Oil for nine years, and that because Glancy came from one of the top oil-producing states in the union they had frequent contact with one another. That was to be expected. What was not to be expected was that he might have had contact with Veronica Cooper.

"I'd seen her in Senator Glancy's office from time to time," Melanfield explained. He was dressed conservatively—a dark pin-striped suit that did the best that could be done with his outsized frame. "Probably said hi once or twice. I don't really remember. I never suspected anything was going on between them. Until the night of September 25."

"What happened that night?"

"I was working late—I'd been pulling double shifts ever since the Alaska wilderness bill left committee. Finished making the rounds about ten, ten thirty. Clerk told me Glancy hadn't left the Russell Building, so I went to his office. The door was unlocked, slightly ajar. Hazel was gone for the day."

Ben shook his head. Imagine how much easier this case would be if Glancy had just learned to lock his doors at quitting time. Or hired a receptionist who didn't require sleep.

"And what did you see in Senator Glancy's office?"

"Well, actually, I heard something before I saw anything. Two voices. Loud. Didn't take long to figure out that they were arguing with each other."

"Could you identify the voices?"

"Yes. But just to be sure, I crept forward a little and peered through the crack in the door. It was Senator Glancy and his intern, Veronica Cooper. Except she wasn't wearing much. Just her underwear. Black lace. And his fly was unzipped."

"Indeed." Padolino lowered his chin, giving the jury a minute to catch up. "Could you make out what they were saying?"

"Objection," Ben said. "Hearsay."

Padolino didn't blink. "As per our brief, your honor, if there is hearsay, it is permitted by bona fide exception in the Federal Rules of Evidence. Any statements made by Senator Glancy are, of course, admissions against interest. And since Ms. Cooper is now deceased, her statements would fall under the exception permitting testimony where the declarant is unavailable."

"The objection is overruled," Herndon declared. Ben wasn't surprised. He had briefed the issue in advance, and Herndon hadn't bought it. But he had to make an in-court objection to preserve the issue for appeal.

"Let me ask again," Padolino said, picking up the thread smoothly. "Could you hear what the parties were saying?"

"Some of it."

"You were eavesdropping?"

Ben grimaced. There Padolino went again, being smart. Bringing it out on direct so Ben couldn't make hay with it on cross. He hated it when prosecutors were smart.

"Look, in my business, information is the coin of the realm. A lobbyist can't know too much, especially about the people he's trying to persuade. Don't get me wrong—I'm not saying listening at keyholes is a great thing. But I genuinely believe my company is doing good, important work for the people of this nation. Securing our political and economic independence. So if I can learn a little something to advance that cause—so much the better."

Jeez Louise, Ben thought. What a patriotic eavesdropper. The man must've rehearsed that speech all night.

"So what exactly did you hear?"

"I heard that Veronica Cooper was very angry. There was something she wanted—I never heard exactly what it was—something Glancy wasn't giving her. She tried everything she could—she begged, she whined, she got flirty. Nothing would change his mind. So she threatened him."

The jury stiffened, almost in unison. They were beginning to see where this testimony was going.

"What exactly did she threaten?"

"She said if Glancy didn't change his mind, she was going to tell everything. She didn't specify what. But given how she was attired and . . . you know . . . the circumstances, I assumed she was going to tell his wife about their affair."

Technically this was speculation, Ben thought, but there seemed little point in objecting. The jury had undoubtedly already reached the same conclusion.

"Was Senator Glancy moved by this threat?"

"No. Just the opposite. He laughed at her. Right in her face. Said she could tell his wife anything and it wouldn't matter a damn bit."

Ben could feel the heat radiating from his client, seated just beside him. But as always, Glancy's sangfroid remained in place. According to him, this entire incident was a politically motivated fabrication. But that couldn't make it easy to listen to. Especially not with his wife sitting just behind him.

"He didn't care what his wife thought?"

"He said she had her own agenda. And she wouldn't let it be screwed up by—this is a quote—'some two-bit tramp whose only real talent was something you couldn't put on a résumé.'"

Padolino paused a moment. "What was Ms. Cooper's reaction to that statement?"

"She was infuriated. Totally lost what little cool she had left. She jabbed Glancy in the chest and said, 'If you don't give me what I want, I'll ruin you.'"

There was a silence in the courtroom—not a good one.

"Was there any further discussion?"

"If there was, I didn't hear it." Melanfield turned to face the jury. "After that last blowup, Ms. Cooper grabbed her clothes and headed toward the door. I didn't want to be caught playing Peeping Tom, so I ducked out of the office and ran downstairs."

"Thank you," Padolino said. He turned to Ben with a sad smile. "Your witness."

Loving tried to think of a question quickly, something, anything to distract Morticia. She was sitting much too close to him, her bosom was too near his nose, and was staring at his neck in a way that made him supremely uncomfortable.

"So, I guess, all these guys." Loving waved his hand generally about the room. "All Goths?"

"Oh, no. No, no, no." She drew in her breath, her chest heaving. "No, despite the superficial similarities, there are two distinct groups. Goths are children, amateurs. Pretenders. Nothing like us. In fact, sometimes I wear colors other than black."

"Like what?"

"A very dark midnight blue."

Loving heard a cracking sound behind him.

"Bend over!"

He turned just in time to see a young woman with a supermodel figure and an endless mass of black curls bend over the back of a chair, which had the effect of hoisting her ridiculously short skirt and exposing her perfectly rounded snowy white cheeks. While Loving stared, a short, stout man—presumably he who had issued the command—brought his hand around and slapped her bottom with a wooden paddle. The woman winced as the paddle made contact—but her ecstatic smile grew broader with each smack.

"You have got to be kiddin'." Loving turned back to Morticia. "Should I do somethin'?"

"Like what?"

"Like give that creep a taste of his own paddle."

She brushed her hand against his. "My friend, he's not doing anything she doesn't want. Just getting her in the mood for the Ceremony."

"But—"

"There is a decided correspondence between the Circle and the dark fetish world."

"You mean—"

"Dominance and submission. Bondage and discipline. Sadomasochism."

"Right out in public?"

"This isn't the public. This is the Circle. We understand one another."

"But isn't this all a little . . . twistedish?"

She laughed, a surprisingly high-pitched giggle. "Don't ask me. I've been into scarification since I was fifteen."

"And that's—"

"Hurting myself. Cutting myself. I used a razor blade. Sometimes I'd draw patterns, shapes."

Loving winced. "Bet that stung."

"Wonderfully so. After I was done cutting, I'd pour alcohol over the wounds. To prevent infection—but also because it hurt so good."

Loving's eyes narrowed.

"Once the welts formed I'd have the image of a raven, an ankh, whatever design I'd crafted."

"But—why?"

She shrugged. "Who can explain why they like what they like? There's no logic to it. We're just hardwired that way. Some say it's endorphins—the body releases them to help you deal with pain and you get a head rush. A natural high. It's a deeply spiritual experience. Try it sometime."

"Mmm . . . maybe later."

"It beats living the usual life of quiet, desperate mimesis."

"Uhhh . . ."

"Imitation. Doing what everyone else does, just because they do it. Never doing anything to please yourself."

"Which is what these folks are planning to do, right? Tonight. What's the Ceremony? Some big orgy?"

She glared at him. "Don't be absurd. The Circle is not about sex. Sex is nothing. Anyone can do that. Animals do it. The Circle is about true blood intimacy."

"Blood intimacy?"

"When you offer your own life energy, you give a part of your self, your essence. You need your blood to live. Nonetheless, you share it with someone else to give them pleasure. It's a beautiful thing. Sex—that's just selfishness. Two people gratifying their carnal desires. Blood intimacy is exactly the opposite."

"And this doesn't seem a little . . . whacked?"

"Who's to say what's whacked? I don't smoke. I don't do drugs. I don't drink . . . wine." She giggled at her little joke. "Most of the people you see in here are perfectly normal citizens who work during the day at perfectly normal jobs. No different from anyone else."

Whatever. Time to get back to the reason he was here. "Do you know a woman named Beatrice? I think she may be a member of the Circle."

"No. But we rarely use our real names here. In fact, we rarely use names. What does she look like?"

"Unfortunately, I don't really know. I believe she may have been blond. She's been described as mousy—not by me—and as being, um, somewhat large around the hips."

"Last name?"

"Don't know that, either."

"Then how did you expect to find her?"

Good question. He thought for a moment. "Any other places the Circle Thirteen crowd frequents?"

"Well, many of us are members of the Playground. But if you couldn't handle that little spanking episode, I wouldn't recommend it to you."

"Anyone disappeared from the Circle recently?"

"Disappeared? No. Sometimes the minions select recruits for the Inner Circle, but—"

"Where do they go?"

"I don't know. I'm not in the Inner Circle."

"Who are these . . . minions?"

"The minions of the Sire, of course."

"And these people—what? Take women against their will? Kidnap them for human sacrifices?"

"Don't be absurd. I told you—we're perfectly normal citizens who happen to share a common interest. We're not even unique. There are vampire clubs across the nation. Take my word for it— I've traveled. There's a network of them; the insiders know where they are and how to find them. My girlfriend runs vampire workshops—"

"*Workshops?*"

"Yeah, at science fiction and bondage conventions all over the country. Did you realize there are at least three hundred and fifty thousand bona fide blood drinkers in this country? Some people believe that we have a genetic quirk that makes us crave satisfaction in a manner . . . different from other people. 'Course, that's the same thing they started saying about gay people a few years ago, right? 'They're not mentally abnormal—they're just different.' The Circle network is not unlike the gay bar world twenty years ago. We're a minority, so we have to keep a low profile. The middle-class majority always fears anything that's different. But that will change. Gay bars, gay men and women, gay marriages—they've come out of the closet. I think we're next."

"So you're tellin' me that you folks—every one of you think—" He wasn't sure he could make himself say it. "You think you're vampires?"

"Not necessarily. Some of these folks are just batting."

"Excuse me?"

"Pretending. Playing dress-up. Plastic fangs, white makeup, scary contact lenses. It's like a big role-playing game for them. We let them hang out here, but they aren't actually members of the Circle. Some girls I know do it just so they can cruise the clubs. You know—Looking for Mr. Goodvampire. They're in love with the undead mythology but aren't actually—how to say it?—drinking from the well."

"And that's battin'?"

"Right. You know—like in the movies. Where the vamps turn into bats." She paused. "Of course, real vampires don't turn into bats."

"And that's what everyone else is? A real vampire?"

"No. Many are wannabes—they're into vampires, they act like vampires. But they aren't. Some are here for the S-and-M stuff. Some are casual blood sippers—like, from a cup. Only a relatively small fraction of the Circle are actual bloodsuckers who—you know, drink it in the traditional manner. They call themselves classicals or, worse, *vampyrs*." She pronounced the last syllable as if it were *piers*. "So pretentious. True vampires are immortal and dead, or undead, if you prefer. They've been made a vampire by another vampire. They have inverted circadian rhythms—in other words, they're genetically 'night people.' They are usually photosensitive—meaning they don't like sunlight. In addition to those made vampires by another vampire, there are also Inheritors—people born into it, who are either immortal or exceedingly long-lived. They tend to be the bad boys—the ones who earned our community its negative reputation. Nighttimers are regular people who have been altered to become vampires. Like me. Not immortal. Not undead. But we don't turn to ashes if we go out in the noonday sun, either."

She stopped, licked her lips. "Enough with the lecture. All this talk and no action is making me hungry. You ready to go yet?"

Loving looked at her blank-faced. "Go where?"

"You know what I mean. You must be curious. What do you say?" She leaned forward and brushed her lips against the side of his neck. "Ready for a little suck?"

"You mentioned the Alaskan wilderness bill, Mr. Melanfield," Ben said. "Could you explain to the jury exactly what that is?"

Melanfield took in a deep breath, starting a spiel Ben knew he had delivered countless times before. "It's a bipartisan bill designed to increase our domestic production of oil and thus reduce our reliance on foreign oil."

"And how does this bill propose to do that?"

"By stimulating production in undeveloped fields."

"Undeveloped—why?"

A tiny crease spread across Melanfield's forehead. "I'm not sure what you mean."

"Those oil fields you're talking about haven't been tapped in the past because they're located in the federally protected Alaskan wilderness, correct?"

"That would, uh, technically be correct. The purpose of the bill, of course, would be to alleviate the federal protection."

"And thus allow developers to destroy the last untouched wilderness area in the entire United States."

Melanfield blew out his cheeks. "Look, Mr. Kincaid, I didn't expect a rational response from you. I know about your past work for the eco-terrorist group."

"Move to strike!" Ben rang out.

Judge Herndon gave the witness a stern look. "The lawyers are advocates, not defendants, sir. I will not permit any aspersions on counsel in my courtroom." Especially, Ben thought, since it's almost certain grounds for a mistrial or an appeal.

"Yes, your honor. I'm sorry. But as I said, I've worked with this company for a long time, and this is an issue I feel strongly about. I care about the environment as much as the next fellow. But I also care about this nation. And we need more oil. Our dependence on foreign oil has been disastrous. Fifty years of meddling in the Middle East have made us worldwide pariahs. How many governments have we propped up or torn down? How many times have we sent our troops into combat? And why? It isn't about Israel, it isn't about stabilizing the region, and it isn't about weapons of mass destruction. It's about oil."

"That's a lovely speech," Ben said, "but you're not answering my question."

"I think I am." Ben knew he was doing a lousy job of controlling the witness—the most important principle of cross-examination. But that was a difficult task when you were dealing with a man who talked persuasively for a living. "Studies have shown that if we could just reduce our energy consumption—or increase our production—by ten percent, we could eliminate our need for foreign oil. Problem is, we can't. Good grief—Jimmy Carter asked us to drive

slower and wear sweaters in the winter and we practically impeached him for it. No politician has had the guts to advocate conservation ever since—it's considered political suicide. Americans think
it's their constitutional right to drive gas-guzzling SUVs and leave
their lights on when no one is in the room. So we must increase domestic production. And the only way we can economically do that is
by passing this bill. I regret the inevitable damage to the Alaskan
wilderness, too. But I prefer that to sending more troops to die in the
Middle East. Or God forbid, seeing a repeat of 9/11."

"My purpose was not to give you a forum for your canned lob-
bying spiel," Ben said. "My purpose was to find out why you
haven't been able to pass the bill."

"I think you already know the answer to that question. Two
words: Todd Glancy."

"Despite your best efforts, Senator Glancy wouldn't support the
bill, right?"

"Worse. He led the opposition. And as a senator from a top oil-
producing state, he had a lot of clout."

"So it would be fair to say that your job would be a lot easier if
Todd Glancy was out of the Senate."

Melanfield looked as if he were taken aback by the very idea. "If
you're suggesting that I made my testimony up, I can—"

"Just answer the question, sir. Senator Glancy is your political
opponent. And your job would be a lot easier if he was gone.
Right?"

"I . . . suppose I can't deny it."

"And if he loses this trial, he will be gone. He'll be replaced by
an appointee of the Oklahoma governor, a Republican with deep
ties to the oil industry, right?"

"I don't know what the governor will—"

"What's more, Brad Tidwell will become the senior senator
from Oklahoma. And he already backs this bill, right?"

"He has had the foresight to lend us his support, yes."

"So a conviction against Senator Glancy is a win–win for you,
isn't it?"

"Objection," Padolino said. "This is becoming offensive."

"Overruled," Herndon said. "But I do think you've made your
point, Mr. Kincaid. Is there anything else?"

"Yes. After this alleged eavesdropping incident, sir, did you tell anyone what you had heard?"

"No. Why would I?"

"You're saying you caught a U.S. senator engaging in ethically and perhaps legally improper behavior. Implying that he either was blackmailing her and was being blackmailed. Did you report this to the Senate Ethics Committee?"

"Becoming a tattletale isn't exactly the key to popularity for a lobbyist."

"Did you tell the police?"

"No."

"Did you tell anyone? A friend? Your boss? Your wife?"

"No."

"But now, after all these months of silence, you expect the jury to believe this heretofore unmentioned story?"

"Look, it was one thing when I thought the man was diddling around with his intern. That's not exactly unprecedented. But when she turned up dead, that was different. Of course I went to the authorities."

"With what? Did you hear Senator Glancy make any threats against Veronica Cooper?"

"No."

"According to your testimony, she threatened him."

"Right. Said she was going to ruin him."

"I submit, sir, that your testimony makes no sense. We knew from the videotape that, at or around the time you heard this alleged conversation, Veronica Cooper was having intimate relations with Senator Glancy. That she was even instigating the encounter, at least to some degree. That's an odd way to ruin someone."

Melanfield smiled. "My guess is she made the videotape."

All at once, Ben felt as if the air had been sucked out of the room, as if his heart had stopped beating.

It hadn't even occurred to him, but it made perfect sense. What was more likely, that the tape was made by a political opponent, or by one of the persons involved? She made the tape—and made sure it got out—to bury her boss. To set up a lawsuit that could make her rich for the rest of her life. If she had lived.

"Move to strike," Ben said, much too late to be effective. "Witness is speculating. His testimony is not based upon personal knowledge."

"Sustained," the judge ruled. "The jury will disregard the witness's statement." But Ben knew it would make no difference. Whether Melanfield's theory had any proof was irrelevant. It made sense. It fit. And even the most persuasive lawyer on earth would have a hard time convincing a jury to disregard their common sense.

"You're tellin' me you really suck people's blood?" Loving asked, leaning as far away from Morticia as possible. He wished he'd worn a turtleneck.

"I wouldn't lie to you," she replied. "Why should I? There's nothing new about it. Human beings have drunk blood since the dawn of time. Vampires were reported by the ancient Sumerians." She scooted closer. "All my life, I've felt like an outsider. Someone who didn't belong. But as soon as I was introduced to Circle Thirteen, I thought—I've found my tribe! These are my people. I don't need scarification, now. I have something else to take its place."

"And that would be . . . ?"

She looked at him levelly. "I think you already know the answer to that question." She slipped a finger under the shoulder strap of her dress and wriggled it down, revealing what was hidden beneath.

Wounds. Several slashes running down her shoulder.

"I—I thought vamps bit people in the neck."

"Some do. Unfortunately, you can kill someone that way. Shoulder wounds are less dangerous, easier to get to, and easier to conceal afterward. They bleed a lot, but there's no chance of bleeding to death from a shoulder cut. It's perfect, really." She pulled the strap back up. "So I can do all the things my body wants me to do, and still wear hot clothes."

Loving shook his head. "I can't believe you actually—"

"Have you not listened to anything I've said? Wake up and smell the bloodlust, handsome." She beckoned toward someone at the other end of the room. A moment later, they were joined by a tall and thin, stubble-cheeked, midtwenties man wearing a leather shirt, leather pants, leather lace-up sandals, and a black cloak. His ears and a good part of his face were covered with piercings, and he wore a thick silver band around his neck. The man had also shaved his head, except for one twisted strand that dangled down in front of his eyes. His face was abnormally white: Loving suspected he used makeup to create the effect. And he was supposed to believe this guy had a normal nine-to-five job?

"Charles," Morticia said, "show the man your teeth."

"Why should I?" he replied. His voice was low and guttural.

"So that he can believe."

"I don't get 'em out unless I plan to use them."

"Please," Morticia insisted. "I'll make it worth your while later." She looked at him sheepishly. "Say cheese."

The man shrugged, then, after a moment's more hesitation, smiled.

They were properly called canines, Loving knew, or eyeteeth, but at the moment it was impossible to think of them as anything but fangs. They were prominent, long, and extremely sharp. Sharp enough to cut through almost anything. Or anyone.

15

"I'm taking you two out to dinner tonight," Senator Glancy announced, after Judge Herndon ended the day's session. "Special permission from the judge—don't have to be back to my cell till ten. So what do you say? It'll be just the three of us, plus my dear, sweet federal marshals. We need to talk."

"We could try Stan's," Christina suggested. "It's nearby. It's mentioned in all my guidebooks."

Glancy shook his head. "Too close to the *Washington Post* offices. I don't want to be spotted by a bunch of reporters. Especially reporters who've had too much to drink."

"What about Two Quail? I hear it's very elegant."

"And packed with lobbyists. Who are even worse than reporters. At least the reporters don't offer to fix you up with women."

Ben's jaw lowered. "Lobbyists do that?"

"Ben, they've got gorgeous babes standing by to provide a BJ in the bathroom if you're on their A list. Or they'll pick up a hottie and deliver her to your place—so you won't be seen doing it. And as fun as that sounds, we need someplace our privacy will be respected."

"Then you'd better pick."

Glancy smiled broadly. "I was hoping you'd say that."

"The usual table, Senator Glancy?"

"If it's convenient."

"Of course. Right this way."

Glancy turned back toward Ben and Christina and winked. "You gotta love it. The man acts as if nothing has changed. No shocked expression, no double take. He's a pro."

Just as well, Ben thought, because he noticed a lot of double takes from the patrons as they passed through the elegant and ex-quisitely chic Four Seasons restaurant on Pennsylvania Avenue. Just a stone's throw from the POTUS himself, Glancy had said. The Man with the Big O. Which in this case stood for the Oval Office. "I sup-posed they're used to scandals in this town."

"It's not that they're jaded," Glancy replied quietly, as they ap-proached the secluded table in an alcove in the rear of the restau-rant's dining area. "It's that they're cautious. A politician can be down one minute, up the next. No way of predicting. One day Newt Gingrich is practically running the country; a year later he's writing bad science fiction novels and reviewing books for Amazon.com. One day Nixon is humiliated and retired from politics; next thing you know he's the damn president. In the long run, it's smart to be nice to everyone of importance. Or who might be. Or ever was."

"Or," Christina said, "you could just be nice to everyone. Pe-riod."

"You could. But you'll never get yourself elected to the U.S. Sen-ate that way." He took the menu from the waiter and smiled. "Thanks for humoring me. I get the impression this fancy-schmancy haute cuisine isn't your usual bill of fare. But I wanted to make the most of my night out."

"Not at all," Ben said, as he gazed at the menu. The prices were not listed, which was never a good sign. "If I don't eat this way often, it's not by choice, it's because . . . um, because . . ."

"Food allergies," Christina said, bailing him out. "Has to be very careful or he gets heat flashes. Believe me, it's a mess."

Glancy smiled. "You shouldn't have any problem here. The original owner set a standard for quality that has never been compromised. The four-star chef is probably the best in DC. Get this—the filets are dry-hung to age for four weeks before serving. Four weeks! And this is top-grade USDA-prime triple-plus beef. The best there is."

Christina gazed at the menu. "Despite hailing from Oklahoma, I'm more of a fish person."

"Of course you are." Glancy flashed a quick smile. "Fish is brain food." He reached across, brushing her hair with his hand, pointing at her menu. "Let me recommend the terrine of baby coho salmon with truffles and pistachios. It's better than sex."

"Really?"

"Well, no. But you know. It's a thing people say." He grinned again, the high-wattage smile that got him elected.

Was it Ben's imagination, or did it seem as if everyone in this whole damn case was trying to hit on his partner?

"We should have brought Shandy," Ben said, trying not to be too obvious.

"Oh, she's been here before. And she pretends to enjoy it, for my sake. But she's a girl of simple tastes at heart. A good girl, loyal. Not a dishonest bone in her body. But more the quarter-pounder type, if you know what I mean."

"And Amanda?"

"Amanda gets off on work. It's all she knows, all she loves. Spinning a PR disaster into a triumph, that's her natural high. Nothing I could give her could ever compete with that."

After they ordered, Glancy predictably wanted to discuss the case. "Don't take this as criticism, Ben. Maybe it's just my imagination, but—are we getting creamed?"

Ben took a long draw from his water crystal. "It's much too soon to predict—"

"It's slaughtersville, right?"

"Things always look bad when the prosecution is putting on their evidence," Christina said.

"Naturally," Ben added. "I mean, we knew they had a case. If they hadn't, they never would've gone to trial. Not against you. We're just going to have to tough it out until Padolino finishes." He paused. "I am sorry about the trouble with your wife."

"Marie?" Glancy waved his hand in the air. "Don't worry about her. She gets it. She knows how the game is played."

"She looked pretty upset . . ."

"Well, that's the best way for her to play it, don't you think?"

"I'm not quite sure I follow . . ."

"Then let me spell it out. If she didn't cry or act distraught, people would say she's a coldhearted bitch, Little Miss Iceberg, which is the stereotype every woman in politics has to fight against. If she acted as if she didn't care what I did, it would suggest she didn't care about me, which would lose her the support of the middle-American housewife—the stand-by-your-man crowd. And her being supposedly shocked about my affair isn't going to do me any harm with the jury—this case isn't about whether I slept with the girl, it's about whether I killed her. No, I'd say Marie played it very smart." He grabbed a roll and slathered it with butter. "Don't worry about my Marie. She's a smart woman. She'll always be on top." He blinked, then quickly turned to Christina. "I didn't mean that in a sexual way."

Ben grimaced. As if anyone thought he had—until he raised the suggestion. To Christina.

"And once Padolino has done his worst and rested," Glancy continued. "Then what?"

Ben cleared his throat. "Then we put on our defense. Start turning the jurors' minds around."

"And how exactly do we do that?"

"My investigator, Loving, has been tracking the friends of Veronica Cooper. Last time I was able to talk to him, he thought he was onto something."

"But he hasn't been able to find them."

"He found one—but she's in the hospital, unconscious."

"And that's it?"

"Well, the main point we'll be making is that the prosecution evidence really only shows that you and Ms. Cooper were, um, you know—" He coughed in his hand. "Involved."

Glancy smiled at Ben's discomfort. "That would be one way of putting it."

"But they have precious little that suggests you committed the murder. Sure, Padolino's created a motive for you. But he hasn't proven Opportunity. In fact, just the opposite. One of his own witnesses said you were in a committee meeting at the time of the murder."

"I'm sure the prosecutor has some way around that."

"Even if he does, it won't prove you murdered Veronica Cooper. What he has is entirely circumstantial."

"As I recall, aren't most murder convictions based upon circumstantial evidence?"

Ben fidgeted with his fork. It was harder to comfort a client who was so blisteringly smart. "True. Eyewitness testimony is rare—murderers don't normally commit their crimes while third parties are watching. But these days, science has made forensic evidence the star of the show. And juries are actually listening. Thanks to TV shows like *CSI,* the parts of the trial that used to be the most boring and least persuasive have become what jurors give the greatest credence. And Padolino has precious little forensic evidence against you."

"He can trace me and the corpse to my hideaway."

"As far as I'm concerned, that cuts against him," Christina opined. "I mean, after all, if you really were the murderer, would you leave the corpse in a place so obviously linked to you?"

"If I was desperate," Glancy answered. "If I had no other choice—no time to find another hiding place. Which is undoubtedly what Padolino will say."

"We can also put on character witnesses who will tell the jury that given your upright character you couldn't commit possibly a murder."

"After that video? You'll never convince the jury I have any character. They think I'm capable of doing anything."

"I think maybe you're being a little—"

"No, I'm being a lot. But I have to be. My entire future is on the line." He buttered his last piece of bread. "Sorry to be Mr. Funsucky, Ben, but I'm doing it for a reason. I suspect you're not planning to put me on the witness stand."

Ben and Christina exchanged glances. "There are obvious

dangers in calling you. Especially after the video. With any public figure, there's always plenty of grist for cross-ex character assassination."

"I get that, but you have no choice. Moreover, I *want* you to put me on."

Ben shook his head. "Todd, I'm not sure you appreciate how dangerous that is."

"I can handle myself."

"We're not talking about a press conference. We're not talking about reporters tossing out softball questions from which you can pick and choose. We're talking about cross-examination by a very experienced, very determined attorney who will not give you any quarter."

"I repeat: I can handle myself."

"And there are other dangers," Christina added. "Some forms of evidence the prosecution can only bring in if you take the stand. Prior bad acts or convictions. Propensity for truth telling. You don't want to deal with that."

"If it saves my career—not to mention my life—I do."

"Senator, I know you've had a lot of experience here in Washington, but when it comes to the courtroom, you'd be wise to listen to Ben. He—"

Glancy held up his hand. "You don't have to tell me about Ben. I know everything there is to know; I wouldn't have chosen him to represent me if I didn't." Ben felt his face reddening—it was awkward being talked about as if he weren't there. "I remember when he won the National Moot Court Championship back in law school, whipping all those private school butts for good ol' OU. Brilliant argument, great command of the material. Hell, I remember seeing you at all those hideously boring debutante parties our parents forced us to attend back in Nichols Hills. I remember admiring you."

"M—me?"

"Yeah. Because while I was off trying to be everyone's friend and bed every girl on the list and making a fool of myself drinking Everclear tornadoes—you didn't."

Ben squinted. "And the point of this is—"

"I must be losing my touch. I thought I'd already made it." He smiled pleasantly at the waiter, who had just arrived with the food. "The point is, when it comes to smart, you win hands down. I got no bones about that. But when it comes to understanding people, I've got the edge. Because while I was making a fool of myself getting to know people, how they think, what makes them tick, you were off by yourself being smart."

Glancy inhaled deeply, absorbing the ravishing beef-and-pecan aroma arising from his plate. "Isn't that magnificent? A perfect sensual experience—it almost spoils it to take a bite." He picked up a fork and began to slice. "I will be testifying, Ben. Count on it."

Loving masterfully maintained a straight face. "So you're tellin' me you use those big sharp fangs of yours to suck blood?"

"Yes," Morticia answered, her voice gurgling with excitement. She rubbed her tummy with one hand. "'S yummy."

"Like liquid energy," Charles added, lisping slightly, no doubt due to the inch-long teeth protruding from the front of his mouth.

Loving shook his head. "I'm assumin', even if you're an Inheritor, that you weren't born with those. Otherwise your mommy would've signed you up for some serious orthodontic work."

"'Course not," Morticia explained. "He had 'em filed."

"And where do you find a dentist who would do somethin' like that?"

"We've got connections. The Sire takes care of us."

Loving's chin rose. "That's the second time you've mentioned him. Who's this Sire?"

"He's the leader of the Inner Circle."

"Did he get you a nice set of fangs, too?"

Morticia opened her mouth wide, smiled, and sure enough she had a more petite but still discernible pair of fangs. "The difference," she said, mouth still open, "is that mine can be removed." She reached up and snapped off her front row of teeth like a pair of fake fingernails. "Acrylic. Snap-ons. Cost me seventy-five bucks. But that's a lot less than Charles paid. And I have the option of not wearing them to work—unlike him."

"I work at home," Charles explained, still lisping.

Just as well, Loving thought. "And you really drink blood?"

"With gusto. The commingling of bloodlines is the ultimate gratification, the sharing of life force. There is no greater stimulation than that derived from walking the narrow tightrope between pleasure and pain. Just thinking about it gets me—"

"Thanks for sharin'," Loving said, cutting him off. "But I notice all your pals are gatherin'." The rest of the Circle was congregating in the center of the room, hands joined, facing one another.

"Time for the Ceremony," Morticia explained.

"And that is . . . ?"

"You'll see."

"I can participate?"

"Sure. Open to all comers."

And why was that? Did visitors become the human sacrifice? Loving was willing to do a great deal for Ben, but becoming a walking, talking blood bag for a coven of vampires was pushing it.

They finished their meals, which all three agreed were fabulous. Glancy assured Ben that the dinner was going on his running tab, which was a considerable relief, and Glancy was in the process of talking them into dessert ("The crème brûlée is like ambrosia in a baking dish, but I prefer the cheese plate, being a devoted turophile") when they were visited by Brad Tidwell, the junior senator from Oklahoma.

Tidwell seemed genuinely surprised to see Glancy, even though Ben thought it was virtually impossible that anyone could've spotted them in this alcove if he hadn't already known they were there. "Glad to see you were able to get out for a night, Todd. You know, we're all rooting for you."

"Oh, I rather doubt everyone is," Glancy said, dabbing his mouth with a napkin. "But thank you."

"I meant everyone from Oklahoma," Tidwell corrected. "We Sooners stand by our own."

"About that," Glancy said. "I did notice that your name is on the prosecution's witness list."

"Doesn't that beat all? I don't know what the deal is."

"I don't, either," Ben added. "And I interviewed you as soon as I saw the list."

"I guess it's because I'm on that committee with you, Todd. Did you know I have the best attendance record of anyone in the entire group?"

"Is that a fact," Glancy said quietly.

Tidwell slapped his hand on Glancy's shoulder. "I do wish you'd think about reconsidering your position on that Alaska bill, though. I know Melanfield's an ass, but I think he's right about this one."

"It's our last untouched wilderness area, Brad."

"I know, but we've got to get ourselves out of the Middle East. It would be the best thing for the country." He hesitated just the slightest second. "I think it would be the best thing for you, too."

Glancy turned his head slowly. For a long, protracted moment, the two men stared into each other's eyes.

"I can't do that, Brad. The price is too high."

Tidwell nodded slowly. "I'm sorry to hear that, Todd. I really am."

Glancy did not reply.

"But no hard feelings, right?" Tidwell outstretched his hand. "You just remember that, no matter what happens, I'm behind you all the way, okay? You can count on the delegation from Oklahoma." He shook Glancy's hand vigorously, then strolled away.

Christina stared at them both, lips parted. "Did what I think just happened just happen?"

Glancy turned to her. "Now I understand why you're such a good partner for my friend Ben. You get the subtext."

"Subtext?" Ben said, turning from one to the other. "What are you two talking about?"

"Opportunity," Glancy said. "I think I know now how that will be established."

"And that handshake?" Ben asked. "That promise of support. That wasn't a peace offering?"

Glancy shook his head gravely. "The Judas kiss."

Not that Loving was looking for trouble. He really wasn't. But when you're hanging with vampires, and someone announces that the Ceremony is about to begin, you form certain expectations. Visions of kidnapped babies being drained. Vestal virgins thrown to the flames. Lucifer the Goat conjured from the netherworld.

Anything but this. Because this was nothing but a glorified AA meeting where all the attendees have the same bad fashion sense.

"I tried to talk to my parents," a young man in a dark sweater said. "But they wouldn't listen. They didn't understand. They said—get this—'Have you ever tried *not* being a vampire?'"

Several sympathetic hands were laid upon his shoulder.

"We feel your pain," the others chanted together.

More likely they cause his pain, Loving thought. With their teeth.

Daily whispered into Loving's ear. "How much more of this are we going to endure? I've talked to everyone in the room. None of them knows a Beatrice."

"Did you learn anythin' about the girls that disappear? The ones the Sire's minions select for the Inner Circle?"

"No one seems to know much about that."

Loving grunted. He was equally stymied. He hated to give up on a promising lead, but this was getting them nowhere. "Amber's last words before she fell unconscious—"

"She was out of her head. Probably didn't know what she was saying."

Another member of the Circle was speaking. "And then she threw the engagement ring back at me, screaming, 'You said you were going to be a lawyer!' And I told her, 'I can still be a lawyer, honey. I'll just have to stick to night court.'"

"Okay, let's get outta here." Loving headed out, but to his surprise Morticia left the group and ran in front of him just as he passed through the outer door, blocking his way.

"You can't just leave. I told you. We're destined to be together." She grabbed him by the collar and pulled him close. "Just let me take a little nip. You won't be disappointed. I promise you." Once again she was all over him, her heaving bosom pressed against his ample chest. "It would be an experience you'd never forget."

"That I don't doubt. But—"

"Give it up, you gorgeous infidel." All at once, she lurched forward, placed her acrylic teeth against his neck, and bit down hard.

Loving pulled away. "Stop that!"

"Why? Afraid you might like it?" She wiped her mouth dry.

"You shouldn't withdraw prematurely. Haven't you heard? Women don't like that."

"Be seein' you." Loving started for the door, tugging Daily as he went.

"You know you want it. Deep down," Morticia called after him. "You'll come back. Wait and see. I'll still be here. When you're ready."

Loving ran down the front steps and breathed in the night air. Strong with carbon monoxide, but refreshing, just the same. It was a relief to be outside, away from that pack of nutcases.

Vampires. Jeez Louise. What next? It can't possibly get any weirder than that . . .

A voice emerged from the darkness. "Freeze, or I'll stake you where you stand, you unholy beasts."

Loving and Daily both pivoted at once. There was a woman standing behind them, emerging from the shadows of a side alley. She was young, slender but sturdy. She had long blond hair and a tanned complexion. Her eyes were fixed intently upon her targets.

She was holding a crossbow. Not a gun. A crossbow.

"Now you're going to do exactly what I say," she said, moving forward but never blinking, never moving her finger from the trigger. "And if either of you so much as takes a baby step toward me, you'll get a bolt through your undead heart."

16

Ben was not surprised when the prosecution called Brad Tidwell, the junior senator from Oklahoma. Padolino made a great show of explaining in open court that Tidwell was a "hostile witness," and was appearing only because he had been subpoenaed—probably a condition of his agreement to testify. Tidwell opened with several stories of how he had once admired Senator Glancy and how helpful the man was during his early days in the Senate, despite the fact that they were from opposite parties. Together, he and Padolino did everything imaginable to dispel the idea that this testimony had partisan motivations.

"On September 26 of last year, did you attend the morning meeting of the Committee on Health, Education, Labor and Pensions?" Padolino asked.

"I did, sir. I'm proud to say I have the best attendance record of any member currently serving. I've never missed an entire day. I even attended when I had strep and a temperature of one hundred and four."

Well, I bet the other committee members appreciated that, Ben mused.

"And was the defendant present on September 26?"

"He was, sir. He's still vice chair, and I believe he handled some of the parliamentary rigmarole at the opening."

"And did he remain in the committee chambers for the entire morning?"

Ben wondered if he had been coached to pause at this dramatic juncture, or if his political experience had given him sufficient instinct to work these things out for himself. "No, sir. He did not."

A small stir from the gallery. Not quite enough to get Herndon's gavel rattling, but close.

"At what time did Senator Glancy leave the room?"

"I can't be certain. I was very busy, and I didn't know then that it would be important. But it was in the first hour or so of the session."

"Say around nine thirty?"

"Objection!" Ben rushed in. "Leading."

"Sustained."

"I really didn't notice the time," Tidwell continued. "But it was early. Before ten, certainly."

The earliest time the coroner said the killing could have occurred, Ben noted. How terribly convenient.

"Thank you. I have no more questions."

But Ben did. More than a few.

"Could we possibly get some specifics on this previously unmentioned absence?" Ben thought it was an appropriate time to allow some indignation to show.

"What would you like to know? I told you as much as I can about when he left."

"How long was Senator Glancy gone? According to you."

"I really couldn't say. I had other things to do than monitor his comings and goings."

"Give me a ballpark figure."

"I can't."

"Was it a bathroom break? Or was he gone a good long time?"

"It was more than a bathroom break. I was trying to float a redraft by him, but he wasn't anywhere in the chamber. I searched the whole place, waited, finally had to move on to something else. It was at least ten minutes before I saw him in the chamber again. Maybe as much as twenty."

More than enough time, Ben realized. He played the best card he had. "Senator Tidwell, I interviewed you two days after the murder occurred, along with every other member of that committee. You told me you were working on a new formulation of a bill and couldn't remember whether Senator Glancy was present the whole time or not."

"And that was true. At the time. But I've had a long while to think about it since then. Time to reflect and to review my notes. Now I distinctly remember looking around for Todd, and not finding him."

The man was so smooth he could make anything sound reasonable. Ben had one last impeachment card, a pretty feeble one. But he had to play it.

"Despite being from the same state, you're not a member of the same political party as Senator Glancy, are you?"

"I think I made that clear."

"The current Senate has only a bare Republican majority. You'd probably like to see a few Democrats replaced by Republicans, right?"

"I don't see what that has to do with anything."

"Answer the question."

"Well . . ." He grinned a little. "I wouldn't object."

"And you'd probably enjoy being the senior senator from your state, wouldn't you?"

That got a rise out of him. "If you're trying to suggest that I'm making this up just to get Senator Glancy out of the Senate, you're wasting your time. I wouldn't do that. We may be political opponents, but we're still brother senators. Politics is one thing, but loyalty is another. I put loyalty first."

"So you say," Ben rejoined. "But that didn't stop you from testifying today, did it? No more questions."

Padolino would try to patch that up on redirect, Ben well knew. But at least it gave him an exit line.

As Glancy had predicted last night, Opportunity had arrived. Coupled with Motive, the prosecution had made their case. They'd given the jury everything they needed to convict. For all intents and purposes, the burden of proof was now on Ben—and if he failed, Todd Glancy was a dead man.

It was overkill, Ben thought, and the flaw with overkill was not just that the jury would get bored but also that eventually some witness might make a mistake that would undermine everything. Padolino had made his case; the only sensible thing to do was rest. But instead, he opted for the anticlimactic introduction of character assassination. For what purpose? Ben wondered. What character was there left to assassinate?

Ben did his best to exclude all such witnesses, but Herndon ruled that it went to the issue of both motive and the likelihood that Glancy might leave a meeting to engage in "inappropriate relationships." So it came in. Padolino put a succession of three women on the stand—all of them young, all of them pretty.

The first, a senatorial aide, claimed that during a meeting of the Atomic Energy Commission, Glancy put his hand under the conference table and between her legs. According to her, when she looked at him, shocked, he whispered, "My dear, you're as cold as ice. Would you like to conduct a little science experiment? Let's see if we can generate some spontaneous combustion." The second, a member of the Senate secretarial pool, claimed Glancy had stumbled into her elevator late one evening, drunk as a skunk, belched, put his hand on her breast, and slurred, "Sssorry. I missstook you for a doorknob."

Christina whispered into Ben's ear. "Am I the only one who's like, *ickk*?"

"No, I'm pretty sure there are others," Ben whispered back. "Sixteen of them, to be exact. And they're all sitting together."

Glancy remained quietly impassive throughout the testimony.

The most damaging was the third, which was undoubtedly why Padolino had saved her for last. She claimed to have been interviewing for an intern's position in Glancy's office, the position later held by Veronica Cooper. This put it in the realm of employment-related sexual harassment, which was not only contrary to federal law and actionable in civil court, but also grounds for immediate expulsion from the Senate, as Senator Packwood had learned several years before.

"He kept saying, 'Hiring is so difficult. You can't make an informed decision unless you're aware of all the candidate's talents.' And then he unzipped his fly."

"Did he . . . make a request?" Padolino asked.

"He didn't have to. It was obvious what he wanted. I told him I wouldn't have sex with a stranger just to get a job. And you know what he said? He said, 'Hey, it's not like it would be real sex.'" She pursed her lips. "Obviously, he was a Democrat."

Ben didn't bother asking his client if any of these incidents actually happened. They didn't directly pertain to the murder. And Ben didn't really want to hear the answer. He was much more concerned about what was going on at the prosecution table. Padolino had effectively completed the day with what at best could be called filler witnesses. Damaging, perhaps, but not *that* damaging.

If this was the best he had left, he would've ended with Tidwell. Which led Ben to an inescapable conclusion. There was something more. Some*one* more. Some killer witness Padolino had saved so he could end with a bang. But who could it be? What could there possibly be left to say?

The question troubled him deeply. Because as every good attorney knew, the key to a successful defense was anticipation. No matter how bad the testimony, if you can see it coming, you can come up with some way to deflect it, to undermine it, to deflate it, to make it seem less than it at first appeared to be.

But if you didn't know what was coming, you were like a floundering fish waiting to be speared. Dead in the water.

Loving stared at the young woman bearing both the determined expression and the crossbow aimed at his chest. "Have I . . . uh . . . done somethin' to offend you?" he asked.

"Your very existence offends me, Dracula."

Loving furrowed his brow. "I think you may be confused."

"Am I?" She was so close now the tip of the crossbow bolt was barely a foot away. "How do you figure?"

Loving pointed to Daily. "He's Count Dracula. I'm Renfield."

Daily spun around. "Now wait a minute—"

"You think that's funny?" She pushed the tip of the bolt to his chest, right over his heart. "You won't be laughing once I send you into instant cremation."

Loving held up his hands. "Look, lady, you've got the wrong idea. We're not vampires."

"I suppose you were in there just for the free crudités."

"I was in there as part of an investigation. That's my job. I'm a private investigator."

"Do you think I'm stupid? I was watching you. I saw that rouged-up Vampirella bite your neck."

Ah. Now Loving was beginning to understand where the woman was coming from. "And why do you care?"

"Because that's *my* job," she spat back. "I'm a vampire hunter."

Loving and Daily exchanged a look. "Did you say what I think you just said?"

"Don't get smart with me!" She jabbed him with the tip of the bolt. "I won't take any crap from a reanimated corpse."

Loving held up his hands. "Lady—do you have a name?"

"Why should I tell you?"

"I'd just like to know who I'm talkin' to before you, uh, slay me."

She hesitated, her narrowed eyes spewing anger. "You can call me Shalimar."

"And you're a . . . vampire slayer."

"*Hunter!* Not slayer!"

"What's the difference?"

"The difference is this is real life, not some TV show."

"Fine. Vampire *hunter.*" He paused. "Do you need a hunting license for that?"

Her teeth clenched together. "Wiseass undead hellspawn. I'm taking you down."

"Look, Shalimar, I'm not a vampire. You fire that bolt, you'll be committin' murder."

"Prove it."

"Prove it? How do I prove I'm not a vampire?" He snapped his fingers. "I got it. I'll follow you home."

"What? Why?"

"If I can sneak into your place without an invitation, that means I'm not a vampire, right?"

She raised the crossbow higher. "I warned you—"

"Or we could get Italian. After you see how much garlic I put on everythin'—"

"Cut it out!"

Loving tried another tack. "You got a cross on you?"

She hesitated. "Several."

"How did I guess? Gimme one."

"Why?"

"So when I don't burst into flames or cower or hiss or anythin', you'll know I'm not undead."

Slowly, Shalimar reached inside her Windbreaker and produced a small wooden cross. She held it out to him. Loving took it into his hand . . .

And screamed. "Aaaaaah!" He dropped the cross and pressed his hand to his chest.

Shalimar jumped, crossbow at the ready. "*What?* You monstrous—"

Loving held up his hands. "Jokin', jokin'." He picked the cross up off the pavement and squeezed it. "See. Nothin'. I'm not a vampire."

Shalimar pursed her lips, furious. "Him, too."

Daily took the cross, didn't joke around, didn't turn to flames.

Slowly Shalimar lowered her crossbow. "I guess you're clean. You should be more careful about who you make out with." She shrugged. "Sorry if I startled you."

"Think nothin' of it," Loving replied. "Happens every day. But lemme tell you—there's nothing in there but a lotta pathetic whack jobs tryin' to convince themselves they're special by copyin' scenes from bad horror movies. I didn't see anyone who didn't reflect in the mirror over the hearth."

"More pretenders." She released the bolt from her crossbow and slowly edged it back into the quiver on her back. "Damn."

"Lady, they're all pretenders. There's no such thing as vampires."

"You're wrong. They do exist."

"Where? Universal Studios?"

"History is replete with documented vampires. The novel *Dracula* was based on a real vampire. Lady Caroline Lamb, the Victorian poet, was a vampire. There have been many books written on the subject."

"Ma'am," Loving said, "with all due respect, I've been known to buy any number of off-the-wall theories. But even I don't believe some lady poet was really a vampire. Know why? 'Cause there's no such thing!"

She looked at him with a sad, pitying expression. "That's what they want you to believe."

"Oh, for Pete's—"

"Are you familiar with Rousseau?"

"The actress?"

"No, the eighteenth-century French philosopher and writer. One of the smartest men who ever lived. He said—and this is an exact quote—'If ever there was in the world a warranted and proven history, it is that of vampires: nothing is lacking, official reports, testimonials of persons of standing, of surgeons, of clergymen, of judges; the judicial evidence is all-embracing.'"

"The man was cracked. With all due respect, Miss Shalimar, people don't rise from the dead, no matter who they've been suckin' on."

"Do you know the disease porphyria? It's a genetic disorder that causes receding gums—which can make people look like they have fangs—and also creates hypersensitivity to sunlight and an enzyme deficiency that can cause people to crave blood."

Loving pinched the bridge of his nose. "Lady, you're . . . what? Twenty-one, twenty-two? You should be in a sorority or the Junior Service League or somethin'. When did you get started chasin' vampires?"

Her eyes narrowed to a dull pinpoint of light. "After they took my sister."

A synapse fired somewhere inside Loving's brain. "What was your sister's name?"

She looked at him for a long while, as if trying to evaluate whether she could trust him, before finally answering. "My sister's name was Beatrice. Why do you ask?"

17

Ben waited quietly, wringing his hands under the defense table, desperate to know who the prosecution's pièce de résistance would be. He'd pored over their witness list, but that was no help—there were at least thirty uncalled witnesses remaining, and as far as he knew none of them had anything sensational to say. He'd tried to wheedle the information out of Padolino, who wouldn't give up anything but kept pestering Ben for Christina's phone number. His associates were apparently under threat of bodily injury not to talk. Ben had scanned the courtroom, the hallway outside, even the men's room, but hadn't been able to spot anyone who wasn't normally present.

"Maybe you're wrong," Christina said, with an attempt at solace that was painfully unavailing. "Maybe there is no killer finale. They've already put on enough to make their case."

"But possibly not enough to win it." Ben shook his head. "No, if this was all he had, Padolino would've closed with Senator Tidwell. Or the video. There has to be something more."

"Don't feel bad," Glancy grunted. "My staff is equally clueless."

"Not for want of trying." Amanda Burton stood behind her man, the usual unpleasant expression on her face. "I've called all my connections in the Senate and the law enforcement world. They haven't been able to tell me anything."

Shandy, her blond hair tucked behind her ears, nodded. "Marshall's come up dry, too. And if Marshall can't find it, it isn't available. Oh—I almost forgot." She pulled a sealed envelope out of her satchel. "This is for you, Boss."

Glancy held the letter between his fingers. "Should I read it now, dear? Or in private?"

She smiled. "It can wait till later."

"Thanks." He tucked it into his coat pocket. "It's a comfort to know I have such dedicated people taking care of business while I'm stuck in this trial."

"Speaking of which," Shandy said, turning toward Ben, "you look cute as a bug in Todd's navy-blue Brooks Brothers."

Ben glanced at the suit he was wearing. "What, this old thing?"

Shandy laughed. "Fits you much better than that blue rag you were wearing twice a week. What's 'Dillard's,' anyway?"

Ben stiffened slightly. "Dillard's is a first-rate Oklahoma-based chain of department stores—"

"But Ben doesn't shop there," Christina interjected. "He shops at a consignment store and buys the hand-me-downs of people who shop at Dillard's."

Ben adjusted the knot in his necktie. "Nothing wrong with a little frugality."

Judge Herndon's clerk entered the courtroom, closely trailed by the man himself. The judge greeted everyone, gave the usual admonitions to his sequestered jury, then got down to business. "I especially want to remind the members of the press in the audience that no disturbances, outbursts, or unruly behavior will be tolerated. And that goes for the nonpress personages in the gallery as well."

Herndon had never started the day with anything like this before. Did he know something Ben didn't? Was there some reason he foresaw the possibility of an outburst?

"Mr. Padolino," the judge said, leaning back in his chair, "please call your next witness."

"With pleasure." Padolino rose, smoothed the crease in his jacket, then addressed the court. "The District calls Miss Shandy Craig."

"*What?*" Ben hadn't meant to say it aloud, wasn't really even conscious he was speaking. He turned, along with everyone else sitting at counsel table, to face the rear of the gallery. Sure enough, lovely Shandy rose to her feet.

She was not surprised.

"I don't believe it," Glancy said, under his breath.

Christina, Marie, the rest of Glancy's staff, and everyone in the gallery who knew the players seemed equally stunned, including a few of the people sitting at Padolino's table. Well, that's the best way to keep a secret, Ben thought grimly. Tell no one.

Shandy started down the nave of the gallery, composed, her chin slightly raised, moving without hesitation. Marshall Bressler was seated in his wheelchair toward the front on the defense side. As she approached, he turned his wheels outward slightly, blocking her progress.

Shandy stopped. The two made eye contact. Even without telepathic powers, Ben felt confident he knew what message was being communicated by the senator's administrative assistant to his young protégée.

You traitor.

Shandy calmly sidestepped him, passed through the swinging doors, and was sworn in by the bailiff.

Ben had assumed—had hoped, really—that Shandy's testimony would focus on the discovery of Veronica Cooper's body. Unfortunately, he was incorrect.

"Was there anything unusual about the hiring process?" Padolino asked.

"Well," Shandy replied, "I couldn't help but notice that all the other applicants for the vacated intern position—there were four of us—were about my age, and I don't want to seem egotistical, but no one there was hard on the eyes."

"During the interview process, were you asked any . . . unusual questions?"

Ben and Christina looked at each other. Here we go again.

"It wasn't so much his questions as the remarks he made in between. I didn't get the joke some of the time. But I did think he was making remarks that were sexually suggestive. He'd laugh and his eyebrows would dance up and down."

"Perhaps he was just trying to learn a little something about you," Padolino suggested. "So he could assess your qualifications for the job."

"Well, at one point he asked if I was wearing a thong. You know, underwear. I had a hard time seeing how that fit into a congressional intern's job description."

"Anything else?"

"Not really. I think he wanted to talk to me more, but he was pressed for time. As you know, the video had just hit the airwaves the day before. He had reporters practically beating down his door, he had a committee about to go into session and, he said, 'many other important meetings.' So he gave me the job and I went to work. I was in the committee room when the meeting began at nine."

Ben slowly released his breath. That wasn't so bad. It wasn't good, but they could survive it. If that was where it stopped.

"Could you please explain to the jury why you were at the meeting for the Committee on Health, Education, Labor and Pensions on the day in question?"

"Of course." Shandy shifted slightly to face the jury, adjusting her skirt to keep her knees covered. Now that Ben thought about it, she was dressed much more conservatively than she had been in the past. Padolino had coached her well. "As I said, it was my first day on the job, my first day working for Senator Glancy. He told me to follow him around all day long, just to get the lay of the land. That didn't last long—his office was so overrun by the media that the senator's PR adviser, Amanda Burton, paged me and instructed me to return to the office. But I was at the committee meeting for a good long while."

"And were you there between the hours of nine and ten?"

"I was."

"A previous witness, Senator Tidwell, has testified that he saw Senator Glancy leave the conference room during that time." He paused, making the jury wait for it. "Did you?"

"Yes, sir. I did."

Ben closed his eyes. There it was. The clincher. Verification from Glancy's own staff member, albeit a new one. Ben had interviewed Shandy after he took the case, of course, as he had every member of Glancy's staff and everyone else on the prosecution's witness list. She had given no indication of any sexual misconduct by the senator, during her job interview or later. And she certainly had said nothing about seeing the senator leave the committee meeting—even though she knew that meeting was key to his alibi.

"Did you see where he went?"

"I did not. I just looked up one moment and he was gone. But I had a hunch."

Ben tensed, ready to spring. This wasn't speculation yet, but it sounded as if it might be on the verge.

"And what was the basis for this hunch?"

"I knew how Senator Glancy got to the meeting. Because he brought me along. We didn't come the usual way, through the marble corridors like the other senators. We took what he called his 'secret passageway.'"

"And that was?"

"A back stairwell. Through a rear door in his private office he could enter the emergency stairway, wind through some maze-like hallways, and end up in the committee room, without ever once emerging in any of the public areas of the building. He said it was very exclusive—only a few of the senators even knew about it. He also told me about his hideaway and how you could get to it via these back passageways without being spotted."

Ben felt Christina kicking him in the shins under the table. She knew where this was going as well as he did.

"Did this behavior strike you as . . . unusual?"

"He said he wanted to avoid the press, which under the circumstances I could understand. So when he disappeared during the meeting, I assumed he went the same way he had come."

"What did you do?"

"I followed him."

Ben felt his heart sink into the pit of his stomach. Was it possible? Could Padolino finally have what he needed most? An eyewitness?

"What did you do?"

"I entered the stairwell through the door we had used to get to the committee room and tried to thread my way to his hideaway. But remember—this was my first day, and I'd only been in this place once. I got lost. There are very few exit doors. So I wasted a lot of time wandering around, not really knowing where I was." She paused. "I probably never would've found them—if I hadn't heard the noise."

"The noise? Could you please be more specific? What did you hear?"

"I heard two voices, a man and a woman, even though the door was closed. But that wasn't the main noise."

"What was the main noise?"

Shandy took a deep breath. "The sound of two people . . . doing it. You know what I mean. Making love."

Jaws dropped in the jury box. And elsewhere as well.

"What did it sound like?"

"It's a little hard to describe, but—we've all heard it. It's a pretty distinctive sound. There was . . . jeez . . ." She rubbed her brow for a moment. "Rhythmic grunting. Low-pitched. The sound of someone being knocked against the wall at a steady rhythm. Some crying out."

"Crying out? As in pain?"

"No. As in . . . you know. Orgasmic ecstasy."

"Are you sure?" Padolino asked. "The two might sound alike. And if you couldn't see them—"

"Yes, I'm sure. And no, actually, they don't sound anything alike. I'm no tramp, but I know an orgasm when I hear it."

Ben cast a quick look at Glancy, who was remarkably stone-faced. He couldn't tell what was going on in that brain, but the wheels were definitely turning. And he didn't want to know what Marie was thinking.

"How long did these . . . noises go on?"

"Oh, I'd guess around two minutes. I didn't know what to do. Part of me wanted to stay. Part of me wanted to go. I couldn't decide. Then I heard the man speak."

"What did he say?"

"Objection," Ben said. "Hearsay."

"You must be joking," Judge Herndon said. He was hunched forward over his bench, hanging on Shandy's every word. "The witness will answer the question."

"It was more of a whisper, actually," Shandy explained. "But I could make it out, just barely. He said. 'I'm glad you enjoyed yourself. Because it's the last time for you. Forever.'"

The buzz in the gallery had been growing for the past several minutes, but at this point it reached a distracting crescendo. Herndon banged his gavel several times. "Don't make me clear this courtroom!"

That quieted the crowd. No one wanted to risk missing what came next.

"Was there anything more?" Padolino asked.

"Yes. I heard the woman give out a little gasp, and then there was this—this—really strange sound, almost like air being sucked in. I heard a sudden thud—as if one of the parties had hit the floor. After that, the room was silent."

"What did you do then?"

"I turned back the way I had come and found the committee room, in a lot less time than it took me to stumble upon those two. Amazing how much better your brain works when you really don't want to be caught somewhere. I came back later, trying to get a break from all the chaos upstairs. I assumed they would both be gone but . . . that was when I found her. Veronica Cooper. Dead."

Padolino nodded sympathetically. "Thank you, Miss Craig. Pass the witness." Padolino looked pointedly at Ben.

He wasn't the only one in the courtroom looking that way. Ben had learned to watch the expressions on the jurors' faces surreptitiously and frequently—and what he was reading now he didn't like at all. What he was reading was that every juror on the bench thought Glancy was a murderer—and a disgusting, perverted, cradle-robbing, sex-addicted murderer at that.

"Will there be any cross?" Judge Herndon asked.

Ben rose to his feet. "Oh yeah."

Once they got Shalimar to put away the crossbow, Loving and Daily escorted her to a nearby Georgetown all-night coffeehouse so they could exchange notes.

"Why do you think vampires were responsible for Beatrice's disappearance?" Loving asked.

She drank deeply from her coffee cup—almost an entire cup at once. If Loving had done that, he'd never get to sleep, but it didn't seem to be a problem for her. Or maybe vampire hunters didn't sleep nights. "I was going to school in Philadelphia—Bryn Mawr—but I have friends in DC, and they kept an eye on my little sister for me. Told me she was changing, going out almost every night, dressing in black, wearing turtlenecks even though it was hot as blazes out. Then she started disappearing, not coming back to her apartment, sometimes for days. At first I just assumed she had a new boyfriend. But one of my friends managed to get a look under the collar of her sweater—and found two unhealed puncture wounds. Bite marks."

"And before that you had no hint that your sister was . . . gettin' into some seriously weird stuff?"

"None at all. Last time I saw her, she was an All-American straight-A student. The next—she's Sabrina the Teenage Witch. Except without the laugh track."

"So what did you do?"

"What choice did I have? I came up here as soon as possible. But it was too late. She was gone. She hasn't been seen since."

"My daughter disappeared, too," Daily said, clenching his fists. "Now she's in the ICU unit of the hospital. If I'd only been smarter. Moved a little faster."

"I kept saying the same thing. Blaming myself. But that didn't help. So I dropped out of school and started spending all my time looking for Beatrice, learning about these vampire cults. I went from one vamp club to the next—gay vamp bars, straight vamp bars—places where they actually serve blood over the counter, like it was a cocktail. You wouldn't believe how many of them there are. No one ever wanted to talk to me—so I had to get tough. That's when I became a vampire hunter. Whether they're real vampires or pretenders, the mythos of the vampire hunter—Van Helsing, Captain Kronos, Kolchak, whoever—terrifies them."

"And that's what brought you to Circle Thirteen tonight?"

"Took me forever to get a lead on that place. But I was told there were some vampires in there."

"Some? It's a regular Vampapalooza. But it's all up here."

Loving tapped a temple. "I mean, they're not really hell demons or 'vampyrs' or whatever the politically correct term would be. Undead Americans? They're just basket cases trying to convince themselves they're special by affecting this Bela Lugosi fetish."

"You mean . . . they're normals?"

"Well, I don't think you're gonna see any of them on the cover of *Sanity Fair*. But I'm pretty damn sure they're not walking corpses."

Shalimar's chin sagged. "Then it's a dead end."

"Maybe not. Someone I talked to said women sometimes disappeared—said they were chosen by the minions of someone called the Sire for . . . the Inner Circle. She also mentioned a place called the Playground." He paused. "Shalimar, I think we should team up. We're all looking for the same girl. Maybe if we pool our knowledge—"

He was interrupted by the sound of Daily's cell phone ringing. "Yes?"

Less than ten seconds later, Daily snapped it shut. "It's Amber. She's awake."

Loving hurriedly tossed some money on the table, pulled a card out of his wallet, and slid it across the table to Shalimar. "Here's my number. Call me tomorrow."

"You'll ask Amber if she knows anything about Beatrice?"

"Promise. I'll tell you anything we learn."

Daily was obviously anxious. "I've got to go."

"I know. I'm coming with you." Loving slid out of the booth. "Thanks for talking with us." He gave her a wink. "Look forward to working with you, Buffy."

Despite the fact that Loving was already halfway across the coffeehouse, Shalimar rose to her feet. *"Don't call me Buffy!"*

Even though it broke protocol as well as one of his primary rules for courtroom decorum, Ben had to talk to his client. He leaned over and whispered into Glancy's ear. "Is any of what she said true?"

"Abso-fucking-lutely not," Glancy shot back. "I've told you before. The only time I left the conference room was when I went to the restroom. And I wasn't gone more than ten minutes."

"Just asking." Ben rose. He wondered if Christina might not be a better choice to cross this witness. He would be forced to tread the line between being firm and appearing to beat up on a helpless young woman. But thanks to his prior objection, the witness was his now, whether he liked it or not.

"Point of clarification, Miss Craig. Did you ever see the faces of the two people who were allegedly in the hideaway?"

"I never saw their faces, no, but I think it's obvious—"

"To be blunt, ma'am, I don't care what you think. I want to hear what you know. Did you see their faces?"

Shandy grasped that the tone of the questioning had changed and resigned herself to answering questions succinctly. "No."

"Were you able to positively identify either of them?"

"I'd never met Veronica Cooper. But I thought the male voice sounded a lot like Senator Glancy."

"Whom you had just met that morning, right?"

"Well, yes."

"And what does that mean exactly, when you say you 'thought it sounded like him'?"

"Well, the voice was low and deep. Kinda slow talking."

"That would be true for half the men over thirteen on this planet."

"It's not just that." She began fidgeting with her well-shaped fingernails, which Ben could only take as a good sign. "I thought he had sort of an Oklahoma accent."

Ben wasn't giving any ground. "And what exactly would that be? Like how I talk?"

"Well . . . I don't really hear it in your voice."

"Why not? I've lived in Oklahoma almost my entire life." Of course, he was educated at a private school in a big city, but for that matter so was Todd Glancy.

"No, it was more like the senator talks. Kinda slow and . . . you know. Drawn out. Lots of extra syllables."

"Give me an example."

Shandy glanced toward Padolino, obviously hoping he could bail her out, but there was nothing he could do. "Well . . . like when he said 'forever.' It was more like he was saying, 'Fuhr-eve-uhhhh.'"

"And that's supposed to be Oklahoma? It sounds more like *Gone With the Wind*."

"Your honor," Padolino said. "He's badgering this poor girl."

Herndon shook his head. "They don't call it cross-examination because it's supposed to be fun. You may continue, Mr. Kincaid."

"It would be fair to assume that anyone engaged in an intimate encounter might speak slowly and dramatically, don't you think?"

"Well . . ."

"And you said you could barely hear the voices. The fact is, you couldn't positively identify either of the two people involved. Not then and not now."

"But I'm sure it was Senator Glancy and that poor girl. Why do you think I followed him in the first place?"

"Good question. Why did you?"

"Because I knew Veronica Cooper was in the building."

Now Ben was confused. "I thought you said—"

"I said Senator Glancy told me she hadn't come in that day. But he was lying. I'd asked the front desk clerk about her when I entered the building and he told me she was there. Well, that's no surprise— we all know she was there now. But why would Senator Glancy lie about it? Unless maybe he was planning to meet her in secret."

"Move to strike," Ben said. "Supposition without foundation."

Herndon inhaled heavily, then said, "Sustained." Which was surely his way of saying that although Ben was technically correct, he couldn't see that it made much difference.

"You use the word *lie* in pretty cavalier fashion, ma'am. Is it possible that Senator Glancy didn't know she was in the building? That she didn't report in to his office?" That was what Glancy had told Ben.

"Then why would she come?" Shandy asked, exasperated. "She couldn't work for him if he didn't know she was there." Her voice dropped a notch. "And she couldn't blackmail him or have sex with him, either."

"Your honor!" Ben protested, but the judge was already on it.

"Miss Craig, you know what is and is not permitted on the witness stand. You will confine your testimony to what you have seen and heard."

"Yes, your honor."

"I won't tolerate any more such remarks, particularly not with testimony of this importance. Do that again and I'll have you removed from the courtroom."

"Yes, your honor. Sorry."

Herndon leaned back, obviously still angry. But there wasn't much he could do to such a contrite witness. "The jury will disregard the witness's last statement. You may proceed, Mr. Kincaid."

Ben tried to salvage what little he could. "You keep saying you 'followed' Senator Glancy. But that isn't really accurate, is it?"

"I don't understand."

"Well, you said yourself that you didn't see him leave. You only guessed what door he exited through. You can't 'follow' someone if you don't actually know where they are."

"I thought I knew. And I proved I was right when I found him."

"Found *someone*," Ben insisted, but even to himself he was sounding increasingly desperate. "All you can say for sure is that Senator Glancy left and you found someone in his hideaway. If he in fact just went to the men's room, you weren't *following* anyone, right? You *discovered* someone."

"I don't think that's what happened," she said sullenly.

Ben decided to let it drop. He'd made his point, and she was never going to agree with him. "Miss Craig, why didn't you say anything about this when it happened?"

"I did."

Ben did a double take. "Miss Craig, I've probably seen you almost every day for the last five months, and you never once—"

"I'm not talking about you. Why would I tell you? You work for—" She looked at Senator Glancy with such contempt it was palpable. "—him. I went to the police."

Ben turned slowly toward Padolino. "You told the police all this? Months ago?"

"Yes," she said.

"But you continued to work for Senator Glancy."

"They asked me to. Just in case I might see or hear something incriminating."

"You were—you—" He looked back at Christina, searching for help. He'd never encountered anything like this in his entire career. "You were an undercover mole in the senator's office?"

"If you want to put it that way."

Ben looked at her harshly. "Miss Craig, did the police—or anyone in the prosecutor's office—instruct you to withhold what you knew from me?"

"Absolutely not. They said I didn't have to volunteer anything. But they told me that if you asked, I had to tell what I knew." She paused, her eyebrows rising. "As it turned out, you never asked. Neither you nor your partner nor any other member of the defense team asked if I knew anything about Senator Glancy's relationship with Veronica Cooper."

And why would we? Shandy had just started work the day of the murder. Padolino had calculated this perfectly.

"For that matter," Shandy continued, "I was told not to eavesdrop on any conversations between Senator Glancy and his lawyers, and that if I did by chance overhear any communications between them, I was not to repeat the information to the police."

So Padolino had covered his ass perfectly. Small wonder he always knew what Ben was doing, that he never made any decent plea offers. He had a mole in Glancy's camp the whole time.

"Let me ask you one more thing, Miss Craig. Do you have a conscience?"

Padolino rose. "Your honor, please."

Shandy held up her hands. "No, let me answer that. I don't mind. Mr. Kincaid, helping the police capture a murderer does not in any way offend my conscience."

"Move to strike," Ben shot back. "You don't know—"

"Sure, I've had to pretend to be Senator Glancy's friend. I've had to put up with him staring at my boobs when he thinks I'm not looking, dropping things on the floor and asking me to pick them up, asking me to adjust his tie so he can press up against me, finding accidental excuses to paw me one place or another. But I put up with it—waiting for this moment. The moment when I could help put away the man who killed Veronica Cooper."

There was more cross-examination after that, more redirect, lots of shouting, many arguments before the judge, and several carefully drafted instructions to the jury on exactly what they could and could not consider as evidence. Ben filed a motion to suppress based on the prosecution's withholding of information, but given that he'd had complete access to Shandy during the pretrial period—more than Padolino, in fact—he knew it wouldn't fly. In the end, none of it mattered, because the true bellwether of a trial was written on the faces of the jurors—and when he looked into their eyes he could see exactly what they thought. They thought Todd Glancy was a murderer, and they were ready and willing to give him the punishment he deserved. Barring an unforeseen miracle, this case was over and Glancy was going to death row.

"You don't understand. I have to talk to her!"

Loving and Daily stood outside the Bethesda ICU, as they had been for the last twenty minutes, arguing with Dr. Aljuwani.

"I understand your pain," the doctor answered, "but I believe it is you who does not understand the situation."

"You said she was awake."

"Her eyes are open, yes, and she is stable. But she has not spoken or in any way indicated that she is aware of her surroundings. She is breathing through a respirator. She cannot talk and you cannot talk to her. She would not understand what you were saying."

"I don't care about that. I just—" His voice choked. Tears began to form in his eyes. "Please. I need to see my little girl. Just—just to know that she's safe. I've been looking for her, waiting for this, wanting it, for so long. *Please.*"

Aljuwani blew out his cheeks. "You will not attempt to question her? Not even talk to her?"

"No. Not if you say I shouldn't."

The doctor was obviously conflicted. But Loving could also see a great deal of kindness and sympathy in his eyes. "Very well. But only for five minutes. And only you. I will not have a crowd in there."

"Understood." Daily turned to Loving. "See you in five?"

"I'll be here. Give Amber my best."

Daily entered the private room in the ICU alone, as the doctor had instructed. No one else was present, not even an attending nurse.

"Amber?"

Her eyes were open, as the doctor had said, but there was no light in them, no indication that she heard him.

"Amber?" he repeated, but still there was no sign of recognition, no indication of consciousness.

He walked to the side of her bed. "Good." He switched off the respirator unit, then removed the plastic cup from her mouth. Almost immediately, her breathing became strained, irregular. Her body heaved. She gasped for air.

"And just in case that isn't fast enough . . ."

He pulled the pillow out from under her head and shoved it down on her face. She began to convulse, to thrash back and forth on the bed. Her arms flailed and grasped at the air, as if some subconscious spirit was struggling to get free. But he held the pillow down tight. And less than a minute later, the thrashing stopped. The heart monitor flatlined.

"Guess you weren't immortal after all," he said, smiling to himself. He put the pillow back where it had been under her head, then started quietly for the door. "Farewell, my princess of the night. Sweet dreams."

Part Three

Stupid
Lasts
Forever

18

She did not know how long she had been lying on the uncovered mattress in this immense room, nothing to cover herself but the soiled damp sheet that clung to her naked flesh. She had no sense of time or space, perhaps because of the drugs, perhaps because the extended separation from the outside world, from the normal diurnal cycles of day and night, had so thoroughly eliminated her sense of time and place.

She knew she was no longer in the chapel. This room had no rose window, no windows at all, no source of light but the glaring fluorescent bulbs that hung directly overhead. Her face and hair were sticky with blood. The pattern had repeated itself over and over again—the bright lights, the sharp pain, the electric current rippling through her body, the physical punishment, the moments of calm interrupted by more agonizing pain. The draining. And the questions, the never-ending questions. She had told them everything she knew but they acted as if they did not believe her, as if she might actually lie to them. For what? For Colleen? She was beyond help. For Veronica? She, too, was long gone. And she had no idea where Amber was, or even if she was still alive. There was nothing she could tell them. And yet, the needle remained in her arm and the relentless questioning went on and on and on . . .

Her vision was a turbid fog, just like her brain, and since they all wore identical robes, she couldn't be sure who it was when the door opened. The sound of his voice told her—it was the Sire. He stood beside the bed upon which she lay. She gazed at his long hair, his thin blood-red lips and the phlegmatic expression she had come to interpret as a smile of pleasure.

"I must know everything," he said simply.

"I've told you everything."

"What you have told me is useless."

"I don't know anything about Amber."

"Never mind that. I found Amber on my own."

"Is she here?"

"No. I couldn't get her away. There were too many people around. I had to simply . . . eliminate the threat."

"What does that mean?"

"What I need to know now is who else you have spoken to. Friends? Family? Your sister? My minions tell me she's in town. Looking for you. What did you tell her, Beatrice?"

"Nothing. I promise you. Nothing!"

He leaned closer, letting her feel his heat, his breath, his intoxicating scent. Despite herself, she was aroused beyond anything she had ever imagined in her life; her need was so intense she would do anything.

"I can give you so much," he said, whispering into her ear. "Make you feel like you've never felt before."

"Oh please. Oh please yes please." She squirmed on the table, her legs thrashing, her hips grinding. "Please. Give it to me. Give it to me!"

"Only when there are no more secrets. When there is nothing between us."

"There is nothing!" she screamed, and even though her arm was hooked to the IV, she jerked forward, teeth gnashing, biting at him. "Please! I burn, master. I burn!"

"And if I give you what you want, what will you give me, my darling?"

She jerked back and forth on the table, growling like a feral beast. "Punish me, master."

"Do you deserve to be punished?"

"I want to feel the hurt," she gasped. "I need the hurt."

"You must control yourself, my child."

"*Hurt me!*" she screamed, an earsplitting cry that reverberated through the room. All at once he reared back his hand and hit her, his knuckles smashing against her face. A trickle of blood flowed from the corner of her lips. She thrust her tongue out and licked it up, rubbing it across her lips, savoring the taste. "I need more, master." Her voice was low and guttural. "You know what I need."

"Very well." He leaned back, walking a finger across her barely covered chest, pinning her to the table not with his finger but with the intensity of his eyes. "I believe you are sincere. I will give you what you crave. Because you can still be of use to us. Soon we will perform the final rite of purification. And then, my dear—" He brushed the matted hair from her face. "—then we will have all of eternity before us."

19

"I still can't believe it," Glancy said, pounding his fist on the conference table. "As long as I've been in politics, I've never been played like that. I might have believed it from anyone else, but not Shandy. Not in a million years."

Ben tried to be sympathetic. "Just shows to go you. You can never really know a person."

"But I did know her, Ben. I did. I just didn't see this coming."

"Well, it's over now. We have to move on." They were seated around a conference table in Ben's borrowed law offices. After hours of being grilled by the police about the death of Amber Daily, Loving had dropped by to deliver an update, then left again to resume his investigation. Christina and Jones were present, though, as well as all the members—all the remaining members—of Glancy's staff. Amanda Burton was fielding phone calls from the press, Marshall Bressler was on his cell trying to minimize the political damage, and Hazel was keyboarding a flurry of documents, some legal, some political. "What was in that letter Shandy gave you, anyway? Before court was in session."

"The height of objurgation." Glancy flung it across the table. "Her letter of resignation."

"How decent of her," Christina said. "Saved you the trouble of firing her."

"And gave her an out in the event that she might be held in contempt of Congress for testifying against me," Glancy said. "Not that any charges are likely to be brought now. The press are treating her like some heroic whistle-blower, not like the b—" He glanced up and caught Christina's eye. "Okay, the unsavory person that she is. Amanda tells me that *60 Minutes* and *20/20* are engaged in a bidding war to get her on as a guest."

"I thought they weren't allowed to pay for interviews," Ben said.

"Oh, they won't pay her anything directly. They'll just . . . make a contribution to her elderly father's pension fund or something. Maybe they'll give her a free hour of prime-time TV to promote her new CD. That's how they got Michael Jackson." He snorted. "Next they'll be offering to pay for the film rights to her life. *Erin Brockovich,* Part Two. Except without the cleavage."

"Do you have anything we might use to impeach her testimony?" Ben inquired. He'd asked before, of course, but it never hurt to try again. "Judge Herndon knows Shandy took us by surprise. I think he'd let me call her back as part of the defense case, if we had a decent reason."

"I hardly know anything about the girl. Contrary to the picture painted by Mr. Padolino, I am not a serial sex addict. And it isn't because I'm such a pure soul—it's because I know you cannot keep a secret in this town. I strayed once—only once—and of course the whole damn world knows about that now."

"So Shandy—"

"I hired her in a rush the day this mess began. I never had a chance to socialize with her."

"You've said some very complimentary things about her since. Talked about how she was taking care of you. You're still saying you thought you knew her," Christina pointed out.

"After the murder. When she was spying on us. I thought she was trustworthy."

"And there was never anything . . . untoward?"

"When would I have had a chance? Yes, I do tend to hire attractive interns. It's not because I want to sleep with them; it's because it's good politics. Even interns have a role, and a good intern can sometimes make the difference between a bill that passes and a bill that fails. We all are more persuaded by attractive people; it's just human nature. Hiring young pretties isn't sexist—it's smart."

"Glad you hadn't figured that out yet when I came on board," Marshall said, his hand covering his cell phone.

Glancy grinned. "And just for the record, I did not ask if she was wearing thong underwear. Why would I? I'm a senator, for God's sake. You make one remark like that and you're on the six o'clock news." He bristled. "I don't know what the big fuss is about those damn thongs, anyway. I never liked them. I much prefer—" He caught himself. "Well, never mind."

"What about the others?" Christina asked. "The other interns and job applicants who testified."

"Look, I'm not going to pretend I've never done a little flirting. I am a human being, and moreover, I'm a politician. If I can work a little charm on someone to get what I want, I will. There's nothing wrong with that."

"The incident with the zipper—"

"Didn't happen. If my fly was open, which I doubt, it was an unfortunate accident, and I certainly didn't do it for that woman's benefit. Ask yourself this: if all these incidents are true, why didn't anyone say anything about it at the time? We've got a Senate watchdog oversight committee, an Ethics Committee, and a hound-dog press. Any one of them would love to get their hands on a story like that. Plus it would guarantee the tattletale tubs of TV time and probably a job. Why would they remain silent?" He balled his fists and pressed them together. "This is just like what they did to Clarence Thomas. Not that he's any great gem. But how is it all those women who were sexually harassed never said a word about it—until he was appearing on televised hearings?"

"So you think she's lying about you just out of spite?"

"Spite? Hell, I think she's on the payroll. It's Paula Jones time, all over again. Give me enough money and I'll say anything."

"And who would want to bankroll Shandy's lies?"

"Anyone who doesn't want to see me on a national Democratic ticket. And believe me, there are a lot of them."

"A right-wing conspiracy?" Christina said, arching an eyebrow.

He grimaced. "Count on Hillary to express something real in a way that makes it sound like a paranoid fantasy. I'm not talking about some secret society. I'm talking about rich Republicans, period. Even though there are more registered Democrats in this country than Republicans, the Republicans typically fund-raise more than three times as much money for national elections—and produce twice as many attack ads."

"What about the Delia Collins incident?" Christina asked. "The one Representative MacReady told the jury about?"

"Never happened. I remember that woman—I met with her on several occasions. But I did not have sex with her. Not under anyone's definition of the word."

Christina stared at him, trying not to appear dubious. "You're sure about that."

He stared right back at her. "Believe me, Ms. McCall—if that woman had given me head on the floor of my office, I'd remember."

"But you didn't vote for the bill she wanted passed."

"There never was any vote. I killed it in committee. Didn't want to. I hate it when insurance companies play games to avoid giving treatment to people who need it. I would've loved to have helped that woman. But I have too many insurance companies making large contributions to my campaign coffers. There aren't that many big businesses in my district, and most of them predictably support the Republicans. I can't afford to alienate the insurance money. Sorry to be blunt about it, but that's just the way it was."

"And Delia Collins couldn't change your mind?"

Glancy looked across the room at his administrative assistant, who was still whipping people into line over his cell phone. "Marshall Bressler couldn't change my mind, and I'd do almost anything on earth for that man. He lobbied hard to get me to change my position. When he went through his auto accident, his insurance company didn't pony up for half of the therapy he received, which they deemed either 'optional' or 'nonmedical.' If I hadn't bankrolled his recovery, he might not have made it. So he was naturally sympathetic to this insurance reform bill. He'd mapped out an entire campaign detailing how we'd drum up enough popular support to replace the insurance money. 'Let Delia Live' was going to be the operation slogan. But it was just too risky. I couldn't do it." His head lowered, and when his voice returned, several moments later, it was considerably quieter than before. "I was greatly saddened a few months later to read that Delia Collins had died."

"Well," Ben said, trying to be consoling, "to be fair, most experimental or untested therapies don't turn out to be worth much. Desperate people turn to desperate remedies."

"I know. But still."

Amanda Burton slammed down her phone. "Look, Kincaid, I've been trying to go easy on you, now that I know how sensitive you are and how easily intimidated you are by any woman with balls, but you've got to give me something."

Ben blinked several times. "Could you . . . be more specific?"

"I need something to tell the press. They keep asking me for our take on the Shifty Shandy testimony. Who are we calling to launch our defense? What's our story? They want to know. And I can't give them satisfactory answers, because I don't have any! I can't tell them our story when I have no idea what it is!" She hunched across the table, poised on her fingertips, her blouse gaping. "I'm good, Todd. You know I am. But I can't spin air!"

Ben tried to remain calm. "Tell them we have no comment at this time."

"We might as well confess! The East Coast evening news cycle will start in twenty minutes. I can guarantee they'll have more coverage of the Gospel According to Shandy. We need something to counter that."

"As soon as we've made up our minds—"

"It will be too late!" She glared at her boss. "I'm not kidding here. If this goes unrefuted in the press, your career is over. I don't care if you're totally exonerated. I don't care if the Pope himself declares you his next saint. Your career in politics will be extinguished."

"Thank you for your concern," Glancy said calmly. "I'm not sure, but I think everyone at the table understands your position."

She turned toward Ben. "We've been paying that investigator of yours a fortune. What has he got for us?"

Ben coughed into his hand. "Well, none of this is verified as yet, but he believes that Veronica Cooper may have been involved with . . . um . . . how to say it? Involved with some occult figures."

"Occult figures?" She was practically screaming. "What, like Casper the Friendly Ghost?"

Ben carefully scrutinized the grain of the tabletop. "No. More like . . . vampires."

Amanda pressed the heel of her hand against the bridge of her nose. "You're telling me Veronica Cooper was a vampire?"

"Of course we don't mean to say that she really was a vampire," Ben quickly added, hoping this sounded better to her than it did to him. "Just that she thought she was a vampire. Or . . . wanted to be a vampire. Or . . . something like that."

"Loving is still working on it," Christina added. "But one of Veronica's friends—whom we believe was also involved in this group—has turned up dead. Strangled in her hospital bed."

Amanda swore. "Fat lot of help she's going to be."

"The point is," Ben said emphatically, "if someone felt the need to kill her, Loving must be onto something."

"Yeah, he's onto a bunch of crackpots. How do we know it has anything to do with this case? Listen to me, Kincaid—if you go into the courtroom with this vampire crap, they'll laugh you all the way back to Oklahoma."

"You're out of line, Amanda," Christina interjected. "Whether you appreciate it or not, Ben is handling this defense very well. Brilliantly, I'd say."

"Look, Goldilocks, you may think your partner walks on water, but he'll never be able to sell this vampire crock to a DC jury."

"We weren't planning to lead with the vampire crock. I mean—"

"What else have you got?"

"Well, numerous compurgators . . ."

"Character witnesses? You can't lead with toady testimony!"

"We weren't planning to lead with toad—I mean—"

"Then what were you planning to lead with?"

Christina cleared her throat. "Well, to tell you the truth, we haven't decided."

"What?" She clenched her fists again. "Todd, I begged you to hire DC counsel. I *begged* you."

"Even if you had, they'd be telling you the same thing, if they had any sense." Christina's cheeks were flushing. "You should just tell the press 'no comment,' whether they like it or not. And let us get on with our work."

"I know what you're thinking, sweet cheeks," Amanda said, drawing up to her full and considerable height. "I know what you're all thinking. Amanda's just a PR flak. A petty annoyance. Nothing to do with this case. But let me tell you something. I've got my finger on the pulse of the people. People just like the sixteen sequestered souls on your jury. If you don't start listening to me—and if you don't come up with something better than anything I've heard in here today—Senator Todd Glancy of Oklahoma is going to be convicted of murder in the first degree. That's not a prediction. It's a guarantee."

"What the hell did you think you were doing!"

Lieutenant Albertson threw himself down into his desk chair. His office was not large, and with both Dr. Aljuwani and Loving's considerable bulk in there, they were pressed close enough together to feel each other's breath.

"He told me he was the girl's father," Dr. Aljuwani explained.

"Told me the same thing," Loving said. "Even showed me his ID."

Albertson tossed his hands up in the air. "Well let me give you a news flash. Three days ago, a DC traffic cop found a '97 Jaguar coupe registered to Robert Daily on the side of I-349. It appeared to have been abandoned. Upon inspection, he found Robert Daily stuffed in the trunk. He'd been shot three times in the heart."

"Jeez Louise." Loving ran his fingers through his hair. "That's how the creep got Daily's wallet."

"It gets worse. He appears to have been tortured—extensively—before he was killed."

"The killer must've been trying to get information about Amber's whereabouts," Loving reasoned. "When he couldn't get what he wanted from Daily, he killed him, stole his wallet, and masqueraded as his victim."

"Given what forensics is telling me, he must've run into you only an hour or so after he finished killing Daily."

Loving pounded his forehead. "I saw blood on his shirt. But he told me he'd scraped himself when he clocked me in the alley."

"And you believed him?"

"I had no reason not to!" Loving rose out of his chair, frustrated by his own stupidity. "He was totally convincing. His eyes teared up every time he talked about Amber." He paused, lowering himself back into his seat. "And I led him straight to her. Even left him alone with the poor girl." Loving pounded his fist into his hand. "Damn! What an idiot I've been."

"You'll get no argument from me."

"He could not have known," Dr. Aljuwani said. "I, too, was convinced that this man was a despondent, loving father."

"That doesn't cut it with me," Albertson shot back. "You're an experienced private investigator, Loving. You should know better. Give me one reason I shouldn't yank your license or charge you with aiding and abetting a homicide."

Loving's broad, square jaw was firmly set. "Because I'm going to find that man for you."

"How are you going to do that? You know where he is?"

"No. But I know what he wants." Loving's focus seemed to turn inward, his forehead creased by determination. "Now that Amber is gone, there's only one thing he could want. The same thing I want. The last surviving member of the Goth Girls Party of Four. Beatrice." He paused. "If he doesn't have her already."

A few minutes later, the temperature in the conference room had fallen, because most of the players had left. Only Ben and Glancy remained, not counting the federal marshals outside.

Ben checked his watch. "You're sure Marie understands I meant tonight?"

Glancy appeared calm and worry-free. "If Marie says she'll be here, she'll be here. She's very dependable." He smiled a little. "But she's not opposed to making people wait a little. Just to remind them how much they need her. Women." He shook his head. "Speaking of which."

Ben looked up from the directed verdict motion he was revising. "What?"

"Why didn't you stick up for Christina?"

Ben's head tilted an inch to the side. "What are you talking about?"

"Just now. When Amanda lit into her."

Ben waved a hand in the air. "Christina can take care of herself."

"I'm sure she can. But she shouldn't have to."

"I . . . don't get you."

"You're the senior partner in the firm, right? You should protect your associates."

"From our clients?"

"Amanda is not your client, and the fact that she works for me hasn't once stopped you from telling her where she can get off."

"I'm not the smothering kind of boss. I'm not even really the boss."

"But there's more to it than that, Ben. Everyone here knows that you and Christina are involved."

"You do?"

"We do. And moreover, I have to tell you there's a general feeling that . . . well, that you're not doing right by her."

"What is that supposed to mean?"

Glancy kicked his legs up on the table. "Well, as I understand it, Ben, Christina has faithfully put up with your other girlfriends, each of them chosen with immense stupidity, a former fiancée who put you off romance for something like a decade, as well as a host of other neuroses and commitment issues."

Ben raised his hands. "Where are you getting all this?"

"I'm a senator, Ben. I have sources. And I'm telling you, just because we're old friends, that it's time you took the next step. Have you asked her to move in with you?"

Ben fidgeted with his legal pad. "Are you crazy? Do you know how small my place is?"

"Not as small as Christina's, I'll wager."

"My mother would never approve."

"When did you ever do anything your mother wanted? Besides, Christina told me she gets on with your mom very well. Better than you do, actually."

"Plus I'm a lousy conversationalist, a poor cook, I work all the time, I'm messy, and . . . and . . . my cats would be insanely jealous."

"Uh-huh." He gave Ben a long look. "You're afraid she might say no, aren't you?"

Ben fell quiet for a moment. "Not really. Actually, she's suggested it several times. I mean, not in so many words, but—"

"Then for God's sake, man, what are you waiting for?"

Ben fell silent.

"Are you afraid it might damage your working relationship?"

"There's nothing I could do that's worse than the stuff she's already put up with."

"Then what is it?"

Ben didn't answer him. He couldn't. He didn't have an answer to give. "There's no rush."

"You don't know that. Hell, look at me. One day I'm being touted as a potential presidential candidate, the next I'm practically on death row. None of us knows what the future holds, or how much future we'll have. But I know this—you and Christina are a good match. And you're both well into your thirties. She's been very patient with you, Ben. But if you mess around much longer, you could lose her."

Ben's shoulders sagged. "I couldn't work if Christina left. I couldn't function without her."

"Have you told her that?"

"Told her what?"

"What you just said. Your somewhat neurotic way of admitting that you love her."

"Have I—?" He stared at Glancy, wide-eyed. "Of course not. That would be . . . that would be . . ."

"Honest?"

Ben wrung his hands. "No. It would be . . . it's just too . . . I don't know. I'm not ready."

Glancy looked at Ben for a long time, then sighed. "Well, I hope you get over that, Ben. I truly do. And soon. Because Christina is a wonderful woman, and very devoted to you. But she's ready to move forward. And if you're not—" He shook his head sadly. "She's going to move on without you."

*   *   *

"Thank you for coming," Ben said as he pulled out a chair at the conference table for Marie Glancy. "I know how stressful this trial has been for you."

"Do you? I wonder if that's possible." Ben thought he detected a grain of sadness in her eyes, but as always she was perfectly coiffed and attired, her makeup unsmudged. "But I'm ready to do whatever you ask. Where is Todd, anyway?"

"I asked him to step out. I wanted to talk to you alone."

"Why?" Her brow furrowed. "What could you possibly want to say to me that Todd can't hear?"

"I'm not saying he can't hear it. He'll learn soon enough. But it doesn't have to be now."

Ben saw her back stiffen, observed the hard lines creasing her face. "Marie, I know your husband has been unfaithful to you."

Her chin lowered. "Am I supposed to act shocked? I knew about the Cooper affair long before that video broke."

"But then why, in the courtroom—"

"Did I put on the big teary-eyed dog-and-pony show? Because that's what people expect, Ben. They want to be entertained. They want drama."

"But racing out of the courtroom—"

"Do you think I overdid it?"

"I didn't think you were 'doing it' at all. Christina told me how she had to fight to get you back into the courtroom. Why would you want—"

"My people did extensive polling on the subject and everyone concurred that this was the best way to go."

"So it was all an act? A performance?"

"Ben, my husband may be the senator, but I'm not exactly a silent partner. I visit the Russell Senate Building every day, even when Todd isn't there. I know what's going on. People talk to me. I have access. I knew about the hideaway, the underground tunnel system. I've got keys to every room in the building. I'm there so often the security guards sometimes don't even bother to pat me down. Probably afraid I'll slap them with some sort of harassment suit." She paused. "What I'm trying to say is, my husband couldn't have an affair without my knowing. My husband couldn't pluck a nose hair without my knowing. So this great revelation was not exactly news to me."

"What might be news," Ben said quietly, "is that I know you've hired a private detective to follow your husband around. That you were having Todd tailed for something like six months before the murder."

Marie settled back into her seat, her hands folded. "I had my reasons."

"Planning a divorce?"

She removed her glasses and rubbed the bridge of her nose. Ben had noticed that she never wore the specs in court or at social functions, but always wore them at press conferences, interviews, or anywhere else she wanted to appear smart. A prop? he wondered. Or a distancing mechanism? "I have no intention of divorcing Todd."

"Forgive and forget?"

Her lips thinned. "Divorce is not an option. It would destroy both—" She checked herself. "It wouldn't be prudent."

"Then why the detective?"

She peered at Ben with an expression he thought she must've practiced on *Meet the Press*. "I would think that was perfectly obvious. I don't like surprises."

"You must've suspected something was going on or you wouldn't have hired the man in the first place."

"Suspecting is one thing. Knowing is quite another. Having details is useful. Having photographs is even better."

"But why go to the trouble of gathering information if you don't intend to use it?"

"Isn't it obvious?" She snapped the glasses back on with the heel of her hand. "I didn't want to be perceived as some pathetic Hillary Clinton clone. 'I was misinformed.' Give me a break. If my husband decides to adopt a new cuddle-bunny, I want to know everything about it. I want to be ready when the news breaks. I want to be positioned."

"Positioned?"

"Ready to deal. Ready to spin. Ready with my well-calculated coping strategy. These things can't be concocted overnight, you know. It requires thought, planning. Polling. Brainstorming with consultants."

Ben stared at her, uncomprehending. Or to be more accurate, he comprehended every word. He just couldn't believe it. It was too strange, too foreign to his usual reasons for dealing with a client's spouse. The woman wasn't concerned that her husband was having an affair. She wasn't even concerned about what it might do to his career. She was concerned about the possible ramifications on her public image.

"You have your own political ambitions."

"People always say that because I won't act like the typical token congressional Stepford spouse who lives only to serve her master's political career. They want me to be Malibu Marie. Why should I? Why shouldn't I think about myself? Women are allowed to be more than just a subservient spouse in almost every other field. When are politics going to catch up to the rest of the world?"

"Here's the thing," Ben said. "I want access to your detective's records. Files, photos, movies. Whatever he's got."

"Are you kidding? I can assure you there's nothing there that will make Todd look better to a jury."

"Right now, there's nothing short of bestiality photos that could make him look worse to the jury. I want to know what your man dug up on Veronica Cooper."

"What makes you think he has anything?"

"He was on Todd for months. I'm betting he spent some time digging into Veronica's background, her lifestyle, her recreational activities."

"So that's your defense strategy. You're going to put the victim on trial."

Ben squirmed. "It's a possibility."

"Do you think that could work? I mean—good or evil, the woman was still murdered."

"In the eyes of the law, you're correct. But in the eyes of a jury, who the victim was can make a huge difference. Up till now, the press has played her as a poor innocent, a naïve waif who went to Washington to serve her country and ended up being abused and debased by a depraved senator—despite a video that to me shows her to be anything but naïve and innocent. We need to turn that around.

Loving tells me she was into some really weird stuff, and I've got at least one witness at an escort service who can give the jury some insight on Ms. Cooper's secret life. But I need more. I'm hoping your detective can give that to me. If he does, it will do a lot more than tarnish the victim's image. If we can prove she was all wrapped up with some bizarre vampire cult—"

"Reasonable doubt," Marie whispered.

"Exactly. Parade in a coven of vampires, and suddenly the list of possible suspects gets a lot longer. Everyone has been assuming Todd was guilty because of the video, where the body was found, and because there were no other likely suspects. But if we can show she was involved with all sorts of dangerous characters—"

"That's brilliant," she said, slowly nodding her head. "I mean, it's evil. Bogus. Lies and calumny." She smiled. "But brilliant. I'm finally beginning to see why Todd hired you."

"We aim to please."

She laid her hand on Ben's wrist. "You're an experienced trial attorney, Ben. Tell me the truth. Are you going to get my husband off?"

"It's impossible to say," he replied, trying to resist his instinctive impulse to brush her hand away. "We haven't put on our case. Juries are unpredictable. The evidence is massively stacked against Todd." He paused. "But I think we have a shot. A small shot, perhaps. But a shot."

She removed her hand. "That's good to know."

"Now, I don't mean to give you false hope."

"It's not about hope," she said, pushing herself out of the chair. "It's about intel. I like to know what the contingencies are. So I can lay my plans accordingly."

Loving and Shalimar stayed hidden in the shadows of an alley off one of the seediest streets in Georgetown, staring at a tall brownstone building across the darkened street.

"That's the Playground?" Shalimar whispered.

"So my sources tell me."

"The whole building?"

"Probably not. Someone's private suite, I bet. Somewhere they can restrict access."

"Then how are we going to get in?"

"I'm workin' on it." Loving had spent the entire day turning over every slimy rock in the city to get a lead on the place.

"I can't believe my sister would be involved in—in anything like this."

"Why? She hung out with vampires."

"But I never—" She stopped short, biting a knuckle. "I imagined—pretended, perhaps—that she'd been taken against her will. Like white slavers or something. But from what you told me, she did it all by choice. She did it for fun."

"Maybe up to a point," Loving said. "But I've got a hunch her power of choice was removed. Otherwise you woulda heard from her." He slowly pulled out of the shadows. "C'mon, Slayer. Let's go find your sister."

They crossed the street and approached the front door of the building. The front door was locked. Just to the right, he saw an intercom speaker. He pushed the button.

"Yes?" the electronic voice crackled.

"Umm . . . could you please open the door?"

"Are you a resident?"

"No. Visitor."

"And who are you visiting?"

Loving looked at Shalimar. She shrugged. He tried, "The Playground."

"Just a moment. I'll transfer you." As if he had asked for nothing out of the ordinary.

A few moments later, the speaker crackled to life again. The voice was different. "Yes?"

"We're here for the Playground," Loving said.

"Do you have an appointment?"

"No, we're—" Looking for someone? Loving thought better of it. "New. This is our first time."

"Are you cops? Or in any way associated with the law enforcement community?"

"Nah. We're just . . . you know. Here for a good time. Into it." Whatever *it* was.

"I'm sorry. I can't let you in without an appointment or a referral. We have to enforce our rules to ensure—"

"The Sire sent us," Loving said. And waited.

The air went dead for several seconds. Then: "Stand back, I'll release the door." He heard a sound something like the turning of an idled engine, then a few seconds later the dead bolt in the door retracted. "Come up to the top floor. The penthouse."

"Will do." He grabbed Shalimar's arm and whispered: "We're in!"

She did not move. "I don't know about this."

"Don't be afraid," Loving said, patting her arm reassuringly. "We'll be together. Besides, whatever it is, it couldn't possibly be worse than that vampire club."

As it turned out, Loving was dead wrong.

20

"Glad to know they still care," Glancy said as he gazed out the limo window at the crowd outside. The courthouse steps were filled to capacity, and the security forces were working overtime to hold the throngs behind the ropes.

"Like you thought they'd forget about this case?" Ben asked.

"You never know," Glancy replied, smoothing the line of his trousers. "If a governor had been caught in the back of a cab with a transvestite last night, no one would remember this case existed."

Ben knew the press could be fickle—he'd seen for himself how press coverage of a case would surge with a dramatic inciting incident, then predictably wane as time passed, spurting briefly when the trial began, then continuing its downward spiral. By the time it was over, sometimes the verdict didn't even make the papers. But this case was something else again. Just looking into the eyes of the people on the courthouse steps informed him that this case was important to them, that it had become a part of their lives.

"This is the big day, at least to many spectators," Ben said. "After all, they already pretty much knew what Padolino was going to say. They've got no clue what you're going to say. They're anxious to hear your story."

"I thought you told me I wasn't taking the stand today."

"They don't know that. Press conference this morning?"

"I don't think so."

"The press is dying to know what your defense will be."

"Yes, but I'm not sure I'm quite ready to say the 'v-word' on national television. I need to practice in the mirror. Make sure I can keep a straight face."

As before, the advance men had worked their magic—all the people most supportive of Senator Glancy were closest to the roped-off trail up the steps. Ben tried to hurry his client, but it was like dragging an elephant. He was an addict, powerless to prevent himself from shaking every outstretched hand, signing every autograph book.

"We know what they're tryin' to do to you," a plus-sized Latino woman said, as she flung her arm around Glancy, hugging him so tightly it made the federal marshals tense. "You hang in there."

"That's my fervent intent, ma'am," Glancy said, flashing that award-winning smile.

He flew up the steps, brushing his hands against theirs like Leno coming onstage for *The Tonight Show,* till he had almost reached the top of the steps. A middle-aged man in a flak jacket ducked under the rope and stood in front of him.

"You killed my daughter, you bloodsucker!" Darrin Cooper flew at Glancy and Ben with a wild walleyed look, but he never had a chance. One of the security cops and both federal marshals tackled him, knocking him to the hard stone steps. His jaw made an ugly brittle sound as it smashed onto the granite. Ben suspected Cooper was going to lose a few teeth over this attack.

"Ben, I think you need to reconsider." Christina was behind him, whispering in his ear. "I understand why you didn't want to prefer charges before. But neither you nor Glancy will be safe if this clown isn't locked up. I mean, I know he seems pathetic, but even a pathetic loser could get lucky. Especially if he starts employing weapons."

Ben nodded, but he knew he couldn't do it. Neither Glancy nor his lawyer could be responsible for incarcerating the victim's father, regardless of the situation. The PR fallout would be brutal.

The officials hauled Cooper to his feet and dragged him up the steps to a holding room. Glancy was unflappable; he went right on smiling and waving as if nothing had happened.

"Interesting choice of words, don't you think?" Ben said.

Christina was puzzled. "I don't follow you."

"Cooper. Just now. Cooper always calls me a money-grubbing bastard, or some variation on the theme." He paused. "But Glancy he called a 'bloodsucker.'"

As soon as the woman opened the door to the penthouse apartment, Loving knew he was in the right place. And wished he weren't.

The first thing he noticed was that she was wearing a dog collar cinched around her neck. She was also wearing a tight leather corset that left most of her buttocks exposed. It was only upon closer—and extremely unpleasant—inspection that Loving realized that she was a he. A somewhat pudgy, heavily made up, he.

Vampire drag. Jeez Louise, what next?

"Would you like me to show you around?" he/she said, and of course Loving didn't, but he said that he did. "If you're with the Sire, I, and my humble establishment, are at your complete disposal. You can call me Mina." And so the tour began. Giggling, mincing, and occasionally attempting to be scary—which was even funnier than the mincing—their leather-clad tour guide strolled them through a maze of darkened rooms, some vacant, most not, all of them equipped with a different top-quality device for the infliction of pain.

"We do have some open rooms," Mina explained. "And remember if you have the desire—and the cash—you can rent this place for the night. Have an exclusive. Just you and your friends."

Loving was pretty sure he didn't have any friends who would want to come here. And if they did, they were off his friends list.

The people they encountered, in the halls and the darkened rooms, were clad much like what he had seen in the vamp club and the Goth bar, when they were clad at all. Too often he had to avert his eyes—and resist the temptation to cover Shalimar's—to avoid seeing something he didn't ever want to see people doing to one another. In one room equipped with a vaulting horse, which they were able to view through a voyeuristic one-way mirror, Loving heard smacking sounds followed by cries of ecstatic pleasure.

"Spanking," Loving whispered to Shalimar knowingly. "Some of these vamps are really into it."

But when their tour guide turned up the lights slightly, they were able to view a spectacle for which neither of them was prepared. A woman, obese and naked, was strapped across the horse. An equally heavy and equally naked man stood behind her teasing her with a cat-o'-nine-tails, whipping her lightly, tickling her legs and breasts and stomach. She moaned in pleasure with each new slap of the leather against her exposed jiggling skin. And, to make it even more interesting, there were at least half a dozen other people in the room, just watching.

In the next room, they found a young woman, this one slender, and as far as Loving could tell quite attractive. She was wearing only black lacy panties and was handcuffed, her hands hoisted above her head and fastened to what looked like a large meat hook suspended from the ceiling. The man standing in the rear was caning her, striking her again and again, all up and down the back of her legs, while she let loose high-pitched whimpers of erotic delight. She writhed back and forth, which did amazing things to her suspended body, titillating not only her and her master—but the audience of spectators as well.

"My sister is not here," Shalimar whispered. Loving noticed she was inhaling in deep quick gulps. "She would not have anything to do with this . . . disgusting place."

Loving put his arm around her and gave her a squeeze. He just hoped she was right. For once, he didn't want to find Beatrice. At least not here.

Ben had adjusted over the years to the fact that he was simply not, by anyone's definition, flashy. Not that he would mind. To the contrary, he thought being flashy sounded rather fun. It just wasn't

in him. So he'd learned to content himself with being thorough, prepared, and good. If he couldn't gain prosperity via flamboyance,
then at least he could gain notoriety by winning.

Nonetheless, he couldn't help but notice the contrast between
Padolino's announcement of his final prosecution witness, and his
own announcement of his first defense witness. The former had triggered gasping and astonishment; the latter was met by, well, nothing. An absence of reaction. Boredom. Ben consoled himself that it
wasn't a reflection on his style as a litigator; it was simply that no
one in the gallery knew who Sid Bartmann was.

That was about to change.

Interest in the witness increased, at least in the jury box, when
the Virginia state troopers walked Bartmann into the courtroom.
They removed his handcuffs but left the leg restraints chaining his
two legs together. He was wearing his prison grays, which informed
all the world that he was Prisoner XK-24637. His face was pale and
pocked; his hair, what little he had left, was unwashed.

"Jesus," Glancy muttered under his breath. "That's my lead witness? He looks like the scum of the earth."

"Yes," Ben replied quietly. "He does."

"Couldn't you have . . . I don't know. Dressed him up a little
bit? Loaned him a bar of soap?"

"Yes," Ben answered. "I could have."

Ben wasted no time establishing that Bartmann had several
prior offenses but that he had most recently been incarcerated during a raid (if you could call what Loving did a raid) on a club in
Georgetown called Stigmata. He was arrested for possession of an
illegal designer hallucinogen derived in part from OxyContin.

"You were a habitué—" Ben checked himself; what was he
thinking? "—you were at Stigmata a lot, correct?"

"Oh yeah. Almost every night. I worked for the owner, Randy
Lorenz."

"And do you know where Mr. Lorenz is at this time?"

"In lockup. Bail was denied."

"What exactly was your position at the club?"

"What, ya mean like my job title or somethin'? I don't think I
ever had one. I just did what the man told me. Randy snapped his
fingers, I come runnin'."

"And what was your rate of payment?"

"I don't think I had one of them, neither. Basically, whenever Randy got a wad of cash, he threw some of it my way. Fortunately, he got a wad of cash like every night."

"And that was because he was peddling a designer drug to a select group of women who were admitted to his apartment on the second level of the club above the dance floor, correct?"

Ben could see the man blinking, trying to understand. Must use short sentences and one- or two-syllable words, he reminded himself. "Randy had some chicks up to his place, yeah. Some of them were usin'. But the club itself was rakin' in dough. It was very popular with . . . you know. A certain crowd."

"And what crowd would that be?"

Bartmann coughed, a long grotesque grinding noise that sounded as if he were peeling off the lining of his lungs. "The Goth freaks."

"Interesting. So you and the other . . . freaks . . . were using this designer drug?"

"Hell, no. I couldn't afford the stuff. Rather have a tall cool one, myself."

"But you were arrested in possession—"

"Randy gave me the package and I held it for him. He was my boss. I did what I was told."

"Even holding on to illegal drugs."

"Hell, I woulda held on to illegal turds if he'd asked me." Judge Herndon glared at the witness but remained silent. "He was the man, you know? He took care of me and I took care of him. He was like the brother I never had."

The brother he never had. Ben was reminded of Aristophanes: youth ages, immaturity is outgrown, ignorance can be educated, drunkenness sobered—but stupid lasts forever. He removed a photograph from his trial notebook and held it up. "Mr. Bartmann, have you ever seen this woman before?"

Bartmann looked at the photo with an expression that was positively repulsive. "Oh, hell, yeah. That's Rapid Ronnie."

Ben cleared his throat. "Rapid Ronnie?"

"Yeah." He laughed so hard it became a sort of snort, a repetitive pig noise in the back of his throat. "She was fast. Fast like you've never seen fast."

Ben felt the inevitable red blotches creeping up his neck. "Sir, are you talking about Veronica Cooper being fast . . . sexually?"

Bartmann touched his nose. "Got it in one!"

"And . . . how do you know this?"

"From personal experience." He winked, and this was possibly even more grotesque than the lascivious expression that preceded it. "She was hot."

"Are you suggesting that you had . . . intimate relations with Ms. Cooper?"

"Damn straight."

"How many times?"

"More than you could count. When that girl wanted it, she wouldn't take no for an answer."

"And when would that be?"

"When she was high on the drug, mostly. Affects different people different ways. Her it made horny. Major horny. Upped her desire—and her pleasure. She couldn't control herself. It was all she could do to wait long enough to get my pants off."

"Did you have . . . someplace you went for these liaisons?"

"Nope. Right there in the apartment at the club. Most times everyone else was high and doing it, so we didn't attract much attention. They were too busy with their own action to notice us." He paused. "'Cept Randy. He liked to watch."

Ben tried to envision the orgy Bartmann was describing—and then decided he'd rather not. "Were you the only person with whom Ms. Cooper had sexual relations?"

"Hell no. She'd do anyone when she was high. All she cared was that you were breathing and male." He reflected a moment. "Come to think of it, some of the time she didn't even care if her partner was male."

"And I gather from the nickname that Miss Cooper tended to be . . . fast?"

"Like you wouldn't believe. A male fantasy come true. No jawboning about foreplay. No screwin' around waiting for her to get in the mood. She was always in the mood. Sometimes she got there before I did. She liked it fast and rough."

"Rough?" Ben said, coughing.

"Very. Violent, almost. Kicking and slapping and spanking and biting."

"Biting?"

"Oh yeah. That always turned her on. And not just some wimpy pecking, either—she wanted a good hard bite. The kind that mattered. I mean, when I pressed my teeth into her neck, she squealed like a pig."

Out the corner of his eye, Ben saw the jury scrutinizing the man, trying to decide if they thought it was remotely credible that the beautiful young intern Padolino had painted as a virtual nun could have sex with this walking waste dump. Verdict: no.

"Mr. Bartmann, when was the last time you had sexual relations with Miss Cooper?"

"The night before she was killed."

Almost as one, the jury members' chins lowered.

"Within twenty-four hours of the time of death?"

"Less than ten, from what I hear. She was killed like around ten in the morning, right?"

"Something like that."

He folded his arms across his chest, obviously proud of himself. "And I had her around midnight. So I'm saying it was ten hours."

"The coroner found evidence of sexual activity . . ."

Bartmann jabbed a thumb to his chest. "I'm your man."

Ben heard the rustling in the gallery, saw the jury shifting in their seats. He knew everyone was uncomfortable with this testimony, with the ugly and bizarre possibility that these allegations could be true. But there was something about the man—his brashness, his lack of shame, the impression that he lacked the smarts to exercise guile—that made his testimony strangely believable.

"And on the occasion of your last encounter, did you bite Ms. Cooper?"

He shrugged. "I don't really remember, but it seems likely. I mean, she loved that move. Once I sunk some teeth into her, she just got all—"

"Thank you, sir," Ben said, holding up his hands. "I think we get the idea." But he still had to convince the jury that this walking talking pond scum had been with Veronica Cooper. He reached into his notebook and produced two documents. "Mr. Bartmann, my apologies, but I'm going to ask you to look at some photographs that were taken of Ms. Cooper postmortem." He paused. "That means after she was dead."

"Do I have to?"

"I'm afraid so. Here's a photo of her right shoulder, the wound that killed her." As he held it up, the jury winced. "She was cut with a large knife, but there was also evidence of a smaller, more subtle incision to her jugular vein made by some other instrument. Like maybe a tooth."

"Objection," Padolino said. "He's just telling the man what he wants to hear. Leading."

"I only offered that by way of example," Ben said innocently.

"It's not like we don't all know where this is going," Judge Herndon said. "Overruled."

"I didn't do it," Bartmann said, cutting in before Ben could ask a question. "I would never hurt Veronica like that."

"I believe you." Ben held up the other photo. "This is an enlargement of a much less severe bite wound that was found on the victim's left shoulder. The bite mark was barely visible when the coroner examined the body; this photo was taken under ultraviolet light."

"Okay. So?"

"Mr. Bartmann . . ." Ben paused, trying to think how best to put this. "Say cheese."

"Huh?"

"I want you to smile. Smile for the jury."

Bartmann looked understandably confused, but after a moment's hesitation, he shrugged and replied, "Whatever you say, counselor." He turned to the jury and grinned.

All his center teeth were missing. Tops and bottoms. From the canines inward. Gone.

"Mr. Bartmann, how did you lose your teeth? Was there an accident?"

"No." He looked down at his hands. "Least not the way you mean. Happened the last time I was in the joint. Cedars. Rough as hell. On my first day. The cell-block boss had two of his goons hold me down while another one knocked out my teeth. With a hammer."

Ben heard a satisfying gasp from the gallery. "Were there no guards present?"

"Not present in the room. They were around. They knew what was happening."

"Then—"

"They had what you might call a special relationship with the cell-block boss. They stayed out of his way, within reason, and he took care of them. Arranged for gifts to be delivered to their homes, their families. Very nice gifts."

"But why would he want to knock out your front teeth?"

Bartmann looked back at Ben stonily. "That way, if someone shoves something in your mouth, you can't bite down on it."

Ben laid a hand on the podium, steadying himself. "Permission to publish the photo to the jury."

"It's already been entered into evidence," Judge Herndon said. "You may proceed."

Ben walked to the jury box and held it up so they could see the enlarged view of the deceased's left shoulder. Two things were immediately clear. The first was that it bore a bite mark. And the second was that this most unusual bite mark was missing its center teeth.

"Why's it always women gettin' the rough stuff in here?" Loving asked Mina.

"It isn't," their indifferently gendered guide explained. "Although that is more common. I've got a man tied up in the next room if you'd like to see—"

"No thanks," Loving said. "I get the picture. All your rooms have people beatin' on one another."

"Not necessarily. There are other forms of pleasure. We cater to all types here. We're a nonjudgmental, equal opportunity pleasure service. You can find people into suffocation, mutilation—"

"Wait a minute. Suffocation?"

"It's a well-known fact that near-death experiences heighten orgasm. Have you never heard of autoerotic asphyxiation? Not that it's the only way to get there. Some of our clients apply jumper cables to their nipples, so they can give themselves an added charge at just the right moment. Some wrap up their testicles with leather cords. Some—"

"I think I got the general idea," Loving said, cutting Mina off. "What about bloodsuckin'?"

"Ah. Some of my clients live for it. But there can be complications. Too much will make you sick. And even a little can—" Mina's voice dropped to a whisper. "—give you diarrhea. Like, all day long. I hear it's very erotic when taken to the extreme, or combined with sexual orgasm. But I guess you already know that."

"What?"

Mina brushed a finger against the left side of Loving's neck. "Looks like someone took a little nibble on you recently."

Loving moved his hand to his neck, covering the impression. "Blast. I meant to cover that up."

"Did you? You know what Freud said. There are no accidents." Mina smiled—leered, actually. "You liked it, didn't you?"

"No!" Loving glanced at Shalimar, whom he noticed was inching away. "I did not like it. Not a bit!"

"Right. That's why you're here tonight." Mina leaned close to Shalimar and whispered, "Deep denial."

Shalimar gave Loving a look he couldn't read.

"So." Mina fluttered obviously false eyelashes and eyed Loving mischievously. "See anything that interests you?"

"Uh, maybe. But I . . . I don't have my partner."

"This young lady seems perfectly suitable," Mina said, motioning toward Shalimar. "Or if you'd prefer something more exotic—"

"No, it has to be the right girl. Otherwise it just doesn't work for me. I need Beatrice."

"And who would that lucky lady be?"

"You don't know Beatrice?" Loving paused. "I thought everyone knew Beatrice."

"Haven't heard the name, but we don't use names much around here. For obvious reasons."

Loving showed Mina the picture Shalimar had given him, but it was no help.

"Is there anyone else I could talk to? Any membership lists I could review?"

"In our community?" Mina seemed appalled by the very suggestion. "I don't know of anyone who would—or would want to— keep those kinds of records. It isn't as if we take attendance. No one keeps track of who comes and who doesn't. Except maybe the Church."

Church? These people? "And that would be . . . ?"

"You know. Surely you've been."

Shalimar cleared her throat. "We're, uh, new here."

"But the Church is everywhere, all across the nation." Mina seemed flabbergasted. "Do you really not know? The Temple of the Vampire."

Loving shook his head. It just got weirder and weirder. "There's a church called the Temple of the Vampire?"

"Absolutely. It's a bona fide, national, federally registered church. Protected by the First Amendment. Tax exempt. But let's not talk about that now. You must've come here for a reason. What kind of pleasure suite can I arrange for you?"

"Nothin' just now," Loving said, guiding Shalimar away. He wondered if he could find his way out of this maze by himself. "I'm not in the mood for pleasure anymore. For some reason, I'm suddenly feelin' very religious."

21

"Your honor, the defense calls his wife, Marie Glancy, to the stand."

Now that was more like it, Ben thought, as he heard an appreciable murmur rising from the gallery and saw one of the reporters run to the back doors, crack them open, and wave for his fifth-estate buddies to come inside. Everyone knew who Marie Glancy was. And everyone, whether they believed her to be a tragic victim taken advantage of by a wayward husband or a shrewd politico with her own agenda, wanted to hear what she had to say.

Ben wasted as little time as possible on the introductory material. The jury already knew who she was, either liked her or didn't, and was well aware of her relevance to the case. He wondered how many minds in the courtroom were comparing the petite, somewhat plain figure in the witness stand to the video's lusty feral child in the lacy undergarments.

"How long have you and your husband been married?"

"Almost sixteen years now. We wed when we were in college. We were very much in love."

"And you went to law school—"

"At the University of Oklahoma." She glanced up at Ben. "As did several other distinguished members of the bar."

Ben had to hand it to her. She was doing a great job of staying cool, but not cold. Calm, but not unemotional. She was even allowing herself a little wry humor, though nothing that might seem sarcastic or flippant. She was dressed professionally but neither too richly nor too austerely. The woman knew her audience.

"And you graduated? Got your juris doctorate?"

"Yes. But I never practiced. Todd took over his father's oil business, then went to the DA's office, then onward and upward into politics."

"And you?"

"I was his wife. I did what was necessary to make his career possible."

Fair enough. And said in a way that made her point without seeming martyrish. For perhaps the first moment ever, Ben began to think this just might possibly work.

"Mrs. Glancy," Ben continued, "much of the prosecution case has centered on allegations that your husband had an . . . an—" *Dammit,* he had practiced this three times just to make sure he didn't stutter. "—an extramarital affair. Did you ever suspect that your husband was . . . doing anything like that?"

"Oh, I did a lot more than suspect." She folded her hands in her lap and directed her attention to the jury. "I knew all about it."

That raised more than one eyebrow in the jury box. "You knew about the affair with Veronica Cooper?"

"Absolutely."

"For how long?"

"Virtually from the moment it started. For that matter, I think I knew it was going to happen before Todd did."

"You seem to have taken it well."

"No," she replied, for the first time allowing her lips to turn slightly downward. "I didn't take it well at all. Not then and not now. But I know my husband. Like many great men throughout history, he has had . . . appetites to match his ambition. And tastes that were, well, somewhat outside the norm. I knew I couldn't satisfy him. I don't think any one woman could, at least not so long as he had options."

"When you learned of the affair, did you attempt to end it?"

"Not then, no. What would be the point? He would be angry and would only move on to someone else." Back at counsel table, Ben noted a concerned expression on Christina's face. Was this testimony supposed to be helping them? "I couldn't stop my husband from straying. So I resolved to simply remain informed of the situation. I couldn't prevent my husband from philandering. But I could certainly prevent myself from being left in the dark."

"So what steps did you take?"

"I hired a private detective." A definite stir in the courtroom. Even Judge Herndon appeared extremely attentive.

"To follow your husband?"

"No. With all the security at the Capitol, that would be next to impossible. Plus there's a good chance he'd spot the tail, and then the game would be up." She turned, crossed, then recrossed her legs. "I hired the man to follow Veronica Cooper."

Point made, Ben thought, and convincingly done, too. The foundation for his next witness was laid. Now he could proceed with Marie.

"Mrs. Glancy, another great linchpin of the prosecution case has been a certain videotape. I believe you were in the courtroom when it was played. It appeared to portray—"

Marie held up her hand. "I know the one you're talking about. I don't need a description."

Several of the jurors almost laughed. She was handling this very well.

"Before it aired on C-SPAN, did you have any prior knowledge of the video?"

"Yes."

Jurors' necks craned. A few lips parted.

"You did?" He paused. "Did your detective—?"

"Make the video? Absolutely not. He took notes, not pictures. But he did find out about the video, and he told me immediately. You see, on this point, the distinguished junior senator from Oklahoma was right—and this may be the first time that's happened in his entire career." A full-fledged round of laughter. She was charming them, absolutely winning them over. "Veronica Cooper made the videotape herself. She set up the camcorder, hid it, and made copies of the tape afterward."

"Objection," Padolino said, rising to his feet. "Since Ms. Glancy is relating what was told to her by this alleged detective, this is hearsay."

"That's not entirely true," Marie said, before Ben had a chance to respond.

"Ma'am," Judge Herndon said, "you should allow counsel to handle the objections."

"Why? I'm a lawyer, too." More laughter, even louder than before. "It's true that I got a report from my detective. But less than twenty-four hours later, I had personal knowledge of the tape. Because I saw it. In Veronica Cooper's grubby little hands."

"She came to you?" Ben asked.

"No. It's not my style to wait for the inevitable, especially when it could be so potentially dangerous. I went to her apartment and confronted her."

"Why would you do that?"

"It was pretty obvious that she made that video for a reason, and it wasn't just so she could spend nostalgic evenings remembering how fabulous my husband had been. My mission was damage control. Find out what she wanted and get it to her before she did something stupid—and irreversible."

"Wouldn't it have been smarter to tell your husband? Let him handle this?"

"Absolutely not. Todd is an intelligent man and an excellent politician, but that in itself can be very limiting. No telling how he might react. And quite frankly, there are some things a U.S. senator simply cannot do—but a wife can."

Ben nodded, slowly scanning the eyes of the jurors. Even those he thought had been most hostile to her at the outset were beginning to melt. That was good. Very good.

"What was it Ms. Cooper wanted?"

"Oh, I'm sure you've already guessed. She needed money, of course. Lots of it. Apparently she had quite an active nightlife—I guess the previous witness gave you some idea of that—and she was using this designer drug that was very expensive. She'd gotten herself deeply into debt, with the kind of people who don't take IOUs. She wanted to leave town, but her meager intern's salary wouldn't permit it. She basically had two options: prostitution, or blackmail."

"And she chose blackmail."

"Exactly, although I'm not sure she'd ruled the other out altogether, if the blackmail didn't work. It's pretty clear at this point that she was . . . not exactly inhibited when it came to having sex."

"Nonresponsive," Padolino said. "Move to strike."

"As you wish," Judge Herndon said. "The jury will disregard the witness's last statement."

"Did she make a specific request?"

"She did. She told me she wanted a quarter of a million dollars, in cash, by the end of the week. And if I didn't comply, she would release the tape to the press and destroy my husband's career."

"What was your response?"

"Well, I wanted to tell her to go—" She stopped herself. "Jump in a lake." More scattered laughter. "But I couldn't. She had the goods, and if anything her request was fairly modest."

"So you considered her offer?"

"I had no choice. I tried to read her the riot act and threaten and scare her, but she wasn't budging. She said she'd already sent a copy of the tape in a sealed envelope to a reporter friend of hers, and if anything happened to her he was under instructions to open the envelope. Which, I assume, is how the damn thing got out. Anyway, bottom line, a quarter of a mil wasn't that much to salvage the career of a man who was being touted as a potential vice presidential or even presidential candidate. I suspect the Democratic National Committee would've put that up in a heartbeat."

Padolino rose again. "Your honor . . ."

"I'm sorry," Marie said quickly. "I'll take that one back myself. Anyway, money wasn't the issue. Trust was the issue. I knew she'd made copies of the tape. How did I know she wouldn't come back for more money later? Addicts always need money and are often willing to do anything to get it. For that matter, how did I know this little minx wouldn't take the money and then leak the tape anyway? I'd learned enough about her to be cautious."

"So what did you do?"

"I gave her my Evelyn look."

"Excuse me?"

She smiled. "My Evelyn look. Evelyn was my mother. And when she got angry, or she had a point to make, she had a look that told you in no uncertain terms that she was not a woman with whom you wanted to be messing around. So I gave this tramp my Evelyn look." She sampled the expression for the jury, who appeared to be suitably impressed. "I told her that she might have some damn tape, but I knew more about her than her own mother, and I could do a lot worse to her than she could ever dream about doing to me or Todd." She took a deep breath, then smiled. "I thought she got the message, so we set a time for the exchange. My money in exchange for her tape and all the copies, and a promise to quit her job and have nothing further to do with my husband."

"Did you tell your husband what you had done?"

"Of course. If I hadn't, the woman might've tried to get money out of both of us. But it was important that he stay out of it. Private citizens can pay blackmail without breaking the law. But a politician can't—that's called hush money." She smiled. "You'll find that in the encyclopedia under Nixon, Richard M. You have to remember, I was doing a lot more here than saving my husband's political career. I was saving our lives, our futures. Regardless of what Todd may or may not have done, I believe in the sanctity of marriage, of the importance of the family unit. And I was determined to see that this woman didn't destroy mine."

Ben nodded slowly, giving everyone time to absorb her answer. "And did you in fact consummate the deal with Ms. Cooper?"

"Yes. I'd rounded up the cash and was all ready to go. Todd asked me to wait until he could talk to her, but I knew that was inane—no amount of charisma was going to persuade this cheap bit of—you know. Anyway, I paid her, but apparently she decided to two-time me, because the next day the video broke. I wanted to confront her, but when I tried to contact her at her apartment, she had disappeared. And then I learned the truth. She was dead."

"Do you have any idea what happened to Veronica Cooper? Who killed her?"

"No. Unfortunately, I'd called my detective off after she agreed not to see Todd anymore, so I didn't have anyone trailing her. But here's my point." She tilted her head toward the prosecution table. "These people keep saying Todd had a motive to silence Veronica Cooper. It isn't true. In the first place, Todd may have trouble keeping his zipper zipped, but he's not a murderer. No way, no how—it just isn't in him. He couldn't kill someone if his life depended on it. But it doesn't matter, because his life didn't depend on it. The situation had been handled. Cooper's silence had been bought. And after the reporter leaked the tape—something I personally don't think Veronica Cooper meant to happen—she could do him no more harm. There was no reason to kill her."

"Thank you," Ben said. He turned to Padolino. "Your witness."

"Are we really going into this place?" Shalimar asked, as they stared at the dark gabled Victorian-style brownstone on the other side of the dark, rainy Georgetown street. "We don't have a warrant. Isn't this kind of . . . breaking-and-enterish?"

"I don't have enough to get a warrant. But if Beatrice is in there—"

"Right, right." She shuddered. "Just looking at it gives me the wiggins."

"Hey, I'm lookin' forward to this. After all the places we've been so far, it'll be a relief to be inside a church."

"It's a vampire church, Loving."

"I don't care if it's the Church of the Zombie-Eaters-of-the-Dead. It's still gotta be better than the other places I've been."

Once again, Loving was very wrong.

The room at the front of the building was small, Loving thought, but it was without doubt a church. It had all the hallmarks: a high steepled ceiling, pews, an altar, an altar rail, and an organ. But there were significant distinctions, too. Instead of electrical lighting, ornate gold candelabra provided the principal illumination. The altar rail was lined with golden goblets, stained-glass pentagrams, and similar gimcracks Loving suspected were more for show than use. The woodwork as well as the stained-glass window behind the altar incorporated bones, skulls, cups spilling with blood, and the ankh—which Loving now recognized as the shape

Lucille had drawn in the air for him. Shalimar explained that it was the Egyptian symbol for immortality and had become the vampire's logo. Of course, Loving rationalized, the Catholic Church he'd grown up in had talked a lot about drinking blood and, for that matter, eating flesh. But somehow he sensed this was very different.

No one was in sight, but the fact that the candles were lit suggested that someone was not far away. Loving tiptoed forward. "Did you see this?" He pulled a black hardbound book out of the cradle on the back of the pew before him. The gold embossed lettering on the cover read: THE VAMPIRE BIBLE. The title page explained that it contained "the underlying pagan and mystical lore derived from our forebears, with selections from Sherpu Kishpu and sacred mystical works."

"What exactly do the parishioners here believe?" Shalimar whispered.

"Funny you should ask." He pulled out a service bulletin he found underneath one of the pews. It was dated the previous Saturday—apparently that was their Sabbath day. " 'The Church is an exclusive society dating back to the time of the Annunaki—Those Who From the Dark Heavens Came. Our Brotherhood is composed of those genetically drawn by the ancient mysteries, those born to the Blood, or those who have heard and heeded the Call of the Night. Our mission is to find our Brethren, the Lost Children of the Blood, and to convert them to the ancient ways before the time of the Final Harvest is upon us. We, the descendants of the ancient priesthood of Ur, call upon the Undead Gods, the ancient Sumerian vampire dragon goddess, Tiamat, and the way of the Magick, to protect and defend us as we find the pathway into the Master Adepti—the Inner Circle.' "

"This is the place," Shalimar murmured. "And the Final Harvest? You don't suppose—"

"Let's hope not." Loving pulled out another document he'd found behind the altar. "Wanna hear the Vampiric Creed?"

"Actually, no. Federally registered or not, I don't believe this place would keep membership rolls any more than the S-and-M palace did. And I don't believe my sister has become a nun in the Temple of the Vampire."

Certainly not a nun, Loving thought silently. But he wondered about some other disturbing possibilities. "Shalimar, I'm gonna take another look around and—"

He froze. Footsteps. Just outside the front door.

He and Shalimar ducked behind a pew.

A few moments later they heard the heavy front wooden doors open. Two people came inside, talking animatedly. Loving could make out one of their voices.

"Then tonight will be the night?"

Deep Throat. Back at the Reflecting Pool. The informant who got him started on this crazy quest.

"Yes," his companion replied. "Are you certain you have no doubts, my brother?"

"Oh, yes, yes." Deep Throat seemed nervous, just as he had when Loving talked to him at the Reflecting Pool. "That was only temporary. I know we're doing the right thing. The Inner Circle must be protected at all costs."

At least that's what he's telling you, Loving mused. Not what he told me.

"Are we the last to arrive?" Deep Throat asked.

"Yes. The preparations have been made. We cannot afford to delay any longer. We must deal with her immediately."

"As you say, Sire."

The two figures moved down the center nave of the sanctuary. Behind the altar, they unlocked and then passed through a door recessed in the back wall.

Loving and Shalimar looked at each other. It wasn't necessary to speak the words; they both knew what the other was thinking. They were getting ready to deal with Beatrice.

"I'm goin' in there," Loving said.

Shalimar grabbed his arm. "You heard what he said. There are others."

"Doesn't matter. I'm goin' in."

"That's crazy. We'll call the police."

"And tell them what, exactly? Even if they take us seriously, which I doubt, they might not be in time." To save your sister, he left unspoken.

Shalimar squared her jaw. "Then I'm coming with you."

"No, you're not."

"Don't treat me like—"

"Listen to me. We need to make sure someone's alive to go to the police. And if I go missin', you'll have somethin' to tell them they'll have to listen to."

"But—"

"It's for the best, Shalimar. You wait outside. If I'm not back in an hour, call the cops and tell them I've been abducted by a satanic cult. That should get their attention."

"But—"

"You heard me," Loving said firmly. "And you know I'm right. So please—wait outside. I'm countin' on you. You've got my back."

Shalimar's eyes blazed. "You're just saying this because you know it's dangerous. You're trying to keep me from being hurt. But you're going to need help and—"

"I'm sayin' this because I'm not as dumb as I look. It's a good plan. So do it already."

Her lips were pressed tightly together. Loving could see she didn't like it.

She laid both hands on his shoulders. "Take care of yourself in there," she said, barely above a whisper.

"That's a promise." He started toward the rear door. "See you outside, Buffy."

Her eyes blazed. "Don't call me Buffy!"

"First of all, Ms. Glancy," Padolino began, "let's set the record straight. All this business about your detective and allegedly offering to bribe the deceased—you didn't tell the police any of this, did you?"

"Todd and I were advised by counsel that we had the right to remain silent and that it would be smart to do so."

"The defendant has a right to remain silent, ma'am, but the defendant's spouse—"

"Is protected by the husband–wife confidentiality rule, as you and I both know, so let's not pretend otherwise."

"That law does not—"

"That law exists to protect marriages—the same thing I was doing."

Ben could see the wheels turning in Padolino's head as he

struggled to find an opening. If he'd ever imagined this was going to be an easy cross, he knew better now.

"Blackmail," he said finally, "is a crime."

"Yes, but being blackmailed isn't. We were the victims, not the perpetrators."

"Failure to report a crime—"

"Honestly, climb off your high horse and come back to earth." She allowed herself to show some mild irritation—just enough, Ben thought. "People being blackmailed never go to the police. If the blackmailers thought there was any chance of it, they wouldn't blackmail them in the first place."

"So instead, according to your testimony, you aided and abetted a criminal act."

"I gave money to a pathetic drug-addicted, brain-addled nymphomaniac who was threatening to bring down one of the best senators this country has ever had just so she could get her next fix. Was that such a horrible thing?"

Ben leaned in close to Christina. "I think she's magnificent," he whispered. "You agree?"

"Big-time," she whispered back. "Just don't fall in love. I've got a few Evelyn looks of my own."

"According to your testimony," Padolino continued, "you told the deceased you could 'do a lot worse to her than she could do to you.' That, I think, could be interpreted as a threat."

"A threat designed to save my husband and marriage."

"Making threats is also against the law."

"Oh, fine." She held out her wrists. "Cuff me. Take me away."

Several of the jurors had to cover their mouths.

"Your sarcasm is not appreciated, Ms. Glancy. This is a serious matter."

"No, it isn't. I mean, murder is a serious crime, but Todd didn't do it, and you'd know that if you hadn't done such a slipshod investigation and settled for arresting the most obvious and available suspect."

"Your honor!" Padolino said angrily. "I ask the court to strike that remark and admonish the witness."

Judge Herndon tilted his head to one side. "The court is inclined to think you pretty much asked for it."

Now several of the jurors were laughing, not even bothering

to cover their mouths. Ben could sense Padolino's desperation. He needed to score a point—and fast.

"You mentioned that you had the money ready to pay off Ms. Cooper."

"I did pay her off."

"I assume that money came from a bank account."

"You would be correct."

"That's the funny thing. You see, back when we were doing our slipshod investigation, I went to the trouble of subpoenaing your bank account records. Both yours and your husband's. We were obviously interested to know if you had made any large withdrawals— or deposits—on or about the time of the murder. As a matter of fact, I have those statements right here."

Back at the prosecution table, some poor legal assistant was riffling through her files, trying to make good on her boss's promise. After an admirably brief wait, she produced the statements in question.

"I don't have to go over them now," Padolino explained, "because I've been over them many many times before. And I know for a fact, Ms. Glancy, that there are no major withdrawals. Certainly nothing in the nature of a quarter of a million dollars." He slid the statements defiantly under her nose.

"Wrong bank," she said, without even looking.

"Excuse me?"

"Wrong bank, Mr. Prosecutor. These are our domestic personal accounts. The money I withdrew came from an offshore account held at a bank on Grand Cayman Island."

"I find that difficult to—"

"The account number is 00945623819. If you call, they will confirm the existence of the account. They won't give you any information about it without permission from Todd or me, but I will grant you that for the limited purpose of checking withdrawals at or around the time of Veronica Cooper's death." She paused. "I think you'll find a rather large one."

"But—but—" Padolino was sputtering now, never a good sign. "Why would a U.S. senator have an offshore bank account?"

"Objection," Ben said dutifully. "Not relevant to the charge at bar."

Judge Herndon considered for a moment. "Although the existence of the account is relevant, it is true that the reasons for having it in the first place may not be." He inhaled deeply. "But I think I'll allow it."

You mean, you just want to hear the poor woman try to explain it to this jury of lower-middle-class taxpayers, Ben thought.

"I haven't really been involved in the creation of the bank accounts for this family," Marie said coolly. "But I believe these offshore accounts may have certain tax advantages."

"More like a tax dodge, isn't it?"

Marie drew herself up and looked squarely at him, without a hint of embarrassment. "Mr. Padolino, I understood your goal here to be prosecuting someone you genuinely believed to be guilty of murder, not generally slandering someone just for the pleasure of doing so. I've allowed you to confirm the existence of the account and the withdrawal. I think that puts an end to the inquiry."

It wasn't often in his career that Ben had seen a witness so thoroughly take command of a cross-examination, much less effectively overrule the judge without anyone in the courtroom daring to saying a word about it. He stopped wondering if she might conceivably have political ambitions, and started wondering how long it would be before she was sitting in the Oval Office.

Beads of sweat dripped down the sides of the prosecutor's face, always pleasurable for a defense attorney to observe. At the same time, Ben knew that when smart men became desperate, they did desperate things. And that certainly proved to be the case.

"Ms. Glancy, you mentioned before that your husband had unusual tastes. I gathered from the context that you were describing his sexual predilections. Would you please explain exactly what you meant?"

Glancy leaned toward Ben. "You've got to stop this," he whispered, but it was unnecessary, because Ben was already on his feet.

"Objection!" Ben said emphatically. "Not relevant."

The judge disagreed. "I think she opened the door to this. Overruled."

"Your honor," Ben insisted, "this is obviously just a prosecutorial ploy to salvage his case by slandering the defendant. There is—"

"I've ruled, counsel."

"Your honor, this is the defendant's wife!"

"And I said I've ruled, Mr. Kincaid!" Herndon rose slightly out of his seat. "That's my nice way of saying sit down and shut up."

Ben reluctantly did as he was told.

"So," Padolino continued, "could you please describe these unusual tastes? And don't spare us the details."

For the first time, the jury could see Marie hesitating, gathering her thoughts.

"Damn," Christina whispered into Ben's ear. "Why did she have to bring this up in the first place?"

A very good question, Ben thought. It certainly wasn't in her testimony when they had rehearsed it the night before.

"Well," she said, drawing in her breath, "you've seen the video."

"We certainly have. Your point?"

"Todd," she said, sighing heavily. "Todd is very into the whole subjugation–domination thing. He likes—well, you can see it in his whole life, everything he's ever done. He wants to be in power. He wants to be in control."

"Like in the video, when he forced himself on Veronica Cooper?"

"Oh, I think that was more playacting than anything else. They were both willing participants. But it was playacting Todd liked." Her eyes moved downward. "Unfortunately . . . I didn't."

Glancy squeezed Ben's arm. "You've got to shut this down," he hissed. "Isn't there any way?"

"I already gave it everything I had," Ben replied. "More objections now would only remind the jury how badly we want to keep this out."

Padolino resumed. "Would this subjugation fetish involve . . . certain positions?"

"Obviously. The woman in any position of powerlessness. Restrained. Bent over a chair."

"Would it involve violence?"

"Objection!" Ben shouted, genuinely outraged. "This has gone far beyond all reasonable claims of relevance. This is nothing less than a prurient intrusion into a public figure's private sex life."

"It's a character issue," Padolino answered.

"Well, isn't that what they always say," Ben shot back.

"It goes to the likeliness of the affair, or affairs. Which goes directly to motive. And the propensity for sexual violence—well, the relevance of that is obvious."

"I'll allow it," Herndon said. He didn't even have to think about it. And as painful as it was, Ben knew his decision was correct.

"Pain was—*is*—a turn-on for Todd," Marie continued. "But it's more than that. It's not just the pain, it's the . . . debasement. The sense that he's reducing the woman to a piece of meat. A plaything. Something that exists only for his pleasure. That's what he gets off on. I wouldn't let him do that to me. So he found other women who would."

"Like an employee who thought she had to please her boss?" Padolino asked.

Marie scoffed. "Like a desperate drug addict who liked sex and lacked the strength to say no."

Padolino had the sense to know this was as good as it was going to get. He ended on a high note and sat down. Ben declined to redirect.

"What the hell was that?" Ben whispered to Christina. "Her testimony was going brilliantly. Even the cross was going brilliantly. And then, at the very end, she tanks. Destroys her husband's reputation."

"Nothing she said proved Todd was a murderer," Christina noted. "She cast serious doubt on the prosecutor's theory of motive."

"Who cares? She made him look so ugly, so perverted, I'll never be able to generate any sympathy for him in closing. I couldn't rehabilitate Mother Teresa after testimony like that." He wiped his hand across his brow. "And it wasn't necessary. Why would she do that? Why would she do that to him?"

Christina watched Marie carefully as she walked coolly down the nave and out of the courtroom. "A woman scorned," she said succinctly. "Hell hath no greater fury."

Peering over the balcony, almost all Loving could see on the inlaid tile floor on the level beneath him was the five-sided star enclosed in a circle—a huge pentagram in the center of the darkened room. The twelve figures surrounding the circle were wearing brown hooded cloaks, like monastic friars of an ancient order, all participating in an uncanny ritual. In the center was a large stone block—the altar, no doubt. A sheet was draped over the top of the altar, but Loving could tell there was something, or someone, under the sheet. Much as he wanted to find Beatrice, he hoped it wasn't her, because the entire time he'd been in here he'd never once detected the slightest movement under the sheet.

After Loving passed through the rear door of the chapel and a long corridor, he found himself on this balcony. A spiral staircase led to the lower floor, but he decided to stay here where he had a better view, and it would be more difficult for the hoods below to spot him. The low lighting cut both ways: it made it harder for him to detect what was going on down there, but it also made it harder for them to see him watching—which was good, because he was fairly certain they would not be pleased.

The men had been chanting for almost ten minutes. He suspected it was Latin, but he couldn't really be sure—he hadn't gone to college and they hadn't covered this in the truck-driving class he'd taken at the Tulsa Vo-Tech Center. At long last, they fell silent. One man stepped forward, entered the pentagram, and laid his hands upon whatever was under the sheet.

"Let us pray."

As one, the rest of the men did not bow their heads, but instead raised them, pressing their hands together and lifting them above their hoods.

"Oh, blessed Tiamat, Guardian of the Darkness, hear our plea. Help us to find the Lost Children of the Blood."

As one, the rest of the assemblage chanted, "Goddess, hear our prayer."

"Help us find the path to immortality and reclaim the spirit of our ancestors, the Nephilim of the Annunaki."

"Goddess, hear our prayer."

"Lead us not unto the wicked ways of the pretender, the Killer of the Spirit, the cursed Nazarene, the Perverter of Souls."

"Goddess, hear our prayer."

"Please accept our sacrifice—"

Loving's head jerked up.

"—as a token of our fealty, our unyielding devotion to your psychic strength. Hear me, the Sire of the Circle, and all your servants in the Inner Circle as we ask your blessing. Offer unto us your greater glory and our nourishment."

"Goddess, hear our prayer."

The room fell deadly silent. The leader—the Sire—reached up and removed the cowl from his head.

Just as Loving had thought. It was Daily—or rather, the man who pretended to be Daily. The man who killed Daily, and Amber. He was the Sire!

His spine tingling, Loving watched as the man slowly drew back the sheet from the sacrifice upon the table. It was a woman, very young, blond, and medium weight. Even with her face silent and ashen, Loving recognized her from the picture Shalimar had shown him. It was Beatrice.

She was not moving, hadn't moved since the ceremony had begun, which meant she was either sleeping, drugged—or worse.

There were too many of them for Loving to try a frontal assault. Even assuming he was the best fighter in the room, he was massively outnumbered. A failed attempt could leave him dead, or Beatrice, or both. The smartest thing would be to get back outside, call in the cops, then create some kind of disturbance—something to interrupt the ceremony and prevent them from sacrificing Beatrice before the police arrived.

He turned and started for the door—

Someone was standing in his way.

The cultist obstructing his passage was wearing a brown hood, but it did not entirely conceal his face. Even in the darkness, his visage was hideous. Gold fangs descended from his mouth. His eyes glowed red. His face was scarred, apparently by design.

"Why are you here?" the voice within the cowl hissed. "You are not of the Circle."

Loving bolted. His best hope now was to outrun them. But just as he was hitting his stride, someone tripped him, causing him to tumble to the floor. He pulled himself up as quickly as he could, but by that time he was surrounded.

"Look," Loving said, "I can explain. I was lookin' for the Presbyterian church and I got lost and—"

He never got to finish his sentence. He heard the whistle of something swinging around in the darkness, something solid, moving fast. For an instant he felt the impact upon the back of his skull. And then the world was consumed by blackness.

22

No one who hasn't done it can understand what it is to try a case, Ben thought as he wiped the sleep out of his eyes and tried to focus on the witness outline he held in his hands. Civil or criminal, it was all the same, at least from one standpoint—the enormous all-consuming immersive nature of the experience. Once the trial began, the rest of the world disappeared. There were no more lunches with friends, no phone calls to Mom, no trips to the local cineplex. During a trial, Ben usually existed on four hours of sleep a night, and he sometimes suspected Christina never slept at all. Despite the pressure, the exhaustion, and the sleep deprivation, he had to keep himself in peak condition and clearheaded. The key to success was to always remain one step ahead—not only planning his case but also anticipating its flaws and preparing for the responses of his opponents. It was a daunting, hellishly difficult task. Even still, he had often thought that trial practice wouldn't be so bad if you could just eliminate one element.

Clients.

"Congratulations, Kincaid. You've really screwed things up now."

Amanda, naturally. He pinched the bridge of his nose. "Have I? I thought yesterday went rather well."

"Shows what you know. You've fucked us royally, and we're going to sit down right now and figure out how to fix it."

Ben pushed away from the table. There was no point in explaining to this woman that he had gotten up three hours before court began so he could prepare his defense, not so he could talk about its PR ramifications.

"We did a lot of overnight polling, after the evening news reports. The results were not good."

"I thought Marie did the prosecution serious damage on motive, and also gave us back a feasible alibi. Our jury has a lot more reasonable doubt running through their brains now than they had before."

"I wasn't polling the jury," Amanda said curtly. "I was polling the voters. The men and women who put Todd Glancy into office."

"I'm not concerned about them."

"I know. That's the problem."

Ben felt his neck stiffening. "If we lose this trial, what your voters think isn't going to matter anymore."

"What do you mean, *if* we lose. You've been hired to win, you schmuck. And we expect you to deliver. My job is to make sure Todd still has a career after the trial. And that's not going to happen if you keep painting him as some depraved sex pervert!"

"That part wasn't my idea. Marie put that in on her own."

"You should've stopped it."

"I tried."

"Don't give me *try!*" The woman was almost shouting. "This isn't the 4-H Club, farm boy. I don't care about *try*. I care about results. That testimony should never have come in."

"I agree. But it did, so now we have to live with it."

She sat on the edge of the table, flipped her hair back, and extended her chest. "We're going to do a lot more than that. We're going to make sure nothing like that ever happens again."

"And how exactly are we going to do that?"

"Easy. I want you to kill the private investigator."

Ben assumed that by *kill* she meant "don't call him to the stand," but given who was speaking, he wondered if he should check. "You must be kidding."

"I'm not. If you put him on the stand, Padolino will spend all of cross quizzing him on everything he knows about Todd's sexual practices and preferences."

"Very likely."

"And given that he was apparently following that bimbo intern around for months, he's probably going to have a lot to tell."

"That's the price we pay to get his testimony about Veronica Cooper."

She shook her head emphatically. "The price is too high."

Ben was just as resolute. "We have no choice."

"Of course we do. And I just made it."

Ben's face crinkled together like aluminum foil. "Do you want to destroy Todd's case? We *have* to use the investigator."

"We should just go with Todd."

"Just go with the defendant? His own self-serving testimony? When we have someone who can corroborate it? You're out of your blinking mind!"

Amanda leaned in so close Ben could feel the darts of her blouse pressing against his shirt. "I can assure you I'm perfectly sane. I can also assure you that I know what's best for Todd, and if you don't listen to me, I'll string you up feetfirst from the Washington Monument."

"Lady, how can I say this nicely? Buzz off." He returned his attention to his outline.

She grabbed his collar. "Don't you turn away from me. Don't you dare turn away from me! I've taken down bigger men than you, Okie. Much bigger. All it would take is a few phone calls and you'll never practice law again!"

"Amanda?"

Both heads whipped around to see Marshall Bressler wheeling himself into the room. He was holding a bottle of blue-colored pills. "Anyone got a bottle of water? I'm a wreck without my morning medication." He looked up. "Oh. Is this a bad time?"

"Depends on your definition of a bad time," Ben said, removing

Amanda's hands. "I think Amanda was about to commit her first murder. That we know of, anyway."

Amanda clenched her fists and made a sonorous growling noise. "You are so . . . infuriating!" She whipped around to face Marshall. "This man is trying to destroy everything I've worked so hard for!"

Marshall raised an eyebrow. "Shouldn't that be what *we've* worked so hard for?"

"He insists on calling that damn detective."

"Did you read his report?" Marshall asked. "I think it's safe to say his testimony will end the media portrayal of Veronica as an angelic innocent."

"What the hell do you know about the media!" She looked as if she were about to pull her hair out by the roots. "All the media will report is the talk about sex. And Padolino will make sure there's lots of it. Enough to fill the front three sections of the *Post*. Did you see the poll results I e-mailed to you?"

Marshall waved a hand in the air. "You know I never look at e-mail, and you should never put anything important in one. Republican eyes are everywhere."

"Paranoid much?" Ben asked.

"Yeah, that's what they were saying back in '04, and then we found out the Republican staff members of the Judiciary Committee had been hacking into our restricted e-mail messages for more than a year, sometimes even leaking them to right-wing pundits. Remember that story?"

Ben frowned. He did.

"These poll results are irrelevant," Ben said. "Any negative fall-out is irrelevant, as I've been trying to explain to Amanda. It's an unfortunate consequence of what we have to do to make sure our favorite politician doesn't get a lethal injection."

Marshall tilted his head to one side. "I'm not sure trashing Veronica will do it."

"It won't hurt."

"What we really need," Marshall continued, "is to give the jury an alternate suspect."

Both Ben and Amanda stared at him.

"Reasonable doubt is fine, but once Padolino starts talking his trash in closing, he'll wash all their doubts away. We need more. We need doubt plus a bogeyman. A good one. That might do the trick."

Ben laid his pencil to rest. "Did you have anyone in particular in mind?"

"Does it matter? Just pick someone."

"Okay. I pick Amanda."

She shot invisible poison daggers at him.

"I'm serious, Ben," Marshall said.

"I am, too. And if we had a viable potential suspect, I'd be the first to put the theory before the jury. But I won't pick someone at random and trump something up."

"It could work."

Ben shook his head. "You've been watching too much television."

"At least give it some thought. How about the junior senator from Oklahoma? He had plenty of motive to want Todd out of the way."

"I won't do it," Ben said emphatically. "Given the way this case is being covered, even the slightest courtroom accusation could destroy someone's life. It's a totally unethical tactic."

Marshall pursed his lips. "You're sure about this. No Mister X?"

"Not unless it's a Mister X whom I really believe might've done the deed."

Marshall nodded slowly, then pivoted his chair around and wheeled himself toward the doorway. "Then let's hope one turns up."

"Psst!"

Christina looked up and saw Padolino leaning out the hallway door of his office, motioning. "Can you come in for a moment?"

"Ooo-kay." She stepped inside. He slammed the door quickly behind her. "Is there some reason for the secrecy?"

"Well . . . I thought it best we not be seen talking together. You know, before the trial is over. Wouldn't want people to get the wrong idea."

"That you're conspiring with the enemy?"

"Something like that. And I didn't want to get you in trouble with your boss."

"I don't think you have to worry about that." Christina stared at him, at the way he was twitching his fingers, pacing back and forth. He never acted this nervous in the courtroom—or for that matter when he was speaking on national television. "What can I do for you?"

"I was just wondering . . ." He fidgeted with the edge of his desk. "I wondered if maybe, you know, when this case is over you and I could, like . . . get a drink together. Or something. I know your boss doesn't drink. Do you?"

"Absolutely," she answered. "I'm a fiend for club soda. Are you serious?"

"What? Did I do something wrong? Do I not seem serious? I just thought, maybe, you know, you and I—"

"Is this some sort of psych-out plan? Some dastardly plot to weaken the defense by making advances to opposing counsel?"

"No! Not at all." He pressed his hands together. "I've just been, you know, watching you. I mean, not in a bad way. Just during the case and all. And I thought maybe you and I should get to know each other better."

Christina's eyes narrowed. She didn't know whether to believe the man or not. And it didn't much matter, in any case. "Thanks for the offer, but I don't think my boss—who by the way is actually my partner—would appreciate it."

"But I already asked him."

Christina froze. "What?"

"I asked him. If it would be all right if I asked you out. I mean, for all I knew there could be something going on between the two of you. Some of my staff thought there was. So I did the honorable thing. I asked him."

"And he said . . ."

"He told me to go right ahead. Do whatever I wanted to do."

"Is that a fact." Christina turned, careful to keep her face from registering emotion. "Well, in that case—"

The door swung open so fast it almost hit her in the face. Steve Melanfield came barreling through. "Paul! Great news. We—" He saw Christina and stopped. "Oh. Hello."

"Back at you," Christina said. "What's the good news?"

He looked at her, then back at Padolino, then back at her. "What the hell. I suppose it doesn't matter. Everyone will know soon. My people in Oklahoma City tell me it's at least ninety percent certain we're going to have a new senator."

"Excuse me?" Christina said. "We haven't lost this case yet."

He shrugged. "Win or lose, the governor has had it. He's going to call for Glancy's resignation. 'Course, Glancy could refuse, but given all that's been revealed, it puts him in a pretty tough spot."

"And if Glancy resigns?"

"The governor gets to pick someone to fill out the remainder of his term."

"And who do you suppose that will be?"

"Don't know, don't care. But I know this—the governor owes Kodiak Oil big time. He'll make sure we're taken care of. He won't pick anyone hostile to me."

"Or me," said another voice from the hallway. This time it was Oklahoma's junior senator, Brad Tidwell, and he appeared just as jubilant as Melanfield. "And since I'll become the senior senator, I think I can arrange to assume most or all of Glancy's former committee assignments." He squeezed Melanfield tightly on the shoulder. "Steve, I think this is the start of a beautiful friendship. Alaska or bust!"

"You people are making me sick," Christina said. "Have you totally forgotten why we're here? This isn't some campaign-headquarters smoke-filled room. It's a courtroom. A man is on trial for his life."

Tidwell was not impressed. "We're all on trial for our lives, lady. From the moment we declare our candidacy to the day we die. Todd knows that as well as I do. But he screwed up. Now he's paying for it." He shrugged, then let loose another grin. "No reason why others shouldn't profit from his mistake."

Christina started for the door. "You're disgusting."

Padolino held out his hand. "Christina—about my . . ."

"Forget it." She pushed Tidwell out of her way. "Buy these two jackals a drink. While you're at it, buy them a conscience." She slammed the door behind her.

When Loving awoke, his head was throbbing and he felt as if he was being tortured. It took a few more moments of consciousness to gather his senses sufficiently to comprehend the reason—he *was* being tortured.

He was strung up, literally, his hands tied together with wire, dangling from the ceiling. His feet did not quite touch the floor. He'd been stripped bare to the waist. Am I hanging from a meat hook, he wondered, like that woman back at the S&M palace? Didn't really matter, not while his arms felt as if they were being ripped out of their sockets. Regardless of what he was hanging from, it hurt like hell.

"Ah, Loving, we're awake, are we? That's good. I was becoming anxious."

Loving didn't have to adjust his vision to know who was speaking to him. "Look who's here. Amber's alleged daddy. Also known as the Sire."

He smiled thinly. "How smart you are. I suspected you'd find us, eventually. So I made preparations." From a rack on the wall, he took the end of a long large fire hose into both hands, then turned the spigot. Water spewed out—slamming into Loving's chest.

"*Ahhhh!*" Loving felt the harsh blast tearing at him, knocking him backward, putting even more strain on his aching arms. "*Stoooop!*"

The Sire turned off the water. "Since you asked nicely. I just wanted you to get nice and wet. Water is such a good conductor."

"You killed Amber," Loving said, gasping. It was difficult to breathe while hanging like this. Almost impossible to speak. "And you killed Colleen and Veronica Cooper, too."

"To the contrary, I never kill anyone." He smiled through thin, blood-red lips. "I merely release them from their bodies. But they still live. They become a part of me. A part of my immortal essence."

Loving could taste blood in his mouth. He spat it out. "Have you killed Beatrice?"

"And why would I do that?"

"I saw you in there! Your sick little ceremony."

The Sire stepped closer—though not near enough for Loving to wrap his legs around his throat. "You misapprehend the nature of our ceremony. We never intended to kill her, at least not there. What purpose would that serve?" He smiled. "We ate her. We took turns, sucking her dry."

Despite his pain, Loving felt his temper rising. "She's still alive?"

"For now. Until she outlives her usefulness to us." He waited until Loving looked him in the eyes before he continued. "What have you told the police about me? Or that attorney you work for?"

"Nothing."

"You're lying."

"Okay, everythin'. They know all about your sick little church. You'd better get the hell out of here."

"Again, you're lying."

"Are you sure?"

"Yes," he sighed. "I'm sure. How much do you know about my little church?"

"Everything there is to know. Everything those girls knew, and then some. Enough to put you behind bars for the rest of your life."

The Sire pondered. "You could be telling the truth. But I don't think so. Let me ask again. What do you know about my church?"

"You run a church? Damn. I thought this was an IHOP."

The Sire frowned. "I can see this is going to be useless. You require persuasion."

"Listen, creep, you can shoot me with your little hose all night long. It won't make any difference."

"I suspect it would, after a few days. But I don't have a few days. Dr. Usher?"

Loving heard a door creak somewhere in the darkness. A figure emerged. He was wearing a white coat, like a surgeon, but that didn't prevent Loving from recognizing him.

It was Deep Throat. And he was carrying a little black bag.

"Dr. Usher did a residency in surgery. Did you know?"

Loving felt a cold chill envelop his body.

"I think you should start with the scalpel, Doctor. What do you think?"

"As you wish, Sire." His expression was flat, almost blank. He was like an automaton, a slave with no choice but to do his master's bidding.

"Very well. You may begin."

"Look," Loving said, "I don't know what you're thinkin', but I'm not gonna—"

In the blink of an eye Deep Throat—or Dr. Usher—lunged forward, scalpel extended. The blade entered the soft part of Loving's abdomen, just above the waist, just below the kidneys.

Loving screamed.

As soon as Ben entered the courtroom, he saw that his next witness was already present, which alleviated one potential worry. On the other hand, his witness was talking to Shawn MacReady, the congressman from Arkansas and former witness for the prosecution, which tended to create additional worries.

Ben approached them. "All ready to go?"

His witness was a tall, exceedingly thin man, almost gaunt in appearance, but with a sinewy strength to him. John Carradine in his prime. Not someone Ben would want to arm wrestle. "I think so. If you're sure you want to do this."

"I'm sure." He shifted his gaze to MacReady. "Anything I can do for you?"

"No. I was just discussing the possibility of employing your witness. I've had a few security concerns of late. Thought he might be able to help." He paused. "For that matter, from what I hear, you've had a few security concerns yourself, Kincaid."

"You could say that. Guard out front told me Darrin Cooper tried to get into the courtroom again today. Fortunately they stopped him."

The bailiff brought the court into session and a few moments later, the judge and jury were back in place. Ben called his next witness.

"The defense calls Max Capshaw."

The tall man shuffled when he walked, with a slight hunch to his shoulders. He was wearing a suit that could be described as ill fitting at best: Ben guessed that it was borrowed and that he didn't normally work with a Windsor knot pressed against his neck.

Ben wasted no time establishing that Capshaw was a licensed private detective in the District of Columbia and that he was the man Marie Glancy had hired to follow Veronica Cooper. With great detail and considerable verve, Capshaw told the jury everything he had witnessed over the course of six months tailing the woman. Todd Glancy barely figured in the narrative, and when he did, Capshaw glossed over it quickly. What he spent his time on was Veronica Cooper's nightlife. Amber and Colleen and Beatrice. Stigmata. The Chosen. Even Circle Thirteen. Veronica's addiction to the designer drug. And her addiction to sex. Lots and lots of sex. Not just with Todd Glancy—not even primarily with Todd Glancy. With all kinds of men. And women. As Capshaw described her sexual encounters, they seemed so patternless and indiscriminate that the jury was left wondering if she had even been aware of what she was doing or who she was doing it with. Padolino objected repeatedly, but Herndon consistently overruled him, reminding Padolino that only yesterday he had been allowed to delve into the parties' sex lives with great abandon. Sauce for the goose.

"During the time that you observed Ms. Cooper, how often would you say that she engaged in sexual relations?" Ben asked.

Capshaw screwed up his face. "Jeez, I don't know. Some nights she did it three, four times, with that many different guys. Some nights in that upstairs orgy apartment she went from one person to the next, one right after the other. Never even went out for a smoke." He shook his head. "I've never seen a girl with energy like that. 'Course a lot of that was being fueled by the drug."

"So it would be fair to say that Ms. Cooper engaged in sexual activity on a regular basis with a wide variety of sexual partners."

"Definitely. Hell, I was telling my friend last night—the big surprise isn't that the senator got caught having sex with that chick. The surprise is that he didn't catch something worse."

Thank you so much, Ben thought, moving quickly to his next question.

"And you're certain she was a member of this . . . Circle Thirteen? The vampire club. And the Inner Circle."

"You betcha. I saw her there, back at that so-called church where they hold all their ceremonies. I watched the whole thing with night-vision binoculars through this rose window. She was wearing robes and chanting and the whole sick nine yards. They even slaughtered a chicken and splattered its blood all over the floor. Disgusting."

"And Ms. Cooper participated in these black magic exercises?"

Capshaw chuckled. "Well, she wasn't Wendy the Good Witch, that's for damn sure."

Ben searched for the right words. "And did you ever see Ms. Cooper physically engaged with one of these . . . vampires?"

"Engaged? I watched one bite her in the neck."

Ben stared at him. "You mean . . . for real?"

"Hell yes. Some of those guys actually have their teeth filed to a sharp point so they can do that sick stuff. You remember the Bartmann guy saying how he turned her on? And he didn't even have all his teeth. Now imagine her with one of these dudes with the big sharpened canines. I'm tellin' ya, she was creamin'. Er, you know— very excited. In a sexual sort of way."

"I think we get the picture, sir." Ben returned to the enlargements from the coroner's report he had used before. "Earlier we heard Dr. Bukowsky admit under cross-examination that there was a wound to Ms. Cooper's jugular vein too small to have been made by a knife." He held up the enlargement and pointed. "You've seen these men, sir, and you've seen how they interacted with Ms. Cooper. I know you're not a coroner, but do you think it's possible this puncture wound was made by . . . a fang?"

"Objection!" Padolino cried. "The witness has no medical expertise. This whole line of questioning is becoming ridiculous. Counsel is turning the trial into a Hammer horror show."

"I'll allow it," Herndon said firmly. "Overruled."

"It's more than possible," Capshaw said, not missing a beat. "It would've been easy. Some of those guys had fangs so long and sharp they could rip your whole head off."

"Based upon your observations, sir, would you say these people with whom Ms. Cooper consorted could be described as dangerous?"

"I'd say that anyone who has their teeth sharpened so they can bite someone in the neck is by definition dangerous," he replied. "And you mix in the drugs and the booze and the loose sex—well, I've heard of living on the edge, but this chick was practically dangling over the precipice. God forbid she ever did anything to make one of those guys mad. Any of them could've gotten to her. Anything could've happened to her. Anything at all."

"Well, that was all very thrilling," Padolino said, as he strolled to the podium to cross-examine. "Almost like watching the late late show, complete with ghouls and goblins and vampires. But Veronica Cooper wasn't killed by a vampire or his fangs, was she? She was killed by a big thick knife. I don't believe you're refuting the coroner's testimony on that point, are you, *Dr.* Capshaw?"

Capshaw gave him a wry look. "No, I'm not disputing that the girl was killed by a knife." Padolino started to move on, but Capshaw cut him off. "The question is, who was holding the knife. And from what I saw of the girl's lifestyle, the possible suspects range somewhere in the four-digit numbers."

"Move to strike," Padolino said angrily. "Mr. Capshaw, did you in fact see anyone kill Ms. Cooper?"

"No, obviously not. Mrs. Glancy ended my employment a few days before Cooper was killed."

"Did you ever see any of these—" He made a show of suppressing his smirk. "—*vampires* hurt Ms. Cooper?"

"Not as such. Not in a way she didn't like, anyhow."

"Did you ever see any of these people threaten Ms. Cooper?"

"No."

"Do you even know of any reason any of them would have to kill her? Sounds like they were all one big happy coven."

"Well, it's possible that—"

"Excuse me, sir, but I don't want to hear about possibilities. I asked if you know—note the word—*know* of any reason these people would have to kill Veronica Cooper."

"No."

"And to your knowledge, did any of these vampires have access to the hallways of the U.S. Senate?"

"Not that I know of."

"Then I submit, sir, that your thousands of mythical unnamed suspects are a smokescreen. There's only one person who had a motive to kill Ms. Cooper, much less had access to her or the place where her body was found."

"Is it time for closing arguments?" Ben said, rising to his feet. "'Cause I had some more witnesses I wanted to call first."

Judge Herndon suppressed a smile. "Mr. Padolino, you're up here to ask questions, not to make speeches."

"My apologies, your honor. I just don't want to see the jury misled by all this nonsensical—" The judge gave him a sharp look.

"Right, right. Questions." He returned his attention to the witness. "Sir, you've talked a great deal about Ms. Cooper's other alleged sexual partners. But you've said next to nothing about the one we're all certain of, whom we saw in living color. Did you ever observe Ms. Cooper with the defendant?"

"Yes," he said succinctly.

"How often?"

"About once a week. Occasionally twice."

"Really. You've described Ms. Cooper as having such tremendous sexual appetites. I'm surprised it wasn't more often."

"Well, the senator is a busy man. Interns have more time on their hands."

"Marie Glancy told us you witnessed Ms. Cooper setting up the camera to make the videotape. So you must know for a fact that sexual relations did in fact occur."

He blew out his cheeks. "Right."

"And how exactly was it you saw her set up the camera?"

Capshaw tugged at his tie. "Her apartment was on the ground floor. There was a bedroom window. She pulled the shades, but they were made of that thin, gauzy stuff and . . . well, if you get close enough to it, you can see through it pretty good."

"So you invaded her privacy?"

"That's more or less my job description, sir."

"And you trespassed. Do you know I could have your license yanked for that?"

"I believe you've already tried, right?" Capshaw gave the prosecutor a sharp look. "But I'm sure that attempt to discredit me and destroy my livelihood had nothing to do with wanting to squelch my testimony in this case. You were just doing your duty as a public servant."

Ben and Christina exchanged a probing look. Ben hadn't known about this. He was beginning to understand why Capshaw was being such a strong witness for them—and was doing his best not to give Padolino an inch.

"So you had a close-up view of our senator in action, so to speak. Could you tell us a little something about his sexual preferences?"

"I don't see that there's any cause for that."

"Oh come on now, sir. The defendant's wife talked about it."
And opened the door to this tacky field of inquiry, Ben thought.
"Why should you have any reluctance?"

"Mrs. Glancy told it pretty much the way it was," Capshaw
said, frowning. "He likes to be in control. He likes to dominate."

"So describe some of his favored positions."

Capshaw looked up at the judge, but saw no relief from that quarter. "It was mostly playacting. More often than not, he'd try to subdue
her. Put her in a position of powerlessness. He had one deal where
he'd bend her over a desk or table, facedown, then stretch out her
arms and tie them in place with ropes or socks or whatever was available. And then . . . you know. Take her from behind. Call her dirty
names. Insult her. Sometimes he'd handcuff her to the bed. Slap her
around a bit, make her scream till he got aroused. Stuff like that."

"Such a wide variety of experiences you seem to have observed.
Tell us, Mr. Capshaw. Did Senator Glancy to your knowledge have
affairs with any women other than Ms. Cooper?"

"Objection," Ben said quickly. "Relevance."

"Overruled. The witness will answer."

"But this can't possibly relate to the relationship between the defendant and—"

"I've overruled you," Judge Herndon said harshly. "The witness
will answer the question."

Capshaw's eyes lowered. "Yes. He did."

A heavy silence blanketed the courtroom.

"How many others?"

"I'm aware of three."

Next to Ben, Glancy's chin fell. Behind him, Marie Glancy tried
to make herself invisible.

"Three? Well, I suppose you were only on the case for six
months, and you spent most of that time tailing Ms. Cooper." Capshaw gave him a cold look. "How often did he see these three other
women?"

"One of them only once. The other two, about once a week.
They met at hotels, mostly."

"Once a week. Just like Ms. Cooper. My goodness, when you add
all these women up, you wonder how the man had time to attend any
committee meetings at all." No one laughed, but Ben would've rather

they had. At least it would've broken the pallor cast by this ugly tidbit of information. "And were these other women young?"

"Yeah. All of them. Young, thin, pretty. Blond. He really liked the blondes."

"So I gather." Padolino drew himself up and faced the jury. "So we're not just talking about a philandering husband. We're talking about a sex addict!"

Ben jumped to his feet, but the judge was already pounding his gavel, trying to quiet the crowd. "Mr. Padolino, you have been warned!"

Padolino didn't stop. "And we're supposed to believe that this sex addict was going to pay one of his many lovers a quarter of a million dollars? When it would be so much easier just to kill her and stuff her in his hideaway?"

"Mr. Padolino!" Judge Herndon shouted, even louder than Ben objected, but it didn't matter. The courtroom was out of control. Reporters were racing out the doors, hoping to be the first to file the story. Calls would be made, trying to track down the other lovers and book them on the earliest possible nighttime talk show. *The National Enquirer* would make them all millionaires.

But at the moment, Ben's main concern was the broken man sitting beside him. "All right then," Glancy whispered, sounding as if he were on the verge of tears. "So maybe I'm not going to be on the national ticket." He clutched at Ben's arm. "Just don't let them kill me, Ben. I did not kill that woman—Miss Cooper. And I don't want to die for a crime I didn't commit."

Ben squeezed his hand and tried to sound reassuring. But as he looked around the courtroom, at the frenzy in the gallery, the anger behind the bench, and worst of all, the faces of the jurors, he knew that every one of them would probably not object if a posse rode into the courtroom and hung Glancy from the nearest tree.

Their only possible course of action now was to put Glancy on the stand, to let him tell his story for himself. But given what had been done to his reputation in the courtroom this day, Ben doubted very seriously that it would be enough.

Loving had experienced a lot of pain in his life, but never anything like this. Every inch of his wet flesh was on fire. Deep Throat had not only jabbed him with the knife, he'd turned the blade, twisting it back and forth, cutting Loving inside and out. He was not content merely to cause injury. He wanted to create pain. And he was doing a very good job.

"Ready to talk yet?"

Loving tried to respond, but the agony was too intense. He had to hold it together, had to keep going until he had a chance to escape. But how could he possibly escape when he was strung up like a slab of meat in the back room of a vampire church?

"I want to know everything you've told the police. Or your Mr. Kincaid." The Sire pushed himself into Loving's face. "Answer me!"

Loving glared at him. "I would say 'Go to hell,' except you might consider that home sweet home."

The Sire snarled. "Hurt him again."

Deep Throat jabbed Loving again with the knife, reentering the same wound. Loving tried to keep silent, but it was impossible. It was too excruciating. He let out a ferocious scream.

"Don't taunt him," Deep Throat whispered into Loving's ear. "You have no idea how dangerous he is. How crazy. There's nothing he won't do."

Loving was breathing heavily. Lightbulbs were flashing before his eyes. His heart was thumping out of control. This must be what it was like to be crucified, he thought. Having your body torn, stretched, until your heart gave out or you finally died of suffocation. Strong as he was, he knew he couldn't take this much longer. Already he was fading . . .

"Oh no, my investigating friend, we can't have you dozing off. We need something to stimulate you. Here—I think you'll get a charge out of this."

All at once, Loving's entire body felt as if it had been ignited. He cried out, bellowing nonstop, writhing this way and that.

The Sire had a two-pronged electric cattle prod pressed up against him, right on the knife wound. Worse, Loving was still wet from the hose and he wasn't grounded, so the electrical shock waves radiated all over him, crashing down his spine, sending his brain into sensory overload.

"Still not feeling talkative? Let's try it again."

He jabbed Loving again, this time actually pressing the prod inside the knife wound. Loving felt as if he were being rent apart, torn from the inside out. There was no way he could endure this pain—no one could. His heart, already racing, accelerated even more. He began breathing in short quick gasps, never getting enough.

"Please stop." Loving could barely see him—tears and pain were blurring his vision—but he recognized the voice of Deep Throat talking to his master. "He can't take much more of this," Usher said.

"He knows how to make it stop."

"I'm telling you—if you keep this up, he'll die!"

"Then let him die!" the Sire screamed. "I'm ready for my midnight snack!" He thrust the prod forward again and held it, letting the electricity ripple across Loving's body, over and over again. Loving tried to hold it together, tried to stay awake, because he very much feared that if he passed out he'd never wake. But it was impossible. The pain ate at him, his heart, every nerve ending in his body. The room seemed to swirl. He felt dizzy, then nauseous, until at last the deep swell of a black tidal wave overwhelmed him and he felt nothing at all.

"What happened?" the Sire bellowed, staring at the inanimate limp body dangling from the ceiling. "What's going on?"

"I told you to stop!" Usher shoved him aside and pressed his ear to the man's chest. "Damn."

"What is it? What are you saying?"

"Listen for yourself." He pushed the Sire's head to the man's chest. "Hear anything? No. Want to guess why?"

"I—what are you saying?"

"I'm saying you can cut Loving loose now." He threw his scalpel down in disgust. "He had a cardiac seizure. He's dead."

23

Ben had almost stepped into the elevator before he noticed the other occupant. Judge Herndon, wearing an overcoat instead of the usual black robe, smiled and said, "Going my way?" in an eerily reminiscent voice. Perhaps he was a *Twilight Zone* buff, too.

"If you don't mind."

"I don't mind."

"I mean, I wouldn't want to do anything, you know, improper."

The corners of Herndon's lips turned upward. "I suspect we can ride to the top floor without invoking Mr. Padolino's ire. Even if these are the slowest elevators in all humanity."

Ben stepped inside.

"Turning out to be an entertaining little case, isn't it?"

Ben's lips parted wordlessly. Was the judge actually wanting to chitchat about the trial?

"I mean, I knew it was going to be sensational. But I haven't had many that have been as lively. So many twists and turns. Got to hand it to you, Mr. Kincaid. After twenty-two years on the bench, you've made it fun to be a judge again."

Ben watched as the elevator doors slowly closed.

"Did have one concern, though."

"Look, if it's about the vampire thing—"

Herndon made a noise that sounded like *pshaw.* Ben had seen that in books, but he wasn't sure he'd ever actually heard anyone say it before. "I've lived in this town since the day I was born. I've seen a lot weirder shit than that."

Ben's eyes ballooned.

"No, I was thinking more about your whole approach to the case. The jury. I know I made some remarks at the outset of the case that might conceivably be construed as disparaging to you and the land you hail from, and I apologize for that. Like to spin the new kids around a little. But you've proven you can handle yourself in the courtroom. One of the best I've seen, to tell the truth. I mean, I've had any number of fancy orators—which you're not, by the way. But when you speak, people get the feeling you really believe what you're saying. I can't tell you how rare that is. Can't be taught—you've either got it or you don't. I can't imagine how you've managed to have a successful law practice and still hang on to that."

A look at our accounting books might answer that question for you, Ben thought.

"Here's the thing, though," the judge continued. "When you're doing your cross, when you talk to the jury, you're pretty matter-of-fact. No high drama, no flamboyance. You're just organized and prepared and make a lot of sense. You don't appeal to people's emotions; you appeal to their intelligence."

Ben watched as the floor buttons lit, one after the other. This really was the slowest elevator in all creation. "Is that bad?"

Herndon shrugged. "I've been out to your part of the world a time or two. Just visiting. Liked what I saw. No matter what the scientists say, people are different, and people in different places learn to behave differently, and I like the folks down your way. They're friendlier. They say hello to people they pass on the street. Cashiers say 'have a nice day' like they really mean it. They remember what courtesy is. And people haven't gotten so wound up with all the newfangled flaky ideas floating around that they've forgotten what common sense is."

"I sense a *but* coming."

He chuckled. "But remember, Toto—you're not in Kansas anymore."

"Oklahoma."

"Close enough. My point is, a DC jury is a very different animal. You're in Homicide Heaven now. This is the land of people wiring themselves with walkies-talkies and pretending they're going to blow up the Washington Monument."

"So you're advising me . . . to avoid common sense?"

"I'm not advising you of anything. That would be grossly improper. I'm just giving you a geography lesson." The bell dinged, and the doors finally opened. "See you in court, Mr. Kincaid."

Sure, Ben thought, nodding. And have a nice day.

It was decided, then. Christina was doing the most important direct examination of them all—the defendant, Senator Todd Glancy.

Predictably, since she and Ben had finalized the decision last night, she hadn't been able to sleep at all. It was not possible to overestimate the importance of this testimony; they had no choice now but to put him on, and they had no chance of winning if it didn't go well. But it made sense for Christina to handle it. First of all, they knew the judge and jury had been appalled by all the talk of sex, weird sex, and violence against women. If Christina acted as if she was Glancy's friend and supporter, if she showed that she, a woman, trusted him and believed him and even liked him, that could help assuage some of the jurors' ill feelings toward him. Moreover, it was certain that Padolino would want to ask Glancy about each and every sexual allegation in detail, now that he was being accused of being some sort of twisted hybrid of JFK and the Terminator. He'd probably cross more about the sex than the murder; it was his strongest punch going into the final round. But if it was a woman asking the questions and objecting, it was just possible he might tone down some of the most lurid, most inflammatory language and accusations.

Worth a try, anyway.

*   *   *

As Christina entered the courtroom, she was shocked to see Shandy Craig, the turncoat intern, sitting behind the prosecution table. She was seated beside Lieutenant Albertson, the detective who had first investigated the murder. They seemed to be getting along famously.

Christina planned to pass by her without comment, but when their eyes met, and Shandy gave her a sort of sneering turn of the lips, Christina couldn't restrain herself. "I'm surprised you have the wherewithal to show your face in this courtroom."

Shandy took it in stride. "All I did was tell the truth. Only a lawyer would think there was something wrong with that."

"Don't try to cast yourself as some crusader," Christina snapped. "You lied. You spied. You pretended to be something you weren't. A friend."

"And a good thing I did," Shandy said defiantly. "If I hadn't, your client might've gotten away with murder."

"My client is not a murderer. And you have no basis for being proud about sneaking around a man's office, sniffing for evidence to use against him, while pretending to be a confidante."

"That's a bit of an exaggeration," Albertson said, cutting in. He was just as rude to her as he'd been the day the body was discovered. "The DA knew all about this plan—and approved it. For that matter, so did I."

Christina hesitated for a moment. Albertson was in on this little sting? Now that she noticed, he and Shandy did appear to be sitting rather close together. Unusually close together.

Well, she had no time for that. She pulled out her files and outlines, the courtroom began to fill, and she took note of all the familiar faces. Almost everyone who had testified, anyone who had been a part of this case, was present. All the senator's staff. His wife. Several other congressmen, including the not-for-long junior senator from Oklahoma and Arkansas's MacReady. Even Darrin Cooper, the victim's father, was present, sitting in the back row, although she noticed one of the several security officers on guard was standing very close beside him. She only hoped they'd stripped him down to his shorts the way they did Ben.

It seemed everyone wanted to hear Senator Glancy testify. What could he possibly say in light of the horrific charges that had been leveled against him?

Glancy was escorted into the courtroom and Ben followed close behind. "Ready to go, slugger?" he said, laying a hand on Christina's shoulder.

"As I'll ever be." Christina took several deep breaths, trying to steady herself, as she watched the bailiff enter through the rear door and call the court to order.

Let the games begin.

"Senator Glancy, we've all seen the video and we've heard the testimony of various witnesses. Were you in fact having an affair with Veronica Cooper?"

"Yes," he answered. He looked at the jurors levelly, composed, soft-spoken. Earnest, but not so much so that he seemed to be trying too hard. Like his wife, Christina observed, he knew how to handle himself, how to communicate to an audience. Which was only to be expected from a politician of his experience, she supposed. "If you can call it that. We had sex on several occasions. I thought I was the only one; I didn't know about all these other men, or her involvement with these clubs and . . . vampires, or whatever they are. And I certainly did not know about her drug addiction."

"What are your feelings now about your relationship with Ms. Cooper?"

"I deeply regret it. And I want to publicly apologize, not only to the people in this room but to all my constituents, for my conduct. What I did was wrong, inexcusable. I made a terrible mistake. And I am sorry."

Padolino rose to his feet. "Move to strike the witness's apology, if that's what it was. Irrelevant."

"Sustained," Herndon replied.

"Would you have acted differently if you had known about her addiction?"

"Of course. I would never have engaged in a relationship with someone who might not be in her right mind. I would've tried to get her some help." He heard some audible scoffing from the prosecution table. "You know, these people have tried to portray me as some sort of predator, someone who wanted to hurt Veronica. Nothing could be further from the truth. I was trying to help her.

Several of the other applicants for her job were more qualified, but I knew that Veronica had a troubled past, a bad childhood, an absentee father. Dirt poor, raised in one of the worst neighborhoods imaginable. I was trying to help her, to give her a chance to better herself. I didn't plan the intimate relationship. It developed over time. We worked a lot together, spent many long hours together . . . and it just happened." He paused. "She was obviously not a virgin when the affair began, and it in no way affected our work. And I might add, what we did was entirely consensual. In fact, she was the initial instigator. Even in that video, awful as it is, I think you can see that she was ready and willing to have sex."

That's enough of that, Christina thought. Move on.

"I don't want to sound self-righteous," Glancy continued, still maintaining his cool, measured tone, "but this really is a case of no good turn going unpunished. If I had forsaken Veronica for one of those spoiled rich kids that usually get these positions, none of this would ever have happened."

Christina tried the Ben trick—watching the jury out the corner of her eye. Were they buying any of this? Too soon to tell.

"The detective who previously testified indicated that in the months preceding Veronica Cooper's death, you had romantic liaisons with other women as well."

"And in most of those cases, he's wrong." Glancy raised his chin, adding a bit of strength to his demeanor. "That's so typical of a detective. Anytime they see a man and a woman enter a room together alone, they assume there's going to be hanky-panky. I find his assumptions sexist and offensive, particularly in this day and age. I notice he didn't claim to have seen anything through a window, even though he appears to be a career Peeping Tom. What he saw, for the most part, was business meetings. I am a workaholic—anyone who knows me can tell you that—and I often work late into the night. Sometimes that work involves meeting people, and sometimes those people are women. Is that a surprise when there are so many female professionals in DC these days? Sometimes those meetings are in hotels, especially when the guests are out-of-towners, but we're talking about places like the Watergate, not Motel 6. I mean, honestly—if I wanted to have an affair with someone, would I go to a hotel? In this town? Of course not. Everyone here knows me on sight. I never did that with Veronica and I would never do it with anyone else."

"I noticed you said most of the detective's accusations were untrue," Christina said, anticipating Padolino's cross. "Was there an exception?"

"One, yes." He lowered his head and seemed supremely ashamed. "A one-night stand. With another Senate employee. I am not going to give her name for obvious reasons. But I have told my wife about it. We've discussed it and come to terms with it. I've agreed to get some help. As soon as this trial is over—if I'm able—I plan to obtain counseling for sex addiction. Or maybe it's power addiction, I don't know. Whatever it is, I understand that I have a problem, and with my wife's help I'm going to overcome it." He raised his hands. "And that's the way it should be. This is a family matter. It's private, or should be, even when it involves public figures. It's really nobody else's business."

Christina paused, letting the jury soak that in. She knew he wouldn't change any minds in the press gallery, but it was just possible he might speak to one of the jurors—especially any who might've had an affair themselves, or who'd had a secret revealed they'd just as soon had stayed private.

"I appreciate what you're saying, Senator. But I'm afraid there is one other matter I have to ask you about. One other woman. One of the prosecution witnesses, Steve Melanfield, the lobbyist who admitted he was a political opponent of yours, claims to have seen you engaged in a sexual act with a woman named Delia Collins."

"Absolutely untrue," Glancy said defiantly. "I met with Ms. Collins on many occasions. My heart bled for her. She had a terminal illness, but she just couldn't accept her fate. She was chasing after all these quack miracle cures—you can't believe how many leeches there are taking advantage of people who have been diagnosed with terminal illnesses. She wanted her insurance company to pay for these treatments. I understood where she was coming from, but if an insurance company gave in to that once, they'd soon have a landslide of similar claims. Everyone's premiums would go up. The companies might well go bankrupt."

"To be specific," Christina said, drawing him out of politics and back to the case, "Mr. Melanfield testified that he saw you in your office receiving sexual favors from Ms. Collins."

"He's wrong," Glancy replied. "And as I recall, he admitted he never saw my face. I don't know what he saw or indeed if he saw anything at all. But I know this—it wasn't me." He stopped, lowering his eyes. "I would never have taken advantage of that dear, strong woman. I was devastated a few months later when I read that she had succumbed to her illness."

Well, they had pretty well covered sex, Christina thought. Now could they possibly talk about the murder?

"Senator Glancy, your wife has testified that when she learned of the existence of the videotape, she gathered funds for the purpose of paying off Ms. Cooper. And she also says she told you about her plan. Is this true?"

"It is. But I disagreed with her actions. I didn't want to pay the woman a cent."

"Why not?"

"I don't think it's appropriate to pay blackmail, especially when you're an elected official. Or married to one. It only encourages more of the same. And it seems clear now that Veronica intended to blow the money on drugs. With all due respect to my dear wife, paying Veronica off was a mistake."

"Did you attempt to prevent your wife from making the payoff?"

Glancy smiled a little. "Christina, I don't have the power to prevent my wife from doing anything. I'm not sure there's anyone on earth who does. But I took actions of my own."

"And what would that be?"

"I called Veronica. Made an appointment to meet her at the Senate the next day. The day she was killed."

Now that got a reaction from the jury. Christina wasn't sure if they believed him, but at least they were listening.

"Did she agree to meet with you?"

"She did. That's why I made the notation in the Gutenberg—my day planner. That's why she was at the Senate that day, even though she didn't come in for work. And that's why I left the Health Committee meeting."

"Then you admit that you met her that day."

"I admit that I tried. But I didn't set up any rendezvous in my hideaway. That would be stupid. I arranged to meet her in the Senate Dining Room. A public place, but one where reporters are not allowed and the staff can be counted on to be discreet. I left by the backstairs door, true, but I turned right, not left, and made my way to the dining room, not to the basement. I don't know who Shandy saw or heard when she was doing her Mata Hari routine, but it wasn't me. I was in the dining room wondering why Veronica hadn't shown up."

"She never arrived?"

"Never. After a while, I returned to the committee meeting, but when it broke for lunch I went back to the dining room, just in case she came late. Stayed there for a long time—you remember. That was when I first met you. I finally returned to my office, and that was when I learned to my horror that Veronica was dead."

Christina closed her notebook. That about covered it. Just one more very important question to ask. "Senator Glancy, did you kill Veronica Cooper?"

"Absolutely not. I would never do that. Never. Not to her or anyone else."

"Thank you, sir," Christina said. That had gone well, she thought. But of course, the hard part was yet to come.

She looked across the courtroom to the prosecution table. "Pass the witness."

"Wha—wha—where am I?"

Slowly the opaque haze lifted from his head, his eyes. Everything throbbed, every part of him. The light hurt his eyes, so he closed them. He had no idea where he was or what had happened. All he knew for sure was that he was alive. And very surprised to be.

"Take it easy. You're still weak. You need rest."

Loving forced his eyes open again. Deep Throat? They were still in that musty basement room. But he wasn't hanging from the ceiling anymore. He was lying on the hard concrete floor. And he was alive!

"You really did start to go into seizure. Too much electricity will do that."

"The—the Sire—"

"He left when I told him you were dead. Fortunately, he didn't have the training or experience to detect your heartbeat, especially when it was so faint. As soon as he was gone, I shot you up with epinephrine to stimulate your heart. Treated the knife wound, too. But you need to take it easy. You've been through a lot, and too much activity after a dose of epinephrine could throw you into seizure all over again."

Loving had no problem following the command to stay put. He felt much too puny to move. "Why did you do all this for me?"

"Look, I'm sorry I got you involved in the first place. It's just—I didn't know what else to do. You may have noticed—he's crazy."

"And the rest of your little club?"

"Don't be a smart-ass. I may be intrigued by the vampire mythology. I even think the bloodsucking ritual is a turn-on, but I draw the line at murder. And what he's got going on in the narthex—that's inhuman. This whole operation—" He shook his head fiercely. "I never wanted to go after those girls—I never wanted any part of it. The Sire lost control and now everyone in the Inner Circle is paying the price."

"But—"

"Shh. Just try to rest. The others have already left. As soon as the Sire leaves, I'll smuggle you out of here. Get you back to your people at the law firm. A big tough guy like you should heal up in no time."

"And you?"

"I think—I think I'm going to leave town. Start somewhere else. It's obvious to me now—no one can take down the Sire. Not me, not you. He really is immortal. Indestructible. The best I can hope for is to go somewhere far away, somewhere safe, someplace he can never hurt me, and then—"

He froze in midsentence. His entire body stiffened. At first, Loving thought he was going to scream, but when the sound actually came out, it was quieter, more like a strange, hollow rattle.

A death rattle.

His body tumbled forward, and there was nothing Loving could do to avoid it. It fell sideways across his abdomen, knocking the air out of his chest, leaving him gasping for breath.

A scalpel was sticking out of the back of his neck.

In the distance, Loving saw a pair of piercing eyes hovering above him.

"So glad to see you're still alive, Mr. Loving." The Sire began to laugh, loud and horribly, hysterically, his dark, deep laughter echoing through the tiny subterranean room. "Now I'll have the pleasure of killing you myself. After I've learned what I want to know. After I've sucked you dry."

"Well now, that was a sweet little story you told," Padolino said, as he strode across the courtroom toward Senator Glancy. "Touching, especially the part about your close relationship with your wife. I felt my eyes getting itchy."

Glancy remained phlegmatic. "Was that a question? If it was, I didn't understand it."

"So now you admit that you were planning to meet Veronica Cooper on the day she died, at about the same time she died, and that you entered the rear stairway that led to your hideaway at just that time. But we're supposed to believe you didn't kill her?"

"That's right. I didn't."

"Must've been someone else. Someone who intercepted her on her way to the cafeteria."

"I really have no idea. I can't imagine who would want to kill her."

"Then we agree on that point, Senator. No one had any reason to kill her. Except you."

Christina started to rise, but Glancy was already answering. "I disagree with that statement. I had no motive at all. As my wife said, she had the situation under control. Sure, I wanted to meet with her, to see if we couldn't come up with some better solution than blackmail payments. I could see she had problems, possibly mental problems, and I knew that video was going to make it impossible for her to work again in DC. I wanted to see if I could help her make a fresh start, find her another job, maybe something in Oklahoma. I have a lot of friends back home. It wouldn't be hard."

"How altruistic of you."

"And even if that didn't work—Marie had given her the money she wanted. Either way, I had no motive to kill her."

"Assuming we believe everything you've told us. Which I for one don't."

Christina gave Ben the eye. Padolino was making a lot of non-question smart remarks. She could object, but she had a hunch that Padolino's sudden resort to arrogance and sarcasm would turn the jury off, which could only work to Todd's favor. Give the man enough rope . . .

"Even if I were going to kill her," Glancy continued, "which I would never, ever do, I certainly wouldn't do it at the U.S. Senate. That's just stupid. And leave the corpse in my own hideaway? That's beyond stupid. That's idiotic."

"So you want us to believe you would never, ever do that, right?"

"Right." Glancy allowed himself a small smile. "Hell, if I really were stupid enough to kill someone at the U.S. Senate, I wouldn't leave the corpse in my hideaway." He paused. "I'd take it to some Republican's hideaway."

Grim as the subject was, that actually got a few chuckles. More important, Christina thought, he'd made his point.

"This all assumes that the murder was carefully planned in advance. But I think it's more likely that you got angry when your attempt to charm her out of her blackmail money failed, lost control, killed her, didn't know what to do with the body, and left her there till you had time to come up with something better."

"Wrong. All of it. And just for the record, Mr. Padolino, I never lose control."

Wrong thing to say. "Yes, we've heard all about how you like to stay in control. How you like to dominate. Especially when you're with your many, many women."

Aw, swell, Christina thought, priming herself to object. Here we go.

"There were two," Glancy said emphatically. "I told you that. No one has proven anything different."

"And what about the handcuffs? Ropes? Is that part of how you like to stay in control?"

Christina rose to object, but Glancy literally waved her down. "Let me say once and for all that I am sick and tired of your use of this courtroom to engage in slanderous statements that don't relate to the murder in any way, shape, or form." He was becoming a little heated, but Christina thought—hoped—that he was okay. "I have admitted that I made mistakes, that I had affairs with two women. What possible business of yours is it how we like to go about it? I know it has been fashionable in the press to pry into politicians' sex lives under the veil of a 'character issue.' Are we now going to start doing that in the courtroom? If you made these statements any-where else, I could sue you for slander, and I for one do not see why courtroom immunity should extend to a prosecutor making gratu-itous sexual innuendos that don't relate to the case at bar."

"Lovely little speech," Padolino said, clapping. "Very dramatic. Move to strike."

To everyone's surprise, Judge Herndon hesitated. "No," he said finally, "I think I'm going to let that stand. It was irrelevant, but then so was your question. I think I'd like to see that remain in the record. Maybe, with luck, one of the reporters in the room will print it. Or perhaps even give it some thought."

Padolino was furious. Christina could see him scanning his out-line, looking for another dramatic topic. "Exactly how many times have you lied to the public now, Senator?"

"I'm not aware of any."

"You lied about your affair."

"At no time did I lie about any affair. I was silent on the matter. There's a big difference."

"I believe that's what, in my church, we call a sin of omission."

"Call it what you like. It wasn't a lie. I didn't lie before and I'm not lying now." He turned to face the jury. "You have my word on that. I will not lie to you."

"You expect us to trust you?" Padolino said indignantly. "Your own wife, the woman who knows you best in all the world, doesn't trust you."

"I beg to differ."

"She hired a private detective to follow your floozies around, Senator. Trusting wives don't do that."

For the first time, Glancy was silent for several moments. "When the issue arose between us, I admitted what I had done im-mediately. I did not lie to her about it."

"Really. And did you tell her about the other girl as well?"

Christina's ears pricked up. Not because of the accusation, but because savvy Mr. Padolino had used the word *girl*. Not the more politically correct *woman*.

"What girl?"

"The other one. The Senate employee with whom you've admitted having an affair."

Glancy thought a long time before answering. "No."

Padolino smiled, triumphant at last. He returned to his table, picked up a small manila folder, then returned to the podium.

"I'm worried," Christina whispered to Ben.

"Why? What's in the folder?"

"I don't know. That's why I'm worried."

"Senator Glancy," Padolino said, breaking the silence, "what was the name of the other woman with whom you had a sexual liaison?"

He exhaled heavily. "I said before, I see no purpose in dragging someone else through—"

"I'm afraid you have no choice, sir. You must answer my question."

"I won't."

"You're under oath."

"To tell the truth. And I have. But that doesn't extend to the unnecessary tarnishing of the reputation of an innocent person."

Padolino pressed his hand against his heart. "Once again, Senator, I am moved by your breathtaking nobility. But in fact, you have another reason for wanting to keep her identity unknown, don't you?"

"This is despicable," Glancy said, increasingly angry. "You're using my silence to imply things that aren't there."

"Who's your other lover, Senator Glancy?"

"I've told you, I refuse to answer the question."

"Are you pleading the Fifth?"

"No. This isn't about self-incrimination. This is about protecting others."

"Let's all remember that he said that."

Judge Herndon cut in. "Mr. Prosecutor, if you so request, the court can order the witness to answer or be held in contempt of court."

"Thank you, your honor, but that won't be necessary." He reached inside his folder and withdrew one sheet of paper. "Senator Glancy, would your lover's name by any chance be Tiffany Dell?"

Glancy didn't answer, but even he couldn't prevent his eyes from widening, his lips from parting.

Where have I heard that name before? Christina asked herself. Somewhere around here . . .

And then she remembered. And realized how bad this really was.

"Thank you for that visual confirmation, sir. Not that I had any doubt. You see, I've spoken to Miss Dell. And she told me all about it."

"Objection!" Christina said, rising to her feet. She didn't care what Glancy thought; it was time to intervene. "We've had no notice of this witness. She is not on the prosecution's list."

"We do not plan to call her," Padolino replied. "She only came to us late last night, after she read an account in the *Post* of Mr. Capshaw's testimony about the senator's other lovers."

"Whether she's taking the stand or not, he's using her testimony. We should've been told."

"Certainly, if she had anything exculpatory to say, we would've notified the defense immediately. But that wasn't the case. Far from it."

"Your honor," Christina insisted, "this is inexcusable. It's trial by ambush!"

Judge Herndon leaned across the bench, gavel pointed, a somber expression on his face. "Mr. Padolino, do you give me your word as an officer of the court that you knew nothing of this informant before last night?"

"Absolutely, your honor."

"And will you make her and any of her records or documents available to the defense should they wish it?"

"We will. She's in the building now, sir."

He fell back into his chair. "Very well. I'll allow it. But you're on a short leash, Mr. Prosecutor."

"Understood, sir."

Christina cut in. "Your honor, I must—"

"I said I'd allow it, counsel!" He slammed his gavel. "The cross-examination will continue."

Padolino turned his gaze back to Glancy, the expression on his face so smug Christina wanted to scrape it off with a pizza knife. "Senator, knowing your strong feelings about truth telling, you're not going to deny that you know Miss Dell, are you?"

"No," he said quietly.

"And you won't deny that you had an affair with her, either, will you?"

"If she's already admitted it publicly, I suppose there's no point."

"Glad you're being so reasonable. Let me ask you, Senator—how old is she?"

Glancy hesitated. "I . . . don't know. She's young, if that's what you're getting at."

"Well, of course, she's young. You only interview, hire, and sleep with women who are young."

"Objection!" Christina shouted.

"Short leash, Mr. Padolino," Judge Herndon said, a fierce tone in his voice. "Very short leash."

"Right, right," Padolino said, holding up his hands. "My apologies. What I want to know, Senator, is her age."

"I don't know her age."

"Don't you? You sponsored her. Because she's not exactly a congressional staffer, as you led the jury to believe. She's a congressional page. A high school student." He paused. "She's seventeen."

Christina's eyes closed. Just as she feared. It was the same Tiffany whom Glancy had sent to meet Ben and Christina when they first came to the Senate.

The stir in the courtroom was almost deafening. Judge Herndon slammed his gavel, but it still took several moments to restore any semblance of order.

"Senator, why did you sponsor Miss Dell?"

Glancy took a deep breath. "She's a bright, ambitious young woman who was raised in a very poor undereducated family in rural Oklahoma. As with Ms. Cooper, I was trying to do her a favor."

"Do *her* a favor? Or do yourself a favor? What did you promise this bright, ambitious girl if she would submit to your disgusting advances?"

"I never did anything of the sort. This is all untrue!"

"I don't think so, Senator. She was a minor and you knew it. You knew it when you sponsored her and you knew it when you took her to bed."

"I object!" Christina bellowed.

"Sustained!" Herndon said, equally loudly. "Consider yourself fined, Mr. Padolino. One more outburst like that and you'll be spending the night in jail."

Padolino plowed ahead just the same. "You didn't suppress her name because you were trying to protect Miss Dell. You were trying to protect yourself. From a rape charge!"

"That's not true!" Glancy insisted. "It was entirely consensual."

"It was statutory rape, at the very least," Padolino continued. "And I wonder if it wasn't more than that."

"Again I must object!" Christina said. "This is pure character assassination. It has nothing to do with the murder."

"Oh, I'm getting to that," Padolino said, in a way that sent chills down Christina's spine. "I'm just laying the foundation here. There's much more yet to come."

"Then get to it," Judge Herndon said. "I've had about as much of this as I'm going to take."

"Senator Glancy," Padolino said, "do you recall the intimate evening you spent with Miss Dell?"

Glancy's whole demeanor, his very presence, had changed. He looked rumpled, confused, uncomfortable. His face was red. Sweat dripped down the side of his face. "Of course I do."

"That's good. Do you remember the part when you bit her on the neck?"

One of the female jurors gasped. They all looked horrified.

"I didn't do anything I thought would be . . . unpleasurable to her."

"Indeed. Do you remember when you cut her?"

And that was when Christina knew. Knew for certain. That was when it became hopeless.

"Again," Glancy said, suddenly looking old, desperate, lecherous, and totally untrustworthy, "it's none of your business what goes on between consenting adults."

"But she's not quite an adult, is she?"

"I didn't do anything she didn't like!"

"Anything she didn't like? Or anything you didn't like?"

Glancy's face was so tight, so flushed, he looked as if he might explode. "She . . . was enjoying it!"

"No, sir. *You* were enjoying it. It was your fetish. Always being in control. She told me she asked you to stop repeatedly. But you wouldn't." The buzz in the courtroom rose, but Padolino continued. "She said you cut her neck, and she cried out for you to stop, but you wouldn't. She said it was as if you lost all reason, as if you became some sort of monster!"

"Objection!" Christina shouted. "Is counsel testifying now or just repeating hearsay from his ambush witness?"

Padolino ignored her. "Tiffany said you cut her, and you wouldn't stop, and she believed that if she hadn't been strong enough to stop you, you would've killed her!"

Christina objected, and Glancy denied, but they were both drowned out by the tumult that swept across the courtroom. It took much gavel pounding before Judge Herndon restored any semblance of order.

"Just answer this for the jury," Padolino said, "and answer truthfully, sir, because I have photographs that were taken by Miss Dell the very night it happened. Do you deny that you cut your young lover on the neck? With a knife?"

The wait seemed interminable. But at last they got their answer.

"No," Glancy said quietly. "I don't deny it."

And then it was over. Not the cross—that went on for another half hour, and then Christina attempted to redirect, for all the good it did. And they would interview Tiffany Dell and try to find some holes in her story. But that had nothing to do with the trial. The trial, as Christina knew all too well, was over. She had no doubts now about whether the jury would convict. She only wondered if they would do her the courtesy of deliberating.

The Sire was dancing around the dead body of his former underling, clapping his hands and shouting in tones that bordered between elation and hysteria. "You thought you could escape the Inner Circle? You thought you could escape my wrath? You *fool*!

Thus to all traitors. Thus to all who challenge the Brotherhood of Miatas. I am the Sire! I cannot be defeated!"

He's insane, Loving thought, as he lay helplessly on the floor. Totally over the edge. He knew it was only a matter of time before the Sire killed him. And in his current condition, he was unable to stop it. Even if he managed to pull himself up, he could never move fast enough to elude that drooling psychopath.

"You thought you could defeat me, didn't you?" He jerked the scalpel out of Deep Throat's neck and pressed it against Loving's throat. "You thought you could take what was mine. Mine! You thought you could steal from me! No one takes what is mine, my sad pathetic friend. I am an immortal! I am a god among men."

"Fine," Loving managed to spit out. "Kill me. But let Beatrice go. There's no reason why you have to kill her."

The Sire shook his head, giving Loving a pitying expression. "How little you understand. After all this time."

Loving felt his gorge rising in his stomach. He had failed—totally and utterly failed. He couldn't save Beatrice. He couldn't even save himself.

"How does it feel to be helpless, my strapping friend? How does it feel to know that your time on this planet is about to come to an end? That I'm going to add your petty life to my collection of souls. That I will drink your blood for my breakfast?"

Loving desperately wanted to tell him what he thought, but he knew that wouldn't be wise.

"Still silent? Very well. Prepare yourself. Say a prayer, if you think it will do you any good." He held up the scalpel; it glistened in the overhead light. "I'm going to cut your throat now. And drink from you like a fountain. Like a fountain!" He crouched down beside Loving. "I'm going to cut you like—"

"I don't think so. Say cheese, Dracula."

"*What?*" The Sire whirled around in the direction of the voice, but before he could complete the turn the room was split by the sound of a projectile whistling through the air. It thudded into the center of the Sire's chest. He screamed, then collapsed.

His hands were clutching the bolt of a crossbow.

"Nice shot, if I do say so myself. Kind of disappointed he didn't turn into dust, though."

Loving leaned forward, struggling to see. "Shalimar!"

She walked beside him, beaming. "Yup. Your friendly neighborhood vampire hunter."

Loving did his best to appear cross. "I told you to stay outside."

"Yeah. Good thing I didn't listen, huh?" She crouched beside him. "How are you?"

Loving grunted and stretched out his arm. "Help me up." He felt extremely woozy, but he was determined to stay at his feet. "The Sire. Is he dead?"

"Nah. Hurting real bad, I hope, but not dead. See? Eyes still open."

Loving bent over the Sire, who was writhing on the floor, trying unsuccessfully to remove the bolt. Loving desperately wanted to kill the fiend on the spot, but he knew that wouldn't be smart, however pleasurable.

He grabbed the end of the crossbow and gave it a twist. The Sire screeched like a banshee. "Not so fun when the sharp instrument is inside *you*, huh? You're bleedin' big-time. The human body only contains eight pints of blood, as I 'spect you know, bein' an expert on the subject. So if you don't tell me what I want to know, immediately, not only am I not gonna call an ambulance, but I'm going to leave you here to die slowly. Then I'm going to let all your henchvamps come in and lap up your blood. And then—" He leaned closer so the Sire could feel his breath. "Then I'm going to take your body to the Playground and put it in the room reserved for necrophiliacs. For the first time in your miserable existence, you'll be bringin' some joy into someone else's life." He paused, giving the man a look that made it clear he was not bluffing. "One chance. Only. Where's Beatrice?"

The Sire raised a shaky hand and pointed up the stairs. Then he jerked his hand to the left.

"You'd better be tellin' the truth, or I'll prove to everyone in the Inner Circle that you're not immortal. Come on, Shalimar."

Shalimar raced upstairs and across the hall, then through the far left door. Loving hobbled behind as best he could. She threw open the door.

"Oh my God."

It was like a wing of a hospital ward, one bed after the next, all of them alike, all of them occupied. By young girls.

"Beatrice!"

Shalimar spotted her long before Loving did. She raced to her sister's side. Loving followed as quickly as possible.

She looked much as she had when he'd seen her earlier, in the Inner Circle ceremony—pale, weak, motionless. But now her eyes were open, and they reacted to the sound of her sister's voice.

"Beatrice! Oh my God. Beatrice!"

Shalimar leaned across the bed and hugged her sister tightly, tears streaming from her eyes. Loving sat on the edge of the bed, tired, hurting, but so so glad. They'd found her. She wasn't dead. She was—

Loving spotted the IV needle in her arm. Beside the bed was a bottle filled with a red fluid.

Her blood.

And as he scanned the room, he saw that on every bed, every girl had an IV needle in her arm, and a half-filled bottle beside her.

Oh my God, Loving thought. This was too much. Too much.

"Call the ambulance," he whispered, the best he could manage. "Call the police. Ask for Lieutenant Albertson."

And then he closed his eyes and tried to make the rest of the world go away.

Oh my God. Oh my dear God.

Part Four

Duende

24

en and Padolino were huddled in the judge's chambers, both hunched over the man's desk while Christina and Padolino's assistants stood barely a foot behind them, each feeding their attorneys case law and citations as the legal wrangling roiled. The court reporter sat just behind them, her fingers rapidly taking down everything that was said.

"This is absolutely unacceptable," Padolino declared. "The trial is over. He was done."

"I never rested," Ben said. "The judge specifically said we could have more time."

"To interrogate Tiffany Dell, yes. Not to drum up some surprise witness."

"Right," Ben shot back. "Only the prosecution is allowed to do that."

"I never put Tiffany Dell on the stand!"

"You used her as a witness just the same."

"Gentlemen, stop!" Herndon put his hands down firmly on his desk. "I've had enough of this bickering. If you have a legal argument to make, then make it. If you have some precedent to present to the court, heaven forbid, please do so. Otherwise, be quiet!"

They both started to speak at once. Herndon raised a finger. "I want you to both sit down. Now. We're going to take turns. You remember about taking turns? Perhaps your mothers introduced the concept one day when you were playing Candy Land."

Both attorneys eyed each other. Lips parted.

"Padolino," Herndon declared, "you're first."

"Your honor, in the name of fundamental fairness, do not allow the defense to pull out some unknown witness at the eleventh hour in a desperate attempt to salvage a case they are going to lose—for good reason. My associates can provide you with a dozen cases in which judges refused to hear testimony from witnesses who were not on the pretrial witness list."

"Nonetheless, this is surely a matter that has to be considered on a case-by-case basis."

"But we didn't even know this woman existed before Mr. Kincaid called us last night. We've had no opportunity to talk to her."

"I have it on the authority of Lieutenant Albertson of the DCPD that Mr. Kincaid himself did not know about this woman or talk to her prior to her discovery by his investigator last night. And the only reason you haven't been able to talk to her is that she's been in the Bethesda intensive care unit along with many other young women discovered on the same premises."

"Just the same—"

Herndon adjusted the direction of his finger. "Okay, you've had your say. Now it's Mr. Kincaid's turn."

"Your honor, the only reason I'm asking the court to permit this testimony is that it is vital to uncovering the truth."

"It always is," he said wearily.

"Moreover, it is critical to understanding what happened to Veronica Cooper."

"Oh honestly," Padolino said, "as if we didn't already know what—"

"Counselor," Herndon admonished, "it is not your turn. Back to the Peppermint Stick Forest."

Padolino clammed up.

Ben continued. "Of course we'll give the prosecutors access to her, the same as we've had, as much as her doctors will permit."

"What about this other person? The one the police chief called 'the Sire'?"

"Real name Barry Dodds, real estate agent by day. Vamp by night." Ben shook his head. "He's not talking—for obvious reasons. Judge, this girl is all we've got."

"And the minor problem of her not being on the witness list?"

"I could show you mounds of case law in which new witnesses were allowed to be added when they were discovered after the trial began—but I don't have to, because you already know all about them. Mr. Padolino was allowed to use a previously unlisted witness, and whether he actually called her or not, her testimony was devastating to my client on cross-examination. All I'm asking for is the same leniency you gave the prosecution."

"But my witness was a young woman of unquestioned integrity," Padolino insisted. "His witness is—is—well, for God's sake. She's a vampire!"

"Not exactly," Ben corrected.

"Okay, she just runs with the wolves, whatever. The point is, the fundamental credibility required of any witness, and especially from an eleventh-hour surprise witness, is utterly lacking."

Herndon batted his finger against his lips. A long time passed in silence while the attorneys waited in excruciating suspense.

"You both make good points," Herndon said, at long last. "And I suspect I could rule either way and not be wrong. The only difference is, if I say no to Mr. Kincaid, he's going to lose, and Appeal Item Number One would be my ruling against his new witness. Why should I let that happen? That's not good for me or the prosecutor's office. Furthermore—" He paused, looking deeply into Ben's eyes. "—I've been watching the defense work for several weeks now. And I tend to think that if Mr. Kincaid says this witness is critical to learning the truth about what really happened—then she probably is. I'm going to allow it."

"But—"

Herndon turned his finger. "Don't bother. The prosecution's

objection is noted. But the jury is going to hear what this woman has to say."

Given all that she had been through, Beatrice looked better than Ben expected, but there was no denying her fragility, the brittle-glass quality of her demeanor. She had been brought to the stand in a wheelchair, and her doctors had insisted that she should testify for no longer than one hour without taking a break of equal length, and that she should be on the stand for no more than four hours a day. Her skin was pale—almost to the point of being translucent—but Ben knew she had suffered severe blood loss and probably had not seen the sun for a very long time.

"It was all fun at first," Beatrice explained. Her voice was quiet and delicate; even with her microphone turned up to its maximum volume, the spectators in the rear of the gallery had to strain to hear what she was saying. "We were just four DC working girls out partying, trying to have a good time. Originally, we frequented the usual twentysomething haunts—the Rhino Bar and Pumphouse, that sort of place. But as we soon learned, we all had a dark side—probably what brought us together in the first place. We were all into Goth, so we started going to those clubs. We thought the whole occult thing was kind of sexy. So it was inevitable that we would end up at Stigmata. The owner's head toady, Sid Bartmann, took a shine to us and invited us to their upstairs apartment one night—and that was when our lives began to fall apart."

"Was that when you first began taking drugs?"

"Yes. Bartmann had a lab not far from the club where he cooked the stuff up. The drugs only increased the intensity of the fun, at first. And the sex . . . well, you got used to it, after a while. If you were high enough, that could be fun, too. Some of the men up there learned about our . . . interests, and they took us to a meeting of Circle Thirteen. That was where the Sire spotted us. His minions invited us into the Inner Circle, allowed us to take part in their secret ceremonies. All very thrilling. Exciting. Sexy. Like I said, fun, fun, fun. Until Colleen got killed."

Beatrice described how the Sire had taken them, while they were all high, and involved them in the Inner Circle's sacrificial rites. Colleen had been chosen to be the first because she was so immersed

in the vampiric mythos. It had long been a fantasy of hers to participate in a gothic vampire sexcapade.

"Her hands were bound behind her back," Beatrice explained,
her voice halting. "She was tied to a chair. And we just stood there
watching, thinking how cool this was, getting more than a little
turned on. We'd been warned that the ceremony required some
small bloodletting, but hey, we were vampires, right? They assured
us the drugs would prevent Colleen from feeling any pain, only
erotic pleasure, and the injury would be small and temporary and
invisible.

"But something went wrong. That was when we realized the
Sire wasn't a wannabe. He truly believed he was a vampire.
'Vampyr,' he liked to say. And he craved blood. Craved it with such
intensity that he lost all control. That's what happened with
Colleen. I don't know how to explain it with any word other than—
bloodlust. Once he stuck his teeth into Colleen and started drinking
from her, he couldn't stop himself. He started on her neck but eventually moved to her jugular. Blood spewed everywhere. Colleen's
eyes bulged. She screamed, but somehow that only seemed to titil-
late him, to urge him on."

"Did you try to stop it?" Ben asked.

"God, yes. All three of us ran to help her, but the other members
of the Inner Circle held us back. They told us not to worry—they'd
seen it happen before." She paused. "I don't think even they realized
just how out of control the Sire was. And by the time they did—it
was too late." Tears poured from her eyes. "Colleen was dead."

Ben gave her a moment to collect herself, then forged ahead.
"What happened next?"

"We didn't know what to do. Amber wanted to go to the police,
but the Sire said we were just as likely to go to jail as he was. We
were accomplices; they'd get us on felony murder charges, he said.
Plus—we needed that drug. If you haven't been dependent on a
drug, you can't know what it's like. Veronica talked about us all
quitting our jobs and getting out of town—but we didn't have the
money to last a week on our own, and we knew it wouldn't be a day
before we came crawling back to Sid or the Sire to get our fix. We
were hooked. We couldn't live without it. We'd do anything for it."
Her head fell. "Even sell out our friend. Even cover up her murder."

"So you . . . just went back to the party-hard swinging vampire life?"

"At first. Then Veronica came up with an idea—a way to make some serious getaway money—enough to buy a huge supply of the drug, enough to last us for years, enough to blow town and start our lives over again somewhere outside the influence of the Sire. Somewhere far away from those hypnotic eyes."

"Do you know what her plan was?"

"More or less. She was going to film Senator Glancy having sex with her—then blackmail him for money."

Several members of the jury stirred. For the first time, the story presented by the Glancys had received some independent verification.

"And did you think that plan was . . . realistic?"

"Definitely. Veronica had a way about her. It wasn't just that she was gorgeous. She knew how to make herself irresistible, how to make men know she was interested, available, or better yet, how to make them think she wanted them. And it wasn't all a show, either. She liked having sex and as with most things in life—practice makes perfect. She was good at it. Veronica was kind of like a drug herself. Men became addicted to her."

"Did you follow the progress of her . . . plan?"

"For a while. Till the morning one of the Sire's Inner Circle goons showed up unannounced at the apartment Amber and I shared after she left the escort service. With a gun."

"Why was he there?"

She pressed a hand against her chest, trying to regain her strength. "The video had been released—the video Veronica made to blackmail Senator Glancy—and suddenly the eyes of the world were on her. The Sire was afraid she'd expose everything. He'd decided it would be best to 'bring us all in.' He'd gone to the Capitol to collect Veronica himself and sent this goon after us. Well, we knew what that meant. We'd heard about the young girls who went to the Inner Circle and disappeared. We'd seen the Sire and some of the other hard-core bloodsuckers going into that secret, always locked, back room, licking their chops. I knew if we cooperated, no one would ever hear from us again. So I made like I was coming on to him, snuggled up close, fiddled with his fly. And while I distracted him, Amber snuck up behind him and clubbed him on the side of the head with a baseball bat."

Ben nodded. Hell of a dramatic story. But was the jury buying it? "What did you do then?"

"What else? We ran. Tried to disappear, become invisible. We knew the Sire had connections everywhere—including with the police, so that was not a realistic option. We had to lie low, deep down under the radar. But how far can you get without using ATMs, credit cards, contacting friends? And just to make everything harder, remember—we were going cold turkey, trying to function without the drug for the first time in months. We were a mess. Couldn't think straight, couldn't plan more than a minute ahead at a time. Stuffing ourselves with sugary foods and booze, trying to make the pain go away. Eventually Amber couldn't stand it anymore. She went back to Stigmata for a fix. Of course, once Randy had her back in his clutches again, he never let her go. Until she ended up getting shot. Through his police connections, the Sire had learned that Amber's father was in town and tracked him down. When her father refused to talk, the Sire killed him, stuffed his body in the trunk of his car, and stole his wallet. They looked enough alike that he could pass using Daily's photo ID, as long as no one looked too closely. He eventually caught up to Amber in the hospital and killed her. I got to hear him brag about it." Her head fell. She pressed her fingers against her forehead, as if trying to extinguish the pain, the grief. "Because he caught me, too."

"But he didn't kill you?"

"No. He'd had to kill Amber, since he couldn't get her out of the hospital without being seen, but there was no reason to be so harsh with me. He pumped me full of drugs that kept me half stoned and tried to brainwash me, torturing me, making me participate in sick ceremonies, slapping me around and then making me beg for more. He broke my nose. But I never gave in to it. I pretended that I did—but I didn't. The problem was—he knew."

"So why didn't he kill you?"

"He wanted me to suffer, just as he said he had suffered after we 'deserted' him. He wanted to put me through hell. So he put me in that room with the others in the back of that church of his, tied me down to the bed—and he sucked my blood. While I was still awake and alive."

Sickened expressions crossed the faces in the jury box. The outpouring of pity was so strong Ben could feel it. If only some of that sympathy would spill over to his client . . .

"Not all at once, mind you. He'd take a pint here, a pint there. When he wasn't around, his assistants would take our blood in the more conventional way. Me and the others—we were his living blood bank. He'd wait till I'd had time to produce more blood, then suck me down again."

"A fact the police can confirm," Ben inserted, and he noticed Padolino didn't object. Because he knew it was true.

"But every day," Beatrice said, "every single day he reminded me that eventually he was going to kill me. He'd . . . play with me. Hurt me. Torment me in any way imaginable, both mental and . . . physical. He never let me move, stretch, go outside. He would spoon-feed me the most disgusting gruel you could imagine. He didn't even let me go to the bathroom—just gave me a chamberpot and told me to do the best I could. I couldn't shower. I got bedsores. My muscles atrophied. I still can't move my left arm. Every day the pain got worse, but he didn't care. He wanted me to live in hell, the sadistic bastard. And I did. I did." Tears again streamed down her cheeks. "And the worst of it was—I knew I had no chance of escape. None. The only thing I had to look forward to was death. A slow painful death caused by that disgusting psycho sucking out all my blood."

Ben paused a moment. Her testimony had been painful, not only for her to give, but for everyone to listen to. But he had a little more ground to cover before they took a break.

"Beatrice . . . who killed Veronica Cooper?"

"The Sire. He told me he was going to do it, then laughed about it after she was dead. Laughed because he'd not only silenced her—he'd made a quarter of a million dollars." She paused, wiped the water from her face, then continued. "He went to the Senate the morning after the video broke—the same morning he sent his flunkie after me and Amber. He bribed some old security guard to put a false name on the 'expected dignitaries' list so he could get in and out without leaving a trace. He found Veronica, overpowered her, bit her, took her money—and gave her that anticoagulant to make sure she bled to death."

"Let the record reflect," Ben said quietly, "that a police search of the so-called Temple of the Vampire, detailed in the report admitted as Exhibit D-235, reveals that a quarter of a million dollars in cash was found in a satchel in the man known as the Sire's bedroom. A comparison of serial numbers has established that this money came from the Glancys' Grand Cayman bank account. And the satchel was splattered with blood that matches that of Veronica Cooper. They also found a bottle of the anticoagulant known as warfarin."

"We never meant for this to happen," Beatrice said, her voice cracking, tears streaming through the fingers spread across her face. "All we wanted was a little fun, something to relieve our stress at the end of the workday. And now—now—" She began to choke, her words mingling with her sobbing. "Now all my friends are dead. All of them. And I don't feel as if I can go on living another day. The doctors watch over me, trying to save me, and I keep thinking— why? Why bother? Why not just let it end and let me finally— finally—find some peace?"

Silence blanketed the courtroom like a shroud. Judge Herndon called for the prearranged break. But no one was listening. Everyone's eyes were on the poor broken girl in the witness stand, not yet even twenty-two, who only a few months ago had a life so vibrant, so promising, that almost anyone might've envied it. And who now was so miserable that she secretly wished her doctors would let her die.

After the break, Padolino attempted to cross-examine Beatrice, but there was little he could do, and he was smart enough not to push her over the brink, an act that would've made the jury despise him. He emphasized how ill she had been, how often she had been on drugs, and naturally suggested that anything she said, anything she thought she remembered, was suspect. The prosecutor repeatedly hammered the fact that she had not seen the Sire commit the murder and was in reality only making surmises about what had happened based upon what this career liar had told her. And he reminded the jury that despite the horrific tragedy these girls had suffered, all the hard-and-fast evidence still pointed to Senator Glancy.

After the drama of Beatrice's testimony, closing arguments were almost anticlimactic—but still of critical importance. Perhaps more than in any previous case in his career, Ben realized that everything could hinge on them, as the jury tried to weigh the credibility of Beatrice's astonishing testimony, whether it could possibly be true, whether it was enough to overcome all the evidence that pointed to Todd Glancy as the killer.

"Ladies and gentlemen of the jury," Padolino began, "when all is said and done, it comes down to this. Which is more likely: that Veronica Cooper was killed by a man who knew her, worked with her, had an illicit affair with her, was being blackmailed by her, had scheduled a meeting with her, left a meeting just before the time of her death, and controlled the hideaway in which she was found? Or that she was killed by some hitherto unknown person with no knowledge of or access to the Senate, who the defense wants you to believe was a—" He rolled his eyes. "—a *vampire,* covering up the evil deeds of his equally diabolical coven. Which one sounds like the truth, the world as we know it, and which one sounds like a preposterous fantasy cooked up by a desperate defense? In the final analysis, I don't think it's all that hard a question to answer."

Padolino proceeded along those lines for nearly an hour, reviewing all the evidence that had been presented during the case and never missing an opportunity to remind the jury of the unsavory secrets that had been revealed about the defendant. "Using a typically disreputable defense tactic, they have attempted to save the defendant by trashing his victim—but it didn't work, did it? They say the victim had an active sex life—the implication being that this makes it okay for Senator Glancy to have sex with one of his young employees, perhaps even to murder her. A detective was called to provide more slander. Even the senator's wife was called to talk trash about poor dead Veronica Cooper—but in each case, what we learned about Senator Glancy was far more illuminating. That he has had not one but many affairs. That he favors aberrant, sickening sexual practices—practices which in many respects resemble the wounds found on the victim. Worst of all, that he has engaged in sexual promiscuity with a minor—a seventeen-year-old girl—and subjected her to the same ugly perversions as the others. That he cut her on the neck, just as Veronica Cooper was cut—fatally. Good God—" Padolino's voice swelled. "You saw that video. What *isn't* this man capable of doing?"

Padolino turned, pivoting, then walked slowly to the edge of the jury box and laid his hand upon the rail. "Don't misunderstand me. My heart bled just like yours did when we heard the testimony of that poor woman, Beatrice Taylor, when she told us about the torment, the horrors that she and her friends endured. But that had nothing to do with the supernatural. That had to do with a megalomaniacal drug pusher. He wasn't controlling those girls with the hypnotic power of his vampire eyes—he was controlling them with drugs. And whether he drank blood or not, it doesn't change the fact that there is no such thing as a vampire and there is no evidence— not the slightest shred of evidence—that this man was ever on the grounds of the Senate, not on the day Veronica Cooper died or at any other time. Ms. Taylor suggests that he bribed a guard to get into the Senate building without recording his name on the daily registry. Well, isn't that convenient? I've heard that you can't see vampires in a mirror. Apparently you can't see them in the United States Capitol building, either."

He paused, looking at each juror in turn. Ben could tell he was winding up for the grand finale. "You know what this is? It's the Big Lie Defense. Tell a little lie, and people may be suspicious, think you're just trying to get yourself off. But if you can concoct something huge, something outrageously unlikely, people are actually more likely to buy it, on the theory that no one would dare tell a tale that tall unless it were true. That's what has happened in this trial, my friends. They couldn't give you another likely suspect. So instead—they gave you Count Dracula."

He stepped closer, and even though his voice grew softer, it seemed more urgent, more insistent. "But you're not that gullible, are you? You're not that easily misled by courtroom shenanigans. You can still distinguish right from wrong, truth from fiction, the likely from the impossible. You know in your hearts what really happened. Senator Glancy and Veronica Cooper were having an illicit sexual relationship. She tried to blackmail him. So he killed her and dumped the body in his private hideaway till he could think of something better to do with it. It's that simple. And that's why I know you'll do the right thing—and find the defendant guilty of the murder of Veronica Cooper. Guilty of murder in the first degree."

"Let's get one thing straight right up front," Ben said, as he approached the jury box. "This case does not come down to which of Mr. Padolino's scenarios you think is most likely. In fact, I will tell you—and the judge will reinforce this later when he gives you your formal instructions before deliberation—that it makes no difference whatsoever which you think is most likely. Because the standard before you is not 'what's more likely.' The standard is whether the prosecution has proven Todd Glancy's guilt beyond a reasonable doubt. If they have done anything less—regardless of what you think is most likely—you must acquit.

"The prosecutor has done his best to belittle the evidence we have presented—even though we have presented tons of it, with one consistent witness after another. Let me tell you something. I am well aware that there is no such thing as a vampire. But what I am telling you is that this nut thought he was a vampire, that he behaved as a vampire, that he led others, with the force of his personality, his sexual prowess, and his drugs, to believe that he was a vampire, and induced them to become a part of his vampiric cult. It is undisputed that he killed Colleen Smith as well as Amber Daily, and more to the point—that he had a motive for killing Veronica Cooper. So let me rephrase Mr. Padolino's question. Which is more likely: that Veronica Cooper was killed by a sadistic maniac who was responsible for the deaths of at least two of her friends and the torture of numerous other women? Or that she was killed by a United States senator, a man with no criminal record whatsoever."

Ben reminded the jury that the evidence against his client was mostly circumstantial. "Contrary to what the prosecutor has said, there is no evidence directly pointing to Senator Glancy. They did all the pointing—the police and the prosecutors—because he was the most obvious and easiest person to accuse."

"Your honor," Padolino said, rising, "I object. This isn't relevant and it slanders the good men and women who are devoted public—"

"Sit down," Herndon said firmly. "And don't get up again."

Ben jerked his thumb toward the prosecutor. "Mr. Padolino

thinks it's unfair for me to insinuate that the police investigation of this case was lazy. But ask yourselves this: why didn't they discover the vampire coven? Why didn't they discover Stigmata, a club the victim had been habituating for months? Why didn't they know she was a drug addict? Why didn't they know she frequently traveled with three other young women—all of whom disappeared? My investigator was able to uncover these secrets—why couldn't they? Answer: because they didn't look. Senator Glancy wasn't arrested because of any overwhelming evidence. He was arrested because the true killer had the sense to implicate someone he knew the cops—and the public—would be predisposed to distrust. Because he was a politician."

Ben faced the jury squarely and ratcheted his voice up a few decibels. "Is this important? You bet it is. Sure, the majority of law enforcement officers in this country are good honest people and we owe them our respect and our thanks. But every time I turn around, it seems as if our civil rights are eroding. We overlook police procedural violations, police brutality, because after all, the suspects are almost always guilty, right? The Second Amendment supposedly protects us from unwarranted intrusions, search and seizures, arrest without charge or probable cause, but every day we see those rights whittled away. We pass laws we know aren't constitutional, but shield the offense by giving them names like the Patriot Act—as if there was something patriotic about violating the constitutional freedoms that are the bedrock upon which this country was founded.

"Is this important?" Ben asked again, this time his voice was even louder than before. "You better believe it. Because this is the United States of America. We created the modern democracy. We invented the Constitution, a written document that guarantees the people's rights—and restricts the powers of the government. I love this country, but every time we let another constitutional right be trampled upon, every time we look the other way while some wrongful act is committed in the name of homeland security, or national defense, or patriotism, we become a little less American. The erosion of one civil right only leads to another, and I would suggest, ladies and gentlemen, that's exactly what's happening here—and it's wrong. Because here in the United States, we don't lock people away because it's fashionable to think the worst of politicians. We don't arrest people because a crime is committed in their workspace. And we don't prosecute people without performing a thorough investigation that has convinced us—*convinced* us—that we have the right man."

Ben took a few steps forward and laid his hands gently upon the rail. "Let me ask you, ladies and gentlemen of the jury. Are you convinced that they have the right man? Has the prosecution proven to you—beyond a reasonable doubt—that Todd Glancy killed Veronica Cooper? Or is it just possible that it was someone else? Is it just possible that it happened exactly as described by Beatrice Taylor, the closest thing we have to an eyewitness in this case, the woman who knows more about what went on in Veronica Cooper's life than anyone else in the world. Is it possible? Do you have a reasonable doubt? Because if you do—if, when you walk back into that jury room, you have a reasonable doubt about what really happened, then you must find my client not guilty. Why? Because this is the United States of America." He let several seconds pass before he added, quietly: "And that's the way we do things here."

25

"Holy smokes, Ben," Glancy said, shaking his head. He was waiting, with Ben and Christina, in a small room just a few doors down from where the jury was deliberating. "If you can give a speech like that every day, you should run for President."

"You're too kind."

"No, I'm a politician—or was, anyway—and I've heard enough orations to know a good one from a bad one. That was a humdinger. All you needed was some facile remark about family values and the invocation of the deity and it would've been perfect." He stopped, then his voice dropped a few notches. "But was it enough to convince the jury?"

Ben had to be honest. "I don't know."

Christina jumped in. "I thought you covered all the main points. Brilliantly and persuasively."

"Perhaps. But we had some bad evidence. The pathetic thing is, the worst of it had nothing to do with who murdered Veronica Cooper. But the jury still heard it."

Glancy didn't respond. They all knew what Ben was talking about.

"What about me?" Glancy asked. "How did I do on the stand? You never said."

Ben chose his words carefully. "I thought you did the best you could . . . given the circumstances."

"You had to handle some tough questions," Christina interjected, trying to add a more upbeat note.

"Yeah, sure, I know all that. But did I have . . . duende?"

Ben frowned. "Would it be a good thing if you did?"

Glancy smiled. That's Spanish. It's like . . . charisma. The power to attract and persuade through personal magnetism and charm. I'm asking you if I seemed . . . charismatic?"

Ben stared at him with weary eyes. Were you charismatic while you were talking about your affair with a minor and your aberrant sexual fetishes? "Juries are more interested in what a witness has to say than how they say it."

Glancy blew Ben a raspberry. "Says you. Charisma is all. If you've got enough of it, you can get away with anything."

"That hasn't been my experience."

"It sure as heck has been mine. Haven't you noticed how no one ever talks about whether a White House candidate is smart or knowledgeable or experienced or capable anymore? They talk about whether he's electable. Whether he seems presidential."

"The legal world operates differently."

"Does it? Answer me this: Why did every single member of Nixon's staff of any importance whatsoever do jail time—except Henry Kissinger, the most active and influential of them all?"

Ben hazarded a guess. "Charisma?"

"Darn tootin'. And he was a funny-looking German Jew with an almost incomprehensible accent. But he courted the press. He had PR people releasing statements about how he was dating Jill St. John or whatever. Meanwhile, he orchestrated the secret and illegal bombing of Cambodia. He authorized the Indonesian invasion of East Timor. He pushed for and got a CIA coup to overthrow the democratically elected Allende government in Chile. If someone had done stuff like

that in Germany during World War II they'd've been tried at Nurem-
berg for war crimes. But when Kissinger did it, what happened?
Criminal charges? No. Instead, he became a wealthy businessman
and a senior statesman on CNN. And you know why?"

"Charisma?"

"Bingo. He was just so charming—no one could believe he
knew about those naughty Watergate plumbers and their friends,
even when common sense tells us he couldn't have been a part of
that administration and not have known about it. Some people
think the whole reason for the Watergate burglary was to see if the
Democrats knew Kissinger had sabotaged the '68 Democratic Vietnam peace initiative which, if successful, would've almost certainly
given Humphrey the presidency. Remember, Nixon won by less than
one percent of the popular vote."

"I think that's a bit of a stretch," Ben said.

"Of course you do. You're a good guy. So you assume everyone
else is, too. But mark my words, Ben—one day that foolish assump-
tion is going to drop-kick you right between the legs."

Actually, Ben thought, it already had, on more than one occasion, but those were stories he didn't care to repeat.

Glancy stretched back into his chair. "So what are the odds?
Fifty-fifty? Better? Worse?"

"I never make predictions," Ben answered. "Juries are too unpredictable."

"Aw, come on. Give me a hint."

"Sorry. I don't know. We'll all find out together."

"Fine." Glancy scrunched down in his seat. "But if we lose, I'm
not inviting your mother to my annual May Day barbecue."

"Just as well," Ben said, smiling slightly. "She wouldn't come."

The outside door whipped open. Padolino leaned inside. "It's
showtime!" He shut the door behind him.

"Already?" Glancy said. "They've barely been out two hours!
What does that mean?"

Ben glanced at Christina, his lips pursed. "It means they didn't
need much time to make up their minds."

Ben thought they got it from television, but Christina's theory
was that every person—and thus every juror—had a secret sadistic

streak, a Mr. Hyde lurking in the back of the cerebral cortex waiting for a proper exercise of power to give it expression. Either way, it was a universal constant that when the jury returned from deliberation, they took great pains to give no indication of their decision. Their faces were blank. They looked at no one.

"Has the jury reached a verdict?" Judge Herndon asked.

"We have," said the foreperson, an older woman sitting on the far left of the front row. The bailiff took the folded verdict form to the judge, who carefully scrutinized it with the same stoic expression that was plastered on the jurors. Finally, without a word of comment, he returned it to the bailiff.

"The defendant will rise."

Glancy did so, followed by his counsel. To their surprise, just behind them, Marie Glancy rose as well.

The foreperson cleared her throat. "We the jury, in the case of the District of Columbia versus Todd K. Glancy, on the charge of first-degree murder—" She stopped.

Ben winced. Why did they always insist on the dramatic pause?

"—on the charge of first-degree murder," she continued, "and for that matter, on the charge of second-degree murder and manslaughter, we find the defendant Todd K. Glancy not guilty."

The courtroom exploded. That was the only way Ben could describe it. Some people were shouting with joy. Some were expressing disgust. But whether out of surprise, relief, or pure cynicism, everyone was talking.

"Oh my God," Ben heard Glancy muttering softly beside him. "Much as I tried to keep my spirits up, I never really believed— never thought it was possible—" His voice choked. "Oh. My. God."

Ben closed his eyes. They had actually managed to pull it off. Against all odds, he and Christina had actually managed to pull it off. *O frabjous day!*

Glancy was nearly in tears. He thanked the jury, then tried to hug Christina and shake Ben's hand, both at once. He looked silly and confused, clearly so overwhelmed he hardly knew what he was doing. Judge Herndon slammed his gavel several times, making a mostly futile effort to quiet the courtroom. When the tumult had finally subsided sufficiently that the judge could be heard, he thanked the jury, gave them a few more final instructions—including reminding them that they were not required to speak to the press and that he personally advised against it—and discharged them. Then he turned his gavel to the main attraction in the courtroom.

"Mr. Glancy," he said sonorously, "you are free to go."

There was more cheering now, less mixed than before. The opposition was leaving the courtroom—Ben had seen both Steve Melanfield and Brad Tidwell depart with shocked expressions on their faces—and Todd's friends and staff were gathering around him, embracing him, congratulating.

"Thank you," he said graciously, "but the accolades should go to Ben and Christina. They're the ones who made this happen."

There was more jubilation, slapping of backs, and aggressive hand-shaking. Marie Glancy stepped up to Ben and quietly whispered in his ear. "Thank you," she said, and she kissed him lightly on the cheek. "You've pulled off a miracle."

"That's why I get paid the big money," he replied.

Christina gave him a wry expression.

"I feel as if I've gotten my whole life back," Glancy said. He still seemed stunned, utterly amazed. "All the anxiety, the turmoil, all these months. And now, it's finally over."

Of course, Ben knew it wasn't. There was still a possibility of statutory rape charges. If Padolino could figure out a way to pursue them that didn't make him look like a poor loser spitefully determined to put Glancy away on any charge he could scrape up. And the only way Glancy could avoid being censured in the Senate would be if he resigned first.

The celebration continued. Ben was surprised to feel a hand tugging on his back. It was Joe Padolino.

"Kudos, counselor," Padolino said graciously. "You tried a fine case. Hell of a closing. I think that's where you won it."

Ben brushed the compliment away. "The evidence won it. The jury knew Beatrice Taylor was telling the truth."

"Yes, but on cross, I—" He stopped himself. "Aren't we lawyers pathetic? We never know when to quit." He smiled, then passed Ben a scrap of paper. "When all the celebrating is over, would you give this to Christina?"

"What is it?"

"My phone number."

"Um—oh."

"I just thought now that the trial was over, she might have more time for . . . you know. Socializing."

Ben nodded slowly. "I'll see that she gets it."

"Great." He slapped Ben's shoulder. "And congratulations again."

Ben returned to the frenzied activity surrounding his client. Hazel had her steno pad out, taking notes. Amanda was doing some scribbling as well. Glancy was firing off one assignment after another. Apparently, now that the trial was over, he wasn't wasting a minute before taking charge again.

"—and I want the Blue Beetle replaced once and for all, even if it has to come out of my own pocket. Next time I'm caught in a national crisis, I don't want my interns running to Kinko's to get the press releases copied."

Everyone laughed. Tears were in many eyes.

"What about a press conference?" Amanda said. "I think we need a press conference."

"No," Glancy said. "We've had a wonderful result, but that doesn't change the fact that a tragedy occurred. We don't want to appear to be taking political advantage of that poor girl's death—or any of the other deaths."

"I suppose you're right." Amanda scribbled a few notes onto her legal pad. "We'll let a day pass, then put out a press release."

Glancy rolled his eyes. "And finally—Marshall?"

His executive assistant wheeled to the forefront. "Yes, sir?"

"Toss me your cell phone."

"Sorry, Boss—I misplaced my briefcase somewhere this morning and my phone was in it."

"Well, when you find it, call that damned overpriced appeals expert we bought—and tell him he's fired. We don't need him anymore!" Another round of cheers filled the courtroom. "All right, you clowns, get me back to the office. I want to see what a mess you've made of it in my absence. And I have a bottle of Dom Pérignon 1963 I've been saving for a special occasion. I don't think they're going to get any more special than this."

Part Five

The Genuine Article

26

Ben and Loving split off from the rest of the group. They had another stop they needed to make before they joined the party back at the senator's office.

Loving knelt beside the hospital bed in Room 342 at Bethesda. He wasn't surprised to see that Shalimar was also there, watching over the patient. He placed his hand on the pale blonde's forehead. "How ya feelin', sweetheart?"

Beatrice looked up at him, a faint smile on her pale, barely red lips. "Doing okay."

Loving jerked his thumb toward Ben. "Didn't I tell you my man would take care of you in the courtroom?"

"Did he ever. Have you heard what they've been saying about him on the radio?"

Ben raised an eyebrow. "About me?"

"Everyone's falling over themselves praising Ben's defense work.

Even Glancy's political enemies, people who still think he's guilty, are complimenting him. Did you hear what the governor said?"

Ben's eyes widened. "The governor?"

"Of Oklahoma, yeah. I don't remember the exact words. But basically it was, It's a shame our trusted senator brought us so much embarrassment—but at least we had Ben Kincaid up there to show the world what it really means to be an Oklahoman."

Ben gaped. He couldn't believe it.

Beatrice grinned, her lips chapped and cracking. "So yeah, I'd say he did okay." She pulled Loving's hand closer and laid it against her cheek. "But you're my hero."

"Mine, too," Shalimar said, jumping in.

Loving turned a bright shade of crimson. "Aw shucks," he said, sounding for all the world as if he had just stepped out of a Goofy cartoon. "I'm no hero. You're the one who pulled my fat outta the fire after I got myself caught."

"After you got yourself caught trying to save my sister's life. You are a hero, Loving. And I'll never forget what you did for us."

"But testifying was so . . . draining," Beatrice added. "They're giving me drugs to ease the withdrawal symptoms, but it's still . . . hard. The docs say I have to stay here at least another week so they can monitor my recovery."

"That's okay," Loving said sheepishly. "We're not going anywhere soon. I'll keep you company."

"Would you really?" her eyes brightened immediately. "That would be wonderful!" She squeezed his hand tighter. "I feel so much safer when you're around."

"Aw, sweetie, you got nothin' to worry about now." Ben noticed that Loving's eyes were almost as moist as Beatrice's. "The Sire is locked up. The Inner Circle has been dissolved. Nothing can harm you."

"I suppose you're right." She paused. "Did they ever find the knife that was used on poor Veronica?"

"No," Loving answered. "I imagine the Sire hid it someplace after he left the Capitol building. Doesn't matter. What matters is—"

"Wait a minute," Ben said. All at once, he felt a cold chill race down his spine. "Wait just a minute."

Loving turned to stare at him. "What's the problem, Skipper?"

"The knife, that's the problem. It *does* matter." He pounded himself on the forehead. "I thought at the time—but then I got so busy with the rest of the trial—my God. Why didn't I see it before?"

"See what?"

"Loving, I think I've made an incredibly stupid mistake. Incredibly stupid—and incredibly dangerous."

"Would you slow down a minute and explain what you're talkin' about?"

Ben didn't answer. "Can I borrow your cell phone?"

Loving fished it out of his pocket. "Yeah. But why? Who're you calling?"

Ben punched in the number from memory. "Marie Glancy."

"Would you wonderful people mind if I had a few minutes alone with my husband?" Marie said. They were gathered in the lobby of Glancy's office—Todd, Marie, Christina, Marshall, and Hazel. Marshall had popped the cork on a bottle of champagne and was pouring it into Dixie cups. Amanda had left to procure more bubbly and some snacks.

"Of course not," Marshall said. "How long have you two been apart now? Five months?" He winked. "Take five minutes. Ten, even."

Marie took her husband by the hand and led him into his private office, then closed the door behind them.

"Think they'll be able to patch things up?" Christina asked.

"Of course they will," Marshall opined. "They're both professionals. A divorce at this juncture wouldn't be helpful to the career of either of them."

"She heard some pretty ugly stuff in that courtroom."

"Trust me," Hazel said, "she's heard it all before. Maybe not in such a public forum. But she knew what her husband was. She knew when she married him." She shook her head. "This won't make a damn bit of difference."

"I hope you're right," Marshall said, wheeling himself up and handing them each a cup of bubbly. "I hate to start drinking without them. But there's no telling how long they may be. And I for one could use a drink. Christina?"

She hesitated. "Well, maybe one. But then I need to start packing up our stuff. No reason to have all this legal garbage cluttering your office."

"You can take a minute," Marshall insisted. They hoisted the cups above their heads. "Here's to Todd Glancy." They all clinked their cups together.

"What do you think he'll do now?" Christina asked. "Politics is out."

"I don't know. But he'll think of something. Maybe he'll teach, maybe he'll practice law. Maybe he'll write a book. Who can say?" Marshall glanced over at the closed office door. "He has so many possibilities. There's no telling what might happen next."

"Damn!" Ben swore. "Still no answer."

"She's probably callin' all her friends," Loving said. "Tellin' 'em the good news."

"As if there's anyone in this town who doesn't already know. It isn't busy, it just isn't ringing." He closed the cell phone with a firm snap. "She probably turned off her phone when she went into the courtroom and hasn't thought to turn it back on yet. Either that or she's ignoring me. Either way—" He turned back to Loving. "—you can stay here, but I have to go."

"Are you sure?"

"Positive."

"Where you headin'?"

"Back to the Russell Building. As quickly as humanly possible."

Why do I always get stuck with the packing? Christina wondered as she loaded the voluminous documents that had been produced into catalog cases and banker's boxes. It was one thing when she was a legal assistant. Legal assistants expected to get stuck with menial assignments, even when they were three times as bright as their bosses. But she was a lawyer now, and a partner, and—

What was the use? She'd never be able to train Ben to clean up after himself, just as she couldn't train him to take cases that might actually turn a profit. Just as she couldn't get him to—oh, what was the use?

She slung a few more piles of documents into the nearest open box. They were tumbling out of order, but what did it matter? In all likelihood, they would never be looked at again and would eventually be tossed out, unless Ben used them to write another book. It would be smarter to concentrate on the supplies and equipment.

She thought she had everything—Post-it notes, perpetual calendar, the stapler shaped like the Eiffel Tower, the legal pads, the laptop—

Wait a minute. The laptop. Where was that, anyway? She'd loaned it to Marshall yesterday so he could review the previous day's transcript, and she hadn't seen it since. Where was he now?

The door to Marshall's office was open, and she was sure he wouldn't mind if she went inside. After all, Marie had been using it as if it were her own ever since the case began. It wasn't as if Christina could leave without the laptop—the gizmo cost more than she made in a month. It wasn't on top of his desk, so she checked the wide middle drawer. No luck. She started with the side drawers, the first, then the second, then . . .

At the bottom of the third drawer, under a hodgepodge of papers, she saw something gray and metallic. At first, she thought it was the laptop, so she pulled it out. Wrong. Even from the back, she recognized it was a picture frame.

Well, she was never one for denying her unquenchable curiosity.

The woman in the picture was not immediately familiar to Christina, but she was almost certain she'd seen the face before. Not in person, but in another photograph. Perhaps a more formal one. Here, she was laughing, her hair whipped behind her, looking out at the photographer with what could only be called eyes of love.

But who was it? Christina racked her brain, searching for the answer.

And then it came to her. And when she remembered, it suddenly became all too clear what had really happened.

In the corridor behind her, Christina heard someone approach.

"Didn't your mother ever tell you it isn't nice to rummage through other people's belongings? Curiosity killed the cat, you know."

Christina slowly turned to confront the person behind her, even though she already knew who it was.

Marshall Bressler sat in his wheelchair, looking just as he always had. Except this time, there was a very large gun in his right hand. Pointed directly at her.

27

"What the hell is going on here?" Todd Glancy said as he emerged from his private office, his wife close behind him. Marshall Bressler was in the main lobby holding a gun on Christina. "Marshall, have you lost your mind?"

"Maybe I have," he said. There was something eerie about his voice, something Christina had never heard in it before. "Maybe it's been coming for a long time."

"How did you get that gun in here?"

He smiled. "Same way I got in the knife."

"What are you talking about?"

At that moment, Hazel entered through the front door. "What on—?"

"Get away from the door!" Marshall ordered. "Now!" The older woman slithered inside, her eyes wide and fixed not so much on Marshall as on the weapon in his hand.

"All of you—get together. Huddle up in the center against the wall—by the Blue Beetle. Get friendly."

Marshall pushed his chair backward to the center of the lobby, waving the gun back and forth to make sure everyone was covered. "I'm sorry it's had to come to this, people. The only one I wanted was you, Todd. All I ever wanted was you."

"I don't know what you're talking about."

"Of course you don't. Because it's about me, not you. And in your world, it's always about you. You don't give a damn about anyone else."

"Marshall, how can you say that? After all the good we've done, you and me, working side by side, fighting the good fight."

Marshall's teeth locked, his whole face displaying his contempt. "You don't know anything about me."

"Then talk to us," Christina said, trying to deflect his attention. It was obvious Marshall was not stable and that he had some sort of grudge against Glancy. If they continued talking like this much longer, that gun was going to fire. "What is it you want?"

"From you, nothing. You've never been anything but a warm, beautiful, caring person. All you had to do was look at that picture for a second and you got it, didn't you?" Christina didn't answer. "I could've put the damn thing out on my desk, and Todd still wouldn't have understood."

"Maybe if you explain it to him. Maybe if we all just calm down and—"

"It's too late for that!" Marshall's voice soared in volume. His hands began to tremble. "I very much regret having to do this to you, Christina. And to you, Marie, and Hazel." He pointed the gun at Glancy. "But now you're all going to have to watch this son of a bitch die."

"Marshall!" Glancy said. "You can't mean it."

"Believe me, I do."

"Marshall!" Marie shrieked. "Please! I beg you."

"Don't waste your breath."

"Marshall," Marie continued, "look at me. Look—at—me!"

He did, and the instant he did, Todd Glancy dove toward the open front door. Marshall wheeled around and fired, but he was well wide of the mark. He swiveled his chair then fired again, this time missing by inches. Glancy did a forward somersault, landed on his feet, then raced through the door.

"Come back, you miserable coward!" Another bullet shattered the jamb. But Glancy escaped.

"Marie—you traitor!" Enraged, eyes wide and red, Marshall whirled himself around to face the three women huddled around the ancient copying machine. Without a moment's hesitation, he raised the gun and fired. Marie Glancy gasped, then tumbled to the floor.

Christina screamed. "Marie!" Hazel began sobbing.

"And I'll kill you two just like I did her. Just like I did Veronica!" he shouted, weaving back and forth in his wheelchair. "Nobody else moves. Nobody else speaks. Do you hear me? *Do you hear me?* Because if you don't do what I say, you're both dead!"

28

By the time Ben arrived at the Russell Building, a siren was wailing and the Capitol police had already cordoned off the area surrounding Glancy's office. People were being evacuated as quickly as possible. The FBI was on the scene as well. Todd Glancy had contacted the authorities as soon as he escaped, and a full-fledged hostage situation had ensued. The federal agents were assembling an operations center and trying to establish contact with Marshall Bressler, the administrative assistant who was now holding three women hostage.

Including Christina.

"I'm Agent Martinez," said a wide-framed officer wearing a standard FBI blue suit and white shirt. "I'm the situation commander." He gestured toward an older woman in a black sweater with a brown leather gun holster slung over her shoulder. "This is Advisory Commander Cross. We understand you know one of the hostages. A Miss McCall."

"I know all of the hostages," Ben explained. "But yes, I know Christina very well. She's my partner. We've worked together for years."

"Good," Martinez said, while simultaneously waving at an operative at the opposite end of the hallway and pulling out his buzzing cell phone. "That could be useful."

"You got here fast," Ben remarked, impressed.

"We're trained for speedy response. After 9/11, we have no choice. Anthrax, ricin, whatever happens next, we have to be able to respond quickly to protect the nation's leaders. Soon as we got the call from Senator Glancy, we roped off the area and began evacuating the senators and their staff across the street to the Library of Congress. We called out the HAZMAT team—the boys in the white space suits. Just to be on the safe side. Tours have been shut down. The restaurants closed. The pages have been given the day off."

"Why the FBI?"

"We're the hostage experts. The Capitol officers are used to dealing with poison in the mail and streakers and such, but they've never had a full-out hostage scenario here before." He flipped open the lid of his phone. "Excuse me. It's Lieutenant Carney, our tactical commander. I have to take it."

He moved to the other side of the corridor where he could talk with some semblance of quiet. Although the passageway had been blocked off and all civilians had been evacuated, there were still dozens of people in the corridor, all of them moving in busy crisscross patterns, pursuing their appointed tasks with great urgency.

A large marker board had been set up at the top of the stairs. Ben didn't comprehend a lot of it, but he did recognize one sketch as a rough outline of Glancy's office. Several names were written to the side, with abbreviated duty assignments reduced to incomprehensible acronyms. And at the top of the board, in bold black letters, someone had recorded THE FOUR STEPS OF SUCCESSFUL HOSTAGE NEGOTIATION: TRUST, CONTAIN, RECONCILE, RESOLVE.

"I know you're busy," Ben said, grabbing the arm of Advisory Commander Cross, "but can you give me some idea what's going on?"

"We still don't know what started it," Cross patiently explained. She had short brunette hair, an efficient cut that would prevent her hair from ever obstructing her vision. "But the Senator's administrative assistant has apparently gone psychotic. He has a gun—we don't know how he got it in the building. Maybe he overcame one of the security guards."

"Bressler? He can't even stand up." Ben shook his head. "I know how he got the gun into the building. Same way he got in the knife." And then Ben explained it to her.

"He's taken prisoners," Cross said. "Senator Glancy managed to escape, barely, but Bressler has at least three other hostages, maybe more. And one of them is wounded."

Ben's heart raced. "Which one?"

"Marie Glancy."

Ben's eyes closed.

"You look relieved."

"No, of course not. How badly is she hurt?"

"We don't know. Bressler has only spoken to us once, by cell, and he wouldn't say much. All he told us was what he wants."

"Which is?"

"Safe passage out of the country. And Todd Glancy."

"He wants to take Glancy out of the country?"

She shook her head curtly. "He wants to kill him."

"Marshall," Christina said, pleading, "why are you doing this?"

"The time comes," Bressler said, his voice slow and menacing, "when a man has to take action. Has to do what's right. Stand up for the woman he loves."

"I've been working with you for months. You've always been logical, reasoned—the one voice of sanity in a crazy politically obsessed world."

He laughed bitterly. "Guess you didn't know me as well as you thought you did. Ben's going to have to get a new psychic."

"But Marshall—taking hostages? In the U.S. Senate? You can't possibly succeed. I don't care what you do to us—they'll never let you leave. This is crazy."

"Don't call me crazy!" he bellowed. "Don't ever call me crazy! That's what that damn doctor said. That's why he kept cramming me full of those blue pills you've seen me taking, day after day. Well, I don't need the doctor, and I don't need his stupid pills."

"All right, all right." Christina held her hands up, trying to placate him. Behind her, Hazel was huddled beside the copying machine, crumpled on the floor. She had totally fallen apart, melted into a useless heap, racked with sobbing. She wasn't going to be any help. And Marie hadn't moved since the bullet caught her in the chest. If she wasn't dead already, she would be soon.

"Marshall, at least let them send in a doctor for Marie. She's seriously wounded."

"Serves her right. She was never any kind of wife to Todd. All she's ever done is lay plots and plans, look ahead to when Todd would be out of the way and she could start her own political career." He snorted bitterly. "There is some justice in that. Todd got exactly the wife he deserved."

"Whatever she may or may not have done, she doesn't deserve to die. Please ask them for—"

"No doctors!" he yelled, his gun hand wobbling with such uncertainty Christina was afraid it might fire at any moment. "If they want to send someone in, send Todd. He said in the courtroom that he'd do anything for his wife. Fine. Let him come in and get her." A thin smile spread across his lips. "I'll have quite a reception waiting for him."

In the charging bay in the left arm of his wheelchair, Marshall's cell phone sounded.

"They want to talk to you," Christina said.

"I've already said everything I have to say."

"Please talk to them. Maybe you can work something out. Some sort of compromise."

"*No compromises!* They give me what I want—*exactly* what I want—or I start shooting." He raised the gun again, wheeling himself closer and closer as Christina pressed up against the wall. "And you're next."

Ben listened attentively as Agent Martinez attempted to reestablish contact with Marshall Bressler. "Pick up the phone, man. Pick up the phone!"

Finally, on the overhead speaker, they all heard the click of the call being answered. "Have you got Glancy?"

Martinez looked down at his legal pad. Ben could see that he was reading from prepared notes, only improvising when necessary. "Mr. Bressler, I want to help you."

"Then bring me Glancy!"

"I will consider any reasonable requests. And I won't lie to you."

Ben realized Martinez was trying to work his way through those key negotiation steps. But Bressler wouldn't even let him get to first base: Trust.

"There's only one thing I want. Todd Glancy."

"Be reasonable, sir. You know I can't do that."

"Then I guess I'll have to shoot someone else!"

"Please don't do that. You'll only make your situation worse."

"Worse? How could I make things worse?"

"Sir, I know what you've been going through."

"No you don't. How dare you say that when you don't. You couldn't possibly! You can't know what it's like to have the only thing you ever cared about in your entire life, the only thing you ever loved or that ever loved you, taken away."

And that was the final piece of the puzzle. Now Ben understood. At long last he grasped what had happened, what was really going on. He wanted to kick himself in the head. He was so stupid, so slow—why hadn't he seen it sooner? He'd become so obsessed with the trial, trying to devise some way of winning, that he'd missed the obvious. When you considered all the facts—it was the only possible answer.

"Mr. Bressler," Martinez continued, "I want to help. I want to give you any reasonable thing you want or need and make sure no one else gets hurt. But we can't give you another hostage."

"Tell Todd his wife is dying!" the voice on the phone shouted back. "Tell him even if he doesn't give a damn about her, his approval ratings will hit the floor if he lets her die."

Martinez took a deep breath. Ben could see he was struggling to maintain that benign mediator's voice. "As it happens, sir, Senator Glancy has offered repeatedly to give himself up as a trade for his wife. But we can't permit it."

"You'd better change your mind."

"Sir, you've been in government a long time. You know we can never put any private citizen in jeopardy, not under any circumstances. And certainly not a United States senator."

"Then you've doomed every woman in this room!" he hissed back, his voice so loud it made the speakers rattle.

"Sir, wait, please, listen to me. I know you're scared, confused. You don't know what's going to happen. You need someone you can trust. I'm your man. Take me as your hostage. I'll go in, unarmed, unbugged. I won't try anything. You have my word on that. Trade me for your hostages. Or at least for Mrs. Glancy."

"No deal."

"She needs medical attention."

"You're damn right she does! And if she doesn't get it soon, she's gonna die. And won't that be ironic? Won't that be the perfect quid pro fucking quo!"

"Sir, let me come in. Just to talk."

"You send Todd Glancy in here in the next ten minutes, or one of the women dies." The line disconnected with a clatter.

"Jesus," Agent Cross muttered under her breath. "He's going to kill them. He's going to kill them all."

Martinez's fists balled up with frustration. "Can someone please explain to me what this guy's problem is?"

"I can," Ben said. "I get it now."

Martinez turned and stared at him. "Then would you please tell me what I'm supposed to do?"

"That's the problem," Ben said, eyes widening. "There's nothing we can do. It's too late."

"Why won't they give me what I want?" Bressler screamed, wheeling himself back and forth across the office lobby. "Is this so hard? All I want is one lousy senator. Hell, they've got a hundred of them. No one will miss one. Especially not that one."

"Marshall," Christina said, "please try to stay calm." She knew she was taking a risk, talking to him, but she had to do something. His eyes were red and inflamed, he was incoherent with rage. Christina was no expert, but it looked to her as if this previously calm, efficient man of logic was totally losing his grip. And if that was the case, there was no telling what he might do. "Maybe you should ask for something else."

"I don't want anything else!"

"They won't give you Glancy. They can't. Why not ask for money? Or just settle for transportation to some country that the

U.S. doesn't have an extradition treaty with. I'm sure you know more about that than I do."

"No!" he bellowed. "I want Glancy. And I'll get Glancy, or they'll see everyone in this room die!"

"P-p-p-please . . ." It was Hazel, hunched down on the floor, her aged hands covering her head. "Please let me go. I don't care what you do to Todd. I don't care what you do to anyone. But please let me go."

For a moment, gazing at the broken, elderly woman he'd known for more than a decade, Marshall almost regained his usual countenance. "I regret that I must do this to you, Hazel. I truly do. But it's necessary."

"I—I can't take it any longer, Marshall. You know how bad my heart is. I'm not going to make it."

"If you die, you die. It happens." His eyes narrowed. "Even to the people you love most."

Christina steeled herself and took a step forward. "Marshall, please. End this nightmare. Let Marie get medical attention. I know you're not a bad person. I don't—I don't understand what's happened to you. But I can't believe you want to hurt anyone." She held out her hand. "Give it up, Marshall. Give me the gun."

"You want it. Here it is." He fired.

Christina's heart raced. The bullet drilled a hole in the carpet between her legs.

"Now stand by the wall and stay put," he growled, waving her back with the gun. "Next time, I won't miss."

"What was that?" Ben asked, grabbing Agent Cross's arm, refusing to let her go. He knew he was pushing his luck. They'd tolerated him so far because he had information that was useful to them, but they could get rid of him with a single word to one of the dozens of agents on duty. "What happened?"

"That's what Agent Martinez is attempting to find out." She looked over Ben's shoulder and saw the situation commander's signal. "He doesn't think anyone was hurt. Just a stray shot."

"This time! Marshall's getting crazier by the minute. We have to do something."

"Mr. Kincaid, I assure you we are doing something. Everything we can. But we have to play this by the book."

"I don't care about your book. I want Christina out of there. And the others." He paused, desperately searching for a solution. "What about tear gas? Can't you flood the room with gas?"

"Not without him knowing about it. He'd have plenty of time to kill the hostages before the gas knocked him out. And he's said if we try anything of that nature that's exactly what he will do."

"What about a sniper? Doesn't your tactical man have snipers on the scene?"

She threw back her shoulders. Ben was obviously starting to get on her nerves. "He has tons of snipers, Mr. Kincaid—but nowhere to put them. There are no buildings or other perches that would give them a line on Senator Glancy's office. For a reason. This is the U.S. Senate, remember? We've never allowed any construction that could be turned into a potential sniper's nest."

"Maybe a SWAT team could rush the door. We don't even know that it's locked."

"That's an option. But if we do that, realistically, he'll kill at least one of the hostages before they get him. Maybe all of them."

Over by the phone station, Ben saw Martinez stick something in his ear. "What's that?"

"An aural implant. Tiny, can't be seen. But it will allow us to talk to him—if Bressler ever gives him the okay to go in."

"What about over there?" Ben pointed toward three men huddled just to the side of the closed door to Glancy's office. "What are they doing?"

"Trying to get a fiber-optic cable inside. One of Bressler's earlier shots went wild and put a hole in the wall. If we can get a videocam cable through it, we can at least see and hear what's going on."

"But how are we going to get the hostages out?" Ben knew he sounded desperate. He was. He'd known Christina so long, had wasted so much time, and now some madman was threatening to take her away from him forever. "He gave us ten minutes."

"Agent Martinez is negotiating for more time."

"He's not going to give you any more time!"

"So what do you want us to do, Kincaid? Send Glancy in to be slaughtered?"

Ben fell silent.

"Please. Just let us do our jobs!"

"Cross!"

Both of them whirled around. It was Carney, the tactical commander. "Just got this tidbit from the computer geeks. Agent Martinez is on the phone with Bressler, so I thought you'd want to see it."

Cross rapidly scanned the document. "Oh my God."

"What?" Ben said. "What is it?"

"How did you get the doctor to release this?"

Carney looked at her stoically. "We didn't ask. You can expect a lawsuit later."

"Would someone please tell me what it is?" Ben pleaded.

Cross looked at him, thought a moment, then decided to cut him a break. "It's about Marshall Bressler. Did you know he was seeing a psychiatrist?"

Ben's heart felt as if it turned to lead. "Why?"

"According to this, the car accident that crippled him also caused damage to the bilateral lobes of his brain, making him susceptible to delusions, paranoia." She paused. "And given to bursts of sudden uncontrollable mania."

"Meaning?"

"In lay terms? He's a walking time bomb."

"I've been working with him for weeks. I've seen no signs of any . . . mania."

"Because he's been heavily medicated with psychotropic drugs. Have you seen him taking pills?"

"Yes. He said they were pain medication."

"Maybe some of them were. But he was also taking a powerful antipsychotic. One little blue pill every six hours. That's what's kept him under control."

Ben took a step backward, staggering. "He lost his briefcase this morning. So he's off his meds. Combine that with seeing Glancy acquitted—"

"This changes everything," Cross snapped to Carney. "Get a message to Martinez. Tell him—"

She was cut off by the sound of a gun firing inside the office. Followed by a piercing scream.

"What happened?" Ben asked, running toward the phone base. "That was Christina's voice. Was someone shot? *Christina!*"

It was her own fault, Christina thought, as she struggled to remain alert and rational through the blinding pain. Whoever was talking to Marshall on the phone was doing a good job; for the first time, Marshall seemed somewhat distracted. He became so angry, so intent on shouting at the man on the other end, that he lowered his gun. And that was when Christina made her move.

It always worked in the movies, she'd thought, as she fell in a heap onto the carpeted floor. But in real life, people don't move faster than bullets. Even before he fired, she had realized that she wasn't going to get there in time and tried to get out of the way. But it was too late. The bullet caught her in the upper right thigh. It hurt like hell and it was bleeding like a river.

All the times she'd watched cop shows on television, through all the westerns she'd seen as a kid, she'd always wondered what it felt like to be shot. Well, now she knew.

It hurt.

"Please let them send in a doctor," Christina begged. Her voice was weak and feeble and she knew it.

"No!" Marshall screamed. "I told you not to try anything! *I told you!*"

"Then—at least let Hazel tie a tourniquet on my leg. I'm bleeding buckets."

Marshall looked at the elderly woman cringing beside the copying machine. "You really think she's capable of anything like that?"

Fine, damn you. I'll do it myself. Christina placed both hands on opposite ends of her blouse and tore off a long strip. She just wished she hadn't worn something so nice. She'd made the mistake of dressing for court rather than for a bullet wound.

Mustering every ounce of strength she had, she wrapped the strip around her leg, just above the wound, and pulled it as tight as possible. The pain was crippling; she felt lights exploding in her head and thought she might pass out. But that was not an option, she told herself. She had to stay awake. She had to. She tied the tourniquet in a knot, then lay back on the carpet, exhausted.

Are you out there, Ben? she wondered. Because I need you. I

really need you. I'll forget about all the problems, the hesitation, the emotional blindness. I'd forget everything if I could just see you walk through that door.

But she was being stupid. There was no way that could happen. She was trapped with a revenge-crazed lunatic. And judging by the way she felt, if the FBI didn't do something soon, she would never see Ben again.

"Just tell us as much as you can," Martinez said to Marshall over the phone. He had already blown step two: Contain. So he was trying for some hope of Reconcile. "Is she hurt badly?"

Ben felt a hollow, sick feeling in his stomach. Someone had tried to get the gun away from Bressler. And since Marie was unconscious and Hazel was in her sixties . . .

"I warned her!" Bressler screamed. "I warned you all!"

"Can you tell where the bullet struck her?"

"I don't know. Looks like the leg."

"Is she bleeding?"

"Yeah. A lot. She's not going to last long."

"Did the bullet pass through?"

"How the hell would I know?" Marshall's voice rose. "What does it matter? If you don't send me Glancy, the next bullet's going into her skull!"

"Mr. Bressler, please let me come in. Let me be your hostage."

"Why should I trust you? You'll try something, I know you will."

"I won't."

"You have two minutes left!" Bressler screeched. "If I don't see Glancy by then, I'll kill them all. If they aren't dead already."

"Mr. Bressler! Mr. Bressler!"

Agent Martinez continued to argue with the man, but Ben knew it would do no good. Marshall wasn't going to change his mind. This far off his meds, he was way past reason. The FBI was stymied. And meanwhile Christina was dying by inches, losing more blood every second.

He made sure no one was looking. Then he quietly picked up one of the aural implants on the desk and pushed it into his left ear.

He walked slowly down the corridor, passing Agent Cross and

the others. By the door, the three officers were still trying to get the fiber-optic cable through the hole in the wall.

"Change of assignment," Ben said, mustering as much authority as he could manage. "Cross says she wants to see you immediately."

"Now? We've almost got this working."

"Sorry. Those are your orders." The three men dropped their tools and started down the hallway.

Ben stood behind the door—knowing that alone made him a potential target—and shouted. "Marshall!"

From inside, he heard, "Who the—?"

"It's Ben Kincaid. I'm coming in, Marshall."

"The hell you are!"

"I am. And you're not going to shoot me, Marshall. I'm unarmed. You said you thought I was the most honest geek on earth, remember? I think you called me a saint. So you know I'm not lying."

"Kincaid!" This was Agent Cross, about twenty feet down the corridor, running his way. "Freeze immediately! Do not compromise this operation. We will use force if necessary to stop you."

"Then you'll have to shoot me in the back," Ben muttered. "I'm coming in, Marshall!" Then he closed his eyes, said a quick, silent prayer, and turned the doorknob.

Before Agent Cross could stop him, he was inside.

"What are you doing in here? What are you doing?" Bressler waved his hands back and forth in the air. Both hands clutched the gun; he had two fingers wrapped around the trigger. Hazel was cowering in the corner, half hidden by the copying machine. Both Marie and Christina were slumped on the floor. The stillness, the pallor in Marie's expression told Ben she was probably already dead. Blood was seeping out of Christina's thigh, but her eyes were still open. Just barely. But open.

She was alive.

"I came for Christina," Ben said. His heart was palpitating; he was breathing in deep staccato gulps. "And Marie. They need medical help. After I take them outside, I'll come back and be your hostage."

"Are you insane?"

"Probably." Ben was having trouble understanding what the man was saying. Apparently the aural implant was affecting his ambient hearing. "But that's what I'm going to do."

"No, you won't!" Marshall wheeled himself forward until he had the gun right under Ben's nose. "You think you're going to pull something. You're trying to fool me!"

"I already told you, I'm not. I'm not armed at all."

"Prove it!"

"All right, I will." Slowly, one step at a time, Ben began removing his clothes. Come to think of it, he thought, this is the second time I've had to strip in a U.S. Senate building. This never happened to him back in Tulsa.

He continued disrobing, all the way down to his boxer shorts.

"Superman?" Bressler said, staring at the big red "S" shield on the front of Ben's boxers.

"Well, people made fun of my last pair. So I switched to something more macho."

"All right, so you're clean. You're still not taking anyone out of here."

"Yes, Marshall, I am. And then I'll come back and be your hostage. I promise you. I'll stay as long as you need me to stay. You can drill me full of holes if that's what you want. But first I'm getting the wounded women out of here."

"You're risking your damn life, you fool. Why would you do that?"

Ben paused and stared straight at the man in the wheelchair. Even off his meds, even totally off his rocker, there had to be some shred of sanity and decency left inside that head. "Because I don't want Christina to die. Any more than you wanted Delia Collins to die."

Ben took a slow small step, then another, toward Christina. He wobbled a bit as he moved. His legs were trembling, and worse, the implant in his ear was affecting his sense of balance.

"I'll shoot you!"

"I don't think you will, Marshall," Ben said, not looking back. "Because you know you can trust me. And you don't want these women to die. They didn't hurt Delia. You have no reason to wish them harm."

Suddenly, Ben heard an intense squawking in his left ear, so loud he initially thought it had burst his eardrum. "Kincaid? Can you hear us?"

Apparently someone noticed one of their implants was missing. He kept on walking.

"Kincaid!" It was Agent Cross. "You have endangered this entire operation. You will be fully prosecuted for interfering with a federal hostage situation."

Ben kept walking.

"But since you're in there, see if you can get some information out of him. We've got the fiber-optic camera working. We can see and hear you."

Ben knelt beside Christina, his bare knees in the huge pool of blood. She could be dead already, he realized. He could be too late.

"I need to talk to her," he told Bressler.

"No!" he shouted. "Not a word."

"Please. I can't let her lose consciousness."

"I said, no!"

"Just let me ask her one question. One lousy question."

Bressler wavered. "Fine. But that's it. One question."

Ben heard the crackling in his ear. Martinez this time. "Ask if there are any other hostages."

Cross chirped in. "Ask if she's seen any other weapons. Does he have a stash of ammo?"

Ben lifted Christina's hand out of the blood, squeezed it between both of his hands, and asked, quietly, "Will you marry me?"

Christina's eyelids fluttered. When she spoke, her voice sounded like rusty hinges. "What do you think I've been hanging around for all these years, you dunderhead? Of course I will. Now get me out of here."

Ben saw the makeshift tourniquet tied around her upper thigh. A piece of her blouse. Damn she was tough. He tightened it, then wrapped his arms under her and lifted her up. He could tell the movement was causing her pain, but she kept it bottled up inside.

"Stay with us," he murmured to her. "Just a little bit longer."

"I'm watching you!" Marshall cried. "One false move and you're dead!"

He carried Christina to the door, opened it. A huddle of agents stood just outside, their weapons drawn. "Stay back," Ben said. "I gave the man my word." He passed Christina to the nearest agent. Almost immediately, paramedics converged around her.

Ben went back inside for Marie Glancy. When he brought her body into the corridor, he heard Cross hiss, "We can go in behind you. Use you for cover."

"If you do, we might lose Hazel."

"If we don't, we might lose you."

Ben shook his head. "I made a promise. I'm sticking to it." He glanced down at Christina, who was already on a stretcher and being taken away. "Take good care of her." And then he went back inside the office. And closed the door behind him.

29

Ben and Marshall talked and talked and talked. No matter how psychotic the man was, no matter how long he'd been off his medication, Ben was certain he wouldn't try anything without provocation. In the first half hour, he watched as Marshall tired and his rage subsided, until he almost came to resemble the steady, wise Marshall Bressler whom Ben had known and admired these past months. After the first hour of talking, he convinced Marshall to let Hazel go, promising to remain as Marshall's hostage. The more time passed, the more weary Marshall became. He still clutched the gun, but Ben could see his eyes growing hazy, his body weakening. Soon he would have to give in to the biological need for rest. And the more time passed, the less and less Marshall talked about Todd Glancy. And the more he talked about Delia Collins.

"She was a beautiful woman," he said, with such sincerity that Ben found himself feeling sympathy for a man who was threatening to kill him.

"I know. I've seen the photos."

"We met the first time she came to Todd's office to try to enlist his support for that damn insurance bill. We hit it off immediately. I couldn't believe my luck. Here was a beautiful, vivacious woman paying attention to a pathetic cripple. No woman had given me the time of day since my accident—until Delia. Of course we knew her time was limited, but somehow we managed to put that out of our minds. We kept dating—always on the sly so no one would accuse Todd of being improperly influenced—and one thing led to another. Fast. We were so in love. We could hardly keep our hands off each other." He chuckled. "That idiot MacReady who stumbled in and saw Delia making love. She wasn't with Todd. She was with me. Can you believe it? Me!"

"That's what I figured," Ben said. "Eventually. I should've seen it earlier." Because Glancy, the control freak, would never have allowed a woman to be on top. Marshall, being crippled, had no choice but to lie on the floor. That's why he didn't get up when MacReady came in—he couldn't.

"I did everything in my power to get Todd to support the bill. But nothing worked. Nothing. And you know why? Not because he didn't believe in it. He did. But he wouldn't support it. He was too dependent upon insurance companies for their campaign contributions. He wanted to remain viable—in the running for a national ticket. That was the worst of it. We like to pretend that this is a democracy, but it isn't. It's the big money, the special interests, the men pulling the strings behind the curtains, they're the ones who decide what laws are passed and what laws aren't. They decide which candidates to support, which candidates get on the ballot. At best, we get to choose between two candidates who have been selected for us by opposing special interests—and even then the political discourse is determined by campaign contributions. Once the candidates are in office, they're so beholden to their financiers that the whole idea of 'government by the people' becomes a joke." He clenched his teeth tightly together. "You talk about your vampires. These are the real vampires, the genuine article, the monsters who take our public trust and suck it dry, who start out caring about the world and end up only caring about reelection."

Ben tried to understand. "So Glancy killed the bill Delia wanted. Still—she was terminal. Todd Glancy didn't kill her."

Bressler looked at Ben, a stony expression on his face. "About six months after Delia died, clinical tests by a team of researchers in Denmark showed that in some cases, an experimental interferon-based cocktail could slow the spread of ovarian cancer, or in some cases induce a full remission. The FDA eventually approved it for general use in the United States. Delia wanted that treatment. But because it hadn't been approved at the time, Delia's insurance company wouldn't pay for it. And since our American health care system only provides health to those who can pay for it, her sole recourse was Congress. And because Todd Glancy cared more about his own reelection than a bill that could save lives—Delia Collins died. My sweet perfect Delia died." His voice was like gravel, racked with sorrow. "My life was over. What chance did I have of ever finding a love like that?"

"What chance does any of us have?" Ben responded quietly, wondering what was going on outside, in a hospital room somewhere, with a beautiful strawberry-blond patient. "So you decided to take revenge."

"I bided my time, waiting for the right moment. Todd is a careful man; he doesn't take many chances. But when he started up with that intern, I knew I had my opportunity. I was just going to expose him, create a scandal, originally. Then I thought of something better."

"Framing him for murder."

He nodded. "After I first conceived the idea, I became obsessed by it. Spent all my spare time thinking of ways to pull it off. Brought the knife to work, even before I knew what I was going to do with it. I couldn't help myself. That man's evil was so enormous I couldn't get it out of my mind."

More likely he was building up an immunity to the antipsychotic drugs that were supposed to keep him under control, Ben thought. After so many years, their effectiveness must have diminished.

"And then one day, the perfect opportunity fell into my lap. I found Veronica in the hideaway—as I told you before, thanks to the

Americans with Disabilities Act, this entire building is wheelchair-accessible. She was making time with that living filth—the one they call the Sire. I heard what they said, what they did. Her vampire lover took the money, had tawdry sex with her, sucked her blood, gave her that drug, and left her for dead. But the amazing thing is— she didn't die. Veronica was stronger than any of us imagined. She might've pulled through—if I hadn't intervened.

"I got the knife and cut her across the shoulder to obscure the bite mark her boyfriend had left behind, and to make a wound so large she couldn't possibly recover. I flipped her upside down, just for dramatic effect and to make her blood drain faster; my legs might be crippled, but my arms are quite strong—I work out, re-member? I was careful not to get blood on me or my chair. And then I left. With all the press we had streaming around the building that day, I knew it was just a matter of time till some snoop discovered the body. Plus I'd spotted Shandy eavesdropping on them—though I made sure she didn't see me. After that video, it wasn't hard to de-duce who would be the cops' primary suspect." He paused. "What put you on to me?"

"I eventually realized you were the only one who could've gotten that big knife into the building," Ben explained. "Security is so tight I couldn't get in with a metal button sewn to my shirttail. But I bet you could get almost anything in. Everyone knows you're going to set off the alarm. Because you're riding around in a wheelchair."

Bressler smiled a little. "At first they made some effort to search me, examine the chair. But it was so hard—someone had to hold me while they sent the chair through separately, and I acted like it really hurt, and after a few months . . ." He shrugged. "Well, what threat could I possibly be? I'm just a harmless old cripple, right? And even if they had patted me down—which they didn't—they wouldn't have found the knife. Just like they didn't find this gun."

"Because you put them in the compartment under the armrest of your chair," Ben guessed. "Very bold of you to show me that, way back when. I tried to call Marie before I came over here, to verify my recollection, because I remembered you telling me she'd had the chair specially designed for you. I'm sure she never imagined you'd use it to . . . well." To smuggle in the gun you used to shoot her.

"Yeah." Marshall took a deep breath. His eyelids fluttered; Ben could see he was barely able to keep them open. "You about ready to go, Ben?"

"I'd appreciate it. Those FBI guys outside must be going nuts. And—I'd really like to see how Christina is doing. And I wouldn't mind putting my clothes back on, either."

Marshall nodded. "I heard what you said, when you carried Christina out of here. Reminded me of Delia. How we were. While it lasted." His eyes filled with tears. He laid down the gun. "I loved her so much, Ben. So much. Did you ever love someone like that? Love them so much—and then lose them?"

"Yes. I mean, she didn't die, but—it hurt just the same."

"You're too young."

"No one's too young," Ben replied. "And my father died, several years ago. That hurt, too. And we didn't even get along. He thought I was wasting my life, that I'd been a traitor to him. But when he died—I couldn't handle it. Probably should've gone into therapy. Instead I ran off to Tulsa and tried to leave my family, my past, far behind." He paused. "It didn't work. Running isn't the answer."

"No." Marshall looked up at him, almost smiling. "And I suppose taking hostages isn't, either."

Ben tilted his head to one side but said nothing.

"You go check on your girl, Ben," Marshall said, still weeping. "And you take good care of her, understand? Remember—every day the two of you have together is a gift. A rare and precious gift. Every single day."

"I won't forget." Ben took the gun and motioned to the FBI officers he knew were watching through the fiber-optic cable. "Thank you, Marshall."

"Thank you for listening. If—if my Delia were still around, I think she'd take a shine to you, Ben."

"She is still around," Ben said. He laid his hand softly on the side of Marshall's face, wiping away the tears. "And thanks to you, she always will be."

30

"Well, I gotta hand it to you, Chrissy," Loving said. "You've worn some crazy getups in the past. But this one takes the cake."

"Ha, ha," she said, with simulated acerbity. She was wearing a hospital gown, a thin pale blue linen number. "I think the floral pattern goes well with my eyes."

They were all standing around her hospital bed—Ben, Jones, Loving, and Lucille. The small private room was festooned with flowers, gifts, and a host of greeting cards dangling from a banner stretched across the head of the bed.

"Wanted you to meet my new, umm, friend," Loving said, gesturing to Lucille. He winked. "I thought the two redheads in my life should meet. She was a big help to the investigation."

"Aw, he did all the hard stuff," Lucille said, blushing. "All I did was dress up like a floozy and play the tease."

"Sounds like hard work to me," Christina said. She turned to Ben. "Has there been any word about Marshall? And Marie?"

"She's going to pull through," Ben replied. "It'll take a while, but the docs say she'll make a full recovery. I'm amazed—but I guess I shouldn't be. She's a tough woman. And Marshall is being treated by some of the best mental health specialists in the country. Todd is paying the bills."

"No criminal charges?"

"Not at this time. I doubt he could be found competent to stand trial. I just hope he gets the help he needs to recover the man he once was."

The phone rang. "Would you get that for me?" Christina asked.

"What?" Ben said. "Just because you got a little bullet wound to the leg, you can't answer your own phone?"

"I could. But I'm currently wearing a gown that exposes my rear end."

"Well, we don't want that," Loving said, rushing to the phone.

There weren't many times in his life when Ben saw his strapping investigator at a loss for words or action, but on this occasion he seemed to be lacking both.

"Loving?" Christina said. She jabbed him gently on the side. "Is it for me?"

Slowly he shrugged off his stupor and found some small measure of animation. "No. It's for Ben."

"Really?" Ben frowned. "Who is it?"

He swallowed. "The governor."

"The governor? Of what?"

"Of Oklahoma," Loving said, eyes bulging. "And he wants to talk to you!"

Ben took the phone. Loving and Lucille excused themselves, saying they wanted to check on Beatrice.

"Congratulations on a job well done, son." Ben immediately recognized the voice of his state's top politician. "Glad it all worked out and your assistant is going to be all right."

"Partner," Ben said, still dumbfounded. "She's my partner."

"Right, right. Listen, I don't want you to feel like you're getting the bum's rush, but I have exactly three minutes until my next meeting, and this has to be dealt with, and I wanted to feel you out before I made any public announcements."

"Public announcements? About—me?"

"Are you kidding, pilgrim? I guess you've been in DC. Back here—you're the local hero."

"I am?"

"Even *The Oklahoman* has had some nice things to say about you and, given your political leanings, that's nothing short of a miracle."

"I didn't know I had political leanings."

"You handled this case with class, and that closing argument you gave was brilliant. Moved me to tears when I read it in the paper. And then when it turned out you were actually right and Glancy wasn't guilty—of murder, anyway—that was even better."

"I still—don't—"

"And then that heroic rescue of your girlfriend. Marvelous stuff. Marvelous. Ballsiest thing I've heard of in my life."

"It was really no big deal."

"Well, the papers are talking about it like you were James Bond. Your approval ratings are sky-high. And not just with women. Wish to God I had ratings like that. Your fame may be fleeting, but I still wouldn't mind leaching a little positive spin off it. Which leads to the reason for my call."

Ben was baffled. The governor was talking fast—much too fast for Ben to process what he was saying, much less anticipate what was coming next.

"There are some preliminary questions I'm required to ask," the governor continued. "Did you vote for me in the last election?"

"Well . . ."

"Didn't think so. Are you even a member of my party?"

"Well . . ."

"My staff was right. And you have no political experience at all, correct?"

"I was briefly at the DA's office but . . . no, not really."

"What the hell. Part of my stump speech has been that blather about overcoming petty partisan concerns and seeking out excellence. And it's only for a year." He paused. "You seem like a hell of a good guy, Kincaid, and the public loves you. Want to be our next senator?"

Ben's jaw dropped with such alacrity he was surprised there was no thudding sound. "Can—can you do that?"

"Can I? I have no choice. Constitution requires it. Glancy has resigned; I have to appoint a substitute to fill his remaining term. So what about it, Ben? Are you my man?"

A thousand thoughts ran through Ben's brain at once. "Can— can I think about it a little while?" He glanced at Christina, who was sitting in the bed staring at him with an extremely puzzled expression. "Talk to some friends and . . . associates?"

"Of course you can. Well, you've got till six o'clock. Then we have to either announce or move on to someone else."

"I'll call you back as soon as I can." He took the governor's number and hung up.

"What was that all about?" Christina asked.

"Tell you in a minute. There's something else I want to discuss first."

"Ben! Don't be such a tease! Was it really the governor?"

"Yup. But—" He paused, shifting awkwardly from one leg to the next. "You know, Christina . . . back at Glancy's office, when you were hurt . . ."

She leaned forward a bit. "Yes?"

"I know you were half out of your head and probably weren't aware—"

"I heard every word you said."

Ben swallowed. "You did?"

"Damn straight. And I haven't forgotten, either."

He looked down at her, the billowing red hair he had become so fond of, the deep blue eyes, the adorable freckles. He couldn't imagine getting through a day without her. And didn't want to try. "I know I've—I've—never really said—"

She reached out and took his hand. "You don't have to, Ben. I already know."

"Really? Really?" He laughed with relief, and she laughed, and then they were both laughing, and then all at once he crouched beside her, picked up a pair of scissors, and snipped off her hospital ID bracelet.

"What on earth are you doing?" she said. "You're going to get thrown out of here."

"A woman like you deserves jewelry of a higher order," he replied. He reached into his coat pocket and withdrew a two-inch-square felt-covered box. And opened it.

Under the bright fluorescent lighting, the diamond sparkled with a thousand colors.

ACKNOWLEDGMENTS

I'd like to tell you that I made up all the information Shalimar and Morticia offer regarding real-life vampires, but of course I didn't. For those who would like to learn more about this growing American subculture, I recommend *Piercing the Darkness: Undercover with Vampires in America Today* by Katherine Ramsland, and *Bloodlust: Conversations with Real Vampires* by Carol Page. In case you're wondering, the epigraph by Ty King comes from "Some Assembly Required," a second-season episode of *Buffy the Vampire Slayer*, easily one of the best-written television shows ever produced. Homages to Buffyspeak and the Buffyverse permeate this book, as seemed appropriate.

I am greatly indebted to the sources who have supplied information about the workings of the U.S. Senate, but who, for some odd reason, have all chosen to remain anonymous. Special thanks to Jodie Nida and James Vance for reading and commenting on an early draft of this manuscript. Friends and readers of this quality are invaluable.

Readers are invited to e-mail me at wb@williambernhardt.com, or to visit my official website at www.williambernhardt.com. See you next time.

—WILLIAM BERNHARDT

ABOUT THE AUTHOR

WILLIAM BERNHARDT is the author of nineteen novels, including *Primary Justice, Double Jeopardy, Hate Crime,* and *Dark Eye.* He has twice won the Oklahoma Book Award for Best Fiction and was presented the H. Louise Cobb Distinguished Author Award "in recognition of an outstanding body of work in which we understand ourselves and American society at large." A former trial attorney, Bernhardt has received several awards for his public service. He lives in Tulsa, Oklahoma.

ABOUT THE TYPE

This book was set in Sabon, a typeface designed by the well-known German typographer Jan Tschichold (1902–74). Sabon's design is based upon the original letter forms of Claude Garamond and was created specifically to be used for three sources: foundry type for hand composition, Linotype, and Monotype. Tschichold named his typeface for the famous Frankfurt typefounder Jacques Sabon, who died in 1580.